PRAISE FOR

LYNSAY SANDS

AND THE ARGENEAU NOVELS

"A masterpiece of fast-paced intelligent action with hot and steamy relationships."
—FreshFiction.com

"Sands' quirky sense of humor shines."
—*RT BOOKreviews*

"Vampire lovers will find themselves laughing throughout."
—*Publishers Weekly*

"Problem?" he asked.

Backing out of the car, she straightened and held up a shoe that had slid out of the plastic bag. "The Explorer ate my shoe."

Scott grinned crookedly. "Ate it, eh?"

Beth stared at the remaining shoe and moaned, "They were my favorite shoes."

Scott shifted his gaze from her pretty, flushed face framed with red hair and looked down at the shoe she held. He then blinked. Good Lord in heaven, the shoe was as red as a candy apple, the heel a good four or five inches high, and he immediately envisioned her wearing them and nothing else. And then he recalled that there was only one now and she'd never again wear them, naked or otherwise, and was nearly as distressed as Beth appeared to be.

By Lynsay Sands

IMMORTALLY YOURS
IMMORTAL UNCHAINED
IMMORTAL NIGHTS
RUNAWAY VAMPIRE • ABOUT A VAMPIRE
THE IMMORTAL WHO LOVED ME
VAMPIRE MOST WANTED • ONE LUCKY VAMPIRE
IMMORTAL EVER AFTER
THE LADY IS A VAMP
UNDER A VAMPIRE MOON
THE RELUCTANT VAMPIRE
HUNGRY FOR YOU • BORN TO BITE
THE RENEGADE HUNTER
THE IMMORTAL HUNTER
THE ROGUE HUNTER
VAMPIRE, INTERRUPTED • VAMPIRES ARE FOREVER
THE ACCIDENTAL VAMPIRE
BITE ME IF YOU CAN
A BITE TO REMEMBER • A QUICK BITE
TALL, DARK & HUNGRY
SINGLE WHITE VAMPIRE
LOVE BITES

FALLING FOR THE HIGHLANDER
THE HIGHLANDER TAKES A BRIDE
TO MARRY A SCOTTISH LAIRD
AN ENGLISH BRIDE IN SCOTLAND
THE HUSBAND HUNT • THE HEIRESS • THE COUNTESS
THE HELLION AND THE HIGHLANDER
TAMING THE HIGHLAND BRIDE
DEVIL OF THE HIGHLANDS

THE LOVING DAYLIGHTS

LYNSAY SANDS

IMMORTALLY YOURS

AN ARGENEAU NOVEL

AVONBOOKS

An Imprint of HarperCollins*Publishers*

This is a work of fiction. Names, characters, places, and incidents are products of the author's imagination or are used fictitiously and are not to be construed as real. Any resemblance to actual events, locales, organizations, or persons, living or dead, is entirely coincidental.

First Avon Books mass market printing: October 2017
First Avon Books hardcover printing: September 2017

Print Edition ISBN: 978-0-06-246895-6
Digital Edition ISBN: 978-0-06-246886-4

Cover design by Nadine Badalaty
Cover and stepback illustration by Tony Mauro
Stepback art © Alin Brotea/Shutterstock (bats and moon)

FIRST EDITION

17 18 19 20 21 QGM 10 9 8 7 6 5 4 3 2 1

IMMORTALLY YOURS

One

"Tybo, it's time to move," Beth said into her headset as she watched the garage door drop closed.

"And thank God for that. We've been camping out here all night in the cold and mud. I'm done in," came the complaint over the headset.

"We all are," Beth said grimly. "So quit your bitchin' and move into position or I'll come find you and kick your arse."

"God, Beth, I love how your accent comes out when you're annoyed. It's so Eliza Doolittle." Tybo's voice was smooth and full of laughter this time. It made her suspect he'd complained just to get a reaction out of her, especially when he added, "I like it best when you talk dirty. It just revs my engine."

"Dirty?" she asked with surprise.

"Ummm hmmm," Tybo crooned. "You said *arse*."

Beth covered the mouthpiece of her headset as a bark of laughter slipped from her lips. She hadn't worked with Tybo long, but was quickly learning the man was a character. Shaking her head, she removed her hand from her mouthpiece and said, "Stop flirting with me, you cheeky bastard, and move into posit—"

A choked sound and the rustle of cloth from her earpiece made her stop talking and listen instead before she said, "Tybo? Tybo?"

Beth paused a heartbeat to wait for a response, and then said, "Valerian? Do you see Tybo?"

Silence was her only answer.

"Ah hell," she muttered. Slipping out from behind the tree she'd been using for cover, Beth started moving quickly in Tybo's direction. She had the dart gun she'd been issued in one hand, but her sword in the other. It was the sword that saved her. Before Beth reached the spot where she'd ordered Tybo to take cover, the dart gun was abruptly kicked from her grip. She never saw it coming, but reacted instinctively, sword hand coming up and swinging hard even as she turned toward her assailant. She caught him at the base of the throat where it met his shoulder. The blade went deep, slicing better than halfway through his neck.

Beth yanked it out, grimacing at the sucking sound it made. She watched the man topple sideways to the ground, and then quickly wiped the blade off on her attacker's coat before grabbing up the dart gun she'd dropped. Shooting him with it to ensure he didn't heal and rise too quickly, she then turned and continued forward. Beth found Tybo on his back in the mud some twelve feet from where she'd been attacked. There was a knife in his chest.

"You should have moved when I told you to," Beth

muttered as she bent to tug the ivory-handled knife from his heart. He didn't open his eyes and sit up at once, but she hadn't expected him to. He'd need some time to heal. Beth reached into the satchel hanging at her side, pulled out a bag of blood and then opened his mouth. She had to massage his upper gums briefly to get his fangs to slide out, but then she slapped the bag to them.

Leaving Tybo where he lay, Beth straightened and glanced around before continuing along the path. Valerian had been positioned another thirty feet ahead in the woods surrounding the house. She found the hunter exactly where she expected, also with a knife to the heart. As she removed it, Beth noted that it was a duplicate of the knife that had been in Tybo's chest.

Tossing the blade aside, Beth slapped a bag of blood onto Valerian's fangs as well before turning to peer through the bushes at the house they'd been watching since just after sunset. It had been empty by the time they'd got their orders from Mortimer at the Enforcer house and made their way here. The inhabitants, a rogue immortal and his minions, had already been gone by then, probably to hunt up new victims. Beth, Tybo, and Valerian had sat here awaiting their return for most of the night and now it was almost dawn, but a few minutes ago a van had pulled into the driveway. The garage door had opened, the van had pulled in, and the door had closed without them ever seeing how many people were in the vehicle. Which was why Beth had ordered Tybo to approach the house. They needed to know how many rogues they were dealing with and what the situation was. It was vital to their approach. If there were innocent mortals who needed saving, for instance, it would affect how they handled everything.

It seemed, however, that their presence hadn't gone unnoticed, and one of the returning rogues had managed to slip out unseen and sneak up on them. Her question now was whether that was the only one. Had the newly turned rogue just been sent out to check around and happened upon them? Or had they been spotted and he was sent out to take care of them? And if so, how many others, if any, were out scouring the trees surrounding the house, looking for them? Aside from whether there were innocents around, Beth also needed to know how many rogues were inside besides Walter Simpson, the master rogue of this group. Unfortunately, getting those answers and doing anything with them would be hard since her entire, and very tiny, team was now incapacitated except for herself.

Cursing under her breath, Beth took a quick glance around and then moved to the nearest tree and swiftly climbed up into the branches. She settled on a large, sturdy branch fifteen feet up, took a moment to be sure that she had a good view of the surrounding area and that no one could sneak up on her, and then slid her cell phone from her pocket.

Mortimer answered on the first ring. "Problem?"

"Oh no, Mortimer. I just called to say hi," she said lightly, rolling her eyes, and then explained grimly, "Tybo and Valerian are both down from knives to the heart. The blades are out, and I think I got their attacker unless there were two. But that leaves me on my own with a rogue who may or may not have others to help him, and who may or may not know people are out here."

"The attacker's not talking?" Mortimer asked.

"Hard to talk with your windpipe hacked open," Beth said dryly.

"I would imagine so," Mortimer agreed, and she was sure she could hear a smile in his voice. "Well, you are in luck. A couple of reinforcements walked in just moments ago. They will be there in twenty minutes. Stay put until they join you."

Beth opened her mouth to answer, but paused as a woman's scream came from the house. It was long, loud and filled with horror.

So, she thought, *there's the answer to one of my questions. Yes, there are innocents inside the house.*

"Beth," Mortimer said, sounding tense now. "*Do not go in there on your own.* Wait for backup."

"Yeah . . . can't promise you that," Beth said solemnly as the terrified scream turned into an agonized one. "Tell them to hurry."

"Beth," Mortimer said with alarm, but she'd already ended the call and slipped the phone back into her pocket so that she could drop out of the tree.

"Feck!" Scotty snapped, bolting toward the door. Mortimer had put the phone on speaker when he checked the caller ID and saw who was calling. They'd all heard Beth's words and the shrieking in the background. Scotty knew damned well that agonized scream would have Beth charging into the house with little care for her own well-being. She needed backup *now*.

"Donny, go with him!" Mortimer barked, slamming the phone back into its cradle when the dial tone announced that the connection had been broken.

"Really?" the young man asked with surprise.

"Move yer arse!" Scotty barked over his shoulder, having heard the exchange. He was already halfway down the hall and didn't slow as he added, "I'll no' be waitin' on ye."

"Go!" Mortimer's bellow was followed by the sound of running feet as Donny obeyed. Scotty was sliding into the SUV and pulling the door closed before the ginger-haired lad caught up to him.

"Keys," he growled, sticking his hand out the open window as the boy slid to a stop next to the driver's door and peered at him uncertainly. The lad had picked him up in the vehicle and so, no doubt, expected to drive, but Scotty didn't care. Giving him a hard look, he ground out, "Now," and was rather amazed when the fellow didn't obey at once. Donny's eyes widened, and there was definitely fear in his expression, but he simply ran around the back of the vehicle.

"Well, ye walkin' bawbag!" Scotty bellowed and opened his door, intending to give chase, but he stopped and swung around in his seat with surprise when the passenger door opened. Scotty raised his eyebrows when the lad slid into the seat and pulled his door closed. But he didn't say anything, merely closed his own door again and held out his hand for the key.

"It's keyless. Just put your foot on the brake and—" Donny didn't bother to finish. The engine was already started. Scotty had driven keyless vehicles before and knew that as long as the key was in the car they were good. However, it didn't escape his notice that Donny was holding on to that key. He didn't care.

"Where to?" he barked, steering the SUV quickly up the driveway toward the gates. When the lad didn't answer at once, Scotty cast a glare his way. "Well?"

"I—" he began helplessly, and then grabbed his phone from his pocket with relief when it rang. "Yes? Oh, Mortimer, thank God, I—" Donny stopped to listen briefly and then said, "Yes, yes. Just a minute."

Scotty brought the car to a stop to wait for the men to open the gates, and then looked to see what the boy was doing. His eyebrows rose when he saw him quickly typing in an address on the GPS. Fortunately, the lad finished just as the gates got wide enough for the SUV to pass through, because Scotty wasn't waiting. He'd rather make Mortimer stay on the phone giving them directions all the way to where Beth was than waste a single minute waiting on typing.

"Which way?" he asked as the SUV surged through the first gate.

"It's calculating a route," Donny muttered, watching the screen.

"Which way?" Scotty insisted as they passed through the second set of gates.

"It's still—Right! Turn right," he said with relief as the route popped up on the screen.

Scotty turned the wheel right and squealed out onto the road.

"The right-hand lane, the right-hand lane!" Donny squawked with alarm as Scotty sped up the road in the left lane.

Mouth tightening, Scotty steered the vehicle onto the other side of the road and silently reminded himself he was in North America now and not his beloved Scotland, or even the land of those bloody English . . . who at least knew which side of the road a car should be driven on.

"The speed limit here is eighty kilometers an hour," Donny said tensely as they continued to gain speed.

"Yer arse and parsley." Scotty muttered the old phrase, basically telling the lad to bugger off, out of habit.

"What?" Donny asked with bewilderment.

Scotty ground his teeth together and shot a glance his way. "Ye're no' a hunter, are ye, lad?"

"Yes. I mean—well, I'm still in training," he said stiffly.

"O' course ye are," Scotty breathed out with disgust and then shook his head. He should have known. He had been made aware of the situation in North America before he flew over from Scotland, and the situation was that they were in a pinch. Nearly three quarters of their Rogue Hunters were down in Venezuela trying to hunt down some mad bastard who had been kidnapping immortals and hiding them away somewhere in that country. That news had spread like wildfire along the immortal grapevine, and with the remaining hunters spread so thin, it seemed like every rogue, or even those bordering on becoming rogue, hadn't been able to resist taking advantage and going haywire. Of course, Mortimer would be utilizing every available hunter and hunter-in-training to try to maintain control of the situation.

"Well now," Scotty said finally in a solemn tone.

"Here's a lesson fer ye then, lad. Speed limits do no' mean shite when ye're racing to the aid o' a hunter who's alone an' in peril. If a bobby spots ye speeding, and tries to pull ye over, then control him and send him on his way."

"Uh-huh," Donny grunted, his hands clenching on the seat and the door arm. "And what if you crash because you're going like a hundred kilometers over the speed limit?"

"Ye do no' crash," he assured him, glancing at the GPS as it started squawking. A turn was coming up, he saw, and began to slow to make it as he added, "But if ye do, ye tuck yer head between yer legs and protect yer neck. Ye can come back from a lot, but no' a beheading."

"Right," Donny muttered, slinking down in his seat.

Scotty noted the action and smiled grimly. "Set a stout heart to a stey brae, lad."

"Huh?" Donny asked, turning a befuddled expression his way, and Scotty shook his head.

"It's from an old Scottish proverb," he explained on a sigh. "I'm tellin' ye to find yer courage fer what lies ahead."

"Oh." They were silent as the car raced through the early dawn, and then Donny frowned and cleared his throat. "You know this hunter Beth we're going to help?"

It started out as a statement, but ended on a question. Scotty supposed the boy had caught some of Mortimer and Scotty's conversation before the phone call. Donny had just entered the room when the phone rang. He could have heard what Scotty had been saying as he'd approached up the hall.

"Aye," he answered shortly.

"You came specifically because of her?"

Scotty nodded. "I came to help her."

"But how did you know she'd need your help?" Donny asked with a frown.

"Because a gowk at Yule'll no' be bright at Beltane," he muttered.

"Huh?" Donny said with confusion.

Scotty clucked his tongue. "It means—Never mind. I kenned she'd be needin' me because I kenned the state o' things here and I ken her temperament. Beth's impetuous, and smart and brave, but she's prone to running into trouble to save others even at risk to hersel'." He cast a swift glance at the other man and arched an eyebrow. "Is that English enough fer ye?"

"Actually, no," the younger immortal said apologetically and then quickly explained, "You have a really thick accent. I don't catch half of what you say."

"Well, at least ye admit it," Scotty said dryly. "That makes ye a cannie lad."

Donny looked uncertain. "Is cannie good?"

"Aye," he said with grim amusement. "Now shut yer geggy. This road is gravel and winding. I need to concentrate at this speed."

Donny hesitated and then asked, "Is geggy—"

"Yer mouth. Shut yer mouth, lad," Scotty growled.

"Aye, sir. I mean yes, sir. I'll shut it," Donny said quickly, and managed to do so for all of two minutes before asking, "But how do you know this Beth? I mean, you're from Scotland and she came from Spain. How—"

"Shut it," Scotty snapped, and then asked, "How much farther?"

When the young man didn't answer right away, Scotty cast a questioning glance his way and noted the battle on Donny's face as he tried to decide which order to obey.

"Well? Do no' be a bampot. Answer me!" he roared.

"We're almost there!" Donny blurted. "Turn right at the end of this road, and then it's half a block up on the left."

Scotty nodded with a grunt, but didn't relax. He had a bad feeling Beth needed him, and he wouldn't relax until she was safe and sound.

Beth leapt back, avoiding being beheaded by mere inches. She actually felt the swish of the wicked-sharp ax the rogue was swinging at her. It stirred her hair in passing, or so she thought, but when she saw the handful of dark red tresses that then dropped to the ground, cut clean off, she snapped, "You bastard! I just got my hair done!"

Furious, Beth leapt forward, her sword singing through the air. Before his head hit the ground, she was turning to ensure there were no other attackers. Her eyes widened incredulously and a low roaring started in her ears as she took in the dozen men and women who had come running from the house and formed a half circle around her.

"You've got to be kidding me," she muttered, her mouth suddenly gone dry. Mortimer hadn't been sure how many minions this rogue might have made, but had guessed that it couldn't be more than three or four. After all, according to the intel he had, Walter

Simpson had been rogue for only a week or so. Yet she'd already taken out four men and two women and now was faced with a dozen more? Either Mortimer's intel was wrong, or Walter was a fast worker, she thought grimly, drawing herself into a battle stance and preparing to skewer the first one to charge on her.

She might not be able to take on twelve at once and win, but she wasn't going down without a fight, Beth thought grimly and gestured with her sword for them to bring it on. No one moved at first, which just irritated her. She had never been a patient person, and frankly, if she was going to die, she'd rather get it over with quickly. Beth just hoped that the whole life-flashing-before-your-eyes business wasn't true. She could really do without witnessing that particular train wreck. Living it had been bad enough.

"Come on," she growled impatiently, raising her sword. "I plan on taking at least four of you with me. Which of you will it be?"

Unfortunately, that just made her would-be killers all take a nervous step back. It seemed no one wanted to die that day.

"What are you waiting for?" a furious voice roared, drawing Beth's attention to the house.

Walter Simpson stood just outside the front door with a whimpering blonde next to him, held upright only by his grip on her upper arm. She was pale, with blood trailing down her throat and soaking into the top of her torn pastel green sweater. But she was alive, and still mortal, Beth thought. She almost started toward them, but was reminded of her own situation when Walter bellowed, "Kill her, dammit!"

The order from the man who had turned them apparently held sway. Beth watched warily as the rogues closed in, crowding together for the approach . . . and then the lot of them were suddenly mowed down by a black SUV that raced past her and toward the house.

Beth gaped as some of her would-be attackers flew up in the air, and others were simply crushed under the wheels. There wasn't a single person left standing once the SUV had passed. The rogues were scattered about the yard in front of her like toppled bowling pins.

It was the sound of the SUV crashing that finally drew her attention from the people in the yard. At the speed it had been going, the driver hadn't been able to stop before plowing into the front of the house. He hit exactly where Walter and his latest victim had been just moments ago, and for a heartbeat Beth was horrified by the thought that the pair had been hit and crushed into the front of the house. Not that she would have mourned Walter Simpson, but the woman had been an innocent, and guilt and regret began to soak into her at the thought that she'd failed her. But then a sob drew her attention to the driveway, and she saw Walter dragging his victim toward a car. It seemed he'd managed to get both himself and her out of the way in time to avoid the vehicle. Now he was making his escape . . . and intent on taking the woman with him.

Issuing a throaty growl, Beth burst after them. She had the advantage. She wasn't trying to drag a struggling victim with her. Beth raised her gun as she ran, then aimed and pulled the trigger, only to curse when nothing happened. She was out of darts. She'd known she was close to empty, but had thought she had one, or maybe even two, left.

Throwing the dart gun aside with disgust, she

brought her sword around in front of her to grasp the hilt in both hands with the blade down. She then raised it over her head and launched herself into the air much as someone would do if they were jumping on someone's back. Only Beth leapt a little higher, and as she came down she punched the blade into Simpson's back just above his shoulder blade. With all her weight crashing on top of it, the sword was forced through flesh, muscle and bone at an almost vertical angle and came out just below his hip bone.

Walter Simpson staggered under the impact and released the blonde as he crashed face-first to the ground. Beth went down with him, but rolled into a somersault that took her right off him. She didn't let go of her sword as she went either, and felt the resistance before it sliced its way out and followed her.

"Gor, that's mingin'! Do ye always have to make such a mess, lass?"

Beth blinked at that voice as she sat up, and then turned to peer with disbelief at the man approaching her. Tall with the kind of shoulders and thick arms only a man raised wielding broadswords in the middle ages could usually obtain, Cullen MacDonald, or Scotty, as he had come to be known, had long hair that was a mixture of deep red and dark chestnut. He looked like a medieval warrior walking toward her, except, instead of a plaid, he was wearing black leather pants with his white linen shirt.

"Scotty?" she said now, sure her eyes were playing tricks on her. But it certainly looked like him, she acknowledged as her gaze slid over his face, taking in the familiar gray eyes with silver specks, aquiline nose, and thin upper lip over a fuller lower one. It was a face she'd seen in person perhaps a handful of times, but had seen repeatedly in her dreams. Usually wet ones.

"Aye." He stopped next to her and held out his hand, offering her aid in rising. "'Tis glad I am to see ye did no' get yerself beheaded ere I could get here and save ye."

"Humble as ever, I see," Beth said with dry amusement, ignoring his hand and getting up on her own.

"Uh, Mr. Scotty?" an anxious voice called. "This guy's waking up."

Beth turned her head to see a young ginger-haired immortal standing by one of the rogues they'd run over. The man was moaning and slowly shifting on the ground.

"Shoot him with the dart gun, then, Donny boy," Scotty ordered, not bothering to glance his way.

"What dart gun?" Donny asked uncertainly.

Biting her lip to keep from grinning, Beth watched Scotty briefly close his eyes and grind his teeth together with impatience. Opening his eyes, he peered at Beth's amused face as he said, "Pray, tell me, lad, that ye did no' come a'huntin' without a gun."

"Okay," Donny said after a hesitation.

Frowning, Scotty turned to eye him. "Okay what, boyo?"

"I won't tell you?" he said, his voice a squeak, and then, clearing his throat, he glanced nervously to the man at his feet who was pulling himself slowly to a sitting position and asked, "Do you have a gun I can use?"

Scotty heaved out an exasperated breath, and turned to walk to the younger immortal's side, withdrawing his short sword as he went. "Nay, lad. I never carry a gun. I use this," he said, and, holding the blade upward with his hand firmly around the bone grip, Scotty whacked the rogue over the head with the brass pommel.

Beth winced at the sound of crunching bone and shook her head as the rogue tumbled back to a prone position.

"I think you cracked his skull," Donny said with awe, staring at the rogue.

"That I did," Scotty said with satisfaction. "Now go get a dart gun and chains out o' the weapons locker in the back of the SUV ere all o' them start waking up. And Donny," he added, bringing the younger man to a halt just as he started away. When the man reluctantly turned back to face him, Scotty said solemnly, "Lesson number two: never go on the hunt without a weapon."

Nodding quickly, Donny turned and rushed to the SUV with its nose presently buried in the front of the house.

Scotty immediately spun back to Beth.

"What are ye doing here in Canada, Scotty?" she asked as he returned to her. "Not enough rogues in the UK right now to keep you busy?"

"It *has* been a bit slow lately," he said with a shrug. When Beth merely raised an eyebrow at that, he added, "As it happens, I was just debating where to go on me vacation when I heard ye were spread thin over here just now, what with most o' yer hunters in Venezuela, so I thought . . ." He didn't bother finishing and merely shrugged.

"You just thought you'd spend your vacation from

hunting rogues in the UK hunting rogues here instead?" she asked with disbelief, and then reached up on tiptoe to knock on his forehead as if it were a door. "Hello! Is there anyone home in there?"

"Oy!" Scotty leaned his head back away from her knocking fist and glowered at her. "I swear, ye're the only lass brave enough to do something like that."

"Because all the other girls think you're the bogeyman and are scared to death of you," Beth said dryly.

"But ye're not," he said with certainty.

Beth snorted. "I've met the bogeyman, and you're not him."

"Aye, I suppose ye have met him," Scotty said solemnly.

Beth's mouth tightened briefly, and then she relaxed and smiled as she shook her head. "Enough of this evasion. Why would you waste your vacation working over here in Canada?"

"A change o' pace," Scotty said with a shrug. "Change is always a good thing. Life can get boring otherwise."

"Humph," Beth said dubiously and narrowed her eyes on the man. He was easy to look at, a whole hunk of sexy manhood, but she didn't trust him as far as she could throw him. He'd popped up in her life repeatedly over the last hundred and twenty-five years since he'd saved her and Dree from a rogue and his mad minions in England. For the first hundred years when he'd popped up, he'd either looked down his nose at her, or treated her distantly, as if she might be infected with something contagious. He'd also been talking to her bosses behind her back, trying to sabotage her position as a hunter. Now he was suddenly acting all charming and friendly? She wasn't buying it. He was up to something.

Honestly, if he didn't smell so good, look so pretty, and feature so frequently in her sexual fantasies, she wouldn't even talk to the man. Unfortunately, he was a sexy beast, and he did feature highly in her sexual fantasies. In fact, he was the only one she had in her wet dreams. The man might not be trustworthy in real life, but in her dreams he was like the Energizer Bunny—he just kept going and going and going. Worse yet, every man she'd slept with over the hundred and twenty-five years since she was turned had worn his face behind her closed eyes. The man just "revved her engine," as Tybo had put it. At least physically.

"I hear ye've left the Spanish hunters and moved here permanently," Scotty said now.

Beth blinked her thoughts away and looked at him through narrowed eyes. While she was English-born, she'd spent the past more than two thirds of her life in Spain. During that time, Scotty, despite living in England himself, had interfered in her life repeatedly and often. She couldn't help but suspect this was another opportunity for him to be sticking his nose in where it didn't belong. However, all she said was, "Dree's found her life mate. She, naturally, wants to settle here with him."

Scotty arched one supercilious eyebrow. "And so ye're jest going to follow her like a puppy and move here too?"

Beth's chin lifted defensively. "She's my family. Of course I'll move here."

"Are ye sure she wants you to?" he asked. "Things

change when an immortal meets their life mate. They tend to—"

"Save it," Beth interrupted, suddenly amused. Scotty could convince her of a lot of things, but not that Dree didn't want her around. They had been thick as thieves for more than a century, and friends even before that. "Dree hasn't changed. She asked me to move here. We're family, and if she wants me here, then here I'll be." Leaning toward him, she smiled sweetly and added, "And since Mortimer is so short-staffed right now, I think you're going to find it impossible to talk him into not letting me work here, if that was your intention."

"I had no intention o'—" he began.

"Save it," Beth repeated with a laugh, and said, "Scotty, I know you tried to talk the Spanish Council out of letting me train to be a hunter way back when, and I know you've interfered since then, trying to keep me off certain jobs." She shook her head. "I don't know why you trouble yourself like that, but while you seem to think I'm useless and little more than a worm that crawled out from under a rock, Dree doesn't. She's a sister to me and—"

"Oh, lass, that's no' why I interfered," Scotty interrupted. "I do no' think ye're a worm, and it fair wounds me to think ye believe that when the truth is I—"

When his words ended on a grunt and his eyes widened, Beth frowned slightly, wondering what was up, and then she stepped quickly out of the way as he fell forward. It was like a huge old oak falling. Beth swore the ground shuddered as he hit it, but then she noticed the dart in his behind and her mouth dropped open.

"Ah, hell," Donny groaned. "He's gonna be so mad when he wakes up."

Beth glanced to the younger immortal to see a dart gun dangling from his hand and a grimace on his face.

"It just went off," he said unhappily. "I swear I didn't pull the trigger . . . I don't think," he added with a frown and then glanced to Beth worriedly. "Just how mad do you think he's going to be when he finds out I shot him?"

Beth glanced down at Scotty, and then shook her head and walked over to the younger immortal. Taking the gun from him with one hand, she patted him on the back with the other and then began to shoot all the slowly healing immortals on the lawn as she said, "He'll not be mad at all. We'll say one of the rogues woke up and grabbed for the dart gun as you were about to shoot, and it went off and hit him."

"But he'll read our minds and know it's not true," Donny pointed out.

"Oh, *we* won't be telling him that," she assured him.

"We won't?" Donny asked with confusion.

"No. I'll call Mortimer and tell him that over the phone so he can't read my mind. And then he'll send more backup to collect all the rogues as well as Scotty, Tybo, and Valerian, and they'll take him back to the house, and Mortimer will tell him our tale, and no one will be the wiser."

Turning to Scotty now, she shot him again in the butt and enjoyed it so much after all the aggravation he'd caused her over the years that she shot him again for good measure. Swinging back to Donny, she smiled and said, "That's just to be sure he doesn't wake up before the backup arrives and we can leave."

Donny didn't look completely convinced of the veracity of the claim, but then he relaxed and said solemnly, "Thank you. I appreciate your doing all of this for me."

"Oh, it's not for you," she said with amusement and then pointed out, "I barely know you."

"Then why are you doing it?" he asked uncertainly.

"For me."

"But you had nothing to do with it," he pointed out.

"True. But that's the first thing to put a smile on my face in decades and I'll not see you punished for it," she said with a grin as she walked back to Simpson and shot him, as well. She glanced around the lawn, her gaze landing last on the blonde mortal who had fallen into a faint when Beth had put her sword through Simpson. She would have liked to go check on the woman and see her comfortable, but she and Donny were the only ones there to tend to matters now. They had the rogues to see to as well as Tybo and Valerian and—which reminded her that there was another rogue in the woods who would be waking soon.

Beth headed for the trees. "Grab another dart gun and start getting these guys into the SUV. If any of them start to stir, shoot them again. I have to go check on Tybo, Valerian, and the rogue who attacked them."

She didn't wait to see if Donny did as instructed, but headed quickly into the woods.

Two

"What is a bampot?"

Beth glanced at Donny with surprise. They'd been driving in silence since leaving Walter Simpson's lair. She looked into the back seat before answering, noting that Scotty was sprawled half on and half off the SUV's bench seat behind them, still sound asleep.

While Mortimer had sent a cleanup crew to take care of the rogues and bring in the injured hunters, Donny had felt so guilty for shooting Scotty, he'd wanted to take him back with them in her SUV. Beth hadn't argued with the young man. It was no skin off her nose if he got himself caught after she'd got him off the hook with her phone call. So, she'd merely climbed in the passenger seat and left him to load Scotty in back and take the steering wheel. She was just a passenger for this ride.

Beth turned forward in the passenger seat and said, "*Bampot* means *idiot* or *crazy person*." Glancing at

Donny curiously, she asked, "Why? Did Scotty call you that?"

"Yes. Well, he said I was cannie, and then asked a question and said, 'Don't be a bampot. Answer me.'"

"Ah." Beth shook her head. "Using his charm on you, then."

"He was all right," Donny said with a shrug. After a minute he added, "He was super worried about you, though. I thought he was going to get us both killed, speeding the way he was to get to the house. I've never seen telephone poles blur together like that before."

That was rather surprising news to Beth. As far as she knew, Scotty didn't think much of her so shouldn't have rushed to her aid. Mind you, he had claimed she was wrong on how he felt about her. Unfortunately, he'd been interrupted before he could explain further, but that might be for the best. If the man said he felt sorry for her or something, she would have had to punch him for ruining any future sexual fantasics that might have included him. She could hardly have sex with a man who felt sorry for her, even if it was only in a dream.

"How come you don't like him?" Donny asked suddenly, and Beth glanced at the ginger-haired man with surprise.

"Who said I don't like him?"

"Well," he said slowly, "if you liked him you wouldn't have enjoyed my accidentally shooting him so much. And you really seemed to enjoy shooting him yourself."

"Oh, that." Beth waved the issue away. "It's not that I don't like him. I just . . ." She hesitated briefly and then blurted, "The man hates me."

"What?" Donny asked, sounding shocked, and then shook his head firmly. "He doesn't."

"He does," she assured him.

"But he—" Donny cut himself off, and instead asked, "What makes you think that?"

"He—" Beth began and then snapped her mouth closed. She'd decided ten years ago not to dwell on bad things anymore. She'd spent more than a hundred years wallowing in the misery of her mortal life and her turning. By doing so, she'd been unable to move forward. It was hard to experience life and be happy when you were sunk in the anger and depression of yesteryear. In a way, by doing that, she herself had continued the torture and humiliation her past abusers had visited on her, and long after they'd stopped and even died. Beth had come to realize she'd wasted all those years, and had decided it was time to let the past go and live only in the moment. The odd thing was, it was a dog that taught her that.

"It doesn't matter," she said now, and then changed the subject. "So, are you originally from Toronto?"

"No. I'm not Canadian. I was born and raised in Kansas," Donny said.

"Kansas?" she asked with surprise.

Donny nodded. "It's where I was turned. Where Leigh was turned too," he added.

"Lucian Argeneau's life mate, Leigh?" Beth asked with interest.

Donny nodded. "We were both turned by the same rogue." He pressed his lips tightly closed briefly, and then blurted, "It's my fault she was turned. I had a crush on her, and my sire read it from my mind and said he'd let me turn her, but the truth was he'd decided to turn her himself. It ended up lucky for me because otherwise . . ." He shook his head. "Well, if not for her, I'd probably be dead. Lucian saved her, and I'm pretty sure she talked him into saving and sparing me too."

"So, like me, you were turned and not born immortal," Beth murmured, watching the telephone poles glide by.

"Yeah. It was pretty awful," Donny muttered.

Beth grunted in response, but her mind was on memories of her own turn. Grinding her teeth, she crossed her arms over her chest to try to dispel the shuddering those memories brought on.

Donny must have noticed the action, because he added almost apologetically, "I guess it probably always is."

"Yes," she agreed solemnly and then took a deep breath, pushed the old memories away and said, "But it's over now. And look at all that we've gained—immortality, good health, good teeth, good everything. Physically we're the best we can be and always will be so long as we don't get ourselves beheaded or burned alive."

"And beheading only works so long as you keep the head separate from the body."

"True," she said with a nod.

"And we're not even dead and soulless," Donny added wryly. "It was a relief to find that out."

Beth looked at him with surprise. "You thought that to be the case when you were first turned?"

"Yeah, of course. That's what all the movies say. Vampires are dead and soulless." He glanced at her with curiosity. "Didn't you think that too?"

"No." She shook her head firmly.

"But you were turned by a rogue too, weren't you?" he said with a frown. "Surely he didn't bother to explain—"

"No, he didn't," she said with a wry smile. "But I knew Dree long before the rogue who turned me came along. She—"

"Dree?" Donny interrupted.

"Alexandrina Argenis Stoyan," Beth explained.

"Wait, you knew Drina Argeneau before this rogue who turned you came along?" he asked with a frown.

"Argenis," she corrected him. "Dree is from the Spanish branch of the family."

Donny snorted at the distinction. "She's Lucian Argeneau's niece. That makes her an Argeneau no matter how they change the name."

Beth opened her mouth to argue the point, but then closed it again and conceded, "I suppose."

"So, how did you know Drina before you were turned? Did you work for her as a maid or something? Those are usually the only mortals who know about our kind. It's hard to hide it from them and—"

"We were friends," Beth interrupted. "And sort of business partners, but mostly friends for a good thirty years before I was turned. And during that time she'd already explained everything to me. It was probably the most interesting conversation of my life," she added with a wry smile as she recalled learning that Atlantis had really existed. That the scientists there had been more advanced technologically than the scientists were even today. That in a search for a better way to deal with illness and internal injuries, they'd developed bioengineered nanos that could be introduced to the body via the bloodstream, which would move throughout the body, fighting disease and repairing injuries.

The thing she'd found most interesting had been that even back then, in a society supposedly so much more advanced, it was laziness that had brought about the invention of the closest thing to immortality man had yet to come up with. Not wanting to have to create hundreds of different programs for the nanos for every illness or possible injury a mortal could suffer, the scientists had simply programmed them with a blueprint of a mortal male and female at their peak condition and given the nanos the directive to ensure or return their host to that condition and then self-destruct.

What the scientists hadn't taken into consideration was that the nanos would consider aging a disease too and would reverse the effects of that aging. They also hadn't considered that the human body was constantly under assault from the sun, from polluted air, even from the simple passage of time, and so the nanos would never finish their work and self-destruct. Instead, they constantly worked at keeping their host at their peak. "Forever young, forever healthy . . ."

Beth didn't realize she'd said that last part aloud until Donny grimaced and added, "And forever needing blood because the nanos use it to make the repairs and fight disease, as well as to propel and reproduce themselves. More blood than we can produce."

"Nothing is perfect," Beth said with a shrug.

"Being a blood-sucking vampire is miles away from not being perfect," Donny argued, his tone dry.

"Blood-sucking vampire?" she echoed with amusement.

"Well, that's what we are," he pointed out.

Beth shook her head and then shrugged. "I prefer to think we're not unlike hemophiliacs. They occasionally need blood transfusions because their blood doesn't clot. We need it more often because we don't produce enough to support the nanos in our bodies. A simple medical need."

"Hemophiliacs don't have fangs," Donny argued.

"And because of that, hemophiliacs died before needles and transfusions were invented," she responded and then added, "And now that there are blood banks and such, thc only thing we puncture with those fangs are blood bags, so what does it matter?"

"I thought you were from Spain?" Donny said suddenly, a frown forming on his face.

"I am. So?" she asked.

"Well, isn't biting mortals allowed in Europe?"

Beth grimaced. "It is. But it's kind of like smoking. There are still some hangers-on to the habit, usually the older immortals, but most don't do it anymore. It's kind of shunned."

"Huh, I didn't know that," Donny murmured, slowing as they approached the driveway to the Hunter house.

Beth glanced into the back seat to check on Scotty as Donny turned the SUV into the driveway and steered up to the first gate. The Scot's eyes were closed and he seemed to still be unconscious, but she could have sworn he'd shifted his position a bit. He could have done that in his sleep, though, she supposed, but continued to watch him to see if he moved. When he hadn't by the time they'd made their way through both sets of gates, she turned forward to glance around as they headed up the driveway.

She was really glad to be done with her assignment and back here, but Beth would be gladder still to get home. It had been a long night . . . and morning, she thought as she glanced at the clock on the dashboard and saw that it was just past noon. Cleanup had taken a while, and she was looking forward to returning to her sublet apartment and getting some sleep.

Mortimer was obviously waiting for them; Donny had barely brought the SUV to a halt in front of the house when the front door opened and he appeared.

"Scotty's still asleep?" Garrett Mortimer asked with surprise as he approached and looked in at the prostrate man on the back seat.

"Yes, and snoring like a bass drum," Beth lied as she got out of the car.

"I was no' snoring," Scotty protested at once, sitting up in the back seat.

Bending at the waist, Beth peered through her open door into the back seat and grinned at him as she said smugly, "I knew you were awake and feigning sleep."

Grumbling under his breath, Scotty opened his door and got out. Once standing, he scowled from her to Donny. "Aye, I was. And I read young Donny's mind. I ken what happened with the dart business."

"Oh . . . er . . ." Donny looked panicked, but Beth merely shrugged.

"He shot you once by accident and I shot you twice on purpose. So if you're going to be bellowing mad at anyone, I guess it'll have to be me. But that'll have to wait until tonight. Right now I'm too tired to listen."

She moved away, intending to walk to the back of the house, where her car was parked. "I'm going home to catch some sleep."

"Ah, Beth?" Mortimer said, bringing her to a halt.

Turning slowly, she raised her eyebrows in question.

"I have another job for you," the man said apologetically.

"Now?" she asked with surprise. They had been working long hours and seven days a week too since this whole mess with Dressler down in Venezuela came up, but usually they were allowed to catch at least *some* sleep between assignments.

"No, not right this minute. You will be able to get some rest first," he assured her quickly. "But not much. The plane is coming for you in a little less than six hours, so you might want to sleep here rather than head home."

"Oh," Beth said weakly. She'd really been looking forward to sleeping in her own bed. Sighing, she started walking back to Mortimer. "Very well. What's the job?"

"We'll talk inside. Scotty could probably use some blood to recoup after fighting off the tranquilizer," he pointed out and then glanced to Donny and said, "Take the SUV around to the garage so it can be cleaned and filled with gas for the next trip."

No doubt eager to avoid Scotty, Donny was back in the SUV and pulling the door closed before the order was completely out.

"That's the fastest I have ever seen him move," Mortimer said dryly as he watched the vehicle speed away. Shaking his head, he gestured for Scotty and Beth to follow as he turned to lead the way into the house. "We'll talk in the kitchen. The blood is there."

Scotty nodded and then waved Beth ahead of him. She followed Mortimer, but had to fight the urge to look over her shoulder to be sure the Scot wasn't planning to shoot her in the butt with a dart gun or some such thing for revenge. Much to her relief, she made it to the kitchen unmolested.

"Nice job rounding up Simpson and his people," Mortimer said as he led them to the refrigerator. "I gather he'd managed to turn a much larger group than we expected."

"Yes," Beth murmured as she watched him retrieve three bags of blood from the fridge. "Either he'd been rogue longer than your intel claimed, or he was turning two or three mortals a night."

"I suspect he was turning several a day. I got a call just before you arrived. He had a setup in the basement, chains and whatnot. Four people were mid-turn down there." Mortimer handed one of the bags of blood to her and another to Scotty as he continued, "And then there was the mortal you saved. Either he planned to chain her up and turn her, as well, or . . ."

"Or she was breakfast . . . for everyone," Beth finished for him, shifting the bag he'd given her from one hand to the other.

"Hmm." Mortimer's expression was grim. "There were several bodies in freezers in the basement. Drained dry and frozen. That could have been her destination, as well."

Beth merely nodded and slapped the bag to her fangs. She was glad the woman was safe, but her mind was now stuck on the bodies in the freezers, the ones she hadn't got there in time to save.

"What will happen to the four who were mid-turn?" Scotty asked.

Mortimer shrugged. "The Council will decide. Usually they read the minds of any new turns the rogues have created, and if they haven't harmed anyone yet, and aren't sociopaths, or likely to harm anyone or go mad, they are taken in by various families and helped to adjust to their new state."

Nodding, Scotty slapped his own bag to his mouth, and Mortimer followed suit. The room was briefly silent as they waited for the bags to empty. They then tore them away one after the other and tossed them in the garbage under the kitchen sink.

"You still look pale, Scotty. Do you want another—?"

"Nay, nay." Scotty waved away the offer. "I do no' think that'd help. What I'd truly like is to find a bed and sleep off the rest o' the effects o' the darts."

"Of course." Mortimer smiled faintly as he straightened from closing the door to the lower cupboard where the garbage was kept. "Sam readied the blue room for you to stay in while here. It is upstairs, the third door on the left. Your bags are already there."

Scotty nodded and turned toward the door. "I'll find it. Thank ye. And thank yer Sam fer me too. I do appreciate it."

Beth watched him go, and found herself suddenly relaxing once he left the room. Facing Mortimer, she asked, "What job is it you have for me?"

He just shook his head. "Sleep first. If I told you now, you would probably forget half of it by the time you woke up anyway. I will explain everything when you wake up."

"As you like," Beth said easily. Normally she would have pressed him for details so that she could mentally prepare herself ahead of time. But she was tired enough to think Mortimer was right and she might do better to wait. Heading for the door, she said, "I'll go sack out on the couch, then."

"No need. Sam prepared a room for you too," Mortimer said, ushering her out of the kitchen and into the hall. "The last room on the right upstairs."

"Thank you," Beth murmured as they reached the stairs. He left her there and continued down the hall to his office, no doubt so that he could complete paperwork on the rogues they'd brought in. She didn't wait to see if that was where he went, but moved quickly up the stairs on light feet.

The room on the right at the end of the hall was painted the palest yellow with pale blue accents. Beth glanced around, noting the nightgown laid out on the bed and the new jeans and T-shirt lying over a chair by the window. There was even a pair of brand-new panties with the tags still in place on top, though no bra. Not that it mattered. Beth wore a bra only for propriety's sake. She hadn't really needed one since the turn. Her breasts now defied gravity.

The thought made her smile as she checked the tags on the jeans and top. Oh yeah, Mortimer's life mate, Sam, was thorough. She had the right size and everything. Setting them back on the chair, Beth walked into the bathroom and found a new toothbrush and toothpaste still in the boxes. There were also soap, shampoo, cream rinse, deodorant and even her brand of perfume as well as a few cosmetics.

Beth washed her face, brushed her teeth and then stripped on her way back to the bed, letting the clothes fall as she removed them so that there was a trail of clothing from the bathroom door. By the time she reached the bed she was wearing nothing more than her own pretty lavender panties. She didn't bother with the nightgown, though. Beth was a restless sleeper, tossing and turning and kicking about. Nightgowns tended to wind up tangled around her waist or even higher, constricting her movement so that she woke up panting and afraid.

The panties were good enough, she thought, and crawled under the covers, only to lie staring at the ceiling and thinking about the often-annoying man down the hall and why he'd appeared in her life again. Scotty was one of those confident, competent, take-charge, manly-type men she always found so damned attractive. And yes, she was attracted to him, but it did her little good. Scotty was kind of a combination of both Lucian and Mortimer in that he sat on the Council in the UK *and* ruled the hunters there. Although really, that was what Lucian did here. Mortimer was supposed to be in charge of the hunters, but when Lucian was around *he* gave the orders.

Scotty was also a laird. He'd been born in 1172, the son of the laird of the MacDonald clan. Beth didn't know much about his life as a mortal, but Dree had once said he'd inherited the title at eighteen and ruled for more than ten years, giving it up only when his being turned prevented his aging and made his remaining with his people risky.

While Scotty might have given up the title, he still had the mindset of a laird, and she was a commoner. Beneath his notice or attention. He'd made that obvious every time they'd met since that first time one hundred twenty-five years ago, usually treating her with cold indifference and looking down his nose at her with a pained grimace as if her very presence offended him. At least, that's what he'd done every time before this, which made her wonder what he was up to now and why he was bothering to be nice to her. Or maybe she was making too much of the few friendly words that had passed between them at the rogue's house. That made her frown and wish she could talk to Dree about it. Unfortunately, her friend was down in Venezuela with most of the North American Rogue Hunters, searching for missing immortals and the mad scientist who'd kidnapped them. Beth was on her own this time.

Ah well, she told herself, turning onto her side. She'd fly out in a few hours and leave the confusion of Laird Cullen MacDonald, aka Scotty, far behind. Hopefully the job would keep her out of Toronto for most if not all of the rest of Scotty's vacation. And she could go back to just fantasizing about him, rather than having to deal with him in the flesh. A gal could hope.

"Hello, Cullen. I hope you slept well."

Scotty glanced toward the stove at that greeting as he entered the kitchen and smiled crookedly when he saw Mortimer's wife, Sam, frying strips of bacon. He wasn't used to people using his true first name.

He'd been called Scotty for as long as he'd been involved with the Rogue Hunters. His first partner had insisted on calling him that because of his Scottish accent and it had stuck. Now it seemed more natural to him than the name his father had given him at birth. But Sam had been addressing him as Cullen since Mortimer had introduced him as Laird Cullen MacDonald, despite his adding that his nickname was Scotty.

"Aye, verra well, thank ye, Samantha," he murmured.

"Well, good," she said, sounding relieved. "I'd feel bad if neither of you were able to get any sleep today."

"Beth did no' sleep well?" he asked mildly, and wasn't surprised when Sam shook her head. He'd already suspected from his lack of dreams that the woman hadn't slept at all.

"Not a wink, apparently. She said her mind was just too wound up after the hunt and she would have done better to go for a run or something before going to bed," Sam told him. "But that's okay. She can sleep on the plane."

"Where is she?" Scotty asked, trying not to sound too interested.

"She decided to drive home and pack some clothes for the trip. I told her that she could buy things in BC and the Council would pay for it, but she said she'd be more comfortable with her own things." Sam's gaze shifted to the clock on the stove, and she frowned as she saw the time. "I would've expected her to be back by now, though. Beth knows what time the plane is supposed to be here, and Mortimer still needs to explain the job to her."

Scotty glanced at the clock now too, and found himself also frowning. From all he'd learned about her over the decades, Beth was the kind of woman who showed up early for everything, rather than risk being even a minute late for anything.

"Maybe I should call and make sure everything is okay," Sam said worriedly. She didn't wait for Scotty to comment, but set down the fork she'd been using to turn the bacon and pulled a cell phone from her pocket. She punched in numbers, placed the phone to her ear and waited . . . and waited . . . and then her eyebrows drew together and she pushed the button to end the call. Setting it down, Sam murmured, "She didn't answer. She must be driving back, maybe."

"Do the SUVs no' have hands-free phone capabilities?" Scotty asked, his eyes narrowing.

"Yes." Sam nodded and bit her lip, her gaze shifting to the phone she'd set on the countertop.

"She would have taken her car and not one of our SUVs," Donny pointed out, drawing their attention to his arrival in the room. "It looked pretty new and probably has hands-free capabilities too, though."

"It does. She used it to call me just the other day," Sam muttered. She picked up the phone and tried to call her again, only to end the call a moment later with a dissatisfied look on her face. Her gaze shifted to the clock on the wall once more, and she shook her head. "I don't think she's the type to be late."

"Ye think right, lass. Beth is never late," Scotty said, getting to his feet. "Donny, fetch a vehicle."

"Are we going after her again?" Donny asked, eyes wide.

"Aye," Scotty said grimly, walking toward him.

Nodding, Donny turned and hurried out of the room.

"I'll explain to Mortimer when he comes looking for you," Sam said solemnly. "Call as soon as you find her."

"I will, lass," Scott assured her as he left the kitchen.

Beth grimaced and glanced to the elevator panel as her phone began to ring again. She didn't try to answer it. Whoever it was could wait until she reached her car, and could set down the box and bags she was carrying to grab her phone. If she ever got off this elevator, she thought with irritation.

The damned thing had stopped on every floor since she'd gotten on board, and it was going to continue to do so all the way down to the parking garage, thanks to an annoying little bugger who had hit every button on the elevator panel before getting off on her floor. If her hands hadn't been full, Beth might have slapped the little brat's mother for not controlling her child and making him behave.

Honestly, what was the matter with people anymore? In her day, the boy wouldn't have dared to do something so bratty for fear of having his behind tanned. Instead, his mother had stood there ineffectively mewling, "Now, Tommy, don't do that. Come along. Daddy's waiting. Tommy."

Sighing as the elevator stopped and the doors opened again, Beth leaned against the back wall of the elevator and briefly closed her eyes. She'd had nothing but delays and detours since heading out to fetch her clothes. Nearly every street she'd taken on the way here had been under construction, and then she'd got caught at train tracks for what had seemed like forever as a train had slowed, gone forward and backed up before starting forward again. It had been like the universe was trying to prevent her getting to her apartment.

Halfway here, Beth had begun to regret that she hadn't just taken up the offer to use the Council credit card and buy all new items when she got to British Columbia. Now she wished she'd turned around then and headed back to the Enforcer house.

"Only twenty floors to the parking garage," she muttered to herself with disgust as the doors closed. Shaking her head, she glanced down at everything she was carrying. She had an overnight bag over each arm, one with a pair of jeans, two T-shirts, a hairbrush, perfume, deodorant, her toothbrush, and all those other things a girl needed for a short trip. The second bag held another pair of jeans, a pair of black dress pants, more T-shirts, a dressier shirt, and the always handy little black dress.

Beth had packed the first bag and started to leave, only to realize that Mortimer hadn't told her how long this job might take or even what it entailed. Concerned that it might take longer than a day or two as she'd originally assumed, and that simple jeans and T-shirts might not suffice, she'd packed the second bag. She'd then also thrown a pair of high-heeled shoes and running shoes into the grocery bag that presently dangled from her left wrist, and then had packed away the set of her favorite knives, two custom-made guns, and her iPad into the zipped-up black carrier that dangled from her right wrist.

On top of all that, Beth was carrying a box filled with food that would go bad if she didn't return within a day or two. If Mortimer told her that she should only be twenty-four hours or so, then she'd simply put it in one of the refrigerators in the garage behind the Enforcer house and bring it back on her return. However, if he said this job would take four days or more, she'd give it to Sam to either use or drop off at the nearest homeless shelter so that at least someone would get to eat it.

The elevator dinged again, and the doors opened. Beth glanced up at the panel to see that it was only the nineteenth floor. She started to scowl, and then pushed away from the wall and moved quickly off the elevator. She would take the stairs. It would be faster, and what she was carrying wasn't really heavy, at least not to her. It was just awkward. The bags on either side bulged outward, bumping into the wall if she got too close on either side, and not having her hands free was a pain, as she learned when she reached the metal door to the stairwell.

"Brilliant," Beth growled as she stared at the doorknob she couldn't turn. Sighing, she set the box on the floor, half straightened to open the door, held it open with her foot, and bent to pick up the box again.

Huffing out a sigh, Beth started down the stairs at a jog, careful not to get too close to the wall or the railing to avoid bumping against one or the other and upsetting her stride. It was much quicker than the elevator with all its stops, and she managed to reach the parking level relatively quickly and without further delay. Beth had to set down the box again to open the door to the parking garage, and then to open the door of her red Ford Explorer and stow her gear inside, but soon she was inside and on her way.

It wasn't until she pulled out of the parking garage

that Beth recalled the two missed phone calls. She almost pulled over to see who they were from, but a glance at the digital clock on the dashboard made her decide against it. She'd already taken much longer than she'd expected, and was going to have to do a bit of speeding on the way back to make up time. Even then Mortimer would no doubt be waiting on her.

The idea made her cluck her tongue. Beth hated to be late for anything and was generally ridiculously early to avoid it. That wasn't going to be the case today, she acknowledged unhappily, and then forced herself to take a couple of deep breaths to relax. There was nothing she could do about it. She should have had more than enough time to get there and back. But things simply had not gone to plan. Life could be like that sometimes.

Having encountered so much construction and so many detours using the back roads to the apartment, Beth chose a different route back to the house, one that put her on the highway for the better part of the drive. It was the route she should have taken on the way out, she supposed. But she liked to avoid the highway if possible. Mostly because she thought the drivers here were crazy. They drove too fast and then too slow and then too fast again, like they did not understand what cruise control was. And—Good Lord!—every time she turned around, someone was switching lanes without bothering to signal or see if anyone was already in that lane.

Beth noticed the semi pulling a flatbed of steel girders before it became a problem. It merged onto the highway from an on-ramp ahead of her, but she was in the middle lane so didn't think anything of it until it suddenly swerved into the center lane just as her front end drew even with the back of it. Beth instinctively hit the brakes and started to turn the steering wheel left but, spotting the blue sedan in that lane, immediately jerked the steering wheel right instead and stood on the brakes, hoping for the best.

Seeing the steel girders coming straight at her head, Beth quickly threw herself to the side, intending to lie flat across the front seat. Unfortunately, she'd forgotten about her seatbelt. She was reminded of it when it snapped tight, holding her in place as the front windshield exploded.

Three

"Do you know where Beth lives?"

"Aye," Scotty answered as he steered the SUV down the driveway. He'd got a lot of information and even maps before flying to Canada. And he'd insisted on driving again. It had seemed obvious from their first drive out to back up Beth that Donny was not comfortable with speed, and he had a bad feeling speed would be of the essence again here.

The young immortal accepted that news without comment, but did eye him curiously. After a moment, though, he said, "You probably want to take the highway. It's summer and the road crews have everything all torn up. She would have taken the highway to avoid that."

Scotty merely grunted. He'd planned to take the highway anyway. It was the only route that had been included with the info he'd been given, and had been listed as the fastest. Which was good, since he felt a certain urgency to get to her quickly.

Donny fell silent for a bit then, and Scotty was just turning onto the ramp leading to the highway when the lad suddenly asked, "What if she's already on her way back and we missed her?"

That was a real possibility and something he hadn't considered. Scotty frowned over it as he merged onto the highway. Once he was safely in traffic, however, he said, "We have trackers on our vehicles in the UK. Do you have anyth—"

"We do too!" Donny interrupted with excitement and pulled out his phone.

Scotty grimaced as the other man called Mortimer. If he'd thought of the trackers back at the house, he might have saved them this trip. At least he would have if all was well with Beth, he thought as he listened to Donny explain what they wanted to Mortimer.

"He's opening the program," Donny announced.

Scotty merely nodded, his concentration on the lanes ahead and the flow of traffic.

A good ten minutes passed before Donny said, "He has it up and sees both our vehicle and hers. He says she's on the other side of the highway, coming our way—" Donny cut himself off abruptly and waited, and then asked with concern, "What?"

"What is it?" Scotty asked tersely.

"He says her vehicle appears to be stopped in the middle of the highway. We should pass her in a couple minutes."

Scotty's mouth tightened. It would be more than a couple of minutes if the slowdown in traffic was anything to go by. The people ahead in all three lanes on this side of the median were slowing to gawk at something, and he suspected it was whatever had stopped Beth's vehicle. Even as he thought that, the traffic on the other side of the median dropped off abruptly, from a steady flow of vehicles to almost nothing. Which meant something had brought oncoming traffic almost to a standstill.

Probably an accident, Scotty thought and shifted into the outside left lane while he had the chance. He wanted to see Beth's vehicle and be sure she was all right and hadn't been involved in whatever was holding up traffic on the other side.

"Looks like an accident," Donny said a moment later.

Scotty merely nodded, his narrowed eyes switching between the road and the accident ahead on their left. There were three lanes of traffic on the other side of the median too, but a flatbed trailer was presently across the two lanes farthest from them, leaving only the inside lane nearest them open. However, the cars weren't whizzing out at one hundred ten or even the speed limit of one hundred kilometers an hour. They were crawling through the opening, the drivers rubbernecking it all the way.

"That explains why she's stopped," Donny murmured, eyeing the accident as they approached. "She must be in an inside lane. Look for a red Explorer. That's what she drives."

Scotty grunted. Their SUV was now crawling as slowly as the rubberneckers on the other side of the median, and he had a huge tight ball of "something's fecking wrong" in the pit of his stomach.

"Can you see any of the other vehicles involved?"

Scotty asked as they drew even with the end of the truck and got their first view of the vehicles behind it.

"Mortimer says we should be right beside her vehicle," Donny murmured, the phone still pressed to his ear as he craned his neck to get a better look around Scotty. "But the only red vehicle I see is . . ."

"The one under the back of the flatbed," Scotty finished grimly when the lad's voice died. He didn't wait for a response, but glanced around to assess the situation. Unfortunately, there was a concrete barrier on this side of the three lanes and no shoulder to pull off onto. He had to get to the outside lane to move the SUV out of traffic. Taking control of several drivers at once, he slowed them to create an opening, and then steered the SUV across the lanes and onto the right shoulder.

Leaving him to it, Donny unsnapped his seat belt and climbed out of his seat and then over the back seat to get to where the weapons locker and blood cooler were.

"Good lad," Scotty muttered as he brought the vehicle to a halt, shifted it into Park and shut it off.

"How are we going to get across traffic?" Donny asked, hurrying to his side with the portable blood cooler in hand as Scotty got out of the vehicle.

"How do ye think?" Scotty asked, shifting his attention to the drivers of several passing cars.

"Mind control to make them stop?" Donny asked.

"Got it in one, lad," Scotty said grimly as he made the drivers slow almost to a stop. He then jogged across their side of the highway with Donny hurrying after him.

They had to climb over the three-foot-high concrete

barrier, cross the grass median and then climb over the concrete barrier on the other side as well. Scotty didn't even have to control the mind of the driver of the first vehicle crawling past the accident. He slowed on his own to allow them to cross. It was probably a good thing, because at that point Scotty could see the vehicle under the back of the flatbed and would have had trouble concentrating enough to control anyone. It was definitely a red Explorer. The girders had sheared off the top of the vehicle, which now lay on the asphalt behind it, leaving a clear view of the blood-covered backs of the front seats.

"Those girders took off the headrests," Donny pointed out with concern. "You don't think—"

That they took off Beth's head too? Scotty finished what the boy wouldn't, or couldn't, say. But he did so silently and didn't respond to the unfinished question. He couldn't bear to think about that, let alone say it. She could not have been decapitated, he assured himself as they approached the damaged vehicle. He had waited too long to—

"She's not here," Donny said with surprise as they reached the ruined vehicle and peered over the front seats that were empty not only of Beth, but blood as well, other than a couple of drops here and there.

Scotty merely nodded, his attention now on the crushed front end of the Explorer where it butted up against the right back tires of the flatbed. The front of the red vehicle hadn't only been crushed accordion-style against the huge tires on impact, but the tires of the flatbed had also blown, dropping the back of the trailer with its stack of girders onto the hood of the engine. He was surprised the combination hadn't caused an explosion and wondered if everyone shouldn't be giving the vehicles some serious space.

"Donny? Scotty?"

Both men turned to see Beth straightening from where she had been kneeling on the roadside beside a somewhat traumatized-looking man in his late fifties.

Surprise evident on her face, she walked toward them now, her eyebrows lifting in question. "What are you doing here?"

"We came looking for you," Donny explained. "You were late, and Mr. Scotty had a feeling something was wrong."

"He's Mr. MacDonald if you want to address him formally," she said with a crooked smile, and then corrected herself. "Well, Laird MacDonald, really. But Mr. Scotty just sounds wrong."

"Oh, sorry, Laird Scotty," the lad said at once.

Scotty merely shook his head, his attention remaining on Beth as his gaze slid over her from top to toe. Much to his relief, she didn't appear injured at all. Although she did have splashes of blood on her back and side. "The blood in yer vehicle?"

"I keep a cooler of bagged blood there in case of emergencies," she explained, glancing to her car and grimacing at the shape it was in.

"Ah," he murmured, relaxing. Obviously, the cooler had spilled, its contents flying about and tearing on impact. That explained the massive amount of blood on the backs of the seats while there was little in the front and on her.

Finally meeting her gaze again, he commented, "Ye managed to avoid injury."

Beth nodded solemnly, and glanced toward the vehicle behind them. "Barely. The seat belt held me up and nearly got me beheaded, but snapped at the last moment."

Scotty paused briefly, sucking in air to calm himself as he realized how close he'd come to losing her, but then asked, "And the driver o' the flatbed?"

Beth gestured over her shoulder to the man sitting on the roadside who she'd been talking to when she spotted them. "He seems fine, but a little out of it. I just got him out of the truck and practically had to carry him. I was going to search his mind to see why he suddenly swerved in front of me, but then noticed you two. It all just happened a few minutes ago."

Scotty nodded. "I'll handle him. Ye see if any o' yer belongings survived the crash."

Beth smiled wryly and shook her head, but muttered, "As you will, m'laird," and headed toward the Explorer.

Scotty's lips twitched at her words. He knew Beth hated it when he got "all laird of the manor bossy," as he'd once heard her put it. But that's what he'd been trained for. He had been laird of the MacDonald clan, expected to take charge and handle any situation that came up. After that he'd had many titles, but every one of them were as a man in charge, right down to his now being head of the UK Council as well as the UK Rogue Hunters. Being "all laird of the manor bossy" just came naturally to him.

More important to him, though, was her reaction to it today. In the past, she would have snarled and snapped at him like a rabid dog. This time, there was little anger. It was more irritation and even some amusement, which seemed to suggest the reports he'd been receiving were correct and she was finally healing from her past. She might actually be ready for him to claim her as his life mate. Something he'd been waiting nearly one hundred twenty-five years to do.

"Donny," he said suddenly, tearing his gaze away from Beth's swaying hips as she walked to her Explorer.

"Yes, Mr. Laird Scotty," Donny said promptly. The boy actually stood at attention.

"Scotty'll do," he growled. "I'm no' a laird anymore. I gave that up shortly after I was turned."

"Oh, right, the aging thing would have forced you to," Donny said with a nod.

"Aye, the aging thing," he agreed and then said, "Call Mortimer and tell him what's happened and that we need a cleanup crew here."

"Yes, sir," he said, pulling out his phone.

Leaving him to it, Scotty then moved over to the truck driver.

Several cars had pulled over on the shoulder, the passengers and drivers all piling out to see if they could help. A lot of them stood crowded around the driver, gazing from the truck to the red Explorer with its crushed front end and sheared-off roof. Scotty sent them away with little effort and then dropped to crouch next to the man and search his mind.

The driver was dazed and confused. He recalled pulling onto the highway and merging with traffic, and then his memory skipped to sitting shaking in his truck, staring into the side-view mirror at the Explorer with its top sheared off.

Disturbed by the absence of memory, Scotty tried

harder and dug deeper into the man's mind, but there was nothing there. The area when the accident had happened was blank. It was as if he hadn't been there during it.

Or as if he'd been under someone's control, Scotty thought with concern. He took a moment to calm the man's mind, and then stood and turned to survey Beth's vehicle.

She was lucky to be alive. Had her seat belt not snapped, allowing her to avoid the girders, she might have been beheaded. And he wasn't quite sure how the Explorer hadn't exploded and burned her alive when the flatbed dropped on it. Those were the only two ways that an immortal could die, beheading or burning, and an accident like this should have resulted in one or the other of those outcomes.

"Mortimer says he's got a team on the way. They'll be here in five minutes."

Scotty glanced to Donny at that announcement and nodded abruptly, then led him to where Beth was leaning into the Explorer. His eyebrows rose as he heard her mutter an unhappy "Damn."

"Problem?" he asked.

Backing out of the car, she straightened and held up a shoe that had slid out of the plastic bag. "The Explorer ate my shoe."

Scotty grinned crookedly. "Ate it, eh?"

Beth stared at the remaining shoe and moaned, "They were my favorite shoes."

Scott shifted his gaze from her pretty, flushed face framed with red hair and looked down at the shoe she held. He then blinked. Good Lord in heaven, the shoe was as red as a candy apple, the heel a good four or five inches high, and he immediately envisioned her wearing them and nothing else. And then he recalled that there was only one now and she'd never again wear them, naked or otherwise, and was nearly as distressed as Beth appeared to be. He really would have liked to have seen her in them.

"Ah well," Beth muttered, tossing that incredible shoe back into the vehicle. "At least my weapons case appears to be all right, and my overnight bags appear to be okay too." She pulled them out of the Explorer one after the other.

Scotty took each item from her, slinging the bags over his shoulder and reaching for the next item until she pulled out a long tubular something. He took it, but then turned it slowly in his hand and sniffed it, asking, "What is this?"

"Huh?" She turned with a brick of something white and stinky in hand and peered at the item he was eyeing with interest. "Oh. Goose sausage. A friend gave it to me. It's really good too, but I was worried that it and these other foods would go bad while I was gone, so I thought I'd best take it all to the Enforcer house. If I'm not going to be gone long, I'll just store it there and collect it when I get back, but if I'll be gone longer, Sam and Mortimer can have it or give it away to charity."

She finished her explanation by plopping the smelly white brick in his free hand and then returned to digging in the car.

The minute she'd turned her back, Scotty handed off the white brick to Donny but held on to that sausage. It smelled delightfully delicious. He could almost take a bite right now.

"I think that's everything," Beth announced, turning with a somewhat crushed box holding several more items of food.

"Good, because if I'm no' mistaken, I believe that truck pullin' up behind our SUV is Mortimer's men," Scotty commented, his gaze narrowed on the vehicle as two men got out, one fair-haired and one dark-haired.

"It's Russell and Francis," Donny said, recognizing them. Concern on his face, he added, "Man, Mortimer must be desperately low on people if he took them off the gate to come out here and handle this."

Scotty frowned at the comment, and reached into his pocket to clasp his phone as they watched the men start across the other side of the highway toward the median. He was considering sending for a half dozen of his own hunters to come help out here . . . just until this business in Venezuela was resolved. He might send a couple down to Venezuela as well to help out there. It would keep his thumb on the pulse of what was happening with that business.

"Hola!"

Blinking his thoughts away, Scotty raised his eyebrows as the dark-haired man leapt over the second concrete barrier and rushed ahead of his partner to greet them. He fairly danced between the slow-moving vehicles in the inside lane and then rushed to Beth and caught her up in his arms.

Scotty stiffened and scowled as the man hugged her tightly and cried, "Elizabeth Argenis! You must be more careful. You cannot get yourself killed after we've just become friends."

"MacDonald."

Scotty heard the greeting as the fair-haired man reached them, but was busy trying to incinerate the darker man with his eyes.

"I do not think you have met my life mate, Francis. Have you?"

That caught his attention, and Scotty blinked and turned to peer at the speaker. "Russell," he said, recognizing the fair-haired man now. His gaze swung back to the man still holding Beth in his arms. "Your life mate?"

"Yes," Russell said, his eyes twinkling with amusement, and then he glanced to the darker man and admonished, "Francis, put Beth down and come meet Scotty."

Francis froze, his head jerking toward them, eyes wide. Setting Beth down, he spun her around to face them and dropped his arm across her shoulders as he stared at Scotty. "Not Scotty the head of the UK Enforcers and the man we have to be nice to if we want to go to London during our European tour so you can introduce me to the Green Giant that Victoria and Julianna were giggling about?"

"He did no' e'en stop to take a breath," Scotty said to Russell in a marveling tone, and then glanced to Francis and added, "But yer bum's out the window, lad."

"My bum's out the window?" Francis echoed with alarm and looked over his shoulder at his behind as if afraid he might have a hole in his trousers.

"It means you are talking nonsense," Russell explained with amusement.

"Aye," Scotty said. "Ye do no' need me permission to visit London. All immortals are welcome so long as they behave."

"And do as he says," Beth teased, offering Scotty a sweet smile when he glanced her way.

Russell's eyebrows rose slightly at her sass, and then he said abruptly, "Well, I am glad you are alive and well, Beth, because Mortimer is waiting on you at the house. Apparently, he has a job for you?"

"Oh, damn, yes, I should get going," she said, her gaze shifting to the destroyed Explorer with a frown.

"We'll drive ye back," Scotty said at once. Taking her arm, he nodded at Russell. "A pleasure to see ye again, Argeneau."

"It's Jones this decade," Russell said with a smile, referring to the last name he was using at the moment. "Francis's family name of Renart is next decade, and then it will be Argeneau again the decade after that."

"Jones, then," Scotty corrected himself and gave a nod to both men before urging Beth away. They had to get back to the house. The plane would be there by now, waiting on them, and as busy as things were, the pilot would not be happy about having to cool his jets. Unfortunately, the delay would not be over even once they reached the house. Mortimer still had to explain the job to Beth . . . and tell her that Scotty would be going with her on this job.

"Wait, what?" Beth blinked in surprise at Mortimer's words. They'd arrived at the house just moments ago. Sam had greeted them at the door and sent them to Mortimer's office, where he had shocked her with the greeting, "I'm glad you were not injured in the accident. I do not think Scotty and Donny could have handled this job without you. It needs a delicate touch."

Shaking her head, she said with confusion, "But I work with Tybo and Valerian. They—"

"Both took a knife to the heart," Mortimer interrupted solemnly. "Rachel, Dr. Argeneau, would like them to take at least another day off to recover fully."

"Oh," Beth said weakly. She would have expected the two men to be mostly healed by now if they'd been given blood transfusions and such, but mostly healed wasn't fully healed and she was no doctor, so it looked like she'd be stuck with Scotty a bit longer.

"Fortunately," Mortimer continued, "Scotty and Donny are available to fill in while Tybo and Valerian are out of commission."

Beth wasn't sure how fortunate that was. She supposed she'd have to wait and see just what Scotty was up to in coming here.

"So," Mortimer continued, moving the subject along, "you will be flying out to Vancouver, British Columbia, for a case that is a bit delicate."

"Delicate how?" Beth asked with interest, trying not to think about the fact that she'd be trapped on a plane with Mr. Sexybeast for a good five-hour flight. At least, she thought that was how long the flight to British Columbia was.

"Delicate because it involves Kira Sarka," Mortimer explained.

"Who is Kira Sarka?" Donny asked before Beth could.

"The youngest daughter of Athanasios Sarka."

Judging by Mortimer's solemn tones, this Sarka person was someone they should all know, and the name did sound vaguely familiar, but Beth had no idea who he might be.

Mortimer must have picked up on that because he explained, "He is the head of the Russian Immortal Council."

Ah, yeah, that's probably why she'd heard the name. Undoubtedly he'd come up in conversation before, and she hadn't paid attention. Beth hated politics. But even more than politics, she hated when people, whether immortal or mortal, got treated differently because of wealth, power, or political connections and such.

"So, he's the head of the Russian Immortal Council," she murmured and then arched an eyebrow. "And that matters why?"

When Mortimer hesitated, Scotty said, "Athanasios means *immortal death* in ancient Greek."

She had no idea what that had to do with anything, but it caught her attention. "His parents gave him a name that means *immortal death*?"

"Nay, his people did when he lived in Greece," Scotty said dryly and then added, "because he seemed immortal to them and brought death to his enemies swiftly and brutally. Athan's always been a bit hotheaded and bloodthirsty."

"Hmm," Beth said, unimpressed.

"He is not someone we want to upset unnecessarily," Mortimer said now. "He's unpredictable and prone to prompt retribution for perceived slights. So his daughter has to be handled with care."

Beth considered that and then asked, "What has she done?"

"She recently moved to British Columbia to attend summer courses at the university. She is living on campus, and apparently has been feeding off the hoof."

"Off the hoof means she's been biting mortals, right?" Donny asked and when Mortimer nodded, he winced and shook his head. "That's bad."

"Definitely," Mortimer agreed.

"So . . ." Beth raised one eyebrow. "You want us to arrange an accident for this Kira? Maybe something like what nearly killed me today?"

"What?" Mortimer gaped at her.

"What, what?" she asked innocently. "Feeding on mortals is not allowed here. It's rogue behavior punishable by beheading. But obviously you don't want to upset her father, Mr. Deathhead, so dragging her in before the Council for judgment isn't possible. Which leaves a punishment that could be seen as an accident having nothing to do with the Council," she reasoned.

"We don't assassinate the children of the leaders of other Councils," Mortimer said firmly.

"Who said anything about assassination?" Beth asked lightly. "I am saying let the Council vote on what to do with her, which, if she is knowingly and deliberately breaking our laws, will probably be beheading. And then we—"

"The Council has already voted," Mortimer said tightly, cutting her off. "They decided to send someone to explain our laws to her, and to inform her of the punishment for breaking those laws. Then she will be watched to see if she continues with those behaviors. If she does, *then* she will be brought in for judgment."

"Ah, I see," Beth said with a solemn nod. "The girl is a dullard, without the mental capacity to understand our laws, so needs them explained."

Mortimer opened his mouth, closed it and then narrowed his eyes on her and accused, "You are trying to get me to decide you cannot be as delicate as we need so I will take you off the assignment."

Beth grimaced at the accusation, but didn't deny it. Instead, she said softly, "We all know she knows the laws here, right?"

"Yes," Mortimer admitted, and then pointed out, "But she may not believe they pertain to her. She is young and apparently rebellious. She enjoys causing her father problems, and she may believe she has some sort of diplomatic immunity here or that we will merely fine her father or some such thing."

Beth considered that briefly, and then let her breath out on a sigh. "Fine. So, we go find her, talk to her, and then watch her to see if she behaves."

"You only have to talk to her, explain our laws and inform her that they do pertain to her too, and then make the consequences clear should she continue to break our laws," Mortimer corrected her. "Someone else is already watching her."

"Then why aren't they doing the talking?" she asked with surprise.

"Because they aren't hunters. It isn't their job. They're only keeping an eye on her as a favor because we're short-staffed."

"Ah." Beth nodded, but then asked, "Is there a reason talking to her would take the three of us?"

"Athanasios has put several bodyguards on Kira. They may take exception to your speaking to her. It is best you not go alone."

"Ah," Beth said again. "So if we're flying out there, I'm guessing we're to rent a vehicle?"

"No. We have a satellite office in Vancouver. There's at least one in every province," he added.

"You mean a house and shop like this one?" Donny asked with interest.

"Basically," Mortimer said and continued, "Someone will collect you from the airport and take you there. Hopefully," he added under his breath.

Beth caught the word and narrowed her eyes. "Hopefully? What does that mean?"

Mortimer paused a heartbeat, but then heaved a sigh and admitted, "I have not been able to get ahold of our agent in Vancouver yet. But I am sure I will before you land," he added quickly, although he didn't sound all that confident.

"And if you don't?" Beth asked.

Mortimer considered the question briefly and then said, "If there is no one waiting at the airport when you land, call me and I will give you further instructions. However, for now, we will go on the assumption someone will be waiting. They will take you to the satellite house, you can settle in and then tomorrow night you can approach Kira Sarka and—"

"Wait, wait, wait," Beth cut in. "Tomorrow night? Why not approach her as soon as we land?"

"Because she is presently out of the country," he admitted and glanced down at the file on his desk before adding, "She is expected back tomorrow by dinnertime, but is presently in Hollywood for a party at some star's house or something. I wrote the name of the actor down here somewhere," he muttered, running a finger down the top page in the file, which was covered with an almost unreadable scrawl.

Not caring whose party the kid was attending, Beth

asked impatiently, "Then why are we flying out to-night? Why not just go tomorrow?"

"Because the plane is available now and may not be tomorrow," Mortimer said, sounding a little annoyed.

"But—" Beth began, only to be interrupted.

"Do not 'but' me, Beth. I have enough on my plate right now without you giving me a hard time. Do you know how difficult it is to get things done around here with seventy-five percent of my people down chasing that damned Dressler? I am working with a handful of real hunters, a bunch of trainees and even volunteers with absolutely no training at all. As for trying to get one of the planes booked for anything, well, that is damned near impossible. I have people driving six, ten, and even twelve hours to look into things that will probably turn out to be nothing, but we have to check out any complaint or tip sent in, because Lord knows if we do not and something happens, I will be the one Lucian—"

"Okay, okay," Beth said soothingly. "I get it. You're crazy busy and stressed out, and we fly down tonight and talk to the kid tomorrow. It's fine. When do we fly back?"

Mortimer stared at her for a moment, looking a bit frustrated that she'd cut off his rant, but after a minute he blew out a long breath and muttered, "I managed to book the plane for the day after. Sunday at noon." Standing, he nodded abruptly. "I think that is every-thing I needed to tell you, so I suppose you had best get to the plane. It has been waiting on the tarmac for the past half hour, and I would not put it past the bastards to fly off on their next assignment if you are not soon boarded."

Nodding, Beth got reluctantly to her feet.

"Your luggage should all be on the plane by now, and the captain has an envelope with credit cards and a small amount of cash for each of you. Bastien sent it with him. He asked me to remind you to please keep all receipts."

"Of course, Mortimer. Don't worry. We'll handle everything," Beth assured him. It seemed she'd be working with Scotty a bit longer. Ah well, she could think of worse things than having to work with a six-foot-three sexy beast of a Scot. He might be annoying at times, but he was always pretty to look at.

Four

"I can't sleep."

Beth heard that complaint from Donny, but didn't open her eyes. She was exhausted and had been dozing in her seat before Donny's words had drawn her back from the edge of slumber. Besides, she didn't think he was addressing her anyway, as was proven by his next words.

"I don't know how Beth can sleep."

"Exhaustion," Scotty said softly. "She didn't sleep at the house."

Beth barely kept from blinking her eyes open with surprise. Not because he knew she hadn't slept at the Enforcer house. She supposed Sam had told him that. She was surprised because his tone had almost been affectionate. Affection was not something she would've connected with Scotty's attitude toward her. This was new and just plain confusing.

"She must've had an interesting life," Donny commented, and then in a wry voice added, "You probably both have."

"Aye," Scotty said. "Living a long time tends to make fer at least a few interestin' interludes."

"Yeah, I suppose so," Donny murmured, and then gave a soft chuckle and said, "Or maybe it's being immortal. It's certainly brought about some interesting events in my life."

Scotty merely grunted at the comment, and silence reigned for a moment before Donny asked, "Do you ever wonder about them?"

"About who, lad?" Scotty asked mildly.

"The Atlanteans."

"Not really," Scotty said dismissively.

"I do," Donny told him.

"And what do ye wonder about them?" Scotty asked indulgently.

"Well, what if Atlantis never fell? I mean, do you think their scientists would have fixed the flaw?"

"What flaw is that?"

"You know, the flaw in the programming of the nanos that keeps them from disintegrating and allowing us to be normal again."

Beth almost sat up and put in her two cents' worth then, but was too tired to bother, so simply stayed put and listened. She couldn't help thinking, though, that if the people of Atlantis were anything like modern people, she didn't imagine they were too upset with the results of that flaw. It was a scientific fountain of youth. Humans reached their peak somewhere between twenty-five and twenty-eight depending on the person, and so that was the state nanos ensured their hosts were returned to and stayed at . . . basically forever, as far as she could tell. Well, barring a beheading or burning up. It was one heck of a flaw.

"Or," Donny continued, "do you think any of those scientists at Argeneau Enterprises might ever find a way to reverse the flaw or something? Reprogram the nanos or whatever?"

Beth waited curiously for Scotty's answer, but he merely asked solemnly, "What do you think, lad?"

"I think they've been working with those nanos an awfully long time and not figured out anything," he answered. "And I think even though they know it's the natural order, maybe people are mostly afraid to die . . . including the scientists. So, maybe they don't really want to find the fix for the flaw in the nanos."

"And I think I was right before. Ye are a cannie lad, boyo," Scotty said, sounding impressed.

"So, that would be a no?" Donny asked in a wry tone. "No, they won't find the way to fix the flaw?"

"Would ye mind if they did no'?" Scotty queried, sounding curious.

"You're asking if I'd mind staying young and strong forever?" he said on a laugh. "Of course not."

They were both silent for a minute and then Donny added solemnly, "I do miss having family, though. I mean, mine weren't the greatest, but they were family."

"I ken family is usually thought o' as forged by blood, lad, but blood does no' always make fer good family. Just look at Cain and Abel, or Constantine. Sometimes a better family can be forged through friendship and time." He paused, apparently to let that sink in, and then added, "Once ye're a full-blown hunter, ye'll find yer partner and coworkers becoming family to ye. Immortals ken the importance o' family and recognize that ye have none now and will adopt ye into theirs."

"Maybe." Donny sounded dubious.

"I'm surprised Leigh and Lucian have no' pulled ye into their family already," Scotty commented.

"So you were awake for that part of the ride back to the house too, were you?" Donny asked on a chuckle. Scotty didn't respond, at least not verbally. He must have nodded or something, though, because Donny grunted, and then said, "As for Leigh and Lucian, they kind of have tried to include me in their family, I think. I mean, Leigh invites me for every holiday and tries to get me to come out, but . . ."

"But ye're no' comfortable with them?" Scotty guessed. "Mayhap ye still feel some guilt for Leigh's getting turned because o' ye?"

"Yeah," Donny said on a sigh. "And then there's the fact that I don't think Lucian likes me much."

"Really? Why would that be?" Scotty asked with interest, and then must have read his mind because he said with certainty, "Ye still ha'e a crush on Leigh."

"Well, sure," Donny said as if that should be a given. "I mean, Leigh's beautiful, and smart and awesome and—"

"I do no' think Lucian does no' like ye," Scotty interrupted dryly.

"Really? Why? Has he said something to you about me?" Donny asked eagerly.

"Nay."

"Then why?" he asked with confusion.

"Because if he's read the thoughts in yer mind about his Leigh and has no' yet beat ye to a pulp, then he must like ye a great deal. He also has more patience than I ever credited him with," Scotty said dryly.

"Oh," Donny muttered, sounding embarrassed.

"Oh, is right," Scotty said with disgust. "Did ye have such X-rated thoughts about *my* life mate, ye'd no' be long fer this world. At the very least ye'd get a sound thrashin'." He paused briefly to let that sink in and then added, "Ye ha'e to learn to control yer thoughts, lad. Ye must remember any immortal older than ye can read every thought out o' yer head."

"Right," Donny said on a dejected sigh.

"Ye need to learn to not think except in private."

"Not think?" Donny echoed with disbelief. "That's not even possible!"

"O' course it is," Scotty assured him. "Ye just pay attention to everything around ye and cut out the commentary in yer head until ye're alone."

"The commentary?" Donny asked uncertainly.

"Aye, that voice in yer head that says, 'Hot damn, those candy-apple-red shoes are fine. I want to strip off every bit o' clothing she has on, licking her from top to bottom as I do, and then, once she's left in only those shoes, back her up against the wall and screw her slow and hard.'"

Beth blinked her eyes open and gawked briefly at the two men before catching herself and closing them again. She couldn't believe those were the words in Donny's head . . . and about Leigh too! Damn, he was lucky Lucian hadn't killed him. That amazed her, but no more than how hot the young man's thoughts were! Especially when spoken in Scotty's deep, sexy voice. She'd actually envisioned all that happening as he spoke the words . . . only to her, wearing her candy-apple-red shoes. And it hadn't been Donny but Scotty doing the stripping, licking, and slow screwing.

Damn, Beth knew what she'd be fantasizing in bed tonight. It was just a shame she couldn't actually act it out with Scotty for real. But the man was over eight hundred years old. Unmated immortals started losing interest in food and sex and things like that sometime after their first hundred years as an immortal. By their two hundredth year they were usually pretty much off both, and they stayed that way until they met their life mate.

Beth had been an immortal for nearly a hundred and twenty-five years now, but hadn't found her hungers waning at all yet. She loved food, all kinds of it, and she enjoyed sex . . . most of the time . . . well, maybe half the time. The truth was, she hadn't really been fussy on sex while mortal, but that probably had more to do with her situation than anything. Since the turn, though, she'd wanted sex, but was most often left feeling unsatisfied by it. Beth had no idea why. It wasn't like she didn't have orgasms or anything. She did. It was just . . . the best way she could think to describe it was that it was like when you were craving cherry pie, but had only apple. It could be the most amazing apple pie in the world, but still wasn't the cherry pie you were really yearning for, and you were left feeling slightly dissatisfied. That's how Beth found sex since the turn. Like it was good, but it just wasn't quite measuring up. Weird.

"But how do you cut out the commentary?" Donny asked now with frustration. "It just comes out. I don't know how to not think."

"Ye do. Ye just ne'er try to censor yourself because ye're used to thinking yer thoughts are yer own," Scotty said firmly. "I'll no' lie, it'll be hard and 'twill take some time fer ye to learn, but ye can do it. We all had to. And 'tis better to make yerself do it ere a stray thought has an older immortal thrash ye, or worse."

"Or worse?" Donny asked warily.

"I ken o' immortals who ha'e been killed fer stray thoughts they did no' control," he said solemnly. "And I'd no' like to see ye added to that list."

"Neither would I," Donny said unhappily.

"I'll do what I can to help ye with it."

"Thank you. I'd appreciate that," Donny said sincerely.

Another brief silence fell and then Donny asked, "Your life mate?"

"What?" Scotty sounded confused.

"Earlier you said, 'Did ye have such X-rated thoughts about *my* life mate, ye'd no' be long fer this world.'" Donny reminded him. "So? You *do* have a life mate?"

"Nay. Well, aye, I do," he confessed. "But I have no' claimed her."

"What! Why?" Donny asked with an amazement shared by Beth.

"'Tis a . . . delicate situation," Scotty said uncomfortably.

"Delicate how?" Donny prodded.

Beth half expected Scotty to tell the boy to mind his own business. Instead, he muttered, "She was no' ready yet."

Donny was silent for a minute, and Beth could almost hear his brain ticking as he tried to work that out. And then he said, "Like she's not ready because she's too young? A kid?"

"Something like that," Scotty muttered evasively.

"How young?" Donny asked with obvious curiosity.

"It does no' matter," Scotty said shortly, and ended the conversation by saying, "I did no' sleep well last night. I'm going to get some shut-eye."

Beth lay awake for a while. At first she was hoping Donny would get Scotty to say more, but then she got to thinking about the fact that Scotty had met his life mate. It might be the reason for his suddenly being nice to her. After all, that would make anyone happy. Of course, his not being able to claim his life mate because she was too young was a wrinkle. Especially since, having met his life mate, all of his hungers would now be reawakened. He'd have a taste for food again . . . and sex. Food wasn't a problem, but if his life mate was too young to claim, he would have no way to sate his reawakened urges for sex other than to look elsewhere.

For a moment, Beth briefly toyed with the idea that he might be open to an affair with her. The idea of actually having real sex with the man instead of the fantasies and dreams she'd been enjoying for over a century was not something she'd ever even considered. Now she did, and just the thought of it set her body tingling.

It wouldn't be like cheating for him either, she assured herself. After all, if his life mate was too young, and he hadn't yet claimed her, they weren't a couple. That sounded reasonable to her.

The stumbling block was that Scotty had never seemed to like her very much. And still might not, she considered. His behavior toward her had been pleasant enough so far, but it wasn't like they'd had much of a chance to talk. No, she was probably the last person he'd be interested in bedding. Which might be a good thing, she decided. After over a century of sexual fantasies about the man . . . well, it wasn't likely that he'd be able to live up to the Scotty of her dreams. That would be terribly disappointing.

Sighing, Beth let the brief idea go and allowed herself to finally drift off to sleep.

"I don't see anybody," Donny said. "Do you see anybody?"

Beth stifled a yawn as she glanced around the small airfield where they'd landed. It was made up of a long strip of tarmac, at the end of which was a large hangar, and a small building with huge glass windows making up the wall that overlooked the landing strip. Not spotting the standard black SUV either parked or driving toward them, she shrugged and suggested, "Maybe they're a little late."

"Maybe," Donny allowed. "Or maybe Mortimer wasn't able to get a hold of anyone. He said to call him if no one was waiting here for us. I better call."

"Be my guest," Beth said wearily. Once she'd fallen asleep, she'd fallen hard and hadn't woken again until Scotty had shaken her awake to let her know they'd landed. She still wasn't quite awake. She needed a coffee. Her gaze focused speculatively on the small building next to the hangar, and then she headed for it. They might have a coffee machine or something. Maybe. Hopefully.

"Wait!" Donny said, lowering his phone when she started away. "Where are you going?"

"I'm going to see if they have any coffee inside. Do you want one too?"

"But—Scotty's still talking to the pilot. Shouldn't we wait for him?"

Scotty had taken on the duty of retrieving the envelope Mortimer had mentioned from the pilot. Beth had been too tired to be annoyed at his taking over again and had merely headed out of the plane to see if their ride was here. Now she paused and turned back to say, "Yeah, and you can do that. I'm getting coffee and coming right back. Again, do you want anything?"

"Uh . . ."

Shaking her head, Beth turned to walk away, saying, "One regular coffee coming up."

"A hazelnut latte if they have them," Donny called after her. "With skim milk, and sweetener."

Beth just shook her head and kept walking. What did he think? Was he expecting there to be a fancy café inside serving lattes, cappuccinos and biscotti? And . . . really? A hazelnut latte with skim milk and sweetener?

"Dear Lord, he's a girl in disguise," Beth muttered to herself as she reached the building. Opening the door, she stepped inside and cast a quick glance around the small, empty waiting area. It wasn't very impressive. The floor was a dull gray tile, the walls a muddy cream. A single row of six upholstered seats sat on a supporting beam that was bolted into the floor facing the windows, but the faux leather of the seats was torn in several places and marked with graffiti. Beth noted two doors on her right—a men's room and ladies' room—and then focused wholly on the vending machines along the wall on the left. She headed for the one with a picture of a cup of coffee on the top and another picture, this time of coffee beans, on the bottom.

Much to Beth's surprise, the machine offered more than standard coffee, and she had her choice of coffee, cappuccino, mocha, Americano, espresso, hot chocolate, tea, apple cider, and yes, even a latte. However, it was just a straight latte, not a flavored one, and she was quite sure it was made with a flavor packet and hot water, not milk of any kind.

"Donny's going to be so disappointed," she murmured with amusement, digging in her pocket for change.

"Who is Donny?"

Beth glanced around with a start to see a tall, good-looking and slender dark-haired man crossing the waiting area toward her. He'd obviously just come out of the men's room. The door was still closing behind him. She stared at him blankly for a minute, surprise battling with recognition, and then whirled around squealing, "Oh my God, Matias!"

Before she'd fully turned, he had crossed the room. Grabbing her by the waist, he whirled her around, laughing.

"Is good to see you, Beth. You are beautiful as ever," he said warmly, pulling her into a bear hug as he stopped turning.

"You too," Beth said with a smile, and then pulled back to look at him. "How long has it been? Two years?"

"*Sí*, so long," he groaned, hugging her tightly again

and this time lifting her off the ground. "I think about you all the time. And I miss you every day."

Beth chuckled at his words, then wrapped her legs around his waist and used the position to force her upper body back so she could look him in the eyes. She did hate dangling in the air like a child. "I think about you often too, Matias," she assured him solemnly. "Spain just wasn't the same after you left."

"And so you followed me here to Canada, *sí*?" he teased with a grin.

"Actually, I followed Drina," she said almost apologetically.

"Ah, *sí*, I heard she found her life mate here," he said seriously. "I am very happy for her. But for me," he added, the solemnity falling away to be replaced by a wide grin, "I am happy because you are here."

"And I'd be happy if someone'd explain just who in the bloody blazes ye are."

Beth blinked in surprise at those words in a deep growl, and turned her head to see Scotty standing just inside the door to the terminal, scowling at her like she was a misbehaving child. Her eyes widened slightly, but she merely smiled and said politely, "Scotty, this is Matias Argenis. My cousin."

"Your cousin," he echoed dubiously.

"*Sí*, she was adopted by the Argenises as a sister to Drina, and family to all," Matias said with a wide smile. "And we are the kissing cousins."

Beth grinned when he kissed her nose, and then leaned forward to kiss his nose back. "Now you'd best put me down ere Scotty has a conniption fit on the spot. I think he believes our behavior is inappropriate."

"Hmm." Matias eyed Scotty's furious face briefly

and then turned back to her and raised one eyebrow. "He is English, no?"

"Scottish," she corrected him.

Matias shrugged, the action jostling her up and down slightly. "Is the same thing. English, Scottish, they are all the cold fish."

Beth grinned in response, but she also unhooked her legs from around his waist, and pushed at his chest until he set her back on the ground. Straightening her clothes, she asked, "Did Mortimer send you to collect us?"

"*Sí.* Mortimer, he is a slave driver. Do this, do that. Collect the beautiful Beth from the airport, take her back to the house, massage her feet, make the mad love to her."

"Idiot! He didn't say that," she protested with a laugh.

"No, but he would have did he know of my great passion for you," he assured her.

Shaking her head, Beth moved around him, muttering, "I need a coffee."

"Coffee is good," Matias said, turning to watch her drag change out of her pocket and pop it in the machine.

"Coffee is bad," Scotty countered. "It affects certain immortals like speed."

"Fortunately, I'm not affected by it," she assured him, and then added honestly, "much."

"Neither am I," Matias announced.

"Hey! Hey! Beth! Scotty!" Donny cried excitedly, rushing into the building with his phone in hand. "Mortimer says he did get a hold of the guy from the satellite house out here. His name is Matias and he should be here somewhere, but I—This is the guy, isn't it?" Donny interrupted himself to say, his gaze sliding between Matias, Beth and Scotty.

"Yes," Beth said with a smile. "Donny, meet Matias Argenis. Our ride, my cousin, and apparently our host here." She watched the men nod to each other in greeting and then turned back to select Americano coffee as she asked, "How did you end up working for the hunters here, Matias? I thought you left Spain to go to college."

"I did," Matias assured her. "I am in school here, but I am a poor student, and needed somewhere to live, so Papa called Lucian, and he said I could stay at the Enforcer house. All I have to do is the odd chore once in a while like collect beautiful ladies from the airport, supply them with a bed, feed them amazing takeout pizza and ply them with Sweet Ecstasy."

"You're not getting me to drink Sweet Ecstasy," she assured him dryly, and then raised her eyebrows and asked, "*Takeout pizza*?"

"You know I cannot cook," he said with a shrug. "But the pizza is amazing. It is nothing like I have ever tasted. You will love it."

"And the reason Mortimer had trouble getting a hold of you?" she asked with a grin as she waited for the machine to make her coffee. "Her name would be?"

"Ah, Justine," he said, clutching his heart and rolling his eyes. "She is the most beautiful girl, but not as beautiful as you," he assured her. "And she is so greedy. She hid my phone and pants and would not let me leave. Naughty girl!"

"Oh, Matias, you're incorrigible," Beth reprimanded

him with a shake of the head as she retrieved the steaming cup.

"I merely live up to my name, my beautiful cousin," Matias protested. "I cannot disappoint the ladies."

Turning to Donny, Beth noted his curious expression and explained, "Matias means *God's gift*. But," she pointed out, turning back to Matias, "nowhere in the description does it include *to women*."

"It doesn't need to be said," Matias said with a shrug. "Who else would a man such as I be a gift to?"

"Your mother?" she suggested.

"*Sí*, her too. I am the best son."

"I think your brothers would argue that point," Beth said on a laugh.

"My brothers would be wrong then," he assured her.

"Of course they would," she said dryly and then glanced to Scotty to note that he was frowning over the exchange.

Turning abruptly to Donny, he asked, "Where's the luggage? Ye were supposed to be watching it."

"I stacked it on a cart thingy and rolled it to the building. It's just there," Donny said, pointing toward the windows, where a luggage cart stacked with their bags could clearly be seen just outside the door. "I thought we'd be picked up out there so didn't want to bring it inside."

"I am in the parking area in front of the building," Matias announced. "They do not like vehicles on the airfield. I will go fetch the SUV and pull up to the door now, though," he said and turned to hurry away.

"Is that for me?"

Beth turned from watching Matias go and followed

Donny's gaze to the drink in her hand. "Oh, no. Sorry, they don't have hazelnut lattes, so I wasn't sure what to get you."

Nodding, Donny turned to the machine, his eyes lighting up as he saw the selections. "Oh, hot chocolate, and mocha and—"

"I'll fetch the baggage cart then, shall I?" Scotty said dryly.

Beth raised her eyebrows at his sarcastic tone, and then smiled and said, "Good idea."

"Right," Scotty spun on his heel.

Enjoying his irritation, Beth took a sip of her coffee and promptly spat it out. "Ugh," she said with disgust and tossed the drink in the garbage can. "Save your money, Donny. That's the worst instant coffee I've ever had."

"Ooooh, but they have mocha! I haven't had that since I was mortal."

Beth turned back to the younger man and raised her eyebrows. "You've had coffee, though, right?"

"No. I've been in training since I was turned," Donny explained, digging in his own pocket for change. "Lucian sent me to this place in Winnipeg for proper training and they're pretty strict. No pizza, no sweets, no pop, no caffeine. It's all steamed veggies, rice, water, and constant lectures about how your body is your temple and eating junk means a need for more blood and stuff," he said with a grimace as he popped change into the machine. "Well, that and weapons training and martial arts, and classes on how to approach a rogue."

"Oh," Beth murmured as she watched him press the Mocha button. She and Dree had gone to a special camp in Spain for training as Rogue Hunters too. But it hadn't been anything like what Donny was describing. Mind you, this was a hundred years ago. There had been no pizza then. At least, they hadn't heard of it there, and there'd been no packaged sweets like they had now. They'd also been encouraged to try things like coffee to see what effect it would have on them while they were in a safe environment.

For some reason, caffeine was one drug nanos did not immediately work to flush out of the system. They didn't seem to recognize it as a drug. Or perhaps they didn't see it as detrimental to the system. Whatever the case, they just let it be, which was weird because it seemed to have a heightened effect on immortals compared to mortals. At least for some. Some didn't feel any effects from it at all. For instance, with Beth it merely woke her up and made her a bit hyper. Drina had done okay with it too. But there *had* been immortals they'd trained with who had been badly affected by caffeine. Apparently they wouldn't find out today if Donny was one of them, she decided with amusement as he spat the sip of mocha he'd just taken back into the cup.

"Disgusting," he agreed, and tossed the drink into the garbage as she had done. But then he turned to put more change in the machine.

"You are not going to waste more money on that machine, are you?" she asked with exasperation, and then suggested, "You might want to wait until we're at the house to try more coffee."

"I'm thirsty," Donny complained. "I'll just try the cider this time. That can't possibly be as bad as the other stuff. But I do want to try an espresso later. You have to promise me I can."

"Promise you can what?" Scotty asked, rolling the baggage cart up to them.

"Try an espresso," Beth explained as she watched the machine produce a steaming cup of what looked like urine. Seriously, the man must be truly thirsty if he was even willing to try that after how horrible her drink and, she imagined, his drink had been. Apparently he was that thirsty, she decided when he blew on the steaming liquid and then took a large gulp.

"Well?" she asked.

"Eh," Donny said with a shrug, but took another sip.

Shaking her head, Beth turned to glance out the front windows. Spotting the SUV pulling up in front of the building, she headed toward the doors. "Come on. Matias is out front."

"So," Matias said as soon as they had stowed their gear in the back and joined him in the SUV. "I will take you to the university. You can be done with your business. And then we relax and enjoy your stay until the plane arrives to take you away."

Beth glanced to Matias with surprise. "I thought Kira was out of town until tomorrow night?"

Matias shook his head. "Mortimer, he had the dates wrong. Tomorrow is the party she is attending in California. Today she is home."

"It's after eleven thirty, though. If she has morning classes, this would be kind of late to go see her, don't you think?" Beth asked after glancing at her watch to note the time. When she'd asked Mortimer why they weren't talking to the girl tonight, she hadn't considered that attending the university as she was, the girl had probably had to modify her hours to match those that mortals kept. She'd thought of that only on the plane. And apparently she'd thought wrong, because Matias snorted with disbelief.

"Eleven thirty is not late," he scoffed. "Besides, you are still on Toronto time. Is only eight thirty-seven here." He tapped on the dashboard clock as proof and then added, "As for the morning classes, Kira is immortal. She will have mostly evening classes and some afternoon classes that were not available at night," he assured her. "In fact, she probably does not even have the classes on Friday. Most students try to avoid the classes on Friday."

"Why?" she asked with curiosity.

"Because then they can start to party on Thursday nights," he explained with a grin.

Beth frowned. "So she probably won't even be there?"

"Oh, *sí*, she will," he assured her. "The bars and dance clubs, they do not get busy until eleven o'clock or midnight. Before that, everyone is getting ready and drinking in their rooms or homes. It is cheaper. Drinks at the bars and clubs are very expensive, so most students get 'half cut' before they hit the bars. She will not have gone out yet."

"Hmm," Beth murmured and then smiled and shrugged. "Then I guess we're going to the university."

Five

"Here we are," Matias announced cheerfully when they pulled into a parking lot at the university campus.

"Thanks." Beth got out and walked around the vehicle, aware that Scotty had got out of the back seat and was following. She slowed and then paused to peer at her cousin with surprise, though, when she saw Matias was out and following Donny toward her. "Where are you going?"

"With you," he said as if that should be obvious, and then, grinning, he said, "It is a building full of young, nubile women. I will be good backup."

"I think it's a mixed-gender residence," Donny commented. "There will be guys too."

"The males are your problem," he said with a shrug. "But the women I can help with. They love me."

Shaking her head, Beth turned to start walking. "Fine. But don't get hurt. Aunt Giulietta would flay me alive if you got hurt."

Matias snorted at the claim. “My mother loves you. She would blame Lucian.”

“Yeah, she would,” Beth agreed with a grin.

“Why does Giulietta love her?” Scotty asked with curiosity, and Matias glanced at him as if he were crazy to even have to ask.

“Because Beth is perfect,” he said. “She is smart, and kind, and good and strong . . . and she used to keep me out of trouble when I was young.”

“I babysat him when he was growing up,” Beth said with affection.

“*Sí*.” Matias nodded. “She was the best aunt ever.”

“I spoiled him rotten,” Beth admitted without apology.

“*Sí*, as I said, the best aunt ever,” Matias repeated.

“I thought you were kissing cousins?” Scotty said dryly.

“As an adopted sister to Drina, she is my cousin,” he said solemnly. “But I called her Aunt Beth when I was very young.”

Scotty merely grunted in response. They’d reached the residence, and all fell silent as they entered the lobby.

Beth took a quick glance around, and then approached the front desk. She smiled in greeting at the twenty-nothing girl behind it, and decided she would try the mortal approach first. “Hello, we’re here to see Kira Sarka. Do we have to sign in before we go up to see her?”

“No. You can’t go up,” the girl said baldly. “Visitors have to stay here in the lobby until the student comes to get you. But I can call and tell her you’re here. What’re your names?” she asked, picking up the phone and starting to punch numbers.

That's when Beth decided that the mortal approach sucked, and slipped into the girl's mind. The last thing she needed was Kira knowing they were coming so she could warn her bodyguards. Making the girl set the phone back in its cradle, she quickly rearranged her thoughts a little so that she would forget they had been there and not notice them heading to the elevator. Easing out of her mind, Beth gestured for the men to follow and led them to the bank of elevators.

"It would seem Kira is not well-liked," Scotty commented as they stepped onto the elevator and Beth pushed the button for the correct floor.

"Yeah, I caught those thoughts myself," Beth murmured as she watched the panel above the door. She had sensed him poking around inside the receptionist's mind, so wasn't surprised by the comment. She had been a little surprised at the level of enmity the receptionist had felt toward the Russian girl, though. Something the receptionist clearly thought was shared by every single person in this building who'd had to deal with "that Russian bitch."

"I suspect the girl will not be easy to deal with," Scotty murmured. "Perhaps I should handle her."

Turning, she eyed him with amusement. "Scotty, I spent most of my mortal years in a house with thirteen women . . . half of whom thought they were prima donnas. That's probably why Mortimer sent me. I can handle this."

"Of course." He nodded solemnly and then actually grinned. "Should be fun."

Beth blinked in surprise, and then glanced to Matias as he chuckled.

Shrugging, he said, "I know you, cousin. Scotty is right. This should be fun."

The *ding* announcing their arrival and the sound of the doors opening forced her to turn away and start off the elevator. Beth spotted Kira's door almost at once. It was hard to miss. There were two huge grim-faced Amazons standing guard in front of it.

"Oh man," Donny muttered behind her. "I can't help you with them, Beth. I can't hit a girl."

Stopping abruptly, she turned on the younger immortal. "Are you kidding me?"

"No. I can't hit a girl," he insisted. "I was raised not to hit them."

"So . . . what?" Beth asked with disbelief. "If we come up against female rogues, you're just going to—"

"Female rogues are different," he said quickly. "They're . . . well, they're rogue. But these women are just doing their job."

"Never fear, Donny," Matias said sympathetically. "I will help. I will seduce them away from the door."

Beth clucked her tongue with exasperation. "There are two of them, Matias. And they're immortal. I can see you seducing two mortals with whatever mojo the nanos give us, but I can't see two immortal women willing to—"

"Is fine, cousin," Matias interrupted reassuringly. "Women love me."

Beth frowned. "I know you think—"

She broke off and they both turned their heads to peer toward the women when two soft hisses were followed by two thuds as the bodyguards hit the floor.

"There," Scotty said easily as he slid his dart gun back into his belt. Catching Beth's eye, he shrugged.

"Now Donny does no' have to hit them, and Matias does no' have to play the Latin lover. That's a teed baw. Can we get on with this?"

Beth bit her lip to hold back the laugh that wanted to escape, and simply nodded and continued forward, saying, "Now maybe you can control the residents who saw that and make sure they don't run screaming to their rooms and dial 911."

"Already on it," Scotty assured her, and she knew it was true. The half dozen young men and women spread throughout the hall had all frozen where they stood.

"Right," she murmured. "Then, Donny and Matias, you get to keep your eyes open for any more bodyguards who might be around."

"You think there are more?" Donny asked, sounding nervous. As he should be if he wasn't willing to hit a woman.

"Mortimer did say Kira's father had sent several of them," she reminded him patiently. "There are probably one or two in the room with Kira, and others on break who could return at any moment."

"Right," Donny muttered. "Can I shoot them?"

That made her stop and turn on him again. "Seriously? You can't hit them, but you can shoot them?"

"It's a dart gun," he pointed out defensively. "A little ouchy and they're out. Besides, Grandma might have said never to hit girls, but she never said don't shoot them."

Beth heard the bark of laughter that slipped from Scotty as well as Matias's chuckle, but held back her own amusement, and merely said dryly, "Yes, you can shoot them."

Shaking her head, she turned on her heel to continue forward again, this time not stopping until she reached the door where the two Russian women had fallen. Stepping between them, Beth raised her hand to knock at the door, and then thought better of it and instead bent to heft one of the women over her shoulder. She then pulled out her dart gun and glanced to Matias expectantly.

Understanding at once, he eased up to the side of the door, grabbed the doorknob and turned it.

The door wasn't locked, thank goodness. That would have completely ruined her entrance. Actually, she would have crashed into the door, looking an idiot, because the moment Matias turned the knob, she started forward, raising her gun as she went.

The room was larger than she'd expected. In fact, if Beth was to guess, she'd have said that the wall between two of the usually tiny dorm rooms had been knocked out to make one large room for the little Russian princess occupying it. It was fitted out like a loft apartment, a large bed in one corner, a kitchenette in another, a dining table in the third. A small sitting area took up the last and the rest of the space.

Beth took all that in at a glance and then focused on the three women in the room. A petite blonde and two more Amazons, one a blonde and one a brunette. She almost shot both of the larger women, but caught herself at the last moment and shot the petite blonde and the large brunette instead. She then dumped the woman she was carrying on the floor and turned toward the door, only to pause when she saw Scotty bending to grab the other bodyguard's wrist. She could see that the people in the hall were moving again as if nothing had happened, and stepped to the side to make room for him to drag the second fallen guard inside as well, and then turned to eye Kira Sarka.

The girl stared back belligerently and then lifted her chin as she gestured to the petite blond and asked, "How did you know she was not me? Most people think Liliya is me and I am one of the bodyguards."

"Then most people must not be looking very closely," Beth said easily. "The bling you're wearing has to be worth a quarter million at least, and your shoes are Jimmy Choos, while your friend there is wearing cheap knockoffs."

"You have good eye," Kira said with a shrug. "But I am not interested in talking. You must go."

Beth chuckled at the order and walked over to sit at the dining table as Scotty straightened and moved to close the door. He then took up position beside it. That left Donny and Matias in the hall to keep an eye out for the return of any absent bodyguards.

Hoping the pair could handle the job, Beth turned back to the Russian and said, "To tell you the truth, Kira, I'm not interested in talking to you either. Unfortunately, that's the job." She arched her eyebrows. "You've been a very bad girl and have been feeding off mortals here in Canada."

"I am Russian," she said with indifference, chin going up even further.

If she wasn't careful, she'd give herself a crick in the neck, Beth thought, but said easily, "And this is North America, where the North American Council rules, and where that kind of thing is against our laws."

"I am Russian," Kira repeated, harshly this time. "And my father is head of Russian Council. He—"

"Yeah, yeah, he's the big chief in Russia." Beth waved her hand dismissively. "But again, this is North America, and you will follow the rules of the North American Immortal Council, or you will be subject to their punishments."

"If you cut off head, my father will—"

"So you do know the punishment for feeding off mortals here," Beth interrupted mildly.

Kira snapped her mouth shut and glared at her.

"The Council was concerned that perhaps you did not know our laws, or that you thought you had some sort of diplomatic immunity because of your father's position in Russia," Beth said lightly. "However, that's obviously not the case."

Beth paused briefly, and then, in a gentle voice, continued, "This is the only warning you will get. They *will* cut off your head if you feed off even one more mortal." She paused again, testing the girl's thoughts before adding, "That seems a very high price to pay to punish your father for being overbearing."

"He *is* overbearing," Kira exclaimed bitterly. "He is the bastard. It is always 'do what I say, go where I send you, be what I want.'"

Beth shrugged without sympathy. "There are worse things fathers can do."

Kira blinked and then narrowed her eyes, obviously reading her thoughts and memories. Beth let her, not trying to hide her history or what her own father had done.

"Your father is bastard too," Kira growled when she finished.

Beth nodded solemnly.

Kira hesitated, and then moved to sit at the table

with her. She stared at Beth in silence for a moment, and then said softly, "I almost would rather my father send me to brothel than kill my love, Bogdan."

Beth opened her mouth, and then paused and read the girl's mind, wincing when she saw a naked young immortal being pulled from a bed of rumpled silk sheets as an equally naked Kira tried to hold on to him and begged for his life. Her cries had no effect, and she had to watch as he was dragged out of her room through a pair of French doors to be beheaded. His blood was vivid crimson against the white snow.

Blinking the visions away, Beth considered the girl, knowing Kira had let her see those memories on purpose. They had been too clear and not at all disjointed as thoughts often were when you were reading someone who was trying to veil their thoughts.

Kira had let her see more than that, though. She'd let Beth see thoughts and feelings that were clearly a cry for help. Frowning, she asked, "Was he your life mate?"

"My father says no," she admitted sadly. "But I loved him."

Beth covered her hand and squeezed gently.

Seeming to take strength from that, Kira sat up straight again and said with disgust, "My father tried to make it up to me by promising I could attend any school I wished."

"And you picked this one," Beth murmured.

"My father hates Lucian Argeneau," she announced, her jaw tight. "Lucian Argeneau is in Canada, and so—"

"So you wanted to attend a school in Canada," Beth finished for her.

"*Da*," Kira said with a nod. "He was furious, but he could not refuse because he had promised."

"Why didn't you pick a university closer to where Lucian lives, then?" Beth asked with curiosity. "Say, in Toronto or something? That would have made him even angrier."

Kira made a sound of disgust. "I did not realize the country was so big. I thought I would be close enough to both California and Toronto."

Beth stared at the girl for a minute, reading her state of mind again, and then said, "You plan to feed off a mortal the moment we leave and force the Council to have you beheaded."

Kira shrugged wearily. "My Bogdan is dead. What is there to live for?"

"I don't know," Beth admitted. "But it's a shame you're willing to give up so easily when there are still so many ways to punish your father. I mean, sure he'll be upset when you die, but he'll get over that and move on. It seems to me there are better ways to make him suffer for longer."

Kira lifted her head and peered at her uncertainly. "Like what?"

Beth shrugged. "You could always drop out of the university here, move to Toronto and see if you couldn't train to become a Rogue Hunter for the North American Council. That would probably really piss him off."

Kira sat up straight again, her eyes narrowing thoughtfully. "That truly would infuriate him."

"Especially since you'd be training and working under Lucian. He runs the hunters. I'd imagine that would be like a thorn in your father's side every single day for as long as you did it."

"*Da*," Kira breathed with building interest.

"But Rogue Hunters cannot feed off the hoof," Beth pointed out.

Kira waved that away. "I prefer my blood cold anyway. Is disgusting to me off the hoof. I only did that to—" Pausing abruptly, she met Beth's gaze and smiled sheepishly. "You knew I did not like to feed directly from mortals."

Beth smiled. "Yeah, I kind of picked up on that when I first read your mind."

Kira nodded, and then asked anxiously, "Do you really think I could be a hunter?"

"I think now is the perfect time for you to sign up for it. We are shorthanded at the moment and desperate for help."

Kira grinned. "I have some training already. I am a good shot with a gun and a bow and arrow. I trained with swords and even took some martial arts."

Beth raised her eyebrows. "Then I definitely think they will be interested in hiring you."

Kira smiled, and then reached out to squeeze Beth's hand. "Thank you. You have given me something to live for."

Squeezing her hand back, Beth nodded and then stood. "We fly back to Toronto the day after tomorrow. The plane leaves at noon. You can come with us if you wish."

"*Da*, I wish," Kira said determinedly. She got to her feet as well and then glanced at her bodyguards with a frown.

"They can come too if you like," Beth assured her. "There is room."

"In truth, I would rather they not come," Kira said with a grimace. "But they will insist, and if I refuse them, my father will probably cut off their heads too."

"Charming," Beth murmured, moving toward the door as Scotty opened it. Spotting Matias across the hall flirting with a young redhead, Beth said, "Matias, give Kira the address of the airport we landed at."

"I will text you!" Matias said, smiling at Kira.

Beth raised her eyebrows and glanced to the Russian girl. "You know each other? He has your number?"

"*Da*. He is terrible flirt . . . and persistent," she added, rolling her eyes. "I gave him number to shut him up."

Chuckling, Beth offered her hand. "I hope to see you there on Sunday."

"*Da*." Kira nodded firmly and shook her hand. "*Dosvedanya.*"

"*Dosvedanya*," Beth murmured the Russian goodbye and then turned to start up the hall.

"It went well?" Matias asked, falling into step beside her as they headed toward the elevators.

Beth nodded, and then said, "So, Matias, am I right in guessing you were the one keeping an eye on Kira?"

"*Sí*," he admitted and shrugged. "It was no trouble. She was in a lot of my classes and likes the same clubs I do."

"Well, it looks like you won't have to keep tabs on her anymore."

"Why?" he asked with surprise.

"She plans to move to Toronto," Beth explained. "In

fact, I think she's flying back with us. So don't forget to text her the address of the airfield."

"Speaking of which," Scotty said before Matias could respond, "I do no' think Mortimer and Lucian are going to thank ye for this."

"The girl was planning on suicide by Council," Beth said solemnly as they reached the elevator. "I had to do something."

"Kira?" Matias asked with surprise, trailing her onto the elevator. "Suicide?"

"Her father cut off her lover's head a couple months ago," Beth explained quietly. "She isn't taking it well."

Eyes widening, Matias raised a hand to his throat, but said, "That explains why she was not receptive to my advances."

"I don't understand," Donny said, and Beth realized he hadn't caught the first part of the conversation when he asked, "Why would Mortimer and Lucian be upset with Beth? What did she do?"

"She suggested the lass move to Toronto and train to be a Rogue Hunter," Scotty explained.

"Really?" Donny asked, and then pursed his lips. "She might do okay. She's big enough for the job."

Beth grimaced at the comment. Kira was a good six feet tall. She was not only voluptuous but muscular as well. The sword training she'd mentioned had shown in her physique. Still, Beth thought as the elevator doors opened and they crossed the lobby to the exit, size didn't make a good Enforcer. Smarts did. She was only five-foot-three and considered herself a damned fine hunter.

"I'm hungry," Donny said suddenly as they headed for the parking lot. "Can we stop at a coffee shop and get doughnuts on the way to the house?"

Beth glanced at him with disbelief. "Seriously? There were probably twenty or thirty food stalls in that place where you could have got food."

"I want a doughnut, though," he said with a shrug.

"They probably had a doughnut shop in there somewhere too," she said with exasperation.

"I will stop at a Tim Hortons on the way to the house," Matias said as they approached the SUV. Beth suspected he made the offer to keep the peace.

"Oh, good." Donny beamed at the man as he followed him around to the driver's side of the SUV. "I like the ones they have with white icing and all those pretty sprinkles."

"Such a girl," Beth muttered under her breath with disgust as she reached for the front passenger door handle.

"Allow me," Scotty said on a chuckle as he got there first and pulled it open for her.

"Thanks," Beth murmured, a little flustered by both his nearness as he leaned around her to get the door, and the chivalry displayed by the action.

"My pleasure," he assured her with a smile as she slid into the seat. He waited until she was settled and then closed the door and got into the seat behind her as Matias and Donny got in on the other side.

"Well!" Matias said cheerfully as he fastened his seat belt and started the engine. "Is this not wonderful? Business is done and now we can play."

Beth turned to him in question. "What did you have in mind?"

"Dancing!" he announced happily. "The girls here, they do not know how to dance, my cousin. You and I will show them."

Beth chuckled at the claim, but shrugged. "Sure. Why not?"

"But doughnuts first, right?" Donny said from the back seat.

"*Sí, sí*, doughnuts first," Matias assured him. "We will stop there on the way back to the house, and then you can all change while I order the pizza, and we will eat properly before we go out."

"Will anything be open by then?" Beth asked dubiously, glancing at the watch on her wrist.

"Cousin, you are forgetting the time difference again. It is not even yet ten o'clock," he said in a pained voice. "I promise we will be at the club by midnight and have hours to dance before it closes."

"Starbucks!" Donny squawked suddenly.

"I see it," Matias said with exasperation.

"Are we sure Donny should have coffee?" Scotty asked, sounding disgruntled. His voice sounded so close she was sure he had leaned forward in his seat.

Turning, she saw that she had been right, but merely shrugged. "Our trainers thought it best to find out how you reacted to things like coffee before you were on the job. We are done with business now, so we might as well let him see how he handles it."

Scotty looked dubious, but merely nodded and sat back in his seat.

Six

"Can you no' turn this music down? I think me ears are bleedin'," Scotty complained from the back seat.

Beth chuckled at the claim, and leaned forward to turn it down, but then asked, "So you'd rather go back to Donny talking?"

"Hey!" Donny bent to peer down into the SUV from where he stood on the back seat with his head, shoulders, and chest out of the vehicle through the sunroof. "What happened to the music? Did you shut it off? Did he shut it off? Do you think it's broken? Maybe it's not the radio. Maybe it's the station. Maybe the satellite was knocked out of the sky or—"

"Turn it back up!" Scotty barked.

"That's what I thought," Beth said with a laugh and cranked up the volume again.

"Yeah!" Donny shouted and straightened to continue playing air guitar in the open night air as they sped down the highway. She should have probably ordered the boy to sit down and put his seat belt on, but honestly, he'd turned into such a chatterbox once the caffeine had hit him, she'd rather risk it. Beth made a mental note to herself to warn Mortimer that Donny shouldn't be allowed coffee. Ever. He was one of the immortals it did affect.

Much to everyone's relief, it was only a couple moments later when Matias slowed as he approached the driveway of a nice ranch-style home she thought might be clad in light brown brick. She wasn't certain. While the increased night vision immortals enjoyed allowed them to see relatively clearly in the dark, it wasn't that great when it came to colors. But between her night vision and the fact that the driveway ran up the edge of the property a good thirty feet to the side of the house, Beth was able to see that while the front yard was small and neat, the backyard was absolutely huge with more than enough room for the large six-car garage and the attached outbuilding it housed.

The driveway led up beside and past the house to those buildings, but it also had a branch that broke off to run along the front of the house. Matias turned onto that, and steered them up to the front door before stopping.

The minute Matias shut off the engine, the loud raucous music died. Donny immediately dropped back into his seat.

"Man, we're here!" he exclaimed as if they might have missed that fact. "I was really rocking it. You have great taste in music, Matias. We should unload, huh?" Throwing the SUV's side door open, he bounded out of the back seat and ran around to the back of the vehicle.

"Ye had to let him drink the coffee, didn't ye?" Scotty said with disgust.

"Espresso," Beth corrected him. "And it's better we know how he reacts to it now than on the job. Fortunately, he has lots of time to get it out of his system. We're on a bit of a vacation right now," she reminded him with a smile.

"Yeah, great," Scotty said, following the younger man out of the vehicle. Beth couldn't help noticing he sounded unimpressed.

"This Scotty, he is a grumpy bastard, no?" Matias commented as he undid his seat belt. Smiling at her then, he added, "And he has the thing for you."

Beth froze in the process of getting out of the vehicle, and jerked around to stare at him with dismay. "No, he doesn't."

Matias just grinned and nodded slowly. "*Sí*, he does. He was wanting to tear my head off at the airport when you were in my arms. He has the thing."

Beth glanced nervously toward the back of the vehicle to make sure that Scotty wasn't hearing any of this. Much to her relief, she could see that Donny was busy chatting his ear off, hopefully preventing his hearing their conversation. Just in case, though, she decided she'd best keep her voice low. Turning back to Matias, she hissed, "He's eight hundred and some years old, long past the days of sex and crushes and whatnot. He doesn't have a 'thing' for me. And if you say that in front of him, I'll scratch your eyes out, wait for them to grow back in and then scratch them out again."

The old threat merely made Matias laugh and shake his head. He did, however, get out of the vehicle rather quickly and hurry around to join the men at the back of the SUV. He probably hoped there'd be safety in numbers, Beth thought with disgust as she got out to follow him.

"So, there are only three bedrooms," Matias was saying as she joined the men. "Two of you will have to share a bed."

Beth scowled at his suggestive tone and the way he waggled his eyebrows as he glanced between her and Scotty. She really should scratch his eyes out, she thought grimly, but merely said, "Scotty and Donny can share."

"If there are three bedrooms, why do we have to share?" Donny asked. "Beth can have one. Scotty can have one. I can have one. That's three bedrooms. That's good. Three bedrooms is good. It's perfect. Like it was made for us. Three bedrooms, three people."

"Three bedrooms and four people," Matias corrected him. "One bedroom is mine already. So, you will share."

"Great," Scotty growled, dragging a large leather bag out of the back of the SUV.

"That's okay. Really. It'll be okay. We can share. I'm a good roommate. I don't snore. Do you snore? Never mind. It doesn't matter. Fine. It'll be fine. We're fine," Donny shot out in staccato sentences as he followed Scotty into the house.

"Oh, *sí*, the Scotty, he has this thing for you and he has it bad," Matias said with delight as they watched the two men disappear into the house.

"Why?" she asked with exasperation as she dragged her bags out one after the other and began to sling them over her shoulders. "Why would you even imagine that?"

"Because he has not killed you for letting Donny drink the espresso. Even though he knows he will be stuck with the man tonight."

Beth tried to hold on to her scowl. She truly did, but couldn't help it and her expression cracked as a laugh slipped from her lips. She covered her mouth quickly and shook her head. "It isn't funny. Donny is going to make him crazy."

"Nah," he said lightly. Taking two of her bags, he reminded her, "We are going dancing. Donny can work the caffeine out of his system on the dance floor and I will finally have a proper rumba partner again. Truly, chiquita, the girls here do not know how to dance."

"Dancing. Right. I forgot about that," Beth said with a smile as they headed into the house.

"Forgot about what?" Scotty asked, meeting them in the entry. His hands were empty, and Beth glanced past him to see that he'd set his own bags on the floor just inside the door of the first room on the left, a small living room decorated in earth tones and overstuffed furniture.

"That we are going dancing and Donny can work off the caffeine on the dance floor," Beth explained.

"Oh, dear God, aye," Scotty said with relief. "If I have to share a room with the lad chattering away like he is now, I'm like to kill him."

"Speaking of which, where is he?" Beth asked.

"Hey! I found the kitchen!" Donny's voice came from the back of the house in answer. "Does anyone else want blood? I found the fridge. And food! Good food! Cheese and sausage. Whipped cream. Dip too.

I love dip. Are there chips? Jeez, this is great stuff. Things I haven't had since I started training. Bologna and salami! Sliced smoked turkey! I could make us Dagwoods!"

"Bologna?" Beth peered at Matias with disbelief. "Your mother would shoot you for even bringing all that junk into the house."

"It tastes good," Matias said helplessly.

"Oh wow! Look at the backyard. It's huge!" Donny cried and then asked excitedly, "Are those dogs back there? Man, they're beautiful. Scary-looking too, but they're probably nice dogs. They just look scary. Right?"

"Dogs?" Beth asked, her eyebrows rising. Matias had always wanted a dog. But his mother, Aunt Giulietta, thought they were messy and smelly and wouldn't let him have one as he was growing up.

"*Sí.*" Matias beamed at her. "Two Dobermans. They are beautiful. I only put them outside when I am not here so they do not ruin the furniture. One of them, Chico, he tried to eat the couch when I left him home alone for a couple hours, so now they must wait in the kennel until I can be with them."

"I see," Beth said and shook her head. "Aunt Giulietta hasn't visited you here yet, has she?"

"*Sí,*" he assured her. "Mama has been here twice, but I had a friend keep the dogs while she was here both times."

The sound of a door slamming made all three of them glance toward the back of the house.

Eyebrows rising, Scotty headed down the hall, with Beth following closely on his heels. There were several doors on the right, each seeming to lead into a bedroom. But there was only one doorway on the left and it was at the far end of the hall. She and Scotty turned in to a family room that took up the near side of the large open space, while a kitchen filled the other half. She spotted the door that had slammed at once. It was in the back corner on the kitchen side, but she didn't move toward it. Instead, she stared out the large windows that seemed to make up the back wall of the house. Through them, she could see the huge backyard, the two outbuildings, and Donny running toward a kennel where two beautiful Doberman pinschers were jumping at the fence, barking excitedly as the ginger-haired man approached.

"Will they bite him?" Beth asked with concern.

"I do not know," Matias admitted with a frown. "He is terribly excited and if he excites them too much . . ."

"Crap," Beth breathed and hurried to the door to go after the young immortal.

"I'm thinking we should take him dancing sooner rather than later," Matias called after them as Scotty followed her.

Beth was too busy running to comment, but she thought that was a damned good idea.

"Have you known Matias long?"

Scotty winced at that loud shout in his ear and tore his gaze away from Beth's gyrating body on the dance floor to peer down at the girl who had cozied up to him on the couch. She was one of the half-dozen women who had been draping themselves all over Matias since they'd arrived here more than an hour ago. He seemed to be popular. But Scotty supposed the little girl with blue hair leaning up against him had tired of trying to vie for the young man's attention and shifted her focus to him.

"Have you?" she asked again. She was shouting to be heard over the music. He wished she wouldn't. Her shouting was giving him a headache. Fortunately, she seemed to realize how unattractive having to shout might appear and made a little moue with her lips. She also blinked her eyelashes at him in a way that made him wonder if she had something in her eye . . . or eyes.

"Nay," he answered her question and then shifted his attention back to the dance floor, finding Beth again as Donny twirled her around to the manic beat.

"Do you like to dance?" the girl tried again.

"Nay," he answered, not even looking at her this time.

"Do you—"

"Matias," Scotty growled. He didn't shout. Immortals had superior hearing and the young Spaniard caught his warning. A moment later the warm weight against his side eased away and then was gone. Scotty supposed the Spaniard had slipped into her thoughts and either urged her back to his side or sent her away. He didn't care which.

"If you keep staring at her like that she will surely burst into flames."

Scotty gave a start at that comment and turned to look around. Matias hadn't sent just the little blue-haired girl away. He'd sent all the women away. He'd also moved next to him on the couch and was eyeing him with curiosity.

"You like my cousin," he said finally.

Scotty merely turned his gaze back to the dance floor.

"Beth says you are over eight hundred years old. Is that true?" he asked.

"Aye," he muttered.

"Interesting," Matias murmured so softly that despite his hearing, Scotty nearly didn't catch it.

Eyes narrowing, he turned to peer at him in question. "Why?"

Matias hesitated and then, instead of answering, asked, "Why didn't you want Beth to be a Rogue Hunter?"

Scotty stiffened. "Who says I did no' want her to be a hunter?"

Matias grinned and raised his eyebrows. "You tried to convince my uncle and Drina not to let her train, and then, once she'd finished training, you traveled to Spain to try to convince the Council to refuse her a position as a hunter. Everyone knows that."

"Beth too?" he asked with alarm.

Matias nodded. "My uncle sat her down and said you didn't think she should be a hunter, and he'd argued on her behalf to the Council. He told her not to screw up and prove him wrong."

Cursing, Scotty glanced back to the dancers. He should have realized that she would find out. Not that it would have stopped him. He'd been desperate to keep her safe. He would have appreciated it had everyone kept their mouths shut, though. It just complicated the situation further, he thought and began to frown, partially because of that, and partially because he couldn't find Beth on the dance floor.

Where the hell had she got to? he wondered, getting to his feet to improve his view of the dancers.

"What is it?" Matias asked, standing up as well.

"I can no' find Beth," he muttered, looking for her little black dress among the dancers. The problem was, there were a ton of women in black. Why the hell would she wear such a common color? She was not a common woman.

"I see Donny," Matias said after a moment. "Beth's not with him. Perhaps she went to the ladies' room."

"Aye," Scotty murmured and settled back on the couch.

Beth flushed the toilet and stepped out of the stall to find the bathroom apparently empty. There had been half a dozen women primping in the mirror or washing their hands when she'd entered, but it seemed they'd finished their business and left.

Shrugging, she quickly walked to the sink and washed her hands. By the time she finished and turned off the tap, the rushing of water from the toilet had stopped too, leaving the room silent except for the somewhat muffled throb of the music coming from the dance floor . . . and heartbreaking sobs coming from one of the stalls.

Frowning, Beth ripped off a section of paper towel and dried her hands, her gaze traveling along the floor under the row of stalls. Two of them were occupied. The one nearest the door, and one two doors over from that. Beth wasn't sure from which one the crying was coming, but suspected it was from the one closest to the door.

"Hello? Are you all right?" she asked, tossing the paper into the wastebasket. When she didn't get an immediate response, Beth walked to the last stall, only to stumble to a stop as it flew open and a young woman hurried out, nearly crashing into her.

"Sorry, sorry," the woman cried and rushed for the exit.

Beth tried to slip into the woman's mind to slow and calm her, but ran up against a wall of pain, confusion, and helplessness that brought her up short. By the time she regained herself, the woman was out the door. Frowning, she followed and stepped out into the hall in time to see the woman disappear through a door marked Emergency Exit at the back of the building.

Hesitating, Beth glanced briefly up the hall toward the dance floor, but then turned to follow the woman's path to the other end of the hall and the waiting door. She couldn't help herself. She recognized all those feelings the woman was experiencing. Fear, pain, helplessness . . . Beth had suffered them often enough when she was young. She knew how debilitating they were, and wanted to help her. If she could.

The emergency exit led to an alley, Beth discovered when she pushed through it. A long, dark alley with boarded windows and large metal garbage bins on one side, she noted as she sought out the source of the fast *tap*, *tap*, *tap* of fleeing high heels. The woman was already halfway up the alley. Beth hesitated again, glancing back to the closing door. The men had no idea where she was and—Her thoughts died abruptly when a loud cry from the woman made Beth turn back toward her. She had stopped at the midway point and was hunched over, sobbing violently.

Mouth tightening, Beth started forward. She would just find out what was wrong. There was a chance she could help, but at the very least, she could slip into her mind and calm and soothe her. The woman had stopped just this side of the metal bins, but as Beth neared her, she suddenly scuttled forward, halfway into the shadows cast by the bins. There she dropped into a squat.

Reaching her, Beth hesitated, but then dropped into a squat as well. Before she could reach for the crying woman, however, a *thunk* overhead made her glance up sharply. She stared blankly at the sword embedded in the boarded-up window above. Had she not dropped when she had, it would have been in her neck right now, she realized as she sought out its owner in the shadows just past the crying woman. All Beth saw was a dark-clad figure holding the sword in a two-handed grip, and then the sword was pulled free, and her survival instinct kicked in.

Jerking upright with a curse, she grabbed for the sword and the figure in the darkness at the same time. Her right hand went for the assailant's throat, nails digging into the skin with vicious intent. With her left, she caught the sword and gripped it, ignoring the pain as it sliced into her skin.

"Beth!"

Startled by the sound of her name, Beth glanced over her shoulder to see Scotty standing in the open club door, concern on his face. That momentary distraction cost her. She didn't see her attacker remove one hand from the sword, and only realized it happened when she was punched in the kidneys.

Gasping in surprised pain, Beth lost her grip on the sword and stepped back, but then instinctively moved her arm up to block the sword as she heard it singing toward her again. Pain immediately sliced through her, radiating out from her arm as she stumbled and leaned back from the blade, trying to get her neck as far from it as possible in case her arm was lobbed off and the sword's momentum carried it into her neck. Fortunately that didn't happen, although the sword did dig deep. Her lower arm and hand were still attached when the sword pulled away, but just barely. Beth was pretty sure the sword had cut most of the way through the bone before being stopped, and she instinctively wrapped her hand around the wound as she glanced around to see the attacker racing away up the alley. Her gaze narrowed on the dark figure moving faster than a mortal could.

The thud of new footsteps heralded Scotty's arrival, and she turned to face him as she squeezed her hand tighter around her wound, trying to keep it closed. The more blood she kept from dripping out, the more blood the nanos had to work with until she could get to the supply in the SUV.

"Here." Scotty wrenched the tail of his linen shirt out of his black leather pants and quickly tore a strip off the bottom.

Beth watched silently as he quickly and efficiently bound the wound. The man had obviously done a lot of that, she thought wryly. But then, most hunters had.

"What happened?" he asked as he tied off the makeshift bandage.

Beth shook her head helplessly. "I was in the bathroom and heard a girl crying."

"Your attacker was a woman?" he asked with surprise.

"No," she said and then shrugged. "I don't know. The person was super tall, wearing a dark suit, and had wide shoulders, so no, probably not," she added on a sigh and then gestured toward the ground behind Scotty and concluded, "She was the woman I heard crying."

Scotty turned and stepped to the side as he noted the woman huddled on the ground at their feet, still sobbing.

"She was hurting and weeping, and I followed her to see if I could help," Beth said and quickly explained what had followed.

"So, she was bait," Scotty murmured, peering at the woman.

They were both silent for a minute, both concentrating on the woman's thoughts, and then Beth gave up and admitted, "I'm not getting anything. You?"

Scotty shook his head. "She was obviously controlled, but her thoughts are so scrambled . . ."

"Yeah, it's like someone put an eggbeater in there," Beth said softly, and then sighed. "We can't leave her like this."

"Nay," Scotty agreed, running one hand wearily through his hair.

"I can't go back inside covered in blood," Beth pointed out. "You go on in and fetch the boys, and I'll take her to the SUV."

"Nay," Scotty said firmly. "I'll walk ye both to the SUV and call Matias and Donny on the way. Yer attacker might be hanging about, waiting for me to leave."

Beth opened her mouth to argue, and then shrugged and closed it again. He was right, of course. Her attacker might still be around, and she was in no shape to take him on now.

Scotty urged the woman to her feet with a hand on her arm. He must have taken control of her mind then because she accompanied them without protest or question.

"You'd best text rather than call," Beth murmured when he started to punch in numbers on the phone. "They won't be able to hear you over the music anyway."

"Right," Scotty grunted and quickly typed out a message. He'd finished sending them both texts by the time they reached the mouth of the alley. The men were swift to respond, and both Matias and Donny caught up to them before they'd reached the vehicle parked a block away from the dance club.

Beth left the explanations to Scotty, her own mind on the attack. It had obviously been planned, the girl used as bait for a direct attempt on her life, but that left the question of how this person had known she would be there to attack. Had she and the others been followed from the Enforcer house to the club? Or had she even been a specific target? It was possible her attacker had just been out to kill any immortal he came across, and came across her.

"Mortimer gave me an address to take the girl to. He says we have people there who can help her," Donny announced as they reached the SUV.

Beth glanced to him with surprise. She'd been so lost in thought, she hadn't realized Scotty had finished the explanations and the younger immortal had called Mortimer.

"We'll take you back to the house first," Donny assured her. "And then Matias and I can take the girl—"

"Don't be silly. I'm fine," Beth said quietly. "Besides, there's blood in the SUV. Isn't there?" she added, glancing to Matias in question.

Her cousin nodded solemnly. "Always."

"I'll grab a couple bags," Donny said, moving to the back of the vehicle.

"Make it four," Scotty ordered, ushering Beth and the girl into the back seat. The other man must have stopped and glanced to him in question, because he added, "The sword cut nearly through the bone. Two bags won't do."

"Right," Donny muttered weakly.

"The lad needs to toughen up if he really wants to be a Rogue Hunter," Scotty said quietly as he slid into the back seat next to Beth.

"He's fine. This is only his second day on the job," she pointed out. "Actually, technically this is still his first. At least, it's his first twenty-four hours."

Scotty grunted at that and lifted his arm to set it along the seat back behind her so that there was more room and he could turn to look at her. He asked, "How is your arm?"

Beth raised her eyebrows at the concern on his face, and admitted, "It hurts like a bugger, but I've had worse."

That made Scotty's mouth tighten, and then Donny closed the back door of the SUV and came around to give him the four bags of blood before getting into the front passenger seat.

"Where to?" Matias asked as he started the engine.

"The house," Scotty said firmly. "Beth needs to rest and heal."

"But what about the girl?" Donny asked with a frown. "Mortimer gave me an address to take her to. He said that they'd tend to her there, make sure there was no damage and retrieve any information they can."

Scotty scowled briefly, but then asked, "What's the address?"

Donny glanced down at his phone and rattled it off.

"That's on the way to the house," Matias said helpfully.

Scotty considered the matter briefly and then nodded as he handed one of the bags of blood to Beth. "Since it's on the way, we'll drop off the lass ere we go home. That way none o' us has to leave the house. I'd rather all three o' us were there to watch out for Elizabeth tonight. At least until we sort out how best to keep an eye on her from now on."

"What?" Beth had been about to pop the bag of blood he'd given her to her fangs, but instead turned on him with surprise as Matias steered the SUV into traffic. "Why? I'm fine. A couple of bags of blood and a bit of time and I'll be good as new. And what's with the Elizabeth thing? I'm Beth. Everyone calls me Beth."

"Beth," he said with emphasis, "someone has targeted ye. Ye were deliberately lured out into that alley, and 'tis an immortal."

"Yes, but—"

"And this is no' even the first attack," Scotty continued right over her.

"What are you talking about?" she asked with amazement.

"The car crash ere we left," Scotty reminded her sharply.

"That was an accident," she said at once.

"Nay," he assured her. "When I read his mind, the driver did no' remember a thing."

"Perhaps he—"

"He was controlled." Scotty's expression didn't hold a bit of doubt as he made that statement.

"What accident?" Matias asked, glancing at her in the rearview mirror.

"A semi hauling girders swerved in front of me on the highway," Beth admitted with a frown. "But I wasn't even hurt."

"Ye should ha'e been," Scotty said with certainty. "Ye should ha'e been beheaded, and then burned to death in an explosion. I still do no' understand how that Explorer o' yers did no' blow up. The weight of the girders landed on your engine when the semi's tires blew."

Beth glanced down at her injured arm, but her mind was on the accident back in Toronto. She'd just started to try to read the driver's mind when she'd heard Donny's and Scotty's voices and had stopped to look around. Still, in the brief glimpse she'd had into the driver's mind, she'd noted the blank spot where his memory of swerving should have been. She'd wondered about that herself, but had just assumed the man had been so traumatized he'd blocked it from his thoughts. But Scotty was saying there had been nothing to find, and suggesting it had also been a deliberate attack and the man had been controlled . . . like the girl tonight.

"My cousin is a wonderful woman. Who would want to kill her?" Matias asked with outrage.

Beth grimaced and admitted, "Probably a lot of people."

"What?" Matias met her gaze angrily in the rear-view mirror. "Do not be ridiculous."

Beth offered his reflection a crooked smile. "I hunt down rogue immortals, Matias," she pointed out gently. "Most of them have families. Sometimes the family understands and knows it has to be done. But other times they're in denial, grief turns to anger, and they want revenge."

Scotty nodded solemnly. "Family members seeking revenge can be more dangerous than the rogues themselves. At least when ye're hunting a rogue ye ken ye're walking into a dangerous situation and are prepared for it. Revenge attacks are unexpected and can be deadly because o' that. I've lost good hunters to relatives seeking revenge."

"Huh," Donny said with a frown. "Nobody mentioned that to me when I was in training."

"They're too busy trying to teach you how to stay alive," Beth said with a wry smile.

"This is the address," Matias said as he slowed to turn into the driveway of a neat white house with a wraparound porch.

"Do you want me to—?" Donny started.

"Nay," Scotty said at once. "I've been controlling the lass since we left the club. I'll take her to the door. Ye lads keep an eye out for trouble, and you," he added, turning to Beth, "stop talking and get some blood in ye. Ye're pale as death."

Beth grimaced and lifted the bag of blood he'd given her earlier. When he then waited, she dutifully popped it to her fangs.

Nodding with satisfaction, Scotty set the other bags in her lap and then slid out of the vehicle. A moment later, he opened the door next to the mortal and she got out.

"I told you Scotty likes you," Matias teased as they watched the Scot walk the girl to the porch.

Unable to talk, Beth merely grunted and glared at her cousin over the bag at her mouth. He was talking like a twelve-year-old mortal boy, and doing so mostly to annoy her, she was sure.

"No, Matias is right," Donny said as if she'd spoken her thoughts out loud. "I know you don't think so, but Scotty worries about you way too much for anyone to believe he doesn't like you."

Beth rolled her eyes as she waited for the last of the blood to be drained. She then ripped the bag away with relief and said, "Now you're both being ridiculous. You make it sound like he has a teenage crush on me."

"Perhaps he does," Matias said with amusement as they watched the front door of the house open. "And why not? I had a teenage crush on you."

"When you were a *teenager*," she agreed dryly. "Scotty is over eight hundred years old, not a horny teenager."

"My mother and father are both well over a millennium old, and they often act like horny teenagers," Matias assured her with a grin.

"Because they are life mates. All immortals act like horny teenagers when they're mated," Beth said with exasperation. "Scotty and I are not life mates."

"This time, she's the one who is right," Donny said almost apologetically to Matias. "Scotty has a life mate. He told me about her on the plane. She's too young for him to claim yet."

"Hmm." Matias didn't sound pleased at this revelation.

Beth merely grimaced. She'd been surprised at learning this on the plane while listening to the men talk, but hadn't really considered it since, and didn't want to either. The man was a hunk of sexy manhood, but usually too annoying for words. At least, he had been in the past. It had allowed her to use him in her sexual fantasies without guilt. At least there, she had been able to keep him from talking. But his suddenly being nice on this trip was just confusing her, and his having found his life mate left her conflicted.

It didn't seem right to use a mated man to find sexual release. It might be only in her mind that she was doing the wild thing with Scotty, but any immortal older than her could read those fantasies from her mind, tell his life mate and make things incredibly awkward. Heck, now that she thought about it, Scotty could have read them from her mind anytime they'd met over the last hundred-plus years . . . and wouldn't that have been embarrassing? Fortunately, she was usually so annoyed with the man when he was near that those nighttime fantasies were far away from her thoughts.

"Are you sure he—" Matias began, but paused when the door next to Beth opened.

"Ye've only had one bag?" Scotty asked with disbelief as he slid back in next to her and saw the three untouched bags still in her lap.

Rather than respond, Beth simply popped another bag to her fangs and slid over to make more room between them now that the mortal was gone. It didn't help much. Scotty simply seemed to expand to fill the space.

"Is the pain worse? Has the healing at least started?" he asked as Matias backed out of the driveway.

Beth nodded silently. Healing always hurt worse than the actual wound. She had no idea why. Someone had once suggested that the nerves went numb after the initial injury, but were brought back to screaming life by the activity of the nanos making their repairs. Whatever the case, there was no doubt she was healing, because her arm was now throbbing with pain.

"Are we still going to have pizza?" Donny asked as they drove through the night.

"*Sí*, I will order it as soon as we get home," Matias promised.

"Give me the number, and I'll order right now," Donny said, pulling his phone out again.

Beth leaned her head back and closed her eyes, trying to focus on something other than the pain as Matias rattled off a phone number, and then Donny made the call. She heard him ask what she liked on her pizza, but couldn't be bothered to answer. It was taking all of her concentration to keep from screaming. Her arm felt like it was full of fire ants or burning porcupine quills. That was the best way she could describe the pain, and even that didn't touch on the severity of it. Fortunately, Matias knew what she liked and answered for her. Not that she was feeling anything as mundane as hunger at that point. However, she would be once the worst of the healing was over, she knew.

Beth was just finishing the fourth bag of blood when

they reached the house. Her arm was still only partially healed and the pain was kicking her ass. When she stumbled getting out of the SUV, Scotty was immediately there to steady her. After one look at her expression and the sweat on her brow, he scooped her into his arms and carried her quickly into the house.

"Do ye have any first aid supplies here?" Scotty asked as he set her on the couch in the living room.

"*Sí*, in the outbuilding. But I do not know what they have. I will show you, though. I have to go fetch the dogs anyway."

Nodding, Scotty straightened and followed the man from the room, barking, "Do no' leave her side, Donny. And stay alert."

Donny nodded and, as soon as the pair were out of earshot, said to Beth, "See, he does like you."

Beth just closed her eyes and shook her head. At that moment, she didn't care what Scotty thought. As much as she lusted after the man, he could prance around naked and, in that moment, she wouldn't even have bothered to open her eyes to see it.

"But why is he after first aid supplies?" Donny asked. "The bleeding was stopped before we got in the SUV and the wound's mostly closed now. At least on the outside."

"He probably meant drugs," Beth said through clenched teeth, and then frowned at her own words. She didn't want drugs. Hunters suffered the healing of injuries without complaint or drugs. It was a point of pride. Besides, she liked to remain in control of her mind and body and had no desire to be knocked out.

Holding herself stiffly against the pain, Beth got

abruptly to her feet, relieved when she managed to do so without crying out or falling over.

"What are you doing?" Donny asked, jumping up with alarm.

"I am going to the bathroom," she answered grimly.

"The bathroom?" He looked dismayed. "But I'm not supposed to leave your side."

"Well, that could be interesting, then, couldn't it?" she asked caustically, and headed out of the room.

"I'll just wait outside the door for you," Donny decided as he followed.

Beth didn't bother to respond.

They'd had a quick tour of the house before leaving. She'd even moved her bags to the room she was to occupy. Well, most of them. One of her bags was still in the bathroom from when she'd prepared to head out to the bar that night . . . which was kind of rude, really, she supposed. It was a communal bathroom, after all. The only room with an en suite bathroom in this house was the master bedroom that Matias was occupying. That meant she, Donny, and Scotty would share the bathroom she was now entering.

Too bad for them, Beth thought dryly as she closed the bathroom door in Donny's face, and then locked it. She wasn't coming out until the worst of the healing was over.

Seven

"I wondered what you wanted from the medical supplies," Matias commented. "If I had realized it was drugs I could have saved you a trip. Beth will not take those."

"Aye, she will," Scotty assured him as he read the labels on the various drug vials. There were few drugs for pain that worked on immortals, and only one that was truly effective. Spotting it, he snatched it off the shelf, and turned to hurry out of the small pharmacy in the outbuilding next to the garage.

"I am telling you she will not agree to taking drugs," Matias warned, following him out of the building and pausing to lock the door.

"I'm no' going to ask her," Scotty responded coldly as he led the way back toward the house.

"Ah . . ." Matias murmured, falling into step behind him. "Well then, this ought to be interesting."

Scotty frowned at the words, but didn't slow or stop,

even when Matias halted at the kennel to release the Dobermans, who had started barking excitedly at their approach. Scotty's one thought was to get back to Beth and end her pain. She'd gone through enough in her life, and would not suffer ever again if he could help it.

Apparently he couldn't help it, because Scotty entered the living room with Matias on his heels to find it empty.

"What—?" Turning sharply, he hurried back past Matias and the dogs and into the hall leading to the bedrooms. It was the only place he could think she might be. Perhaps she had wanted to lie down.

Spotting Donny outside the bathroom door, Scotty hurried to his side.

"Is she in there?" he asked as he reached the younger immortal.

Donny nodded. "She said she had to go to the bathroom."

Scotty listened to the sound of rushing water coming muffled through the door, and frowned. "That does no' sound like the toilet flushin', or the sink tap runnin'."

"I think it's the shower," Donny admitted reluctantly.

"She should no' be in the shower. She could faint and hit her head and just do herself more damage," Scotty said with concern, and knocked at the door.

"She is fine," Matias assured him mildly. "She has had four bags of blood. She will not faint."

"She's in pain," Scotty said grimly.

"She would tell you that life is pain," the Spaniard said with a shrug. "Let her be. She will come out when she is ready."

Scotty shook his head and knocked at the door again. "Beth, open up."

"No! Go away!"

"If ye do no' open the door, I'll break it down," he threatened.

"Try that and I'll shoot you with my dart gun . . . again!" she threatened right back.

That gave him pause. The damned woman had already shot him once. He wouldn't put it past her to do it again. Turning to Donny, he asked, "Does she have her dart gun with her?"

Donny shrugged helplessly. "I saw one of her bags in there before she closed the door, but I don't know if her weapons are in it."

Scotty peered at the door, debating the issue, and then glanced around with surprise when the doorbell rang.

"That will be the pizza," Matias said, turning to head back up the hall. "If you are going to break down the door, please do not do it until I return. I should like to see it when she shoots you."

Scotty stared after him with disbelief and then shook his head and peered at the door once more. He had no doubt that Beth would shoot him if she had her dart gun. Knowing her, she probably did, Scotty decided with displeasure and thought that rather than hunting down painkillers for her, he should have just pulled out his own dart gun and shot her.

"Really?"

Scotty glanced around to see Matias returning up the hall, carrying four medium-size pizza boxes and shaking his head with something between disbelief and amusement. He didn't understand why until the man said, "Your earlier concern has now turned into wishing you had shot her? Really?"

Scotty scowled. The younger man was obviously reading his thoughts. That was the most annoying part of being an immortal who had found their life mate. He was now easy to read, and had been since meeting Beth over a century ago, which was why he had offered to help Donny control his thoughts. He knew how hard it was.

Rather than tell Matias to shut up, Scotty simply asked, "Is one o' those fer me?"

The Spaniard raised an eyebrow. "Do you wish to have it here or at the table in the kitchen, or in the living room?"

"Here."

Shrugging, Matias examined the labels on each box, shifted them to lie on one flat hand and pulled out the second one from the top.

"Thanks." Scotty took the box and slid down the wall to sit on the hardwood floor.

"You?" Matias asked Donny.

"The living room," the young man said firmly, and the pair left Scotty alone to wait.

Beth turned off the shower, but didn't immediately step out of the tub. Instead, she reached back to unzip her sodden dress and then peeled it off her shoulders. She hadn't been able to manage the feat earlier, so had simply kicked off her shoes and stepped under the water spray. Now the dress dropped to the tub floor with a heavy splat.

Grimacing, she stepped out of the circle of wet cloth and toed it aside, then stripped off her panties and bra as well before tugging the shower curtain aside and grabbing a towel off the rack. Beth quickly dried her hair first, and then wrapped the towel around herself sarong-style before stepping out onto the floor mat. She didn't know how much time had passed, but the worst of the healing was over, the throbbing reduced to a mild ache, so she'd guess a couple of hours.

Usually Beth would have lain down and tried to rest while she healed, but there were no locks on the bedroom doors and she hadn't trusted Scotty not to come in and try to force a shot of painkiller on her. So she'd stayed in the shower, and actually, the water had helped somewhat, distracting her from the pain enough to make it more bearable. Especially when the hot water had run out and she'd been left with cold water pouring down over her. That had been extremely distracting.

A check of the bag she'd left in the room earlier proved what Beth had already known—there were a pair of clean jeans, a couple of T-shirts, but no bras or panties. One of the T-shirts was an overlarge one she wore to sleep in, so she tugged it on over her head. The hem fell to midthigh, covering the important bits.

"Good enough," Beth muttered and turned to scoop up her wet clothes. She quickly squeezed as much water out of them as she could and then hung them over the shower rod. Leaving her bag there for now, she told herself she'd collect it on the way to bed and finally unlocked the bathroom door. She pulled it open to find Scotty outside, sitting on the hall floor. He was leaning against the wall opposite the bathroom door with his legs stretched out and crossed at the ankles. His arms were folded over his chest, his head down, eyes closed and an open, empty pizza box rested on the floor next to him.

After a hesitation, Beth started to ease past him in the direction of the kitchen. The sight of the pizza box was enough to make her search out food. She didn't think she made any noise, but with the first step Scotty lifted his head and his eyes opened, making her freeze like a guilty burglar caught in the act. The two of them stared at each other for a moment, and then Scotty got quickly to his feet.

"How're ye feeling?" he asked, his voice rough with sleep as his eyes slid to her arm.

"Better," Beth murmured, and then, shifting self-consciously, added, "You didn't have to wait out here."

"I wanted to be sure I talked to ye ere ye went to bed," he muttered, bending to pick up the pizza box.

Beth peered at it as he straightened and asked, "Donny?"

"He went to bed nearly three hours ago. Matias let him use his bathroom to brush his teeth and such."

"Three hours?" Beth asked, her eyes widening. If Donny had gone to bed that long ago, after eating and whatnot, she'd obviously been in the shower longer than the couple of hours she'd thought.

"Aye," Scotty said. "I'm to wake him up in an hour so that he can keep an eye out for trouble while I rest."

Beth frowned and turned to walk up the hall toward the kitchen. "Surely that's not necessary?"

"There have been two attacks on ye in twenty-four hours, lass," he pointed out, trailing behind her.

Beth didn't comment. She had thought about what had happened while she was in the shower. It had helped to distract her from the pain as her body healed. And she would admit that it did seem like someone was out to get her, but it wasn't the first time and probably wouldn't be the last. Still, now that she was aware of it, she would be more careful and keep her eyes open. She didn't think they really needed to have someone missing sleep to act as a guard.

"Isn't there an alarm system here?" she asked. "There is at the Enforcer house in Toronto. Not that they use it much, what with someone at the gates and the dogs walking the property. Speaking of which, Matias has the dogs here. They'd start barking if they heard or saw anything."

"Aye, Matias brought them in. They're in his room with him," Scotty murmured. "And there *is* an alarm. Matias put it on ere going to bed, so do no' open any doors or windows or ye'll set it off."

"Good, then there's no need for either you or Donny to be standing guard," she pointed out. "Besides, so far they've only attacked me when I was on my own. I doubt they'll attack me here when they probably know there are other immortal hunters around." Glancing over her shoulder, she added, "And I'm not even sure the accident and the attack are connected."

"Beth," Scotty began with exasperation.

"Just listen," she said, pausing in the kitchen and turning to face him. "If the two were connected, that would mean whoever was behind the accident had to have followed us here to Vancouver."

"Aye," he agreed with a nod.

"But they couldn't have," she assured him and

pointed out, "It's not like we drove here in a car they could have followed. We didn't even fly out of an airport where they could have checked the flight we were on. We flew straight from the Enforcer house on a private plane to that landing strip twenty minutes from here. So how did they know we were coming to the Enforcer house *here* in Vancouver?"

Scotty frowned as he considered that and then suggested, "Mayhap they read that ye were going to Vancouver from yer mind."

Beth shook her head. "I didn't even know I was coming here until I got back to the house *after* the accident," she reminded him. "Mortimer told me what the assignment was and where just before we got on the plane. The only people around were you, Donny, Mortimer, and me. And we took off from the house. We didn't go anywhere someone could read me after I learned."

Giving him a moment to think about that, Beth turned and opened the refrigerator to check the contents. Spotting the pizza box inside, she grabbed that as well as a bag of blood.

"As far as I can tell," Beth continued as she carried the pizza box and bag of blood to the counter and set them down, "nobody could have followed us."

"Except perhaps someone connected to the North American Rogue Hunters," he countered. "Anyone working for Mortimer could have found out about this trip easily enough."

Beth opened the pizza box and verified that it was her favorite—pepperoni, mushroom, onion, and tomato—and then turned to retrieve a plate from the cupboard as she agreed, "True. I don't think I've pissed off any of my coworkers yet, but it's possible. Except that doesn't seem likely."

"Why?" he asked at once as he watched her transfer a couple of slices from the box to the plate.

"They wouldn't have the time," she said dryly. "As shorthanded as he is, Mortimer's had us all working overtime and running here, there, and the other place," Beth assured him. Seeing the uncertainty on his face, she added, "But it would only take a phone call to Mortimer to see if one of the other hunters is in the area . . . and trust me, he'll know," she added dryly, moving to set the plate of pizza in the microwave. "He knows exactly where every one of us is at any given moment."

"He can't possibly ken where each o' ye are at all times," Scotty said with disbelief as she closed the microwave door and pushed the button labeled Reheat. "Mayhap he can find and follow yer vehicles with the GPS trackers in them, but if ye're no' using the SUV—"

"The Council supplies us with cell phones," Beth interrupted. "We're to carry them at all times whether working or not. That way they can reach us at all hours and everywhere if there's an emergency. They can also track us with some kind of app . . ." Beth shrugged and explained, "I didn't care if they tracked me so didn't pay close attention to exactly how they do it. But one call to Mortimer and he can tell you who, if any, of our hunters are out here in BC right now."

"They can track yer phones?" Scotty asked with interest.

Nodding, Beth picked up the bag of blood and leaned back against the counter as she added, "There's also a program they put on each phone that allows them to see whatever your phone's camera sees, and even hear what's said near it. I think it can get copies of your text messages, and allows them to listen in on phone calls too. But Mortimer says they don't activate it unless a hunter goes missing. I'm not sure that's true," she added dryly. "But I'd like to think so."

"Really?" Scotty murmured, and she could see his mind ticking that one over. From his perspective, as the head of the UK hunters, it would probably seem like a handy little program to have installed in hunters' phones.

Beth wasn't sure how she felt about it all herself. In situations like this, it was certainly handy to be able to immediately discount the hunters she worked with from being here in BC and possibly behind the attacks on her. But privacy was something in short supply today. The advent of bugs and cameras and even computers had played havoc with that particular commodity, and she had to wonder how much knowledge was too much, and if they all wouldn't be happier with a little less of it. It was the fruit of knowledge of good and evil that got Adam and Eve kicked out of paradise, after all. Maybe knowing everything both good and evil that went on in the world wasn't that grand a thing.

"I'll call Mortimer."

Beth merely nodded and popped the blood bag to her fangs. She was pretty sure her attacker wasn't anyone she worked with. But she wasn't positive.

Scotty got through to Mortimer right away, but was still on the phone with him when the bag at her mouth finished emptying. The microwave began to beep, announcing it was done, as she tore the bag away and tossed it out, so she retrieved the pizza and moved to sit at the kitchen table to eat.

"Mortimer checked and said we're the only hunters in the whole province of British Columbia right now. There isn't even anyone in Alberta at the moment," Scotty said with a frown as he slipped his phone back into his pocket.

Beth merely nodded as she chewed the bite of pizza she'd just taken.

"He also says we're the only ones who knew he was sending us out here."

Swallowing, she added, "And Matias."

"Aye, but he was here in Vancouver so couldn't have caused the accident with the truck, or had the knowledge read from his mind at the accident site." He frowned and then added, "I'll have to ask Donny if Matias was inside during your attack or—"

"Matias would never hurt me," Beth interrupted at once.

"Oh, aye, because he wants ye in his bed," Scotty muttered.

Clucking her tongue with irritation, Beth shook her head. "No, he doesn't. He is just teasing about that. It's his way of trying to make me see him as a man and not the boy whose diapers I changed and whose snotty nose I wiped," she explained with a faint smile. "Everyone treats him like a child still and he's struggling to be seen as a man . . . with everyone."

Scotty's eyes widened slightly as if that possibility hadn't occurred to him, and then he relaxed and murmured, "Oh."

Beth took another bite of pizza, shifting her mind

back to the "accident" and the attack. After swallowing, she heaved a sigh and pointed out, "It seems obvious that the crash and the attack tonight can't be connected."

"Aye, it would seem unlikely that they are," Scotty admitted, not sounding pleased.

She understood that. It certainly would have been easier if they were connected. Then there would be only one person out to get her and not two. But . . . maybe there still was only one, she thought suddenly.

"Since no one knows I'm out here," Beth said slowly, considering a brief thought she'd had earlier, "maybe the attack tonight wasn't directed personally at me."

"What?" Scotty stared at her with bewilderment. "Who was it directed at, then? The mortal? It wasn't her head he was trying to cut off."

"No, but I was thinking, maybe it could be an immortal who's newly gone rogue and was looking to kill just an immortal female, or even just a hunter, and I happened to be there tonight," she pointed out. "The only other option seems to be that it was someone with a beef against me who just happened to spot me at the club and decided it was a perfect opportunity for some revenge."

Scotty scowled, and Beth got the feeling he didn't deal well with not knowing what a situation was.

Shrugging, she finished off her pizza while he mulled over matters, and then stood and rinsed her plate. Beth set it in the dishwasher with the other dishes, and then dried her hands on a dish towel and turned to head for the kitchen door. "I'm going to bed."

"I'll come with ye."

That brought her to an abrupt halt. Turning, she peered at him blankly. "What?"

Scotty eyed her determinedly as he crossed the room. "Ye've been attacked twice now, lass. Whether it's by two different people, or one somehow managing to track ye here, 'tis clear ye're no' safe. Someone should be with ye at all times until we sort this out."

Beth frowned. "So . . . what? You plan to sit in the hall outside my door until Donny gets up to replace you?"

"Nay," he said, and Beth was just relaxing, thinking he meant only to escort her to her door, when he added, "I plan to stay in yer room."

"Oh, hell no!" she said at once. Dear Lord, she had sexual fantasies and wet dreams about this man all the time. Every night. There was no way she was having him actually in her room with her while she moaned and panted his name. Not that Beth knew if she did that, but if she did, she sure as spit didn't want him there to witness it.

"Beth, ye've narrowly escaped death twice now, and were badly injured the last time. I'm trying to keep ye safe," he said reasonably.

"Well, I have news for you, my friend, you're not—" She paused abruptly and then asked with sudden frustration, "What do you care?"

Scotty blinked in surprise. "What?"

Beth scowled at him as various emotions rolled through her. Mostly confusion, with a side order of bewilderment and a touch of hurt. The handful of times she'd encountered him before this, Scotty had treated her with cold disdain. Now, this trip, he was suddenly deigning to smile at her, and talking to her like she was a real human being rather than the scum of the earth he'd seemed to see her as for the better part of one hundred twenty-five years. And he was worried enough about her that he was willing to give up a night's sleep to guard her?

Beth had no idea what had brought on this sudden about-face in him, but she wasn't sure she liked it. The truth was, she was finding it somewhat alarming. It was one thing to lust after a man when you knew he didn't like you. It had ensured she couldn't like him either, so that her passion for him had remained firmly housed in the "he's a hot hunk you can fantasize about, but don't think it will go further" category.

However, now he was here, treating her like a human being and acting all nice and seemingly concerned about her well-being and—frankly—it was scaring her silly. She could like this guy who was nice to her, and that wasn't a good thing, especially when he had a life mate somewhere he was just waiting to claim.

"What do you care?" Beth repeated now. "You barely know me."

"That's not true," he said with surprise. "I've known ye fer nearly a hundred and twenty-five years."

Beth snorted at the claim. "You've popped up in the same area as me a handful of times over one hundred and twenty-five years and looked down your nose and been a thorn in my butt every single time before this. So, what's changed?"

"You have," Scotty responded at once, and then looked as if he'd quite happily snatch the words back.

Tilting her head, Beth eyed him solemnly. "Explain."

Scotty stared at her for a moment, several expressions flashing across his face, but then his mouth tightened and he shook his head. "Never mind. That's a conversation for another day. One when ye're no' swaying on yer feet from exhaustion. Go on to yer bed and get some rest. Ye've had a tough day."

Beth remained where she was, her mind turning everything over. In truth, she knew what he said was true. She had changed a great deal over the last ten years. Before that she'd been a "hurting unit"—angry, bitter, resentful . . . She'd felt like life had kicked her in the teeth, repeatedly . . . and it had. But she'd continued to do that kicking herself afterward. And then, ten years ago, they'd been clearing out a rogue nest and come upon a terribly abused dog. Half starved, burned, beaten, and tortured in ways she couldn't even guess by the rogues in the house, the poor beast had been at death's door. It had also been terrified, growling and snarling viciously, not letting any of them near him.

Deciding it was beyond helping, one of the other hunters had intended to shoot him, but Beth had intervened. To this day she couldn't say why exactly, but she'd looked into his eyes and something had called out to her. Perhaps she'd recognized herself looking back—the young terrified her who had been peering out at the world through her own eyes since she was a child. Whatever the case, she'd offered him part of her lunch, talking to him softly the whole time. It had taken a lot of patience and coaxing, but eventually she'd got the dog to eat. Beth hadn't tried to touch him or get too close—he'd been too skittish for that, and she'd understood. There had been times in her life when she hadn't trusted anyone to get too close or to touch her either. So she'd left him to eat and had gone back to work, helping with cleanup now that the rogues in the nest had been apprehended.

At first the dog had stayed where he was and followed her with his eyes. But when she'd walked around the side of the building, he'd followed, creeping just far enough around the corner that he could see her again. She'd noticed, but ignored it, and just gone about her business. But when he followed her again the next time she moved out of sight, she'd started to talk to him as she worked.

In truth, Beth couldn't recall what she'd said to him, really, except that she'd told him she was going to call him Ruff because he barked and growled anytime anyone got too near, and because he was in such rough shape. By the time cleanup was done and she and Dree had headed to their vehicle, Ruff had reduced the distance he kept between them to two or three feet. He followed them to the SUV and when she opened the back door, he'd hesitated only a moment before hopping inside.

Beth had taken him home, and fed him again, but allowed him the distance he wanted. She'd then gone to bed and had been just dozing off when she'd felt him hop up on the foot of the bed. She'd almost told him to get down. The poor beast was crusted with filth and blood. But in the end she'd let him be. When she woke up it was to find him cuddled up against her in bed. He'd let her pet him, and bathe him, and after eating again had gone docilely with her to the vet.

Within a very short time, Ruff had been a different dog altogether. A beautiful American boxer, he'd grown strong and healthy and had become an affectionate, cheerful, and loyal companion. He'd grown in confidence and lost any hint of skittishness. It was as if the abuse had never happened. He'd let it go and moved on, enjoying his life with her. Beth had been amazed. The vet hadn't. He'd said animals were the smarter creatures, living in the now and not dragging past baggage along with them through life. Ruff had it good now and was enjoying it.

Beth had learned from Ruff. She was nearly a hundred and sixty-five years old by that point, and had dragged the misery of her mortal life around with her for the last hundred and fifteen years since being turned. But she'd determined to be like Ruff, set that past down and travel on without it. It had taken her a little more time and effort than Ruff. Beth had slipped a couple times, and again picked up that baggage she was so used to carrying, but eventually she'd managed to set it down and leave it down so that it became just a part of her past and remained there where it belonged. Doing so had changed Beth's life tremendously. Her anger and bitterness had evaporated, she'd started to enjoy life more, and she'd become the person she suspected she was always meant to be.

So yes, Beth had changed. Apparently it had not gone unnoticed by Scotty, and that in turn had changed his behavior toward her. Interesting.

Breathing out slowly, Beth finally nodded and simply said, "Fine. I'll go to bed. Alone and without a guard," she added firmly, and when he opened his mouth on what she suspected was going to be a protest, she reminded him, "I'm the one in charge of this mission. You and Donny are my backup, so I know you'll listen to me when I say you're not spending the night in my room guarding me like some defenseless child. Understood?"

Scotty's mouth snapped closed, but he nodded stiffly.

"Good." Turning, she walked out of the kitchen with a quiet, "Good sleep."

Eight

Beth pushed through the Emergency Exit door and found herself in the alley again. The *tap tap tap* of high heels drew her gaze to the weeping woman just as she suddenly stopped and dropped to a crouch before the garbage bins. Beth peered at her and then shifted her gaze to the figure standing, hidden in the shadows cast by the bins. Squinting her eyes, she tried to pierce the darkness and get a better look at the person waiting to attack her, but all she could make out was the shape of someone tall in a suit.

"Chestnuts! All 'ot, a penny a score!"

Startled, Beth turned at that cry and peered down the alley in the other direction. Her eyes widened, and for a moment she thought the alley was on fire on the far end. Even as she had the thought, though, she was suddenly standing in the midst of all that light and heat, and she saw that what she had thought was a fire was actually hundreds of lights coming from the stalls lining both sides of the way. Each stall held at least one and sometimes two lights to illuminate the wares. Some had candles, while others had the smoky flame of old-fashioned grease lamps. Together, though, they all worked to light the whole area so that she was nearly dazzled by the colors around her. Here a splash of red apples, there purple pickling cabbage next to a stall of yellow onions, and then a butcher's stall with slabs of meat piled high behind a butcher who paced back and forth, sharpening his knife on a steel that hung from his waist.

It was Saturday night at the market in Tottenham Court, when it was so crowded you could barely move. The smells were overwhelming, and the noises . . .

"Now's your time! A half quire of paper for a penny!"

"A pound of grapes two pence!"

"Pick 'em up cheap here! Three Yarmouth bloaters for a penny!"

"Fine russets, penny a lot!"

The din was incredible and something Beth had forgotten.

She felt a tug on the long blue Victorian gown she was now wearing, and glanced down at a girl of perhaps five or six with a heavy basket in hand.

"Walnuts, miss? Sixteen a penny," the girl said, lifting her basket for Beth to better see.

Noting her hopeful smile and her fingers stained brown from the walnuts, Beth felt around on her person, hoping she had a pocket or purse with coins. The child reminded her of her little sister, and she'd buy every last walnut if she could.

"Here, lass."

Beth glanced around, her eyes widening when she saw Scotty beside her, dressed in a traditional plaid. As she watched, he handed several coins to the girl, but waved away the basket she then happily held up to him.

Scotty shook his head and said kindly, "The coins are fer you, lass. Keep yer walnuts."

"Thank ye, m'laird. Thank ye." The girl rushed off as if afraid he'd change his mind.

"That was kind," Beth said softly, not at all surprised to find him here. Her dreams always included Scotty, and had since she'd met him a hundred and twenty-five years ago.

Turning, she let her gaze sweep around the stalls and milling people. This was where she'd been happiest in her life, at market with her mother and sisters.

"Saturday night market at Tottenham Court," Scotty murmured, glancing around.

"You know it?" she asked with surprise.

"O' course. I've had a home in London since the seventeenth century," he murmured.

Beth frowned, unsure if that was true, or just something she'd dreamt up. She supposed it didn't matter. Whether it was true or not, she liked that he knew this part of her life, if only in her dream.

"I loved the market," Beth murmured, starting to walk along the stalls. "It was always noisy and exciting and colorful. It seemed to always have a fair-like feel to it."

"Aye," Scotty agreed, and then he caught her arm and drew her close as a sharp snap cut the air. But he relaxed when he realized it was just the percussion cap from some boys shooting at targets for nuts.

"Be in time! Be in time! Mr. Fredericks is about to sing the Knife Grinder!" a tall thin man boomed out beside her as she passed.

"I'd forgotten how noisy the market always was," Scotty said with a wry smile, and Beth was again surprised he was speaking her own thoughts aloud. But then, what else would he say? This was her dream, after all.

"Mmm, strawberries," Beth murmured suddenly as she spotted them in the next stall. Smiling at Scotty, she admitted, "I always loved strawberries. They were my favorite as a child."

"But not anymore?" he asked.

Beth made a face. "Nowadays they pick them green and ship them to stores and they aren't as sweet and juicy when you buy them. Unless you find them at a roadside stand or grow your own," she said with a grimace. "Back then they were always red, ripe, sweet, and juicy." She chuckled and added, "Of course they came when in season and were too expensive, so we never had them anyway."

"Then how do ye ken ye loved them?" he asked with amusement.

"I used to follow Mr. Badham when he was carrying his strawberries to the stall in hopes one or two might tumble to the ground," she explained.

"And did they?" he asked with a smile.

"Oh yes, once or twice," Beth said with a nod. "And I'd snatch them up and pop them in my mouth quick as you please. They were delicious, even with the bits of dirt that sometimes got on them in the fall."

Something flickered on his face, she wasn't sure what, but then Scotty suddenly ushered her up to the strawberry stall and tossed a coin at Mr. Badham before taking a wicker quart of the ripe red berries. Turning to Beth, he plucked one out, examined it briefly and then nodded his satisfaction and held it up.

"Dirt-free," he assured her solemnly. "Open yer mouth."

Beth smiled uncertainly, not sure why she was blushing, but she could feel the heat in her cheeks. Flustered, she tried to take the small fruit from him rather than open her mouth, but he immediately moved the strawberry out of her range.

"Tuh uh uh," he said, shaking his head. "Open."

Beth bit her lip briefly, but then dutifully opened her mouth and watched him move the offering closer until she could bite into it. The berry was as plump and sweet and juicy as she recalled from those days, and Beth closed her eyes on a moan as she chewed and swallowed what she'd bitten off. But then her eyes popped open with surprise when Scotty suddenly licked her lower lip, taking away the bit of juice there.

"Delicious," he agreed huskily, and then tossed the quart of berries aside, drew her into his arms and kissed her.

Startled, Beth didn't move at first. This just wasn't like her. Even in a dream she would never start anything in the middle of the market. Despite her history, she had a certain sense of propriety that her mother had drummed into her. Public displays of lust in the middle of the market did not seem proper, and there was no doubting the lust in that moment. While she might be still and docile under his attention, the kiss was ravaging, Scotty's mouth working over hers, his tongue slipping out to thrust between her lips and stir her desires.

When his hands began to roam, Beth tried to protest, but it was difficult with his mouth covering hers. One of his hands held her head in place as he kissed her, while the other dropped to cup her behind through her gown and lift her a bit, even as it urged her forward until their bodies rubbed against each other.

Gasping, Beth managed to break their kiss and glance self-consciously around, only to blink in surprise when she saw that the market was gone. They were now in a large bedroom lit only by the flames that crackled in a fireplace in the wall next to them, and they stood beside a bed with drapes and silk sheets in forest green. They were alone.

That was all Beth really noticed. The moment she broke their kiss, Scotty had begun to nibble on her ear and neck, and her body responded by beginning to tremble.

Beth knew at once that this was going to be one of the knee-knockers. That was what she liked to call the dreams that felt so real she could actually taste the salt on his skin, and feel the heat of his body. Those were the rarer of the dreams she had about Scotty, but they were also the most powerful so that she woke afterward with her body sweaty, sated and still trembling from the pleasure her dream lover had given her.

She was aware that Scotty had begun working on the fastenings of her gown. Beth didn't try to stop his eager hands, but when he nipped at her earlobe, she turned her head so that he could kiss her again. This time, she kissed him back with all the passion that had been missing from her in the market. She also let her own hands roam now, sliding them over his hard, wide chest, and then plucking at the pin that fastened the plaid in place. It undid as if by magic, and the material immediately slithered away to the floor, leaving him standing in a white linen shirt that barely covered his family jewels.

Beth had just taken note of that when her gown too dropped away to pool on the floor. Scotty stepped back to survey her, and she glanced down to see that she was wearing a white bustier and knickers as well as hose and garters. She wondered briefly where those had come from and then Scotty growled, "Beautiful."

Beth shifted her gaze to him. He was smiling warmly.

"I decorated me room with ye in mind. I kenned this color would suit yer alabaster skin and red hair. Ye're like fire and ice in a forest."

Beth's eyes widened in amazement. She'd never been the flowery sort, so had no idea where those words had come from. But she liked them, she decided, and reached down to find him and show him just how much. Only the minute her fingers found the hardness she'd known would be waiting under the linen shirt, Scotty caught her hand and removed it at once.

"Nay," he growled, catching both of her hands in one of his and raising them over her head as he urged her back against one of the columns of the bed. Holding her there with his body, he met her gaze and said firmly, "I'm no' a client to be pleasured. I'll pleasure you."

Confusion clouded her mind again at once at the words, because Beth was quite sure they hadn't come from her. In fact, they were kind of hurtful, perhaps because of the anger that flashed in his eyes that could almost have been disgust. Aside from that, Scotty had never before spoken in her dreams. He had always been more of a doer than a talker. But then usually his mouth was pretty busy with other things, Beth thought, and shifted her attention abruptly back to him as he kissed her again.

Still a little wounded by his words, Beth was at first slow to kiss him back. But when his tongue thrust into her mouth and his free hand glided up her side and then around to knead one breast through her bustier, her body responded like Pavlov's dogs, and she was soon sighing and gasping by turn as he lashed her with his tongue. She felt his hand shift to find the top of her bustier, but was still startled when he tugged at it, forcing it down to free one breast. When he broke off the kiss to lower his mouth to claim the nipple he'd freed, she slid her hands into his hair and cupped his head as he suckled, her focus completely on the sensations he was stirring in her. Sensations that were only magnified when he slid one leg between both of hers and moved it up until his thigh rubbed her where her excitement was building.

Closing her eyes, Beth bit her lip and gave herself over to the need rising in her. Without even realizing it, she began to shift her hips, riding his thigh. But then his free hand slipped under the waistline of her knickers and slid down to delve between her thighs, and Beth cried out, her body bucking.

Letting her nipple slip from his mouth, Scotty straightened and kissed her neck, murmuring, "Do ye like that?" He ran his fingers lightly across her damp skin before pausing to circle the nub of her excitement. "Do ye like it?"

"Yes," Beth gasped, riding his hand now.

"I want to taste ye. Would ye like that?" he growled, nipping at her ear.

"Oh, God," Beth groaned both at the words and at the feel of his finger pressing into her even as his thumb continued to caress her. She pushed down into the intrusion and then gasped with disappointment when he withdrew his skilled fingers. Only to gasp again when he suddenly dropped to kneel before her.

Realizing her garters would prevent him removing her knickers, Beth started to lower her now free hands to help take them off, but then stiffened when Scotty grasped her knickers at the waist. As she watched in amazement, he ripped them wide open rather than bother to remove her garters and hose to get them off. It was a quick and violent action, and one easily performed, although some part of her brain was arguing that it shouldn't have been managed so easily. Beth actually had to remind herself that it was a dream. It just all felt so damned real.

"Oh!" she gasped when Scotty suddenly caught her at the waist and turned to toss her on the bed. She'd barely bounced once on the feather mattress before he caught her under the knees and drew her down on the silk sheets until her bottom was at the edge of the bed. When he then dropped to kneel on the floor and buried his face between her open legs, Beth gasped and half sat up in shock, only to buck and cry out as his tongue rasped across the tender flesh there.

While she was still half-raised, Scotty reached one hand up to squeeze the breast he'd freed earlier, then toyed with the nipple as he lapped at her.

Groaning, Beth covered his hand with one of her

own, but placed the other on the bed to help keep herself upright as she trembled and squirmed under his ministration. When he added his fingers to the mix and began to thrust one in and out of her as he licked and nipped at the center of her enjoyment, Beth cried out and fell back to lie flat. Her body was writhing, her legs locking and unlocking around his head and her hands now tangling in the sheets as she fought to reach that pinnacle he was urging her toward. She was also aware that she was making the most godawful sounds—deep moans and heavy groans interspersed with her crying his name in a pleading voice . . . and she didn't care.

And then her body went taut and stiff for a moment before everything exploded, and Beth began to shudder and almost convulse as she found her pleasure.

Scotty eased from between her legs then and joined her on the bed. He drew her into his arms and shifted them both further up the bed, and then simply held her until her breathing and heart rate calmed.

"Thank you," Beth whispered, caressing his chest. "Can I—"

Her question died when Scotty caught her under the chin and lifted her face for a kiss. It started out sweet and soothing, but soon became more demanding, and his hands began to move over her once more. She was moaning again by the time Scotty rolled her onto her back and covered her. Supporting his own weight with his arms, he ground himself against her as he thrust his tongue into her mouth.

Moaning in response, Beth spread her legs for him and raised her knees so that she could brace her feet flat on the surface of the bed. Scotty answered the invitation and surged into her, and Beth's whole body responded, the full force of her hunger rushing back as if it had never been sated.

Crying his name, she clutched at his shoulders and raised her hips to meet him, urging him on until he stiffened and cried out as he found his own pleasure. Beth knew that wouldn't be the end—it never was in these more intense dreams—so she wasn't surprised when he pushed up and off her to kneel between her legs and urged her to turn over. She sat up at once, but then shifted to her knees in front of him and reached back, managing to catch his hip and urge him closer. Growling, Scotty moved forward on his own knees, his legs framing hers as his chest met her back. He then slid his hands around her waist and up across her stomach to cup her breasts.

Beth groaned and arched against him as he weighed and squeezed her breasts, her hips shifting and rubbing her bottom against the hardness between them. Scotty nipped at her ear and kissed her neck, but when he began to toy with her nipples, she twisted her head around in search of his mouth. He kissed her roughly, and then let one hand drop from her breast to glide down between her legs.

Beth cried out into his mouth, her hips moving into his touch, and then she couldn't stand it anymore, and she broke their kiss and dropped forward to her hands and knees. Clasping her by the hips, Scotty immediately began to . . . lick her face?

Gasping in shock, Beth opened her eyes and gaped at the big black beast standing over her on the bed, panting happily.

"What the—?"

"Chico! Down!"

Beth glanced to the door as Matias pushed it further open and rushed in to hurry around the bed.

"Sorry! I am sorry. I was checking on you and he slipped past me. Chico, come here," he hissed, grabbing for the Doberman's collar and falling on the bed when a second dog rushed in to join the fun and tripped him up, then proceeded to climb on top of him and lick his upper back. Matias's voice was exasperated as he buried his face in the bed and muttered, "No, Piper. Bad."

Chuckling softly as Chico shifted to drop on her legs so that he too could get to his master, Beth sat up to move her legs out of the way of being trampled by the excited dog. She then leaned back against the headboard and simply watched as both dogs descended on her cousin, licking his arms, his legs, his hair . . .

"I love my dogs," Matias said dryly, his voice muffled by the blankets. Both Dobermans immediately shifted their excited attention to his face, trying to get to the parts he'd buried in the blankets.

"They are sweet," Beth said with amusement.

"Hmm." He didn't sound convinced. Pushing first one away and then the other, he struggled to get upright. The minute he was standing again and they were unable to reach his face, Chico and Piper turned to her. Squealing, Beth immediately pulled the blanket defensively over her head to avoid the wet kisses. That just seemed to excite the dogs even more, and they began to try to nose their way under the blanket with her.

Giving up, Beth tossed the blanket aside, grabbed the first dog by the ears and began to rub them while kissing the top of his head and murmuring, "Now I've got you. You're all mine. I've got you now."

"He likes you," Matias said with amusement as Chico calmed down and enjoyed the ear massage. "They both do," he added as Piper settled next to her on the bed and laid her head in her lap.

Smiling, Beth released one of Chico's ears and reached out to scratch behind one of Piper's. When Chico lay down next to her too, she continued to pet them, but glanced to Matias and asked, "Why were you checking on me? You knew my arm would heal well enough."

"Hmm." Matias grinned and settled on the bed next to her. Absently petting Piper, he said, "Well, I feared you were being attacked again."

"Attacked?" she asked with surprise.

"Hmm." Grinning, he explained, "You were moaning, groaning, grunting, and crying out. It was most alarming. I was sure you were either being tortured to death, or you were making the mad, passionate love to someone. But since Donny is up and about, Scotty was in his own bed making the same sounds, and I can now see there was no one in your room let alone your bed with you, I can only assume it was a dream . . . a shared sex dream," Matias added with a wicked grin.

"What?" Beth squawked, sitting up straight.

"*Sí.* I knew there was something between you and Scotty—" he added with satisfaction and then asked, "How was it? Is it as hot as they say? It sounded hot."

"There's nothing between Scotty and me," Beth protested, ignoring his other questions.

"Oh, *chica*, how stupid do you think I am?" he asked with disbelief.

"Apparently really stupid since there's nothing between Scotty and me," she insisted.

"Really?" Matias raised his eyebrows superciliously. "And yet he was worried sick about you last night after you were injured."

Beth snorted at the claim. "He probably worries about everyone that way. The man runs the Rogue Hunters in the UK. It's his job to worry about the hunters."

"Beth, seriously," Matias said with a frown. "I beseech you. You must know he is your life mate? He is showing all the signs," he told her and then counted off, "One, I can read his mind. He's much older than me and I shouldn't be able to, but I can. Two, he is eating. He ate an entire pizza last night by himself. And he is drinking too. I gave him a soda to have with his pizza and he drank the whole thing."

"Yes, he's eating and drinking and he probably can be easily read," she allowed. "And yes, he's met his life mate. But it isn't me, cousin."

"Why are you bothering to lie to me?" Matias asked with exasperation. "You were in here having the shared dream with him. You were moaning and groaning and crying out, 'Scotty, oh, Scotty.'" He mimicked what she guessed was supposed to be her voice with a ridiculous falsetto. "And Scotty was down the hall doing the same thing, but shouting, 'Beth! Oh my God, Beth!'"

"He was?" she asked with surprise.

"*Sí*," Matias said firmly.

Beth frowned over that, but shook her head. "He can't have been. He has a life mate already. He just hasn't claimed her."

"*Sí* . . . you," Matias said with satisfaction.

"No. Scotty told Donny—"

"And *I* am telling *you* I can read his mind. Did I not mention that?" he asked with irritation, and then continued, "And last night when you were in pain, his thoughts were in an uproar. He was in a panic to ease it for you. He was also most concerned that we must guard you well because he would not lose his life mate. Those were his thoughts. 'I will not lose my life mate,'" Matias said with emphasis and then smiled smugly. "You. You are this life mate."

"But how can that be?" she asked with confusion. "I mean, I met the man over a hundred years ago. How could he not be my life mate back then and then suddenly be my life mate now? Wouldn't he have had to be my life mate all along?"

Matias pursed his lips and considered the question. "Perhaps he was."

"What?" Beth glanced at him with surprise.

"Well, he has expended a lot of energy over the years trying to keep you from being a hunter and then trying to keep you off dangerous hunts," he pointed out. "And I read in his mind last night that he's had someone watching over you since shortly after he saved you from Jamieson."

"What?" she repeated, outraged.

Matias nodded. "*Sí*, he was thinking of that last night. It was someone named Magnus, and he recalled him back to England when he decided to fly out here to Canada, but he was thinking he should put him back on you after last night's attack."

"Son of a—I can't believe he had someone watching me all this time," Beth said grimly. "How did I not notice?"

"You are missing the point, *chica*," Matias said with exasperation. "Why would he do that? Why did he have someone watching you even way back then?" he asked, and then answered, "He must have known all along that you were his life mate."

Beth stared at her cousin blankly as everything he'd said circled slowly inside her head. Scotty had set a bodyguard on her. He'd been looking out for her. He was eating and easily read because he'd found his life mate. And the dreams . . . Beth frowned. Were they shared dreams? Life mates were said to have them when in the vicinity of each other . . . but Scotty had played in most of her wet dreams since she'd met him. Even the ones she had when they were on different continents.

Although, she thought suddenly, they had always been more powerful when he'd popped up in Spain, and now here. Beth had just assumed it was because he was on the scene and big as life. Now she realized he'd often stayed in either a house or hotel near wherever she lived. Then the dreams had been much more powerful, more real. She'd been able to smell him, and touching him in her dreams had felt like she was touching him in real life . . . like the dream tonight, she thought with a frown.

"Frankly, I am surprised that you did not realize it yourself," Matias added.

Beth scowled at him. "How was I supposed to know? I was a new turn when I met him. It had only been two weeks since I was turned. I couldn't read anyone, so not being able to read him meant nothing to me. And I was still eating back then. And . . . well, he's a good-looking man. I just assumed I was dreaming about him because he was a hottie."

"All true," Matias decided after a moment's consideration. "So I will accept that you did not know, but *he* definitely must have known."

Beth bit her lip, unwilling to believe that Scotty had known all this time and not claimed her. How much did you have to hate someone that you would bypass claiming them as a possible life mate? The one thing all immortals yearned for and were seeking? And why would they even *be* life mates when he hated her?

"Maybe he wasn't sure," she suggested hopefully.

"Beth," Matias said heavily. "Scotty is not an idiot. He knows the signs of meeting a life mate. His not being able to read you by itself would have told him that is what you are."

"He can't read me?" she asked curiously. "How do you know that?"

"Because he didn't know that you knew about his interfering in your becoming a hunter and some of the jobs you've been on," Matias explained. "If he could read you, he'd know that. But he didn't and was surprised and even dismayed when I told him that you do know."

Beth merely grunted at that. It still annoyed her to think of the way he'd interfered in her being an Enforcer over the years.

"So, he must know," Matias decided, and then frowned and said, "But if so, why has he not yet claimed you? Most immortals would have claimed you right away, yet he has not."

When he peered toward her in question, Beth lowered her head and concentrated on petting Chico as she finally gave in to the truth. Scotty had known they were life mates for over a century and done nothing about it. There was only one reason she could think of for that, and it was both simple and obvious.

"If I had to guess, I would say because he doesn't like me," she said softly.

"What?" Matias shook his head and blew a raspberry. "Impossible! You are beautiful, and charming and strong and smart! You are a goddess among women!"

"And yet he doesn't want me," Beth said wearily. "He hasn't claimed me and usually, at least until this visit, he's been cold as a witch's tit to me."

"I have not seen this cold tit," Matias assured her solemnly. "In fact, I would say from the looks I have seen him give you that the witch's tit is on fire."

"Yes, well, that's only this time," she assured him. "In the past he treated me like I had the plague. He even wanted to have my mind wiped in a three-on-one."

"What?" Matias's eyes widened incredulously and she couldn't blame him. A three-on-one was when three immortals worked together to invade and eradicate another immortal's memories. They erased each memory over and over again to prevent the nanos repairing them, until the individual was as blank as a clean chalkboard. It was a drastic measure, used as a last resort.

"*Yes*," Beth assured him firmly. "When he and his men saved us from Jamieson, he pulled Dree aside and said the Council would want me put down, but he thought I should be given the three-on-one and have my mind wiped," she told him. "In fact, if not for

Dree, I'm sure he would have done it. But she refused to allow it and got us on a boat headed for Spain that very night."

"Thank God for Drina," Matias said with a shake of the head. "I cannot imagine life without you in it as . . . well, as you."

"Apparently, that's what Scotty would have preferred, though," Beth whispered miserably.

Matias's mouth tightened. "Well, screw him and the cow he rode in on. He is out of luck. We will find you another life mate, and Scotty can go wipe someone else's mind to have a pickle for a mate."

Beth's lips twitched at the words. "A pickle?"

"Well, what do you think is the result of a three-on-one?" he asked grimly.

She shook her head. "Marguerite Argeneau's husband did a three-on-one on her, and I'm quite sure he didn't wipe all her memories, leaving her a pickle."

"Then she is lucky. From what I understand, that is very hard to do. It is easier to just wipe the memory completely, and when that happens, the person is no longer themselves. They are a tabula rasa. A blank slate. Their personality gone." Matias snorted and added, "That is probably what he wanted, a blank slate to turn into whatever he wishes."

"Or just a woman who wasn't a prostitute as a mortal," Beth said quietly.

Matias turned on her sharply. "That was not your choice. He cannot blame you for that," he said with outrage. "Your father sold you to those disgusting purveyors of flesh! And they in turn sold you to Danny after your chastity was stolen."

"But I stayed in the business after Dree killed Danny

and I was free," she pointed out solemnly. Matias had known her life history for years. He'd asked her and she'd told him. Beth didn't hide it. Secrets were never a good thing. They tended to give others power over you if they learned of them. Besides, she wasn't ashamed of her history. At least, she hadn't thought she was. But now she wondered if she shouldn't be.

Sighing, Beth leaned back against the headboard and closed her eyes. It was far too early in the day to have to deal with this. Or was it? Opening her eyes, she turned to her cousin and asked, "What time is it?"

"Nearly two o'clock," Matias answered, and then raised his eyebrows. "Since you are awake, can I take you to breakfast?"

"Breakfast?" she asked with interest.

"It will get you away from the house and . . . him," he said apologetically. "And it will give you a chance to clear your head."

Beth smiled crookedly and shrugged. "That's not necessary, Matias. I'll be fine. I mean, I'm not the one who's been running around aware that we're life mates all this time. I thought I just had the lusties for him, so didn't become emotionally involved. I'll just continue to think of him that way."

"Lusties?" Matias asked with amusement.

"That's what Mary and I used to call it when we were attracted to a man," she said with a small smile that faded as she recalled her friend Mary's fate. These last ten years since the arrival of Ruff in her life, Beth had made a practice of finding the bright side of every event. For Mary, she'd told herself that at least her friend enjoyed a couple of years of her retirement before Jamieson had killed her, that at least her death had been quick. It might not seem like much, but Beth knew it was. She'd seen many mortals die slowly over the last century, fading away, suffering terribly over a long period of time as they struggled to live a life that no longer offered them anything but the pain of cancer or some other ailment. She was glad Mary hadn't had to go through that.

"I will take the dogs and go so that you can dress," Matias said and started to get off the bed, only to pause and turn to hug her tightly. "You are a good woman, Beth. If he cannot see that and accept you the way you are, it is his loss."

"Thank you," she murmured, hugging him back. "And you're the best cousin a girl could ask for, Matias. The day Dree and her brother welcomed me into your family was the luckiest of my life."

Matias squeezed her a little tighter, and then released her and got up.

"Chico, Piper, come," he ordered, patting his hip as he headed for the door. The dogs immediately leapt off the bed and followed him out into the hall.

Nine

The moment the door closed behind Matias and the dogs, Beth threw her covers aside and got up as well. But then she just stood there, momentarily overwhelmed by all she'd learned. She was a possible life mate for Scotty, but he didn't want her. How deep must his loathing be that he would pass up the chance of a life mate just because she was that life mate?

Wow. She had lived fifty years as a mortal, and only one hundred and twenty-five more as an immortal. That wasn't even a quarter of his life, but Beth would have jumped at the chance of a life mate. Yet he didn't want her.

For a moment anger and pain tried to drag at her, but she pushed it away and took a deep breath. As Matias had said, it was Scotty's loss. She was a good woman, and she would make a good life mate . . . to someone else.

"They should have dating sites for immortals," she muttered under her breath as she dragged a fresh pair of jeans out of her bag and began to pull them on. Maybe she'd start one. She could hire Marguerite, or someone like her, to interview all the immortals who joined and match them up.

Or maybe young Stephanie, Beth thought as she tugged off her overlarge T-shirt and then grabbed a bra from the bag and donned it. Drina said the kid had some skills in that area. Hell, she could hire both of them and halve the work for each. And she could call it iHarmony for Immortal Harmony.

The thought made her grin as she pulled on a clean T-shirt, but Beth shook her head. That sounded too much like an Apple product.

Immortally Yours, maybe? That one wasn't bad. She'd have to think about it. Actually, she didn't know why someone else hadn't thought of it already. There were so many lonely immortals out there, waiting for a life mate.

Shaking her head, Beth rooted through the bag she'd collected from the bathroom on her way to her room last night and gathered her weapons belt and the small arsenal of weapons she'd brought with her. She made short work of fastening the belt around her waist and quickly filling all the custom holders. Her sword, knives, and a dart gun were quickly tucked away, and then she headed for the door, mentally preparing herself to face Scotty now that she knew the man was aware of the dreams she had about him.

The thought made her grimace. It was one thing to have sexual fantasies and dreams about a man when he didn't know, and quite another for him to know exactly what you wanted to do to him behind closed doors . . . and what a screamer you were.

"You can do this," Beth muttered under her breath. "You can't waste your time worrying about a man who thinks himself better than everyone else. Just deal with him until tomorrow and then you'll fly home and not have to deal with him anymore."

Shoulders straight, she dragged the door open and marched out of her room.

Much to Beth's relief, there was no one in the hall, and she made it to the bathroom without encountering anyone. She continued the inner lecture as she relieved herself, washed her hands and face, and then brushed her teeth and hair. Once she didn't have anything else to do, she forced herself to continue on to the kitchen.

Beth heard the murmur of male voices before she reached the kitchen door and braced herself for what was to come, but it wasn't as hard as she'd expected it to be. She supposed, in a way, while everything had changed, nothing had changed at all. She'd always been attracted to Scotty, and she'd always known he hated her or at least looked down on her. The only added factor here was that he was aware of the wild sexual fantasies she had about him. Oh well. He appeared to enjoy them too, so he couldn't point fingers, Beth told herself firmly and entered as Donny said, "You're kidding me. You're a lawyer?"

"For fifty years," Matias said with a nod as Beth strode to the coffee machine.

"Why are you in university, then?" Donny asked with confusion.

Matias shrugged. "I got bored and thought I would try something else."

"What are you taking?" Donny asked.

"Right now I am taking general courses so I can see what interests me most."

"Man," Donny muttered. "I thought you were like twenty or something."

"Seventy-five," Matias corrected him.

"Matias, where do you keep your cups?" Beth asked before Donny could speak again. The coffee machine was the good old-fashioned drip kind, where a whole pot was made and not a cup, *and* the carafe was nearly full. Matias was the only one with coffee, Donny had a glass of water in front of him and there was an empty blood bag in front of Scotty.

"In the cupboard above the coffeepot," Matias said helpfully.

"Thanks." She opened the cupboard door, picked one of the dozen or so cups and poured coffee into it with a little sigh.

"Thank God you're up," Donny said into the silence. "We have to go out for breakfast, and then we have to go grocery shopping if we want lunch and supper."

"There's plenty of food here," Beth said lightly as she stirred sugar into her drink. "Make toast, or a sandwich or something."

"I can't. There's no bread," Donny said, scowling at Matias. "All that meat and cheese and not a lick of bread in this place."

"Tina forgot to get it when she picked up the groceries for me," her cousin said with a shrug, and then pursed his lips and added thoughtfully, "Although she may not have forgotten. She is on that no-carb diet. Avoiding the bread might have been deliberate."

"Tina?" Beth asked with a smile. "I thought you were mad about Justine."

"*Sí*, but Justine does not like to shop, and Tina does. She is very sweet."

"Uh-huh," Beth said and then asked idly, "Who does your laundry?"

"Nicole. She is very handy with the iron."

"Housecleaning?"

"Michele." He grinned widely. "She wears a French maid outfit when she does it. Afterward, I reward her well."

"I'll bet," Beth said dryly and shook her head. "Good to know you haven't changed and still keep a harem of willing women around."

"I must. I am God's gift to women," Matias reminded her, even managing to keep a straight face as he did.

Chuckling, Beth scooped up her cup and took a sip before asking, "Does Mortimer know you have mortal women running around the Enforcer house and doing your chores for you?"

"No. He has never asked so I have never told," he said with a shrug and then eyed her warily. "You think he would not like it?"

"I think he would definitely not like it," she assured him. "There's too much risk one of them could see or hear something they shouldn't."

"I never let the girls come when there are Enforcers here," Matias assured her. "They just help me take care of things when I am the only one present."

"Hmm," Beth said dubiously.

Matias eyed her with dissatisfaction and then asked, "Are you going to tell him?"

Beth considered the matter briefly and then shrugged. "If he doesn't ask, I won't tell." Matias was just relaxing when she added, "But if he does ask, I will."

Matias grimaced, but before he could protest or respond, Donny complained, "Beth, I'm starved."

Turning her attention to the younger immortal, she raised her eyebrows. "Well, you didn't have to wait for me. Why didn't you go grab yourself some breakfast while I was sleeping?"

"I couldn't leave the house," he protested as if shocked she'd suggest it. "You were attacked last night. Someone is out to get you."

"Oh yeah," Beth muttered into her cup. She supposed she should have expected that Scotty would insist all three men stay to guard her, but she'd been so distracted by everything else, she'd kind of forgotten about that incident in the alley. Besides, she didn't know why the man would bother. He didn't want her, so why worry about her well-being?

Not wanting to get caught up in that painful inner conversation again, Beth sighed and pushed the question away. Lifting her head, she raised an eyebrow in Matias's direction. "You don't happen to have travel mugs?"

"*Sí*." Grinning, he stood and moved to a cupboard at the opposite end of the room. There were half a dozen or so cups in the cupboard. He picked a red one that reminded her of her poor destroyed shoes and carried it to her, murmuring, "It seems we will have company for that breakfast I offered to take you out for."

Beth shrugged as she turned to pour her coffee into the travel mug. "Such is life, cousin."

"*Sí*," he murmured.

Beth quickly rinsed the cup she'd used, snapped the lid on the travel mug and turned back to start across the kitchen. "Come on, boys. It seems breakfast and shopping are on the agenda before anything else today."

"Mortimer called while you were getting ready," Scotty announced, and Beth froze and closed her eyes on a curse.

"I forgot to call him and report on what happened with Kira before we went out last night," she realized out loud.

"Aye," Scotty agreed. "But I would no' feel bad. I forgot about it too. I fear Donny's reaction to caffeine made us all forget. I explained as much to Mortimer and filled him in."

Sighing, Beth forced herself to turn and nod at him. "Thank you."

"Me pleasure," he said, offering her a smile.

Beth bit her lip, and then asked, "How did he take the news that Kira was returning to Toronto with us?"

"He was no' pleased at first, but in the end said it was better than her committing suicide by Council order and starting an international immortal war," Scotty said dryly and then added, "O' course, once I mentioned that she was trained in weapons and martial arts, he warmed to the idea. He's hoping she will no' need much training at all ere he puts her in the field."

Beth snorted. "He already has trainees and volunteers on the job. He won't make her train. He'll just place her with a seasoned hunter and let them train her on the job."

"Maybe not," Scotty said. "After all, she is the daughter of Athanasios Sarka. He'll take care that she is no' hurt on the job."

"Hmm, you're probably right," she said thoughtfully.

"Can we go now?" Donny whined. "Honestly, you could have told her all that in the car, Scotty. I have been up with nothing to eat for hours."

"There was still pizza in the refrigerator," Beth said with irritation. "You could have warmed some up and had that."

"Pizza for breakfast?" Donny asked with disgust.

"What? I thought all young people liked leftover pizza for breakfast," she said. When his expression just became more disgusted, Beth sighed and spun away to walk out of the kitchen, saying, "Fine, we'll go. But grab a bag of blood to bring with you. That should tide you over until we get to the restaurant," she pointed out, and added under her breath, "At least you won't be able to whine with it in your mouth."

"Ewww, blood before breakfast? That's gross."

Beth stopped walking and turned on him with amazement. "Seriously?"

He nodded with a grimace. "I can't stomach blood until after I have some food in my stomach. And I need to eat if you expect me to suffer through shopping."

"I am not making you suffer through anything," she snapped. "You're the one insisting we must go shopping."

Ignoring her argument, Donny just said, "We should

go to one of those breakfast crepe places. I like the ones with berries and lots of whipped cream, or—oh!—apple cinnamon crepes with caramel sauce. Those are yummy. Or the chocolate crepes with cherries."

Beth turned to frown at Scotty. "Did you let him have coffee today?"

"No," he assured her firmly, his lips twitching with amusement. "This, apparently, is just Donny before breaking his fast."

"This is Donny starved," the younger immortal put in grimly. "Now let's go."

He marched past them then, headed for the front door with his nose in the air.

"He reminds me of Phil," Beth murmured with disbelief as she watched him in his huff.

"Who is Phil?" Scotty asked, eyes dancing with laughter and curiosity.

"A twelve-year-old girl we had at the brothel for a while. Her name was Phillipa. We called her Phil. She was always throwing temper tantrums and marching about like she was a princess."

"What happened to her?" Scotty asked solemnly.

"She threw one too many temper tantrums, and Danny sold her to another bullie."

"*Bullie* means *pimp*, *sí*?" Matias asked.

"It did back then. At least, a specific type of pimp, one who kidnapped girls and forced them into the business, or tricked them into it like both Danny and this guy. Sometimes, though, one bullie would sell a girl to another to be rid of her," Beth explained and noted the relief on Scotty's face. She supposed he'd worried she was going to say the girl died in some horrible manner . . . and she did. The next bullie didn't sell her on when he found her annoying. He choked her to death in a fury.

"Are you guys coming or what?" Donny demanded from the door, and then jerked his head toward it when the doorbell sounded. Swinging his head back, he asked uncertainly, "Do I answer it?"

Beth opened her mouth to respond with an exasperated yes but never got the chance. Scotty barked, "No," and suddenly took her arms and maneuvered her quickly back into the kitchen.

"Remain here," he ordered, then told Matias to stay with her and rushed up the hall.

"Huh," Beth grunted. "Go figure. One little cut on the arm and I go from respected Enforcer to damsel in distress."

"It would appear so," Matias agreed.

"Well, that's a problem," Beth said with disgust, and then frowned and moved closer to the door as she heard surprised greetings and male laughter. "Sounds like it's friend and not foe."

"*Sí*," Matias agreed as another burst of laughter reached them.

"Then why are we hiding in the kitchen like a couple of old women?"

Matias shrugged. "I was amazed that you did not hit Scotty when he pushed you in here like a child."

"Right," Beth growled and strode out of the kitchen.

"Ah, there she is," Scotty said with a smile as she approached . . . as if he hadn't shuffled her into the kitchen and ordered her to stay there. "Beth, these are three of my best hunters, Magnus Bjarnesen, Rickart de Caulmont, and Odilia Baignard."

Beth stiffened. Magnus was the man Matias had

said had been watching over her for the last century or more. Realizing that Scotty and the others were waiting for some reaction from her, she nodded and politely murmured, "Hello."

Beth didn't wait for their response, but then turned to Scotty and raised her eyebrows. "And they're here because?"

"I figured Mortimer could use some help and thought I'd bring some o' me people o'er to assist until he gets his own men back from Venezuela," he explained.

"Nice," Beth said with a nod. "But then why are they *here*? Should they not be in Toronto helping Mortimer?"

"Aye. They will be," Scotty assured her. "I actually sent for six. Three flew into Toronto and these three continued on to join us. They'll stay here tonight and then fly back with us tomorrow."

Beth narrowed her eyes. She wasn't stupid. He'd brought in babysitters. To watch over her. Which was just ridiculous. She was a Rogue Hunter. She could take care of herself.

"I know it'll be a bit cramped, but 'tis only for one night," he went on as if oblivious to the fury building in her eyes. "Odilia can bunk with you, and the boys can take the couches in the living room. 'Twill be grand. Like a party . . . without the . . . er . . . party part."

Beth merely smiled at him, nodded and turned to Matias. "I presume you have more vehicles in the garage out back than the SUV you drive around?"

"*Sí*," he said, his lips twitching.

"Another vehicle is no' necessary," Scotty assured her. "Magnus rented a car when they landed. 'Tis how they got here."

Ignoring him, Beth smiled at Matias and asked politely, "May I borrow one?"

"*Sí*," Matias said on a soft chuckle this time.

"Er . . . Beth . . ." Scotty said with a frown.

"Thank you," Beth said to Matias. Taking her cousin's arm, she urged him back up the hall. "I just need to fetch my bags. Are the keys in the house or in the garage?"

"In the garage," he said, and then retrieved a set of keys from his pocket, slid one off the ring and handed it to her. "This is the key to the garage. Return it when you're done."

"Beth!"

There was no mistaking the thundering behind them as anything but Scotty giving pursuit. Beth ignored it and simply thanked Matias again and then continued up the hall to the bedrooms.

"We should talk," Scotty said, following her.

"There's no need to talk," Beth assured him, unperturbed. "Your hunters are welcome here."

"Then why are ye fetchin' yer bags?" Scotty asked, following her into her room.

Shrugging, Beth began gathering her belongings, and said, "That should be obvious. There isn't enough room here for everyone, so I'll go check into a hotel and your people can stay here with you."

"The devil ye will," he said with exasperation. "Ye ken they're only here to watch over ye."

"I don't need watching over," Beth said calmly. "I can take care of myself."

"Goddammit, woman, ye nearly died last night!"

"Only because you distracted me," she growled and, leaving the rest of the bags, headed for the door with just the one over her shoulder. "I was doing fine until you shouted my name and diverted my attention. Another minute and I'd have dragged my attacker into the light and would now know who they were instead of still wondering."

"Fine, ye were distracted," he snapped, following her through the family room to the door at the back of the kitchen. "But that could happen again the next time too. Only now, Magnus, Rickart, Odilia, and me will be watchin' yer back. We'd keep ye safe."

"I don't need you to keep me safe." She slammed the back door open and strode outside. "I will not slip up again. I will be on the alert. And—" whirling on him, she snarled "—what do you care anyway? It's not like you want to claim me as your life mate."

Beth noted his stunned expression, but she was a little busy being stunned herself. That had just come out. Like lava bursting over the top of a volcano, the words had rushed out, carried on a wave of rage and pain she hadn't even realized she was experiencing.

But then, she'd never been very in touch with her feelings, Beth acknowledged. According to Dr. Hewitt, the psychologist she'd switched to on moving to Toronto, who also happened to be married to an Argeneau, she'd learned to disassociate from her feelings while young. It was how she had survived the traumas of her mortal life. It was how she'd survived a childhood with an abusive, alcoholic father, and being sold into a brothel, and being a prostitute, and the horrible, violent turning, as well as everything that had followed directly on it.

Unfortunately, disassociating didn't mean the feelings weren't there, just that you weren't connected to them, so were taken by surprise when they suddenly exploded all over the place. And that was pretty much how she was feeling right now, like she'd vomited her guts out on the lawn in front of Scotty . . . And now he knew that she knew that they were life mates. He also knew it bothered her that he wouldn't claim her.

Sighing, Beth turned and continued to the garage. Much to her relief, Scotty was no longer following.

"Feck," Scotty breathed as he watched Beth enter the garage.

"I did tell you, you were handling it all wrong."

"Aye, ye did," Scotty said wearily, not bothering to glance around to verify that the speaker was Magnus. He'd recognize his voice anywhere. They had been friends for over eight hundred years, nearly since the day Scotty had been turned.

"How much does she know?" Magnus asked, stepping up beside him to peer at the garage as the door closed.

"As far as I can tell?" Scotty said and then shook his head. "Everything."

"Everything?" Magnus asked with a wince.

Scotty nodded on a sigh and ran a hand wearily through his hair. "Except mayhap that I had ye watchin' over her fer the last century. As far as I know, she does no' ken that yet, but according to Matias she and everyone else ken about me trying to prevent her becoming a hunter, and she just said . . . Well, she obviously kens we're life mates and I've no' claimed her."

"Hmm," Magnus murmured. "It would probably

be better if you gave her some time to herself to cool down."

Scotty merely grunted.

"So . . . what do you want me to do?" Magnus asked. "I can follow her to whatever hotel she picks and watch her, or—"

"Nay," Scotty said with frustration. He knew he should probably give her space, but he couldn't afford to. She was safer with them. He just had to convince her of that.

"Nay?" Magnus asked.

"Nay," he repeated. "I'll talk to her."

Leaving Magnus behind, Scotty headed across the yard to the door of the garage, his determination building with every step he took. He entered without hesitation, only to stop abruptly to give his eyes a minute to adjust. The lights weren't on in the garage. The only illumination came from the afternoon sunlight creeping weakly through the small dirty windows on each side of the garage. It took a moment for his eyes to sharpen and begin to define shapes and colors, and then he looked around.

There were five vehicles in the six-car garage. The closest bay was empty. Scotty supposed that was where the SUV Matias drove was supposed to stay. From where he stood, Scotty could make out the tool-strewn work counter along the back of the building, an open door leading into a tiny bathroom and another door leading into a larger office. Beth was in the office, picking through keys on a key rack hanging on the wall.

"What do you want from me, Scotty?" she asked wearily without ever taking her eyes off the keys she was sorting.

Scotty hesitated, and then glanced to the wall on either side of the door he'd just entered to find the light switch. He flicked it on, and then walked to the door of the office to peer at her. "I just want to see ye safe."

"That's kind of you," Beth said, finally settling on a set of keys and turning to face him with them in hand.

They stared at each other silently for a moment, and then Scotty sighed and moved forward, saying, "Lass, I ken ye can look after yerself, but everyone needs help sometimes and—" He paused and blinked in surprise as she suddenly slid around him and scurried out the door.

Damn, Scotty thought. When Beth had simply stood there waiting, he'd believed she was willing to hear him out. But she'd just been waiting for him to stop blocking the door so she could escape, he realized. Mouth tightening, he turned on his heel and hurried after her.

Beth was at the SUV in the second bay when he caught up to her. She already had the door open and was about to slide into the driver's seat. Scotty caught her arm, tugged her back and slammed the door closed.

Cursing, Beth jerked her arm free and whirled on him. "Why are you doing this? You don't even want me."

"Aye, I do," he growled, and then to prove it, he caught her arm again, this time to drag her forward and cover her mouth with his.

That was a big mistake, and Scotty knew it at once. He'd had Beth every which way possible in the more than a century's worth of dreams he'd had about her, not to mention the ones he'd shared with her. But those dreams had offered the equivalent of the heat from a match. The reality, just a kiss, brought on the raging heat of a towering inferno.

Scotty was immediately and painfully excited, his instant erection pressing urgently against the cloth of his tight jeans. His body was also humming and blood was rushing in his ears, sounding like the war cry of a thousand warriors before a battle. He was definitely going to prove he wanted her, but there certainly wouldn't be any talking. They were both being swept up by the passion immortal life mates enjoyed. And he could already tell it was going to be one hell of a ride.

Beth froze when his mouth first covered hers. It was something that had happened perhaps a million times in her dreams over the last hundred and twenty-five years, and still she wasn't ready for the reality of it. None of those kisses had prepared her for the way his heady scent enveloped her, or for the feel of his steel-hard arms enclosing her, or how his firm body now pressed against hers. And they certainly hadn't equipped her for the hungry way his mouth devoured hers, his tongue immediately demanding entrance.

In truth, Beth wasn't sure if she actually opened to him, or Scotty simply forced his way in. But it didn't feel like a taking. She didn't feel invaded. Instead, she was overwhelmed by sensation. The taste of him, the feel, the smell . . . and the need that was suddenly trying to claw its way out of her. That, at least, she recognized. Although it had never felt as strong as this or as violent. It had never left her clinging to him, her body surging against his with a demand of its own.

Beth was still so angry at Scotty that she wanted to slap him, but that didn't stop her from driving her hands into his hair, catching at the strands with her fingers and dragging his head to the angle she wanted as she finally began to kiss him back.

For a moment, it was almost like a battle, each of them trying to devour the other, and then Scotty turned with her in his arms and backed her up against the SUV. The moment he had her trapped there with his body, he tore his mouth from hers and bit at her neck, nipping, but not puncturing, as his hands began to tear at her clothes.

Scotty didn't remove her top—he tore it from her as he had her knickers in the dream the night before. Her bra quickly followed, although he merely dragged the straps off her shoulders and down her arms far enough to free her breasts before leaving the straps there to reach for the plunder he'd revealed.

Moaning, Beth leaned her head back against the SUV and closed her eyes as he squeezed and suckled at first one erect nipple and then the other. But she couldn't stand that for long. Her need was too desperate to bother with foreplay. She'd had more than enough of that in their dream. In fact, she was more excited now than she'd been as she'd waited on her hands and knees for him to enter her before the arrival of the dogs had woken her from their shared dream.

Almost gnashing her teeth with frustration, Beth pushed him back sharply, reached down to grab his linen shirt and began wrenching it out from where it was tucked into his black jeans. She started to work at the buttons then, but her hands were shaking and uncoordinated, and in the end she lost it and simply ripped the shirt open, popping the buttons as she went.

The action seemed to incite Scotty. Growling deep in his throat, he caught the back of her head and dragged her back against him so that he could claim her mouth in another searing kiss. Beth kissed him in return, but her hands were busy, skating over his chest, squeezing his pecs and then gliding down his stomach until one found the hardness between his legs.

Scotty sucked in a sharp breath as she began to rub him through the material, and Beth echoed the action as his excitement swept through her. Craving more of that, she used her free hand to unsnap his jeans as she continued to caress him, but the moment they were undone she released him to push his jeans over his hips and free his erection.

Scotty threw his head back on a guttural shout as her hand closed around him, and Beth muttered something even she didn't understand as his pleasure echoed through her. But when she then began to run her hand firmly up and down, Scotty knocked her hands away and reached for the waist of her jeans. They were undone almost before Beth's mind could catch up with what he was doing, and then Scotty dropped to a crouch before her so that he could drag them down over her hips, taking her underwear with them.

Beth stepped out of first one leg and then the other at his urging, and then gasped as he tossed them aside and leaned forward to press a kiss to the juncture between her legs. It was just a quick kiss, as if in greeting, and then he straightened and stepped into her waiting arms.

There was no more foreplay. Scotty didn't even remove his own jeans. He merely caught her by the waist, lifted her up and then lowered her onto the hard shaft she'd freed. Beth clung to his shoulders and groaned as he filled her. The dreams truly hadn't done him justice. When the man entered her he was hot and hard and filled her to capacity. And then he pressed her back against the SUV again and began to withdraw and thrust into her until the only thing she was aware of was the growing tension in her body.

Beth knew she was feeling his pleasure along with her own, and that was the cause of the overwhelming excitement and wave after wave of mounting pleasure surging through her . . . and she reveled in it. She wanted it to go on forever. She just wanted him to keep on pounding into her until the end of days. But too soon she was throwing her head back and screaming as the tension exploded between them. Those waves of pleasure immediately rolled over her head, drowning her and drawing her down into the waiting darkness.

Ten

Beth shifted sleepily and rolled onto her side, frowning when she searched for her pillow and couldn't find it. Opening her eyes, she found herself staring through a tinted window at Scotty's back.

Blinking in confusion, she glanced around. She was lying naked in the back of an SUV with Scotty's linen shirt laid over her. It was her only covering. The moment Beth saw that, her memory came rushing back.

This was not the first time she'd woken. The first time she'd been on the floor of the garage. Scotty had awoken before her and was leaning over her, suckling at her breast as his hand worked between her legs, stirring her passions again. Beth had taken him by surprise and let him know she was awake by rolling him onto his back and quickly mounting him. The concrete had been cold and hard under her knees, but he'd been hot and hard inside her, and she'd ridden him until they both shouted their pleasure.

The next time, Beth had actually woken first to find herself lying on top of Scotty with her cheek on his chest. After a hesitation, she'd carefully eased herself up. She was standing with her feet on either side of his hips, about to move one leg so that she could go find her clothes, when his eyes opened and his hands rose to grab her calves. They'd stared at each other briefly, and then he'd sat up and kissed her inner thigh, and then higher, and Beth had grabbed his head to help her stay upright as he drove them both back to the edge of madness.

The third time she'd woken up, Scotty was carrying her around to the back of the SUV.

"The floor was cold," he'd explained wryly when he saw she was awake. He'd set her down behind the vehicle then, and when he'd turned to open the hatchback, she couldn't resist running her hands over his strong back and pressing her nose to his skin to inhale his scent. Scotty had stilled with the door open and then had turned with a groan to kiss her, his hands traveling everywhere. The next thing Beth knew, she was leaning into the back of the SUV and he was thrusting into her from behind, and they were both crying out again and embracing the darkness.

This was her fourth time waking up, and they were no longer alone, Beth realized as she became aware of the muffled male voices coming from outside the SUV. Clutching Scotty's shirt to her chest, she sat up and spotted the man Scotty was talking to. It was one of the trio who had arrived that day. Magnus, the one who had apparently been spying on her for the last hundred years.

Turning away from them for now, Beth looked

around for her clothes. But of course those would still be lying on the garage floor beside the SUV, she realized, and then sighed and quickly pulled Scotty's shirt on. Beth tugged it closed in the front, but that was the best she could do. She'd been so desperate to get it off him, she'd ripped the damned thing open, popping all the buttons.

Sighing, Beth glanced out the window again. Scotty and Magnus were still talking, but they were also moving away from the SUV, and she was quite relieved to see that he was wearing his jeans. Whether he'd donned them before or after Magnus had arrived, Beth didn't know, and she really supposed it didn't matter. She doubted it had taken more than a heartbeat for the man to figure out what they'd been doing out here in the garage all this time.

That thought made her wonder just how long they'd been out here. How long did those bliss faints last when life mates mated? Beth had no idea, but if she were to go by the hunger cramping her stomach, she'd guess they'd been out here for several hours at least.

That distracted her for a moment, and then Beth realized Scotty was ushering Magnus out of the garage. Relieved that she could now get out and find her pants, she shifted to crawl to the hatchback and then paused to glance toward the two men. They were at the entrance. Magnus stepped out even as she looked, and Scotty leaned against the open door and nodded at something the man was saying.

Deciding that was probably the best time for her to do it, Beth opened the SUV's hatchback and slid out, then rushed around gathering her clothes. She found her jeans first, and then searched for her underwear.

They were nowhere to be found, but she did find her torn T-shirt and her bra.

Giving up on her panties for now, Beth quickly tugged her jeans on, did them up and found her underwear when they fell out of the bottom of her jeans. Grimacing, she snatched them up and shoved them in her pocket. She then turned her attention to her bra, only to grimace when she saw that it had been torn where it connected at the front between the two cups. Beth didn't recall it happening. Actually, she couldn't remember it being removed at all, but things had gotten a bit wild a time or two, so . . .

"Ye're awake."

Beth glanced around to see Scotty hurrying back toward her. Retreating from his reaching arms, Beth grimaced and said with a little embarrassment, "I need a shower. And we should probably go get those groceries. I'm rather hungry."

"Ah, no need to get the groceries," Scotty told her almost apologetically. "Odilia and Donny took care of that yesterday."

"Yesterday?" Beth echoed blankly, and then understanding struck and she asked with alarm, "It's Sunday? What time—" The question died on her lips as she glanced toward the dirty windows and noted the light managing to get inside. It wasn't the gray light of early dawn. In fact, it looked like the bright light of early afternoon.

"It's all right," he assured her. "It's only eleven o'clock. We have time to get to the airfield."

"Oh my God," Beth breathed, rushing for the door.

"Wait, Beth!" Scotty followed on her heels. "We need to talk."

"Why didn't you wake me?" she cried, pushing out into the sunshine.

"Because I wasn't awake either. Magnus woke me up just moments ago to warn me that it was growing late."

"Dear God, I need to shower, change, make sure I have everything packed and—I didn't even get a proper visit with Matias. He'll be annoyed with me. I—Dammit, I wanted to call Kira and be sure she is still returning with us. Bloody hell, I hope there's room for everyone on the plane. She's bringing her bodyguards, you know."

"Nay, I didn't know. But . . ." Scotty let his words die and slowed to a halt as Beth reached the back door and slipped inside. She was still rattling off things she had to do when the door closed behind her.

"So much for talking," he muttered to himself and then gave a start when a wet nose pressed into his palm.

"Piper likes you," Matias commented, making his presence known.

Scotty petted the Doberman and found it oddly soothing.

"I take it you sorted out everything with Beth?" Matias asked after a brief silence.

Scotty shook his head. "I meant to, but we just . . ." He waved vaguely toward the garage.

"Ah," Matias said, sounding disappointed. "So, she hasn't heard and accepted your explanation for why you had not claimed her?"

"Yet." Scotty stressed the word. "I had not claimed her yet. I was always going to claim her eventually."

Matias eyed him dubiously. "Are you sure about that?"

"Of course," he said firmly, and then added, "When we met she was traumatized by her experiences and her turn. I was just waiting for her to heal."

"Are you sure you were not waiting to see if she would finally fall completely apart and you could have the three-on-one mind wipe performed on her?" Matias asked quietly. "A clean slate. No memories of her days in the brothel, so you could forget about that yourself?"

"That wasn't—" Scotty frowned. "They are bad memories for her. I thought only to ease her suffering."

"Oh, *sí*, of course." Matias didn't sound as if he believed him, and then he said, "When she told me about your wanting to perform the mind wipe on her, I did wonder . . ."

"What?" Scotty asked warily when Matias fell silent.

"I wondered what would have happened if you had managed to convince Dree to let you perform the three-on-one," he admitted. "Would Beth have still been a possible life mate for you? Or would the removal of those memories of her past have changed her personality so that you were no longer suitable to be life mates? We are all shaped by our experiences, after all."

"So you are a Rogue Hunter in the UK? How did you become one?"

Beth smiled faintly as Kira leaned toward Odilia with obvious interest. Other than the fact that Kira was a blonde and Odilia had long dark hair that was a blend of chestnut, umber, hickory and chocolate, the women were very similar. They were both beautiful, both stood about nine inches taller than her and both outweighed her by a good twenty pounds. Beth wasn't surprised that Kira would be interested in the other woman's experiences.

A laugh from the back of the plane drew her gaze, and Beth watched Scotty interacting with the men. He, Donny, Magnus, and Rickart had taken up positions leaning against the wall by the bathrooms when they'd boarded. Kira had shown up with all four of her bodyguards, and as Beth had feared, there weren't enough seats on the plane for everyone. That being the case, the men had left the seats for the women. There would have been just enough seats if Scotty's people hadn't appeared on the scene, but now there was one seat going empty because none of the men would lay claim to it.

Rather like her, Beth thought suddenly. She was an unclaimed seat. Only there was only one man who should claim her, and he wasn't interested. At least, he hadn't said he was claiming her, or even asked if she would let him during all those hours in the garage. They'd just screwed like frantic bunnies until they ran out of time. Some women might have seen that as his staking a claim, but Beth wasn't foolish enough to do so. Thanks to her life as a mortal, she'd had a lot of men in her bed, and watched just as many leave it. Sex—even wild, passionate sex—was not a declaration of anything. It was just sex.

"Please, tell me. *Da?*"

Beth glanced to Kira and shook her head with a small smile. Somehow the girl managed to make her plea sound like a royal command. That was a skill, and one Odilia apparently responded to, because she complied.

"I was turned in 1852 when a rogue immortal invaded our home one night while we were sleeping. I was ten," the woman said, gaining Beth's full attention as she realized that they were contemporaries of a sort. Beth might have been turned forty years later than Odilia, but she had also been forty years older. They had been born the same year. And the year Odilia had been turned was the year Beth's father had sold her to a brothel.

"He roused the whole house," Odilia continued. "And then he killed every living soul one after another—my parents, my sisters, and every last servant. He left me for last, and attacked me just as viciously as the others so that at first I felt sure I should soon join them. However, at the last moment he forced his blood on me and then left me lying in my own blood and that of my loved ones, to turn while he just walked out the door and disappeared—poof." Odilia snapped her fingers to illustrate how quickly he'd left her life. "I woke up after several days of excruciating pain and wandered outside in search of help. Fortunately, Scotty and Magnus found me before I did anything that could make me rogue too.

"Of course, I couldn't return to my home or my old life. I needed to be taught how to feed without harming my host, and how to hide what I was. Scotty took me in and helped me through my transition. He became my guardian. And then later, when I showed interest in becoming a hunter, he trained me to be one. I have been on his team ever since," Odilia ended simply.

"This rogue was a monster," Kira said, sitting back in her seat, her eyes wide. "I thought my father the only monster, but it seems there are worse monsters out there even than him."

"Many, many monsters," Beth said solemnly. "That is why Rogue Hunters are needed."

Kira glanced to her, curiosity filling her expression. "And you, Beth? How were you turned? It was a rogue too, *da*?"

"*Da*," she murmured and then said, "Oddly enough, it is a story very similar to Odilia's." Beth smiled at the other woman as she said that and received a tight smile in return. She'd found the woman a little standoffish since coming in from the garage that morning. At the time, Beth hadn't known if it was just the hunter's personality or if she'd taken an instant dislike to her for some reason. Now Beth wondered if perhaps the woman disapproved of what she and Scotty had got up to in the garage. Or perhaps Odilia didn't think she was good enough for Scotty. He had basically adopted the other woman as a child and raised her. She supposed the woman could be protective of him and not think Beth good enough for the man who was like a father to her. But then, how else would Odilia feel? Scotty apparently didn't think her good enough either . . . well, for anything but sex.

Pushing these thoughts away as unproductive, Beth explained, "As with Odilia's family, a rogue entered our home one night and attacked each of us in turn. Only, he turned every one of us. Like her, we were left lying in our own blood to turn. But once those dark days were over, he hadn't disappeared. He was there to tell us that we were his now, and that he expected us to lure men to the house to murder and rob them."

"Did you do it?" Kira asked, wide-eyed.

Beth shook her head. "I couldn't. I fled to find a friend for help, Alexandrina Argenis. She had been in our lives for many years by then, and we all knew that she was an immortal and what that meant, so I knew she could help. Unfortunately, by the time I found her I was in a bad way. She took care of me and helped me recover. Once I was cogent enough to recall the women at the house, I told her and we returned at once, but by then two weeks had passed and it was too late. They'd gone mad under this rogue's abuses and had been attacking mortals, feeding off and killing them since my leaving. They were beyond help and immediately attacked us. As with Odilia, Scotty and his men saved us, but we did not stay with him. Drina was immortal-born. She took me to her family in Spain to help me through the transition. I was adopted into her family, and we trained together to become Rogue Hunters."

Kira sat back with a gusty sigh. "These rogues, they are bad news. I think I will enjoy helping to stop them."

Beth smiled at the words. "It can be satisfying work. Especially when you are able to save would-be victims."

"*Da*. No doubt." Kira nodded and then peered at her solemnly and admitted, "I suspected you were not an Argenis by birth. It is your eyes. They are green with gold rather than blue with silver. All Argeneaus, whether they go by the name Argenis, Argent, Argentum, or Argeneau, have blue and silver . . . or at least the silver."

Beth merely nodded.

"What was your last name before you became Argenis?" Kira asked with interest.

"Sheppard," Beth answered, surprised to find she

had to think to recall it. The name even felt odd on her tongue. But then, she had carried the name Argenis more than twice as long as she had the name Sheppard. And Beth hadn't felt at all bad at shedding her father's name in the first place. While she had loved her mother, as far as Beth was concerned, she wanted no reminder or attachment to her father, even in name.

"Our footman's name was Sheppard," Odilia said now with surprise, and then added solemnly, "He was a good man. He tried to protect my mother from the rogue. Of course he couldn't, and died horribly for the effort," she finished, and then glanced at Beth curiously and asked, "Do you think he could have been a relation?"

"I don't know," Beth admitted. "I don't recall having any family besides my parents and sisters, but he could have been related, I suppose."

Odilia nodded and then tilted her head and commented, "You are rubbing your stomach. Do you need blood?"

"Probably," Beth admitted with a grimace. "And food wouldn't hurt either."

"Do they keep blood on the plane?" Kira asked, glancing toward the kitchenette.

"Yes, I think so," Beth said and stood to head for the galley, thinking she really should have taken the time to grab something to eat before leaving for the airfield. She'd intended to, but by the time she'd showered, changed and gathered her things together, Matias had been insisting it was time to go.

Stepping into the kitchenette, Beth glanced around at the wood grain cupboard doors, wondering which if any was the refrigerator, and then she just started opening them one after the other in search of blood, crackers or—hell—even peanuts or pretzels. She hadn't eaten since the pizza Friday night. Well, technically, Saturday morning, she supposed. Now it was Sunday afternoon and she was famished.

The first cupboard held glasses and cups, and in the second she found plates and bowls. But the third held small bags of chips, peanuts and, yes, pretzels, but also bread sticks and crackers.

"Oh yeah," Beth murmured, but continued opening doors until she found two small bar-sized refrigerators. One held blood, and Beth took a bag before opening the cupboard next to it to find the second refrigerator, which held fresh fruit, cheese, and dips.

"Jackpot," she said happily and slapped the bag of blood to her fangs as she reached in with her free hand to grab a peach.

"Food."

Startled by that deep rumble, Beth turned sharply and saw Scotty standing behind her, staring at the contents of the refrigerator. Even as she did, his gaze shifted to her and he growled, "I'm hungry."

Judging by the way the silver in his eyes multiplied, Beth suspected he wasn't just talking about food or even blood. She wasn't surprised when he moved in close, caught her by the waist and lifted her to sit on the counter.

Beth's eyes widened above the blood bag, but she merely held on to it and the peach a little more firmly.

"So hungry," Scotty murmured, stepping between her legs. When the peach bumped against his chest, he glanced down at it with interest, and then he smiled and caught her wrist to lift it until the peach was in front of his mouth. He took a large bite, murmuring with pleasure as he chewed and then glanced to her hand and stilled. Beth followed his gaze and saw that juice had run from the open wound in the peach, making little rivulets down her hand and wrist and further to her elbow.

Swallowing the bite in his mouth, Scotty bent his head to catch the drop of juice that dangled from her elbow. He then followed the rivulet upward, making her skin tingle as his tongue scraped over her sensitive flesh, licking away the juices.

Beth was holding her breath as he licked her arm and wrist, but when his tongue slid over and between her fingers, she moaned and let go of the peach.

Scotty caught the fruit as it fell and set it on the counter. Taking advantage of the fact that her hand was now empty, he sucked one finger into his mouth to the base, and then let it slide back out before taking up the next and repeating the exercise.

Beth had never experienced anything so erotic in her life. Her body was trembling, her breasts hard and sore, and her legs were trying to close to ease the ache there. Scotty was between her legs, however, preventing that, and seemingly of their own accord, her legs closed around him, pulling him forward against her.

She moaned around the bag of blood at her mouth as Scotty rubbed against her. Head dropping back, Beth let her eyes close, and then blinked them open and lowered her head with surprise when the blood bag was suddenly tugged from her mouth. It was empty, she saw as Scotty tossed it on the counter, and then his mouth covered hers, his tongue thrusting past her lips as he ground his groin against her.

Beth gasped and then tilted her head and clutched at his shoulders as she kissed him back. She felt him grab her breast, and groaned as he kneaded it, her legs tightening around his hips and her heels pushing him more firmly against her to increase the friction.

Growling into her mouth, Scotty released her breast and then tugged her T-shirt from her jeans and pushed it up above the bra she wore beneath. That was quickly tugged down so that he could claim one swollen nipple.

"Did you find any foo—Oh! Sorry."

Beth and Scotty broke apart at once and she peered blankly over his shoulder at Odilia, briefly confused as to who she even was. And that about summed up what Scotty's touch, his real live touch, did to her, Beth acknowledged. She forgot everyone and everything except for how he made her feel.

"Sorry," the woman repeated, flustered. "I was just hungry, but I'll . . ." Whirling away, she rushed back toward the seats and out of sight.

Scotty remained still after she left, his head turned toward where she'd been, and Beth forced herself to slow her breathing and take deep, calming breaths. Once her heart had stopped thundering and the aching in her body had eased, she withdrew her hands and unhooked her legs from around him and then quickly put her clothes back in order.

"We should join the others," she whispered, pressing on his chest with one hand to ease him back.

Scotty sighed and released her to comply, stepping away from her so that she could slide off the counter.

"Odilia is—"

"Your daughter," Beth finished for him as she turned and retrieved a tray she'd spotted in one of the cupboards. She then quickly began gathering items—a stack of plates, crackers, cheese, fruit, the bread sticks, dip, and even several bags of blood and half a dozen cans of soda.

"You took her in and cared for her after her family was slaughtered and she was turned. That was kind of you," she added.

"She was just a child," Scotty said solemnly. "She'd lost everything."

"She was lucky to have you save her." Beth picked up the tray. Turning, she faced him and added, "I was too. Even if you did want to wipe my mind."

Beth didn't wait for a response, but slid past him with the tray.

"Is anyone hungry or thirsty?" she asked brightly as she carried the snacks toward the chairs where the women were. Beth wasn't surprised when the men all immediately moved forward in the plane, eager to examine the offerings. She was quickly surrounded by both the men and women grabbing for various items, and felt sure she'd soon be returning to get more of everything, but then Scotty came from the kitchenette with a second tray stacked with food and blood.

"Set it on the table," he suggested quietly. "And make sure ye fill a plate yerself and take a bag of blood. It's been more than twenty-four hours since ye ate, and the one bag o' blood ye just had'll no' do ye."

Blushing, mostly because she was now thinking about why she hadn't eaten in more than twenty-four hours, Beth piled food on a plate before snatching a bag of blood and returning to her seat.

She glanced toward Odilia as she sat down, but the woman was sitting silent and still, her eyes closed.

Wondering just how awkward this was going to make things between them, Beth sighed and set the blood aside for now to concentrate on the food. She did her best not to think about Scotty while she ate, but that was impossible. Her body was still humming from what he'd done to her, and really he hadn't done much. A kiss and a squeeze and she was as shaky as a virgin on her wedding night.

Closing her own eyes briefly, Beth pondered what it was he wanted from her. She knew he didn't want her. Well, he did, but only in a physical way. As far as she could tell, Scotty didn't want her for anything else, not as a mate, or he would have claimed her a century ago. So what were they doing? Was it a fling? An affair? And if so, how long was it supposed to last? Was this just a vacation thing for him? Over once he returned to England? Or were they just going to be eternal bed buddies, sleeping together every time they crossed paths over the next millennium or so, or until he came across another possible life mate who was perhaps more suitable?

Suddenly depressed, Beth opened her eyes and set her half-finished plate on the table. She then slapped the blood bag to her fangs and turned to stare out the window at the earth below. Everything looked so small from up here, she thought, and then smiled faintly and closed her eyes. Maybe this insurmountable problem fully occupying her mind, and seeming so large, was really just as small, a hiccup in her life. If so, wouldn't she feel foolish for wasting so much energy on it?

In truth, Beth supposed it was foolish either way. Whether the problem was large or small in her life, sitting here fretting about it wasn't going to solve anything.

It wouldn't even change the situation. She *couldn't* change it. There was no way for her to make Scotty accept what she had done in her past, if that was why he wasn't claiming her. All she could do was change her present behavior, which meant she had a choice—either she accepted that he could not and would not claim her as a life mate because of her past, or she whined and cried about it.

The choice there was an easy one. Whining and crying never achieved anything. So she had to accept it. That being the case, she now had two more choices: enjoy the fling—or whatever this was she was having with Scotty—for as long as it lasted, or protect herself, and avoid him at all costs until he left Canada. He wasn't the only immortal out there. Surely there would be other possible life mates for her? She just might have to wait a millennium or two to find him.

"I would ask you what you are thinking, but since I can read your mind it is unnecessary," Magnus said lightly, drawing a scowl from Scotty.

"Ha ha," he muttered, not bothering to tear his gaze away from Beth to look at his friend. "Yer wit is staggerin', Magnus."

"I like to think so," his friend admitted, and then arched an eyebrow at him. "So what is it that Matias said to you back at the house to get your knickers in such a twist?"

Scotty glanced at him in surprise. "Ye ken Matias said something, but no' what he said?"

Magnus shrugged. "Your thoughts are mostly fretting over whether Matias was wrong or right, but not what about. So . . . what did he say?"

Scotty hesitated, but then admitted, "Matias thinks I wanted the three-on-one mind wipe performed on Beth because I can no' accept that she was a—her past."

"Hmm." Magnus nodded solemnly. "I see."

"Which is ridiculous. I suggested that because she was half-mad when we rescued her and suffering under the memories of what had been done to her. Wiping her mind seemed a kindness then."

"And now?" Magnus asked.

Scotty frowned, but admitted, "She's better now. As ye said in yer reports, she seems to have found a way to deal with it."

"So, now you are glad you did not perform the mind wipe on her," Magnus suggested.

"Nay," he said at once, and then added, "She'd still be better off if it was done. It would be easier on her if she did no' have to carry around all those memories about what happened to her. She'd be much happier without them."

"Hmm."

"I do no' care that she—what she did."

"Hmm."

"That was over a hundred years ago. It has nothing to do with now," Scotty assured him.

"Hmm," Magnus repeated.

"Oh, stop with the *hmm*s and say whatever 'tis ye have to say already," Scotty muttered, turning to look at Beth again. Whenever Magnus nodded and *hmm*ed, he had an opinion he didn't think Scotty would like.

Unfortunately, it was also something he usually needed to hear.

"I just find it interesting that you cannot seem to even bring yourself to give name to Beth's profession as a mortal."

"What?" he asked with surprise.

"You keep avoiding saying what Beth did," Magnus pointed out almost pityingly. "You keep using phrases like 'what she did' and 'her past,' neatly avoiding calling her a prostitute."

Glowering, Scotty turned back to look at Beth. She wore no makeup. Her skin was porcelain, with a light dusting of freckles across the nose. Her sweet, full lips were rosy despite a lack of lipstick, and when she blushed with embarrassment, or flushed with excitement, her cheeks also took on a rosy hue. She was petite, and she was beautiful, with the sweetest smile he'd ever seen. She did not look like a conniving, money-hungry whore.

"Feck," he muttered as that last thought ran through his head. He did have issues with her being a prostitute. All this time he'd been telling himself that he was waiting for her to heal. And he had been, he was quite sure, but so long as he'd been waiting for her to heal and hadn't been able to claim her, Scotty had been able to avoid dealing with the issue he had with her former profession.

"It is understandable that you would have issues with it," Magnus said as if he'd spoken aloud. "We come from an earlier era, one that forged our morals and opinions. We were taught prostitution was an abomination to our Lord God. Of course you would struggle with it," he said gently, and then added, "It is just a shame you were not admitting to yourself that this was a problem for you so that you could have dealt with it earlier."

When Scotty merely grunted and continued to frown unhappily, Magnus said, "I suggest you avoid her for the time being, at least until you can sort yourself out. If you can accept her along with her past, including her years in a brothel, then all is fine and well. However, if you cannot, then it would be kinder to leave her be and allow her to get on with her life. But you cannot have it both ways."

Scotty didn't respond except to tighten his lips. He didn't want to let Beth be. He wanted her in his life. He also wanted her in his bed, naked and moaning. He wanted to plunge himself into her over and over again until she forgot every last man she'd bedded over the years.

"You mean until *you* forget every man she may have had in her bed over the years," Magnus said quietly, still reading his mind. "Because that is the problem, is it not? Beth has already left that past behind. It is you now struggling with it."

Scotty closed his eyes. Magnus was right, of course. He was the one tormented by her past. He'd managed to ignore it and pretend it wasn't an issue all this time because she was so damaged and had needed to heal. But now she had healed. He could claim her . . . if he could just accept her past and get over it.

"I advise you not to confess your issues to Beth," Magnus said now. "She had a tough life as a mortal, and has worked hard to overcome it. I will not have you insulting or hurting her because of your own hang-ups."

"O' course I will no'," Scotty muttered. He had no desire to hurt her. This was *his* problem.

"You should not sleep with her either," Magnus added now, and when Scotty turned a surprised face his way, he pointed out, "Sleeping with her if you cannot ultimately bring yourself to claim her is cruel. And it would make you just as bad as the men in her past who used her for their own pleasure, or for profit."

Magnus left him then, and walked over to sit in the empty seat next to Beth. He didn't speak to her or disturb her rest in any way. He simply leaned back and closed his eyes. He was sending Scotty a message. Magnus was on Beth's side. At least in this.

Frowning, Scotty turned away from the seating area and walked back to rejoin Donny and Rickart. He didn't really enter into their conversation, but simply nodded and made the appropriate sounds at the appropriate times. In truth, his mind was on his own thoughts . . . and his feelings about what Beth had done as a mortal. Now that he was being forced to confront his feelings on the subject, he admitted that before meeting Beth he'd always thought prostitution to be the lowest of trades. He'd been raised to believe prostitutes were shameless, deceitful whores who cared only about coin . . . and he couldn't bear knowing that Beth had once been one.

And that, he acknowledged, was a serious problem.

Eleven

"What think you?"

The whispered question made Beth glance to Kira. She noted the woman's narrow-eyed gaze as she surveyed their surroundings, and then turned back to the barn in the clearing and commented, "It's pretty quiet."

Kira nodded. "Maybe they are sleeping, *da*?"

"Maybe," Beth allowed, but didn't move. Something didn't feel right about the place. It looked like it had been abandoned for a while, which wasn't what bothered her. Actually, *that* was the problem—she couldn't quite put her finger on what was bothering her.

"Is dump," Oksana, one of Kira's bodyguards, growled, not bothering to keep her voice down. "Is perfect place for the disgusting rogues. Let us catch this *dyatel* and leave here."

Beth didn't respond, except to smile slightly at the use of the word *dyatel*. Kira had explained it meant woodpecker, and was considered a terrible insult. It seemed calling a Russian any kind of an animal was insulting. Whether it was *osyol* which meant donkey, or *kosyol* which meant billy goat. Russians did not care for being likened to animals.

"*Da*," Nika, another bodyguard, agreed. "I do not like here."

Turning on the pair, Kira hissed angrily, "Shhh. Would you let them all know we are coming?"

Oksana quickly hid a resentful scowl, and presented an unconcerned face, but her voice was quieter when she said, "Is okay that they know. I am not afraid of some rogue."

"Perhaps not," Beth said in a low voice. "But if they hear us, they could escape before we can catch them."

Oksana shrugged. "Then we no catch them."

Beth closed her eyes briefly and shook her head. "I really should have insisted the four of you went for training."

"We are trained," Oksana growled. "In Russia. Think you Athanasios would make us protectors to Kira if we were not the most skilled warriors? I could beat you in battle with any weapon. I could kill you with—"

"Enough," Kira whispered furiously. "In future, you will keep shut the mouth, or I will send you back to Russia and tell Father you were unsatisfactory bodyguard."

Oksana shielded her expression quickly, but not before Beth saw the flash of fury there. The woman was eventually going to be trouble.

Releasing a small breath, Beth turned to survey the barn again. A tip had been called in to the local police that children had found an empty coffin here. Mortimer kept tabs on all calls to the police, just in case anything came up that was immortal-related. If something suspicious did crop up, he sent Enforcers to check out the claim, as well as to ensure the tip was forgotten by the police. Beth and Kira had got stuck with investigating this claim.

This job was what Beth would've categorized as a joke job, something trainees were normally sent on. Mostly because these missions were a waste of time. They included things like checking on immortals who hadn't been heard from for a while, and traveling to California to just make sure that one celebrity or another wasn't really an immortal in hiding because "they hadn't aged in years," or single solitary coffins found in old abandoned barns.

And why would a single coffin in a barn be considered a joke job? Because rogues tended to gather acolytes—new immortals they turned themselves and convinced to follow them. Which meant they would need many coffins. One by itself simply would not indicate the usual rogue's lair. In fact, on the way out here, Beth had been positive that this single coffin could have nothing to do with immortals. She had even come up with alternate possibilities for the existence of a coffin in an old abandoned barn. For instance, it could be that the former owners of this barn had stored the coffin here for their own future funeral, or . . .

Well, frankly, that was the only excuse Beth could think of for there to be a coffin in a barn, and even that seemed a piss-poor one. No one really bought their coffins ahead of time and stored them for the day they died, did they? Still, it had made more sense to her than that a rogue was living in an old abandoned barn. And she was quite sure it must've struck Mortimer the same way, or he wouldn't have sent her and Kira here.

This wasn't Beth's first case with Kira. Mortimer had been pairing her with the girl ever since they'd landed back in Toronto two weeks ago. Most of the cases he'd sent them on had been pathetic, easy checks of the more ridiculous tips. She quickly realized that Mortimer was trying to keep Kira away from anything dangerous. The problem was that it meant keeping Beth herself away from anything juicy too, and she was too good a hunter to want to spend her time on joke jobs. It was something she fully intended to complain about after they checked out this barn.

Beth understood that Mortimer wanted to keep Kira safe, but while she was coming to like the Russian girl, it was time someone else took over babysitting duty. Two weeks was punishment enough for talking the girl into coming to Toronto.

Two weeks, Beth thought suddenly. Had it really only been fourteen days since they'd returned from Vancouver? It felt like a lifetime to her. And not just because she'd been stuck on babysitting duty. Scotty had been avoiding her since their return. Beth hadn't seen him once during this whole time. Well, not in the flesh. He filled her dreams every night, making love to her in the forest-green bedroom, in the garage in Vancouver, on her kitchen table, in the elevator of her apartment building, in the blue room at the Enforcer house, in the pale yellow room at the Enforcer house, on the beach, in a movie theater, in the bathroom of a nightclub, and, last night, in the cooking section of a bookstore.

The backgrounds for their dream trysts were growing more and more risqué, taking place in spots Beth would never consider in real life. She wasn't choosing the locales. Scotty was. Sort of. Last night she'd been dreaming she was at the shopping mall, trying to figure out what to buy Drina for her coming birthday. Beth had wandered through various stores, trying to find something, and had been in the bookstore when Scotty had appeared in her dream. She'd actually been in the fiction section when he found her, but he'd looked around, caught her hand and dragged her to the nearest display table, which happened to be in the cooking section.

In the past, Scotty would have taken her from the more public spot to a more private spot for their dream sex, but now he wasn't. And she understood exactly why. While their dream sex had always seemed hot and satisfying before, now—after having experienced the incredible, passionate, almost violent need inspired in true life mate sex—the dream sex was somewhat disappointing. It simply couldn't compare, and they were both yearning for that explosive union they'd had in the garage. At least, Beth knew she was, and could only assume that was the reason their private moments were taking place in more public spaces. Scotty was trying to replicate or boost the passion they'd experienced during real sex.

Kira's shifting restlessly beside her forced Beth back to the matter at hand—the dilapidated old barn and the coffin that was supposed to be inside.

After eyeing the building for a moment more, trying

to figure out what bothered her about it, Beth gave it up. "I'm going to go see if I can get a look inside. The rest of you wait here."

"*Nyet*," Kira said at once. "We are team. I go with you."

Beth considered her stubborn expression, and then nodded reluctantly. "Fine. You come. The rest of you stay here," she ordered.

"Where she goes, we go," Oksana announced with a shrug that said there would be no argument on the matter.

"Whatever," Beth said with exasperation and moved out of the bushes in a crouch. Honestly, she was beginning to understand why everybody at the university had seemed to dislike Kira. It wasn't just her attitude, and she did at times have some serious attitude, although there seemed to be less of that every day since she'd come to Toronto. The real problem was the women who guarded her. All but one of them were stubborn, sullen and miserable, and seemed to want to make everyone around them miserable as well.

Beth crept along the edge of the woods toward the barn, very aware that she was being followed by a parade of Kira, Oksana, Nika, Liliya, and Marta. Liliya was the only bodyguard Beth liked. The petite woman, unlike her larger compatriots, was quiet, efficient and easy to get along with. If Beth had a choice, Liliya would have been the only one with them.

Pausing at the edge of the woods adjacent to the corner of the barn, Beth took a moment to survey the building, and then ran lightly across the open area to reach it. Once there, she put her back to the wall of the barn and watched the others follow. The moment they were all standing like her, with their dart guns out and their backs against the building, Beth turned and began to move along the wall.

She hadn't gone far before a nail caught on the material at the shoulder of her long-sleeved black shirt. Beth paused to unhook herself, and then continued. Another nail caught at her at the same place several more feet along, and she paused again, this time taking note that the nail was bright silver and shiny-new . . . and Beth wasn't positive, but she thought the first one might have been too.

She considered that briefly, and then continued on much more slowly, scanning the wall as she went. Three boards later, Beth found the tip of another shiny silver nail poking out of the wood at her shoulder level. She examined that nail briefly and then the wood itself, noting that the board wasn't as thick as the ones on either side of it.

Glancing along the length of wall ahead, Beth saw that every third or fourth slat was recessed a bit. Whoever had built the barn hadn't bought the wood at a Home Depot or some other big-box store where the planks would have been a standard width, depth, and length. Heck, for all she knew, the barn had been built before big-box stores. Whatever the case, the nails were showing only on the slats that weren't as deep as the others. But they were all new and at the same height.

"Those nails are new," Kira whispered by her ear.

Beth turned to nod at her. She almost wanted to pat her on the head and say "good girl" for paying attention and using her brain, but managed to quell the urge. Kira might think she was being condescending or something, so Beth merely whispered, "Something doesn't feel right. Stay alert, remain at least a step behind me, and keep your eyes open. Tell the others."

Kira nodded and turned to pass along the message to Oksana.

Beth watched the Amazon stiffen and narrow her eyes, and knew at once that the woman didn't appreciate orders from her. As far as Oksana was concerned, Beth was a nobody, with no say about anything she did. Fortunately, Kira seemed to realize that too and stepped past the woman to pass the message to the others herself.

Beth waited patiently until Kira'd finished, ignoring the glowering looks Oksana was giving her as she did, but once Kira returned to her side, she continued along the building. This time, Beth didn't stop until she reached the barn doors. Dropping into a crouch just to the side of where the two doors met, she glanced back to see that the others were doing the same . . . all but Oksana.

"You are so slow," the Russian growled with disgust, standing out in the open. "Why you not just walk in there and shoot up rogue if he there? Is no good you skulk around like big English, Spanish, American coward!"

Well, Beth thought wryly, at least the woman had got it mostly right and hit on every continent where she'd lived. Deciding the element of surprise was definitely over now, and stealth and caution were wasted, Beth turned away from the angry woman and eased the far door open enough to poke her head through and glance around.

There wasn't much to see. A couple of moldy old

bales of hay were stacked at the far end of the barn, but other than that it appeared to be empty. Frowning, Beth straightened and pulled open first one door and then the other. She then moved cautiously to stand in the opening to survey the interior of the building again, but now with the aid of the day's dying light coming through the open doors.

"There is nothing," Kira whispered a step back on her left, and Beth was pleased to hear concern in her voice rather than confusion. It told her that the girl seemed to understand that that was wrong. There was supposed to be—

"Where is the coffin?" Liliya asked just as quietly from a step back on her right.

Beth was as proud as a teacher on graduation day. Liliya and Kira would make good hunters in the not-too-distant future.

Not so much Oksana, though, she acknowledged as the woman stomped forward into the seemingly empty building, snapping, "Why you whisper? There is no one here."

"Oksana, get back here," Beth growled, her inner alarm going from a mild blip of warning to a shriek as she took another look around the building. This time she noted the wooden slats with metal in the middle that had been nailed to the walls and ran down each side of the building.

"I no take orders from you," Oksana growled, continuing forward to the middle of the barn. "I no take orders from cowards. Athanasios will be disgusted when I tell how you—"

Beth heard the hissing sound just before Oksana's words died. She instinctively grabbed the arm of each woman on either side of her and dragged them backward out of the barn a good half a dozen steps, nearly tripping over Marta as she did. The woman had obeyed her instructions and stayed behind her. Nika, however, hadn't, and Beth wasn't able to grab her. The woman also didn't immediately follow. Instead, she stayed just inside the door, seeming transfixed.

"Nika?" Beth said worriedly when a moment passed with no sound from Oksana and no movement from Nika. Gesturing for the other women to stay where they were, Beth moved quickly up beside Nika, but stopped just inside the doors when she felt something bump the top of her shoulder. Spotting the razor-thin wire, she reached out to touch it and then noted that it stretched completely across the opening, and in fact from one wall inside the barn to the other. It was attached to what turned out to be a track, which was the metal strip in the middle of the slats she'd noticed stretching nearly to the back of the barn. Something had set it off, sending it shooting forward to the end of the tracks on this end of the barn, slicing through anything in its path . . . like Oksana, she saw, peering into the barn at the woman on the ground . . . in pieces.

Sighing, Beth turned back to Nika and saw that the wire was presently embedded in the taller woman's upper arms and her chest just above her breasts . . . and her heart.

"Yeah, that's gotta hurt," she muttered.

"*Da*," Nika agreed in a trembling voice, and Beth glanced to her face with surprise. She'd thought the woman unconscious, which she supposed was stupid since she was standing upright and stiff as a board.

Must have been wishful thinking, she decided, because getting the woman off the wire was going to be a painful exercise, and she really would have rather had the woman unconscious for it.

"What is it?" Kira called with concern and started to move forward.

"Stay back," Beth ordered.

"But what—"

"It was a trap," she explained. "A wire was rigged to slice through anyone who entered."

"What?" Kira squawked.

"Yeah, that's how I feel," Beth muttered, ducking under the wire to move in front of Nika. As she did, she spared a glance for Oksana, her mouth tightening as she peered at the woman lying on the ground about twenty-five feet in. Her body was in two pieces. Well, four, she corrected herself. Oksana was the same height as Nika, and the wire had cut through her chest and upper arms too. Only it had gone all the way through.

Now that was seriously going to hurt during the healing, Beth thought, and then felt bad because she was glad that if it had had to happen to one of them, Oksana was the one.

Bad Beth, she told herself as she turned to peer at Nika and the wire. There was a slight lip at the door of the barn where she'd been standing a moment ago. Beth had stepped down perhaps two inches when she'd ducked under the wire, and now found that while the wire was at a level just under Nika's armpits, it would have hit her at about the middle of her throat. Unlike the taller Oksana, Beth would have been beheaded and would now be in only two pieces rather than four, she thought absently as she looked over where the wire was embedded in Nika.

There wasn't much to see. The wire was paper-thin, and the nanos had already stopped the bleeding so that there was just a thin red line to show where the wire had cut in. It had gone almost halfway through before being stopped by the end of the track, she noted.

"Nika," she said with a frown. "We have to get you off this wire before the nanos heal your body with it inside."

"What? Heal?" she gasped with alarm, trying to look down at herself.

"If they haven't already started," Beth added under her breath and then grasped the wire on either side of the bodyguard's arms and said, "Just don't move for a minute."

"*Da. Nyet*," Nika said weakly, apparently confused. Although, really, who wouldn't be in this situation?

"I'm sorry," Beth said sincerely. "This might hurt."

"Just do it fast, *da*?" Nika said, trying to be brave.

"*Da*," Beth responded. "On the count of three. One, two—" She yanked the wire toward herself, concentrating on keeping it level, and was amazed when it came right out.

"Back up," she instructed Nika. "Back—Oh!" Beth said with surprise when the woman toppled backward like a felled tree. Releasing the wire, she ducked under it, grabbed Nika's wrist and quickly dragged her away from the building to rest by Kira, Liliya, and Marta.

"Call Mortimer and have him send out blood," Beth barked as she straightened. "Lots of it. And some backup, and a cleanup crew or something. Christ, just tell him to send everyone," she added, turning to hurry back to the barn.

Beth heard Kira bark, "Do it!" but didn't glance back, so was surprised when she stopped just before the wire and Kira whispered, "What do we do now?"

Giving a start, Beth scowled at the girl. "I told you to stay back."

"You cannot do everything yourself. We are team. I will help," Kira said firmly, and then turned to peer into the barn.

"You are worried there is another trap," Liliya said, and Beth's head shot around to where the other woman now stood a step back on her right. Apparently, no one felt they had to listen to her.

"I told you to call Mortimer," Kira snapped at the girl.

"Marta is calling," Liliya assured her and then looked inside the building and pointed out, "If they planned to kill and not just maim, there will be another trap. It will probably be fire."

"Yes. That's what I'm worried about," Beth said on a sigh.

"You think there is another trap?" Kira asked with concern. "Obviously this is trap. There is tip about coffin, yet no coffin here, the cutting wire instead. Maybe that is all."

"I don't know," Beth admitted. "But a secondary trap is a possibility that has to be taken into account."

"*Da*, but we must get Oksana out soon or she will die," Kira murmured with concern, and then frowned. "How long before blood dies when cut off from heart? They tell us in biology class, but I no remember."

"The nanos will keep Oksana's heart pumping for a little while even without directions from the brain, and the nanos can repair or replace the dead brain cells once the head and shoulders are reattached," Beth said solemnly, her gaze sliding slowly around the barn in search of anything that might hint at another trap. A big sign reading Explosives! TNT! or Incendiary Device! might have been nice. Sadly, there was nothing that helpful.

"How long nanos keep heart pumping without head and shoulders attached?" Kira asked.

Beth shrugged. "No one knows."

"Well, they should find out. We should know these things," Kira said with irritation.

"*Da*," Liliya agreed.

Beth eyed them with exasperation. "To find out, you'd have to decapitate immortals and keep the head away from the body so it couldn't heal for increasing lengths of time. Who the hell would volunteer for that?"

Neither woman responded. Presumably, they wouldn't volunteer.

"Okay," Beth said and took a deep breath. "You two stay here and I will run in, grab Oksana and run right back."

"What if there is another wire?" Liliya asked.

Beth glanced at her uncertainly. "Another wire?"

"Well, it would be smart. If one was injured by first wire, the natural instinct is for others to rush in to help. A second wire would take the rest out."

"Damn," Beth breathed and thought she should have considered that herself. Heaving out a sigh now, she said, "Right. I will crawl in, throw the arms out and then drag the upper and lower body quickly back out as fast as I can and pray there isn't a fire trap."

"You cannot crawl and carry both parts of Oksana," Kira said with exasperation. "I will crawl in with you and take the upper, while you take the lower."

"Forgive me, Kira," Liliya murmured. "But I think you should wait here for us while I go in with Beth. Because," she continued firmly when Kira tried to protest, "were you to die in there, your father would have me beheaded anyway. At least this way, if I die it is with honor for having saved you. *Da?*"

Kira hesitated, but then sighed and waved them away. "Very well, I will wait here . . . unless you need my help."

"Good." Beth dropped to her hands and knees and began to crawl forward. A moment later, she spotted movement out of the corner of her eye and knew it was Liliya following her. Beth tried to keep her focus on the ground in front of her as well as scan the area as she went. She was still hoping to spot any potential threat before it became a deadly one.

Her gaze shifted over the track on one side of the barn, and she thought that must be the reason for the new nails poking through the wooden walls. In the next moment, though, Beth frowned as she realized that the track ran along the sides of the building. The nails she'd encountered had been along the front as they'd approached the door. They hadn't gone anywhere near the side of the building.

That realization made Beth stop. She suddenly had a bad feeling creeping along the back of her neck.

"Should I throw the arms to Kira?" Liliya asked uncertainly after a moment when Beth didn't move.

She glanced to the woman, and then down to see that she was just inches from Oksana. Instead of answering, Beth turned her head to glance back the way they'd come. For a moment, she didn't understand what she was looking at. There was, in fact, a set of tracks along the front wall on either side of the doors. There was also a wire running from the end of each track to the outer edge of each door.

Beth stared at the setup silently for a moment and then considered it logically. If the wire was supposed to move on the tracks, and the wire was now hanging loose along the door, then the track must pull the wire back rather than snap it forward . . . which would pull the doors closed.

"Huh," Beth muttered. Why pull the doors closed? To lock them in. But why? Turning her head slowly, she examined as much of the building as she could again. Beth still didn't see anything to raise alarm, but she couldn't see behind the broken bales of hay.

"Liliya," she said solemnly, "I think you should back slowly out the way you came."

"What do you see?" Liliya asked quietly.

"There are wire tracks leading up to the doors. I think they're rigged to pull the doors shut and keep them shut," she admitted.

Liliya was silent for a minute, considering, and then said, "Fire. To prevent escaping fire."

"That would be my guess," Beth agreed and then glanced back to the woman waiting in the doorway. "Kira, I think you should move away from the doors."

"Why?" she asked at once, stepping right up to the wire that had sliced into Nika.

"Because I think the doors are wired to slam shut,

and I don't want you trapped in here with us if we trigger something," Beth explained. "So, back away from the door."

"I will hold door open if starts to close. You hurry. Get Oksana," she ordered.

"Nobody listens to me," Beth muttered, turning her gaze to Oksana.

"Kira is stubborn like our father," Liliya said dryly.

"*Our* father?" Beth asked sharply, and Liliya looked dismayed at her slip.

Closing her eyes, the petite blond blew a breath out and then admitted quietly, "We are half sisters, but you mustn't tell her."

"Why?" Beth asked with amazement.

"Because our father is medieval in his mindset. I am the bastard he had with an old immortal lover. Kira is the daughter of his life mate. He will not have his life mate and daughter hurt by the news that he has bastard children."

"Children? As in more than one?" Beth asked with interest.

"*Da*," she said dryly, and then crawled a couple steps forward, grabbed the closer of Oksana's arms and rose up on her knees as she turned to hurl it toward the doors. It sailed over Kira's head and disappeared behind her.

"Nice," Beth murmured, moved close enough to grab the second arm and did the same.

"Now the hard parts," Liliya said grimly.

"The upper body's closer to you. I'll take the lower," Beth said.

Nodding, Liliya caught Oksana by the hair and then

slowly began to back out the way she'd come, dragging the upper portion of Oksana's body with her.

Beth watched her for a minute and then turned to consider what remained of Oksana. It would be hard to crawl and drag the lower portion of her body. While Liliya had been able to make use of Oksana's long hair, Beth didn't have that option.

Her gaze slid over the large Russian and then settled on her weapons belt. Beth instinctively felt for her own belt, and then nodded and quickly undid and removed Oksana's belt. She looped it through two of the belt loops on the woman's jeans, and then slid it through her own belt and refastened the ends.

Satisfied that Oksana was now tethered safely to her, Beth began back toward the door as Liliya was doing.

The click when it came seemed extremely loud to Beth. Her gaze immediately jerked forward in search of the source, and she spotted the lever Oksana's lower half had been lying on and instinctively flattened herself to the ground just before the world erupted in noise and light. An explosion, and screaming and shouts all sounded at once. Beth ground her teeth and closed her eyes as a wave of terrible heat rolled over her, and then she just leapt up and began to run, hardly aware of Oksana's lower body bouncing against her legs as she went.

Through the smoke and flames, Beth spotted Liliya lying unconscious near the slowly closing doors. Changing direction, she ran toward the other woman, her gaze sliding to the doors as she went to see that Kira was struggling to keep the doors from closing. Pain burning along her back, and terrified they wouldn't make it out in time, Beth screamed and put on a burst of speed.

"Beth needs help."

Scotty's hand tightened convulsively around his phone at those words.

"Where is she?"

Mortimer rattled off an address that Scotty repeated to Rickart. The man immediately pulled a U-turn and headed back the way they'd come. Returning his attention to the phone, Scotty asked, "What's the situation?"

"I don't know. But it must be bad. One of Kira's bodyguards called, Marta I think. She was freaking out. She said Oksana was in pieces, Nika was down, and Beth said to call for blood, cleanup, backup, and just everyone. She'd never say 'just everyone' unless it was a shit storm. Beth doesn't panic."

"What the hell did ye send them into, Mortimer?" Scotty barked with dismay. "Ye were to be sending them on soft calls. Ye promised me that in exchange for me bringing me men o'er!"

"I did!" Mortimer yelled. "At least, it was supposed to be a soft call. Some kids found a coffin in an old barn. It was a joke job, for Christ's sake!"

Scotty forced himself to calm down. "Who's with her?"

"Kira and her bodyguards," Mortimer answered sharply. "There are six of them out there."

"Six minus the one in pieces and the one who's down," Scotty growled and then glanced to Rickart. "How far out are we?"

"Two minutes," Mortimer answered over the phone, having heard the question. "I have your vehicles on the monitor right now. Odilia and Donny are too far out to be of use, but Magnus is closer than you are. You should be able to see him when you turn the next corner. You are practically on his tail."

Scotty glanced forward as they took the corner and grunted when he saw the SUV speeding in front of them.

"You will see the barn after the next corner," Mortimer said as the SUV in front disappeared around the corner in question.

Scotty didn't respond. He just ended the call to climb into the back of the SUV and grab the blood cooler.

"I see it. I—Holy Mother of God!" Rickart shouted as Scotty turned to make his way back to the front of the SUV with the cooler.

Scotty jerked his eyes forward at that and stared in horror at the barn in front of them as it seemed to implode. Fire rushed out through the doors as if they were the gates to hell. The flames receded back into the building just as quickly, but thick, dark smoke immediately began to billow out in its place, almost obscuring the inferno raging inside.

Cursing under his breath, Scotty unstrapped the fire extinguisher next to where the cooler had been, and climbed back to the front of the vehicle with both items as Rickart followed Magnus's SUV almost to the doors . . . the slowly closing doors, Scotty saw with a frown and spotted two women, one on each door, trying to hold them back.

Magnus's SUV stopped and the man was running for the doors first, but Scotty wasn't far behind, leaping from the vehicle before Rickart had quite brought it to a halt.

Magnus ran to the door on the left, adding his weight and strength to the woman's to try to keep it open, so Scotty went to the door on the right. Recognizing Kira Sarka struggling with that door, he dropped his burdens and moved up beside her.

"Where's Beth?" he shouted, slamming into the door and digging in his feet to try to prevent it moving. Much to his amazement, while he slowed the door, he didn't stop it.

"She's inside!" Kira yelled over the roar of the fire.

"I'm on it!" Rickart bellowed, rushing past them and racing into the smoke and flames.

Scotty almost let go of the door and chased in after him, but good sense made him hold his position. They had to keep the door open or Beth didn't have a chance. Grinding his teeth, he put his shoulder to the wood, desperate to stop its movement, but merely slowed it a little more. The doors were more than half-closed now.

Relief raced through him when he spotted Rickart hurrying out of the blinding smoke with Beth in his arms. He stayed where he was until the man carried her past him, and then released the door, grabbed up the cooler of blood and hurried to where Rickart was laying the woman on the ground. It wasn't until he stood over her that he realized it wasn't Beth, but the petite blond bodyguard, Liliya.

A shriek sounded behind him then, and Scotty whirled toward the barn. For a moment, all he saw was smoke and more smoke, and then fire raced out of the closing doors.

"Dear God, she's on fire!" Rickart gasped beside him.

Scotty knew at once that it was Beth. With his heart in his throat, he charged forward, throwing himself on her and rolling her across the ground. It didn't take him long to realize that was a mistake. Rather than put out the flames ravishing her, Scotty was quickly on fire himself. Fortunately, Magnus had more sense than him, and snatched up the fire extinguisher he'd left by the door. Rushing to them, he raised the extinguisher, and Scotty closed his eyes as the foam sprayed out of the nozzle.

Twelve

Scotty was walking along the ocean shore, enjoying the cool soothing water rushing over his feet. When he saw Beth walking toward him in a fiery red dress, a smile claimed his lips. Happy to see her up and well, he hurried to meet her, eager to take her in his arms. She seemed just as eager, and they met and embraced there on the shore's edge. But as he bent to kiss her, Scotty realized it wasn't a dress she wore; Beth was engulfed in flames, and now so was he. The fire licked along his skin and burned his hands, arms, chest, and face as they fell to the ground screaming. They rolled, and rolled, and . . .

His own screams woke him. Scotty sat up abruptly, his heart drumming so loudly in his ears that it took a moment before he became aware of a soothing voice saying, "It's all right. You're safe. I've given you something for the pain. Rest now."

Turning his head, he stared blankly at the woman

speaking, a redhead with soft silver-green eyes. "Who're you?"

"Rachel," she answered easily. "Dr. Rachel Argeneau. Your doctor, so be a good man and lie down and rest. Doctor's orders."

Scotty scowled groggily, and opened his mouth to tell her to bugger off, but for some reason he couldn't seem to get the words out. His mouth drooped and then his eyelids did, and he was pretty sure he fell back on the bed. Before he could worry about it too much, he was asleep.

The next time Scotty woke, it was much more slowly. Pain and hunger drew him inexorably toward consciousness until he blinked his eyes open. He was in the blue room Sam had prepared for him at the Enforcer house. It was dark, the curtains open to reveal a full moon and twinkling stars, and he had to wonder what the hell he was doing in bed. He should have been up and about helping to catch rogues at this hour.

Pushing aside the sheets and blankets that covered him, Scotty sat up and slid his feet to the floor, but then just sat there for a moment. He felt incredibly weak and had no idea why. He probably needed blood, Scotty decided and grabbed the post of the headboard to steady himself as he stood up. His legs trembled, threatening to give out, but he was sure a bit of blood would fix that right up. Determined to find some, he started to move, intending to walk around the bed, but paused abruptly as he bumped into something in the dark. His eyes didn't appear to be focusing properly, and his night vision wasn't working as it should.

Beginning to worry now, Scotty reached for the lamp on the bedside table and flicked it on, startled when the bright light brought a moan from the other side of the bed. Turning, he stared at the figure lying on the opposite side, and then gaped at the horror looking back at him. Charred, black skin mixed with patches of bloody red spots and two eyes presently a solid gold as the nanos did their work. Scotty opened his mouth on an alarmed shout even as the figure in his bed released a terrified shriek, and then the floor was rushing up to meet him.

The next time Scotty woke, he did so abruptly, his eyes opening to stare at the ceiling overhead. Memories from the nightmares he'd endured crowded into his mind, but he forced them away to take stock of himself. He wasn't in pain, wasn't even feeling hunger, the room wasn't on fire, no burning women were dancing before him, and no charred monsters lay in the bed with him. Scotty was quite sure he was awake this time . . . and he didn't feel half-bad.

"Are you just going to lie there staring at the ceiling all day, or did you want to talk to me?"

Scotty turned his head on the pillow to peer at Magnus. He opened his mouth to ask how long he'd been down, and "Where's Beth?" came out.

Magnus's mouth twitched with amusement at the question.

"She is in her room. We thought it best to separate the two of you after you both had fits when you saw each other the last time," he answered easily. "I just came from there and she is doing well. She was burned worse than you, but seems to be healing quicker. Must be because she is younger," he taunted him.

Scotty scowled at him for the attempt to insult him, and sat up abruptly in bed, happy to find there was no weakness or trembling this time as he shifted his feet to the floor and stood. He was wearing one of those horrible hospital gowns, though, he noted with a grimace.

"You should not be out of bed, my friend," Magnus said, standing to move to his side. "You are not finished healing. Rachel will give you hell if she catches you."

"Who the devil is Rachel?" Scotty asked, but had a vague recollection of what he thought had been a dream. Some woman telling him her name was Rachel Argeneau, and she was his doctor. If he recalled correctly, she had ordered him to rest.

"She's the doctor who has been nursing you back to health," Magnus said easily as Scotty started around the bed toward the closet. Scotty had reached and opened the closet door when Magnus announced, "She found you most difficult, and said it was patients like you that made her decide to work with the dead in the morgue rather than live patients."

"The morgue?" Scotty turned on him with horror. "Ye had a mortician doctoring me?"

Magnus shrugged. "Well, she was the only one available and beggars cannot be choosers. Besides, the nanos really do all the work."

"You'd best not let my wife hear you say that. Hell, I'm offended to hear it myself."

Scotty had just turned back to the open closet door, but at that comment, swiveled to glance at the man in the doorway. He raised his eyebrows as he took in his slim build, dirty-blond hair, and silver-blue eyes.

"This is Etienne Argeneau," Magnus announced. "He is Rachel's life mate and husband."

"That I am," Etienne said mildly, and then eyed

Scotty and said, "And you're Cullen MacDonald, the patient who has kept my wife busy for the last three nights and two days trying to keep you asleep and comfortable while you healed."

"Hmm," Magnus murmured. "That is true. She had a devil of a time keeping you under. You would wake up screaming, or get up and try to walk around. She had us put you in restraints at one point. Those tranquilizers they developed do not work well on you at all."

"No," Scotty admitted, turning to the closet to pull out a pair of black jeans. "I was shot with three of them my first day here and wasn't out for long."

"How long?" Donny asked, making his arrival known. The younger immortal narrowed his eyes on Scotty as he entered the room to stand next to Etienne. "You weren't awake when I dragged you to the SUV and hefted you into it, were you? Because you could have saved me a lot of trouble if you'd just let me know you were awake and could walk."

"Aye," Scotty agreed with an evil smile as he dragged his jeans on and did them up. "But then I wouldn't have been able to listen to the conversation ye had with Beth on the way to the house."

"Hear anything interesting?" Magnus asked with amusement.

"Just Donny being a wee clipe, and Beth saying she thinks I hate her," Scotty admitted as he removed the hospital gown and turned back to the closet to search for a shirt. He'd hoped to hear more, but Beth had turned the conversation to the boy rather than talk about herself.

"What's a clipe?" Donny asked with a frown.

"A tattletale," Magnus informed him.

"I don't tattle," Donny protested.

"Ye told her I was speeding to get to her," Scotty pointed out, shrugging into a white linen shirt.

"Well, yeah, but to prove you didn't hate her, not to get you in trouble," Donny pointed out.

"Hmm," Scotty muttered as he finished doing up his buttons. Glancing to Magnus then, he raised an eyebrow. "Where's Beth?"

"I told you, she's in her room," Magnus answered.

"Aye, but where is that?" Scotty asked impatiently.

"Oh, you do not know," Magnus realized and stood up. "Well, I can take you there, but you might give her nightmares."

"What?" Scotty asked with surprise. "Why?"

"Try looking in a mirror and see for yourself," Magnus said dryly.

Scotty hesitated, worry coursing through him when he noted the pity on Donny's and Etienne's faces. Frowning, he turned and walked into the bathroom and then closed the door. He could have just looked in the dresser mirror, but he wasn't sure what to expect, and would rather see what was what while on his own.

"God Almighty," Scotty breathed when he flicked on the light and saw his reflection. His long hair was gone, his scalp a mass of scars and still healing raw skin, and his face . . . He didn't even recognize himself. The skin was the same mess as his head. It just looked like his scalp had slipped down to cover his face. His eyes were alarming too, a solid silver as the nanos tried to repair what the flames had apparently done.

Scotty peered down at his hands now, noting the same knotted skin there, and wondered that he hadn't noticed it while he was dressing. He supposed he'd been distracted by so much company. Now that he was thinking about it, though, Scotty couldn't believe he wasn't in agony. Weren't the nanos working to heal him even now?

A knock at the door drew his attention, and after a hesitation he said, "Come in."

Magnus stepped inside and smiled at him sympathetically as he closed the door.

"Rachel thinks the tranquilizer works differently on you," he said, meeting Scotty's gaze in the mirror. "That for some reason your nanos fixate on flushing those from your system, rather than tending to anything else. So that when she gives them to you, the healing stops . . . which is why you are not presently unconscious. She thought it would be better for you to heal."

Scotty let out a little breath of relief. "So it will heal?"

Magnus nodded, and then warned, "But once the nanos finish flushing the tranquilizer and set back to work on your skin, you will be in agony again."

Scotty nodded, and asked, "How long until that happens?"

Magnus shrugged helplessly. "I would not guess it would be too long from now. After all, you are awake, so the worst of the tranquilizer must already be flushed from your system."

Mouth firming determinedly, Scotty turned and opened the bathroom door. "Show me where Beth's room is. I want to see that she's all right before . . ." He didn't bother finishing. They both knew he meant before the healing set in and he was in agony once more.

Donny and Etienne were gone when Scotty stepped back into his room. He wondered briefly where they'd gone, but didn't ask. He merely followed Magnus into the hall. It turned out that Beth's room was just across the hall and down a room. The door was open, and Magnus stepped up to peer inside, then relaxed and gestured him over.

Scotty moved beside him and peered cautiously around the door frame. This was where Donny and Etienne had gone, he saw. And it was why Magnus had relaxed. The two men made something of a screen, blocking him from being seen by anyone in the room, and, in turn, blocking Beth from his view. He could hear her speaking, though, and she sounded just fine other than her voice being a touch husky. Probably from the smoke she'd inhaled, or maybe the flames, or possibly even from screaming. It was hard to say without seeing her.

"You had sisters?" he heard a woman ask, and supposed it was this Rachel, the doctor and Etienne's wife.

"Two. One older and one younger," Beth answered, her voice soft with affection, and then on a chuckle she added, "I was the dreaded middle child."

"Oh, God, the middle child is always trouble! All the magazines say so," Rachel teased with a laugh. "What were your sisters' names?"

"Ella was the older one," Beth answered, and then added sadly, "She died of the ague when I was nine. Mom tried everything to save her—hot compresses, cold compresses, all the medicines she could get her hands on, but . . ."

"Ague was what they called fevers, right?" Rachel asked curiously. "I know it could be malaria at times too, but they also called anything with fever that, didn't they?"

"Aye," Beth admitted. "They just came on one day, fever and chills. She got hotter and weaker . . . Ella was fair burning up, but nothing would stop it. Ma even tried leeches." She was silent for a minute and Scotty waited, thinking that her accent became thicker and her speech more antiquated when she spoke of the past. He'd noticed it happened when she was upset too.

"Ella used to act as barker for our mom at market," Beth said suddenly. "She had such a clear beautiful voice. It was almost like singing."

"I'm sorry. I don't know what a barker is," Rachel admitted.

"A barker calls out about the pies, selling them." Beth paused briefly and then sang out, "'Pies! Fine, fresh penny pies! Won't you buy some pies, sir! A pie for a penny! Please, sir, won't you buy the pies!'" She ended on a chuckle and then admitted, "I took over when Ella died, but I was never as good as her."

"And your younger sister?" Rachel asked. "What was her name?"

"Little Ruthie," Beth answered, affection clear in her voice. "She was a good one. Used to nap at Mom's feet most of the time at market. Didn't fuss and such as a babe. And stayed close when she got talking gibberish and toddling around."

"Your mom took you all to the market?" Rachel asked with surprise.

"Aye, from the earliest I can remember. There weren't day care then," Beth said wryly. "So aye, Mom took us. We helped sell the pies. Helped make 'em too."

Scotty leaned against the door frame as he listened,

enjoying the almost lyrical sound of her voice and the happiness he heard in it.

"Penny pies, they were. The best in London. Everyone said so," Beth added proudly.

"And your father?" Rachel asked. "What did he do?"

"Drank, mostly." Her voice was cold now and completely devoid of emotion. "He was a drunkard. Beat me mom to get the coin from her for the day's sales and then drank all night and slept the day away. He was a mean drunk too. Mom tried to shield us, but couldn't always, and we learned to move quick when he started his fists in swinging."

Scotty frowned at the picture she was drawing of her childhood. He'd seen enough men like Beth's father to know how it would have gone. Her father would have been unpredictable, laughing and teasing one minute and then in a rage the next. With a father like that the day could go from good to bad in a heartbeat, and it was impossible to know when it would happen. It left the family in a perpetual state of crisis. They might be smiling and seeming to enjoy something on the outside, but inside they were always on the alert for that change, always on the verge of fight-or-flight.

"I'm sorry," Rachel said with sincerity.

"What?" Beth sounded surprised. "Don't be. It was a long time ago. Besides, I may have lost in the father category, but me mom was a wonderful woman. Loving, and kind. She taught me to work hard and be kind to others. I don't know how many times she said to me, 'Never look down on others, Bethie, until ye've walked a mile in their shoes,' and 'Work hard, Bethie, and make yer own way. Don't depend on some worthless man to do it. They'll sore disappoint ye.'"

After a pause, Beth added, "She taught by example too. No one worked harder than me mom. We'd get home from market, and she'd start right into making the pies for the next day, even while making us dinner and such. After we ate, I'd help with making the filling for the penny pies while she concentrated on the pastry, but then she'd send us girls to bed while she worked well into the night. Come morning, Mom'd be up before all of us, firing the stove and starting in baking the pies we'd made the night before.

"That was the secret to why her pies were so popular," Beth assured her. "Others baked them the night before, putting the first batch in while they made the second batch and so on, so they were already a day old by the time they got to market. But Mom wouldn't do that. She baked them all that morning, so they'd still be warm and fresh when we got them to market."

"When did she sleep?" Rachel asked with amazement.

"Truth is, I wondered that myself sometimes," Beth admitted on a chuckle. "But there was a morning or two I caught her napping against the stove while the pies baked, so I know she did get some sleep."

"What was the market like back then?" Rachel asked with interest. "Was it in an enclosed space, or—?"

"They were starting to build those big enclosed markets then, but Tottenham were still just stalls and stands on either side of the lane, and that were us," Beth said.

Etienne shifted slightly, and for a moment, Scotty was able to see Beth. The fire had taken her hair too, but her head was already healed, and her beautiful red hair had grown back a quarter inch or more. Oddly enough, she looked lovely even without the long, rich red locks. Unlike his, her face was healed, and she looked adorable and somehow innocent and sweet as if the fire had burned her sins away.

"I used to love the market. I worked hard, but had friends there too, and on warm beautiful summer days it was great fun. However—" She paused, and he saw her grimace and give a shudder before Etienne shifted again, blocking her from view once more as she continued, "Winter was a different story. It was something awful then. So cold ye were sure yer toes and fingers'd fall off, and ye hardly sold anything anyway on those days. Those penny pies could be fresh from the oven, but by the time we got them to market they were frozen solid."

"So," Rachel asked, "when you grew up did you bake penny pies and sell them at market too? Like your mother?"

There was a brief silence, and Scotty found himself clenching his fingers as he waited for her response, and then she finally said, "Nay. The cholera took me ma and Little Ruthie when I was ten. I don't know why I didn't get it," she added. "I ate the same food as them, drank the same drinks and went all the same places. I even nursed them when they fell ill, but never got it." She paused briefly and then continued, "Unfortunately, while I'd helped with making the filling ere that, Ma never got around to teaching me to make the pastry. When they passed, I tried to take over making the pies, but . . ."

Scotty heard her give a small laugh before she admitted, "I fear ye could have hammered nails with me pies. The pastry was that hard. Course, the first day everyone was expecting me ma's usual fine fare so bought up all me pretty pies right quick. They'd missed them while me ma and Ruthie were sick and I was nursing 'em. The second day I took pies to market, they must have thought that first day's offerings were just a one-time mistake, or mayhap they were bought up by people who hadn't bought any of the ones the day before, but most of the second day's offerings sold too. But by the third day, I hardly sold any at all. I guess I was not made to be me mother."

Scotty waited tensely then, expecting Rachel to ask what she'd done then, but the question never came. Instead, Etienne's wife said, "You're looking a bit pale, Beth. I think we should give you some more blood and let you sleep."

"So are you," Magnus murmured at Scotty's side. "Are you in pain? Are the nanos starting into healing again?"

Scotty hesitated, but then nodded grimly. The pain had started several minutes ago, but he'd wanted to hear about Beth's childhood. It hadn't been what he'd expected. While he wasn't surprised at the kind of father she'd had, what she'd said about her mother had been a revelation. In truth, it sounded like she had a childhood similar to his own in some ways. Oh, certainly, there had been a lot of differences. He was raised a laird's heir, while she'd been the child of poor parents, scratching out a living. But Scotty had had a good and kind father and a vicious, mean whore for a mother, while Beth had had a good, kind mother and a vicious, violent drunkard for a father. They'd each had one good parent and one bad.

Scotty didn't protest when Magnus urged him back to his room. He went quietly, his thoughts in turmoil.

"Should I leave you to rest?" Magnus asked as he ushered him into his room. "Or are you well enough to talk about what to do about Beth?"

"What do you mean, do about her?" Scotty asked with a frown.

"To protect her," he explained. "This latest attack proves the one in Vancouver was not a one-off. Someone is out to get her."

"The fire at the barn was an attack on Beth?" Scotty paused at the side of the bed and turned to face him, alarm rushing through him and briefly displacing the pain that had begun to eat at him.

"Of course! You do not know," Magnus said, sounding irritated with himself. "Sit down and I'll tell you what happened."

Scotty hesitated, but then dropped to sit on the bed and waited.

It seemed to Beth that she barely drifted off to sleep when arguing voices brought her back awake. Scowling, she opened her eyes and glanced around the dark room. No one appeared to be there with her. The voices were coming from the hallway.

"I agree. Someone needs to watch her. But not you," she heard Magnus say. "You need to heal, Scotty. You are a bloody mess at the moment. You will scare the girl half to death if you go in there looking like that."

Beth's eyebrows rose and she wondered what he meant by it. Scotty was a mess? Why? Had he been hurt? No one had mentioned that when she'd woken up.

Frowning, Beth sat up and pushed the sheets and blankets aside to get out of bed. Much to her relief, the room didn't spin around her and she didn't sway on trembling legs. She was done healing for the most part, and Rachel said she just needed a good night's rest as the nanos finished the work inside her and she'd be good as new. The fact that she was no longer suffering pain had made Beth think that the healing must be over. However, Rachel said her pallor and the continued need for extra blood suggested otherwise. The nanos were still working inside, just on things that apparently didn't hurt. Perhaps even only on rebuilding their forces, but whatever the case, she should take the opportunity to rest to help them along, rather than slow their progress by giving them more work.

"Scotty, listen to me," Magnus said now. "Donny, Etienne, Mortimer, and I will take turns sitting with Beth. We will keep her safe. What you need to do now is concentrate on healing."

"I listened to ye the last time and look what happened," Scotty shot back. "She'd be fine, ye insisted. She'd have Kira and her bodyguards there with her to keep her safe, ye assured me. Besides, whoever attacked her in Vancouver wasn't likely to follow her back to Toronto, ye said. And now look! She barely escaped having her head cut off, and was damned near burned to death."

"I know. I was wrong," Magnus said soothingly. "I will not make the same mistake twice, though. Obviously whoever attacked her in Vancouver has followed her back here. We will keep an eye on her now and we will look into who it could be. I am just saying that you should concentrate on healing yourself. Just for the next twenty-four hours. The worst of your healing should be over by then and you can—"

"I can heal and watch her too," Scotty growled, turning away from Magnus and toward her door just as she opened it.

They both froze. Beth noted that Scotty was scowling at her as if expecting her to try to send him away, but she was too busy taking in the ruin of his face and head to do so.

His hair, that long, beautiful hair she'd tangled her hands in and pulled as he loved her, was gone. In its place was a charred mess. It was how she imagined a scorched earth would look from space. But that wasn't even the worst of it. His face too was charred, but the healing had started there so that strips of flaking black skin were interspersed with ribbons of raised, red, ridged scars.

"It'll heal," he growled and Beth shifted her eyes to his, blinking as she noted the solid silver staring back. The nanos were obviously hard at work there, repairing whatever damage the fire had done. At least, she assumed it was fire, although she had no idea how he'd been burned. She'd got out of the fire on her own. Beth remembered that much. Reaching out, she gently touched a section of his face that was already scarred and shouldn't hurt and asked in a soft voice, "How?"

Scotty raised a hand to cover hers and she just managed not to flinch at the mess it was. *Dear God, the pain he must be in*, she thought weakly.

"He tackled you when you came running out of

the barn on fire," Magnus explained when Scotty remained silent. "He rolled on the ground with you, trying to put out the flames."

That made Beth frown, and she glanced to the man and asked, "But why isn't he healing?"

"He is. But apparently where the tranquilizers simply help get others through the pain of healing and the nanos ignore it until they have finished their work, with Scotty the nanos turn all their efforts to removing the drug from his system first and then return to the healing. So the tranquilizer just slows his healing."

"I think he must be allergic to the tranquilizer," Rachel announced, approaching from the stairs. "And highly allergic at that. The nanos in him react as if they're removing a life-threatening poison and turn all their attention to getting it out of him. Thus slowing his healing."

Beth nodded solemnly, and then turned her hand in his to clasp it gently.

"He can stay with me if it makes him feel better," she announced and tugged him into her room.

Beth wasn't surprised when Magnus and Rachel followed, but she simply led Scotty to the bed, urged him into it and tucked him in. She noticed the wide-eyed way he was looking at her as she did it, but ignored that and simply walked around the bed to climb in next to him. She didn't lie down, however, but sat up against the headboard and pulled the blankets up to cover the pale blue hospital gown she wore. Beth then peered from Rachel to Magnus expectantly. "So, you think it was another attack directed at me?"

The pair exchanged a glance, and then Magnus asked, "Do you disagree?"

Beth considered it briefly. "It was definitely a trap, and a well-thought-out one. If I hadn't noticed the new nails sticking out of the wood of the barn as we approached, I might have walked straight in to take a look around when I saw that it appeared empty. We probably all would have."

Magnus nodded solemnly.

"But I don't see how it could have been directed at me specifically," she continued. "I'm not the only Rogue Hunter working for Mortimer. In fact, he has more people to call on right now than he did before you and the others came from England. Any one of us could have walked into that trap."

There was silence for a minute, and then Kira said from the door, "Except it appeared to be a joke job. That is what you call it, *da*? The joke job?"

"*Da*," Beth admitted reluctantly, watching the other woman enter. It was the first time the Russian had visited since she'd woken up, although she'd been told Kira had refused to leave her bedside the first night, insisting on staying to watch over her.

"So," Kira continued, "if this person knows you are stuck with me, going only to the joke job, then they know is likely you will be assigned barn."

"She's right," Scotty said grimly. "Yer team is the only one that would've been sent to that barn."

"But who could have known that?" Beth asked with a frown.

"Pretty much every Enforcer working for me right now knows that," Mortimer said, entering the room as well. Pausing, he glanced around at the people in the room, and raised his eyebrows. "You could have let me know there was going to be a meeting about this."

"It was not planned," Magnus assured him.

Mortimer grunted at that, and then rubbed the back of his neck before saying, "So, here is our problem. That accident on the highway appears to have been deliberate. The driver had been controlled. However, we do not think it can be connected to the attack in Vancouver, because whoever set up the car accident could not have followed you to Vancouver, and none of the Enforcers—who were the only people who could know you were out there—were in Vancouver, except for you three. However, now there has been another attack here, a very well-planned attack. But the only people who could know you would be the one sent to the barn are our people." He raised his eyebrows at her. "Do you have any idea what the hell is going on?"

Beth shook her head solemnly. "Sorry. No."

Mortimer grimaced, but nodded. "I did not think so, but was hoping."

"Each attack was pre-planned," Scotty said now, the words coming through clenched teeth.

Beth was aware that she wasn't the only one to look at him. Everyone was watching him now, waiting for him to continue, and probably noticing—like her—that he was obviously suffering. The man was extremely pale. He was also sweating as he struggled with the pain of healing. And there wasn't a damned thing they could do to help him if he was allergic to the tranquilizers.

"At least somewhat," he added with a frown. "The first one could have been a case of opportunity. The immortal behind this could ha'e been followin' Beth, spotted the truck pullin' girders as it drove onto the highway and then simply took control o' the driver and caused the accident. But the second one . . ." He glanced to Beth. "The mortal was taken control of and sent into the ladies' room to lure ye out to the alley where the immortal was waitin' with a sword. That took a little more plannin'."

"And the last one was all plan," Beth continued for him. "The barn was set with traps, the call was made to bring someone out, presumably me, and then . . ." She shrugged and raised her eyebrows. "What does that mean?"

Scotty closed his eyes. His hands and jaw were clenched, and Beth was sure she could see a difference in him. To her it looked like there was less black on his head and face, and more red, wet, raw skin.

"I do no' ken," he said at last on an expelled breath and shook his head on the pillow. "I think it means something, but I can no' think just now."

Everyone was silent for a moment, and then Magnus said, "Well, perhaps we should all take some time and think about it. In the meantime, you need to rest and heal, Scotty."

"What we need to do is place guards on Beth," Scotty countered, his voice rough with pain. "She is never to be alone. She is to go on no more hunts. In fact, she should no' leave this house until we sort out who is after her and catch them."

Beth had to bite her tongue to keep from protesting. She really, really wanted to, and if Scotty were his normal strong, healthy self, she would. But he wasn't. Scotty was in no shape to argue. He was in a bad way, and it was all thanks to her. To his trying to save her. Beth shook her head slightly, still finding it hard to believe he'd done that. She truly didn't understand the man. Nothing he did made sense to her. He didn't want her, but he risked himself to save her. Because there was nothing riskier to an immortal than fire. It was like putting a match to pure alcohol. *Whoosh*, up they went. It was amazing they were both still alive.

"My bodyguards and I will help guard Beth," Kira offered, although the word *offered* was something of a misnomer. The Russian's offer was actually more of an announcement . . . as usual, Beth thought with amusement, and smiled at the woman as she commented, "You don't appear angry about being sent on joke jobs."

Kira shrugged. "I am new one. New always starts at bottom. Is how you learn . . . and I am learning," she added solemnly.

Magnus smiled faintly. "And what have you learned . . . besides not to throw yourself on a burning immortal?" he added dryly.

"A lot," Kira assured him, and then glanced at Beth and praised her. "You are good teacher. At barn I learn never to rush in. To be patient, like you. And to be cautious, and see everything. You saw both traps before they were sprung."

"Not soon enough," Beth said unhappily. "I should have considered that there might be a second lever where Oksana fell that acted as a secondary trip for another trap once her weight was taken off. As Liliya said, everyone would rush in to help the downed person, and that is when the second trap could do the most damage."

Kira shook her head. "You cannot know everything."

"Still, I'm sorry about Oksana," Beth said solemnly. The first thing she'd asked about on waking the first time was how the Russian had fared. She already knew that Liliya had dropped the Russian Amazon's upper body when the explosion knocked her to the ground, and that she was dazed and confused when Rickart reached her and carried her out. Liliya hadn't recalled about Oksana's upper body until it was too late. Only the woman's lower body and lower arms had survived the fire, and her lower body had got pretty charred along with Beth . . . and Scotty, she added silently, glancing to the man in bed next to her. His eyes were tightly closed, his face a rictus of agony.

"*Da*, that was bad," Kira said, drawing her attention again as she admitted, "I no like Oksana. Was hoping for excuse to send her ass back, but not *just* ass."

A wholly inappropriate giggle tried to slip out of Beth, and she had to cover her mouth to hold it back. There was nothing funny about any of this. The woman was dead.

"Right," Mortimer said suddenly, straightening. "Rachel, do whatever you came up here to do. The rest of us will clear out," he announced and then added, "Magnus, I need you and Kira to come to my office."

Thirteen

The room cleared out quickly, leaving just Rachel, Beth, and Scotty. Rachel immediately retrieved five bags of blood from the refrigerator they'd moved into the room. She offered one to Beth with a small smile. "There's nothing I need do for you. More blood and some rest and you'll be good to go."

"Thank you," Beth murmured, accepting the blood.

Rachel nodded, then turned to set three of the remaining bags on the bed next to Scotty and handed him the fourth as she said, "Unfortunately, there's nothing I *can* do for you except offer you blood. I'm afraid you're just going to have to work through the pain of healing somehow."

Scotty grunted as he accepted the offered bag and then muttered, "It will no' be the first time," before slapping it to his fangs.

Rachel glanced back to Beth and said, "I'll check on you later. Rest now."

Nodding, she slapped her own bag of blood to her fangs as she watched the woman leave, pulling the door closed behind her.

Beth remained sitting upright until the bag was empty, and then ripped it away and took Scotty's as he removed his own. She tossed them both into the small garbage bin next to the bedside table, and then scooted forward in the bed so that she could lie down. When she did, Beth automatically turned on her side toward Scotty. It was the side she always slept on and she did it without thinking, but then paused and stared at him.

Beth almost turned the other way rather than lie facing him, but decided it might seem rude for her to turn her back to him, so she remained where she was and watched silently as he popped another bag of blood to his fangs. She examined his face as he fed. Scotty had his eyes closed, but she noticed lines were beginning to form around them, and his jaw was tightening with each passing moment. The blood he was taking in was speeding up the healing, rushing it along and increasing his pain, she realized, and frowned.

By the time Scotty switched the second empty bag for the third bag of blood, his hand was shaking, and Beth couldn't take it anymore. She hated knowing he was in such agony and there was nothing she could do about it. She was actually relieved when he tugged the third bag from his fangs and turned to peer at her rather than slap the last one on.

After a hesitation, Beth murmured, "Thank you for trying to save me."

Scowling, he muttered, "It was stupid. I'd have done ye more good had I grabbed up the fire extinguisher and sprayed ye like Magnus did afterward to both of us."

Beth grinned. "Are you suggesting you made a mistake and aren't perfect?" she asked with mock disbelief, and then gasped, "No! Say it ain't so!"

Scotty's mouth twitched, fighting to smile, or maybe fighting not to, and he turned his head on the pillow to stare at the ceiling, muttering, "Only you would dare taunt me."

Beth just watched him for a minute and then asked solemnly, "Is it very bad?"

"What?" he asked, glancing at her with confusion.

"The pain," she said dryly. "What else would I be talking about?"

"Oh." Scotty scowled at her. "Well, it is now that ye've got me thinkin' o' it."

"Hmm." Beth picked up the last bag of blood and offered it to him.

His mouth tightened, but Scotty took the bag and popped it to his fangs. His eyes narrowed suspiciously, however, when she immediately smiled.

"The tranquilizers don't work on you," she pointed out.

He grunted around the bag in his mouth.

"But I have an idea how to knock you out so you sleep through the healing."

Rather than look interested in this idea, Scotty's eyes narrowed even further.

That was gratitude for you. It was like he didn't trust her or something, Beth thought with amusement, but merely asked, "What is the extent of your burns?"

That question had him blinking above the nearly full bag at his mouth.

"Is your chest burned?" she asked, and then simply

tugged the blanket down to see. Problem was, she'd tucked him into bed fully clothed. Frowning now, she commented, "That can't be very comfortable for sleeping. You'll not relax that way. Sit up."

Scotty shook his head at once, the blood in the bag sloshing one way, then the other as he did.

"Careful," Beth cautioned. "You'll tear the bag and get blood everywhere."

Scotty just narrowed his eyes again. The closest thing to a scowl he could manage at the moment, she supposed.

"Here, I'll make you more comfortable," Beth said and shifted to her knees next to him so she could set to work quickly unbuttoning his shirt and tugging it from his pants. Scotty tried to stop her, grabbing at her wrists, and she knew for certain that he was in a bad way when she proved faster than him.

"I know you like to be in control, Scotty," she said soothingly as she worked. "But this is for your own good. Think of me like a nurse. I'm just making you more comfortable."

Beth finished undoing and opening his linen shirt, and let out a breath of relief when she saw that his chest seemed undamaged. That was something, anyway. She didn't know if it was because when he'd leapt on her, his chest against hers, it had staunched those flames and he hadn't been burned there, or if it had been only mildly burned and so had already healed, but she was grateful for small mercies as she turned her attention to the button and zipper of his jeans.

"You just relax, and let nurse Beth take care of everything," she instructed him lightly as she snapped the button open, slid down the zipper and then began to work his jeans down over his hips. "I'll have you sleeping in no time. It's the least I can do when you got this way trying to save me."

"Stop," Scotty said sharply, and she glanced around to see that the final bag was empty and he had ripped it from his mouth. "Nay. I do no' want ye to do that."

Beth sat back on her heels and peered at him with frustration. She could make him pass out and sleep through the worst of the pain with a little life mate sex. At least for a while, and she wanted to do it. She didn't like to know he was in such pain, and . . . well . . . actually, though Beth was loath to admit it, she wanted to do it for herself too. Her body was tingling at the very thought of enjoying the shared pleasure with him again. It was like a drug, and she a drug addict who'd been without a fix for two whole very long weeks.

They stared at each other for a moment, and then Beth suddenly relaxed and smiled. He'd said no, so she couldn't continue to touch him. That would feel too much like rape. However, there was more than one way to skin a cat . . . if it worked, she thought with sudden concern.

"What are ye thinking?" Scotty asked suspiciously. "Ye have a scheming look to ye at the moment."

Beth blinked her thoughts away and peered at him innocently. "I don't know what you're on about, Scotty. I was just thinking that if you don't want to be comfortable, that's fine. But I do."

"What does that mean?" he asked warily.

Beth shrugged and straightened on her knees next to him as she said, "I usually sleep in the nude."

Scotty's eyes widened, but he made no protest when she reached back to undo the ties of the hospital gown. He also remained silent when she next settled to sit on her haunches and let the gown shimmy down her arms to pool in her lap, leaving her breasts bare.

"I was badly burned everywhere," Beth told him quietly, peering down at her own chest rather than meet his gaze. She had been naked in front of a lot of men, but for some reason having him look at her in that moment made her shy. Clearing her throat, she continued, "But I healed nicely."

Beth followed the words up by slowly sliding her hands up to cup her own breasts as if to display them.

"Don't you think?" she asked, not surprised to hear her accent thickening. It always did when she was excited or angry or anxious.

"Aye." It was a husky growl.

Beth bit her lip, struggling with her unusual shyness, but then closed her eyes and tilted her head back. Trying to pretend it was him touching her, she began to squeeze and knead her own breasts and then tweaked the tightening nipples. Much to her relief, Beth heard Scotty's breathing grow heavier and more labored, and thought it might be working.

Clearing her throat, she whispered, "I remember in the garage, waking up that first time to find you leaning over me. You were suckling my breast and your hand was . . ." She broke off and moved one hand down beneath the hospital gown to touch herself, sliding her fingers gently across the moist folds.

Beth opened her eyes just enough to peek out from under her eyelids and saw Scotty lick his lips as he stared at where her hand had disappeared. She continued to touch herself for a moment, and then shifted her wrist slightly, sending the soft material of the hospital gown down her legs to lie on the bed, letting him see what she was doing.

"Do you remember?" she asked, her own voice gone husky.

"Aye," he breathed, not taking his eyes away from her hand. "Spread yer legs more."

Beth smiled with relief at the demand. She had him. At least, she thought she did. She wasn't sure. She wasn't feeling any of the shared excitement she'd experienced when they'd made love, just her own milder excitement at having him watch her pleasure herself.

"Spread yer legs more," Scotty repeated.

Beth smiled and obeyed, easing her knees open so he could better see what she was doing. The action brought her left knee into contact with his hip just above the jeans she'd tugged down, and Beth was suddenly assaulted by a confusing wave of sensation. Excitement and pain roared into her brain as one, but the pain was the overriding, overwhelming sensation and she sucked in a draft of air as it punched her in the head.

Scotty closed his eyes as Beth's knee brushed his skin and a shaft of pleasure slipped through his body, battling with the pain for attention. It wasn't until he opened his eyes again that he noticed that Beth had stiffened and stilled, her face twisting with pain.

"Beth?" he said with concern.

She breathed out slowly through her nose, and then

opened her eyes, her gaze landing on his lap. When her eyes widened slightly, Scotty glanced down himself to see that the pleasure that had briefly shot through him had managed to make him semi-erect. Just enough for his penis to push its way out of the top of his open jeans.

He really should have put on boxers or something, Scotty thought, and then sucked in a startled breath when Beth leaned forward and exhaled, her breath brushing lightly over the sensitive tip. His cock didn't suddenly stand up and do the samba, but it did grow a little firmer as another shaft of pleasure slithered through the pain that had been embracing him. It was like a sliver of light in the darkness, and rather than protest this time, Scotty stilled and closed his eyes, focusing all his attention on that one beam of light.

"May I?" Beth asked, and Scotty's eyes popped open at the question to see that her hand was hovering over him, ready to touch him, and despite his earlier protest, he was actually disappointed she'd asked. Because now he had to say aye or nay, and the truth was he wanted her to touch him. He hadn't just been fighting her. He was fighting himself. He wanted her to do it. Not that he'd started out in any kind of mood for sex, and truthfully, he wasn't even quite there yet, though he was certainly interested, but the idea of escaping the pain he was in through the blessed sleep that followed life mate sex was a very attractive one.

However, Scotty could hear Magnus's voice in his head telling him to leave her alone if he couldn't claim her. Otherwise he would be using her . . . like all the other men in her life.

Scotty battled with his conscience briefly, but with every moment the pain those brief shots of pleasure had displaced returned, and he growled, "Aye."

Beth eased his jeans further open, and then took him in hand. Scotty leaned his head back with a sigh of relief as his body responded, the pleasure once again slipping through and chasing away the pain somewhat.

She gave him only two gentle strokes before he heard her moan. The sound made him open his eyes to look down at her. Beth's body was as rigid as stone, her face twisted in agony as she worked.

For a moment, Scotty was confused, and then it occurred to him that during life mate sex, the mates shared their pleasure. It was what made it so overwhelming. He now suspected whatever channel it was that opened up between the couple to allow that must also allow other sensations they were experiencing to be shared. Pain, for instance. Beth was feeling his pain, and while the pleasure she was giving him was helping to mitigate his pain, it was still pretty strong, and she was being hit with it.

Scotty half rose up then, reaching for her, determined to make her stop. But she caught his hands gently with her own, and determinedly closed her mouth over his semi-erect member. The action made him freeze, his head going back as a much stronger, sharper shaft of pleasure raced through him, replacing a good portion of his pain. It was as if his brain couldn't handle the conflicting messages being sent to it, and was choosing the pleasure.

Thank God, Scotty thought as her mouth continued to slide firmly up and down, driving away the pain that had been attacking him. When the last of it had gone and he was experiencing only pleasure, Scotty opened his eyes and watched her work. She no longer seemed to be experiencing pain either, he noted, and was touched that she would have borne it for him. Most women would have moved as far away from him as they could to avoid that kind of agony, he was sure. Instead, she'd taken it to ease his burden.

Scotty slid the mangled fingers of one hand across the short hairs of her scalp, surprised to find them as soft as a puppy's fur. And then he reached for her breast with his other hand and began to fondle her as she worked, gratified to find the pleasure between them increase. But finally, he closed his eyes and just enjoyed what she was doing as they both climbed toward that darkness that would take him away from the pain without stopping his healing.

"You cannot go," Magnus said firmly. "You are to stay here until we sort out who is trying to kill you."

"But I need clothes," Beth protested, glancing between Magnus and Mortimer determinedly.

"There are clothes here in the stockroom," Mortimer pointed out. "We keep them here for just such an occasion."

"I want *my* clothes," she argued. "And my toothbrush, and my—"

"You cannot always get what you want," Magnus said unsympathetically.

"Rolling Stones fan, huh?" Beth asked dryly, and realized he hadn't been purposely misquoting the song only when he peered at her blankly. Sighing, she said, "Never mind. Look, I'm going a little stir-crazy here, guys. I need to get out of the house. But I also really do want to wear my own clothes. I'm not comfortable taking from the stockroom here. Not when I have my own clothes just a short drive away." Beth hesitated briefly, but then added, "And I wouldn't mind some takeout either. No offense to Sam, but I'm a meat eater. I'm not keen on kale salad and vegetable soup."

"I hear you on that one," Mortimer said dryly.

Sam was on a health food kick at the moment, and forcing the rest of them along with her on the journey.

"I swear I'm going to ban magazines from the house if she keeps trying every new trend that comes out," he added grimly, then glanced to Magnus and said, "Take her to her apartment and let her get some clothes, and then pick up some takeout on the way back . . . for all of us," he said heavily and then added, "Well, all of us meat eaters."

"Do I need a jacket?" Beth asked Mortimer.

"Not today. It's nice out," he answered.

Nodding, Beth turned to lead the way out of the office.

"Scotty is not going to like this," Magnus said in warning as he followed.

"Scotty won't know. He is sleeping," Beth assured him. "The first pain-free sleep he's had in days now that the worst of the healing is done."

Beth had "put Scotty to sleep" several times since the day they'd woken up after the fire. And while at first the start of each time had been terribly painful, she'd kept at it because it had worked, and had ended with the sought-for results . . . the unconsciousness that followed release. Well, not that she hadn't felt the pleasure too and passed out. Beth might not have enjoyed the start of the first few sessions, but she had the end . . . too much. The last two days had been spent completely in bed with him. Scotty had slept for hours after that first time she'd tried to ease his pain and lull him into the unconsciousness that followed life mate sex. He'd done the same after the second, and had healed a good deal during those first two rests. By her third effort, she had noticed that his pain wasn't nearly as bad, and the whole exercise was much more pleasurable for both from the beginning.

By the fourth time, his face had cleared up enough that he could kiss her, and Scotty had been the one to initiate the life mate sex. He'd also initiated the fifth and sixth time, stirring her awake with passionate kisses and caressing hands. Beth had woken first the seventh time, though, and noting that his expression in sleep was relaxed and pain-free, but that he was terribly pale, she'd realized they'd been neglecting food and blood. Scotty needed both to finish healing, so she'd snuck below and fetched cheese and crackers—the only things non-vegetable in the house.

Beth had taken her booty back to the room to wake Scotty with an offering of that and the blood she fetched from the refrigerator in their room. They'd spent the day eating, chatting, laughing, and making love.

Beth had woken up first again this last time, and she'd rolled over and just stared at Scotty for the longest time . . . until she'd realized she had a goofy smile on her face and was thinking a bunch of ridiculous things about what they should do today, tomorrow, next week. She was falling for the bastard, Beth had realized with alarm. She was falling for him and planning a future with the man when she didn't even know if there *was* a future for her with him. Certainly he hadn't said anything to suggest there was.

Stunned at how stupid she was turning out to be in the romance department, Beth had slid from bed. After quickly throwing on the clothes Sam had left on the chair for her, she'd come below to find Magnus and Mortimer in the office and demanded she be allowed to leave the house for a bit. And—thank God—they were going to allow it. Or, Mortimer was going to allow it and Magnus was reluctantly going along with it, Beth thought as she followed him out the back door.

They walked to the garage in silence, and then Beth led the way in when Magnus opened the door for her. She nearly crashed into Odilia and Rickart.

"Sorry," she said, jerking back to avoid the collision, and stomped on Magnus's foot and bumped into his chest instead.

There was a moment when they all laughed, and then Rickart said, "It is good to see you up, Beth. How is Scotty doing?"

"Much better. He'll probably be up and about in another hour or so himself," she assured him, and then turned to offer a tentative smile to Odilia and said, "Thank you for the flowers. That was very kind of you."

Looking embarrassed, Odilia shrugged. "I thought it might brighten up the room a bit and give you something to look at other than four walls."

Beth smiled. "Well, thank you. They are beautiful."

"So?" Rickart glanced from her to Magnus. "What are you two doing?"

"Beth wants clothes from her apartment and takeout," Magnus said dryly. "So I am driving her."

"Is that—I mean, should she—Would it not be better—"

"Mortimer okayed it," Magnus said, ending Rickart's struggle. "In fact, he suggested I bring some takeout for everyone. Any requests?"

"Not for me," Odilia said at once, slipping past them. "I am just off shift and ready for a nice soak and some sleep. But thank you," she added, stepping outside and heading for the cars parked in front of the garage.

"Rickart?" Magnus asked.

Beth glanced to the other Enforcer with surprise. She'd thought him older, like Magnus and Scotty, but if he ate, he couldn't be, she thought as he hesitated.

"I will accompany you and think on the way," he said finally. "In fact, we can take my car."

"Good man," Magnus murmured and followed him outside, ushering Beth with a hand at her back.

"Nice car. Not sure about the color, but I like the shape," Beth said as he led them to a mustard-yellow Mustang.

"I was going to rent one in lightning blue, but didn't want Odilia to think I was copying her," Rickart said, speaking with exaggerated volume. Presumably so Odilia could hear.

"Ha ha! Just get it over with and admit you are colorblind," Odilia taunted him through the open window of the next car over.

Beth smiled as she looked over the metallic-blue Mercedes sedan the woman was starting, and said, "I think I like hers better."

"Oh, Dear God, you are breaking my heart," Rickart exclaimed, opening the front passenger door for her. "This is a *Mustang*. There is no better car than this."

"If you say so," she said, settling into the passenger seat. Rickart closed the door for her, and Beth waved out the window when Odilia honked and pulled away. But they were soon following her down the driveway.

Beth sat silent and patient as they headed out of the gates and turned onto the road. She even managed to keep her mouth shut for the first ten minutes of the drive, but finally she couldn't stand it anymore and said, "I notice you seem to know where I live."

Rickart jerked his head toward her and then glanced to Magnus in the back seat before facing forward again and muttering something unintelligible.

"I'm sorry. I didn't catch that," Beth said lightly. "Was that, 'Why yes, Beth, we all know, thanks to Magnus following you around like a dog for the last century, spying on you?'"

Rickart turned to her sharply, his jaw hanging open until Magnus said mildly, "Watch the road, Rickart."

There was silence for a moment after Rickart turned his attention back to traffic, and then Magnus cleared his throat and asked, "Scotty told you?"

"No. Matias read it from his mind," Beth said grimly, crossing her arms over her chest and peering out at the passing cars.

"He asked me to do that only to keep you safe," Magnus said quietly.

"I don't know why. He doesn't seem to want me for his life mate," she snapped, and then couldn't resist asking, "Does he?"

Even Beth winced at the pitifully hopeful tone to

her voice. Cripes, she was turning into one of those pathetic women who chased after men they knew ultimately didn't want them.

"He is struggling," Magnus said solemnly after a moment. Which meant no, he didn't want her, Beth translated.

"Why? With what?" she asked urgently, finally turning in her seat to look at him.

Magnus hesitated and then shook his head apologetically. "I cannot tell you that. You will have to find out for yourself. But I would advise you to get him to talk about his mother."

"His mother," Beth muttered, and flopped back around in her seat. "It always comes down to the mother, doesn't it?"

"Except when it comes down to the father," he said with amusement, and Beth grimaced. She'd had her own daddy issues. No doubt Magnus was reminding her of that. But she'd sorted through those. It'd taken a hundred years, but she'd done it. It seemed, however, if she was understanding Magnus right, that after eight hundred years, Scotty still had mommy issues. Great!

"Here we are," Rickart announced moments later as he pulled into the parking lot of her apartment building. "Do you want me to stay with the car? Or come up with you guys?"

Magnus didn't hesitate. "Accompany us in case there is trouble."

Beth didn't comment. She didn't really think Rickart was needed, but there was no reason to make him wait in the car like some chauffeur either.

There was something about having two six-foot-plus men on either side of you that made an elevator slightly claustrophobic, Beth decided as she watched the floor numbers light up on the panel over the door. This time there was no bratty kid pushing all the buttons, or even anyone else on the elevator needing to get off to slow them down. They reached her floor relatively quickly and Beth led them to her door. But when she went to put her key in, Magnus covered her hand.

"Allow me," he said and took over opening the door.

Beth rolled her eyes with irritation at being treated like a damsel in distress, but stepped back and left him to it.

The apartment didn't blow up when the door opened, but Magnus made her wait in the hall with Rickart while he checked the interior. Presumably for intruders or traps. She didn't ask. Beth was too busy resenting the fact that she was being treated like some mortal civilian. She could've checked for traps and intruders too, or at least helped him do it. She was a Rogue Hunter too.

"All clear," Magnus announced when he finally returned to the door.

"Thank you," Beth said dryly, and entered her temporary home.

"Nice place," Rickart commented as he followed.

"It's a sublet," she told him, heading into the kitchen to grab a bag of blood. She should have had one when she'd woken up but had been too eager to get out of the bedroom before Scotty woke to bother. "I took it until the start of fall. Hopefully by then Dree and the others will be back, and I'll have a better idea where I'll be stationed."

"You do not think you will continue to work here?" Magnus asked with curiosity.

"I don't know," Beth admitted. "Dree and Harper have a place here in Toronto, but they spend a lot of time in some little town further south, Port something or other." She shrugged. "We'll see."

Taking the bag with her, she moved out of the kitchen and started across the living room toward the bedroom, saying, "There's juice and blood in the fridge. The TV remote's on the table. Make yourselves at home. I shouldn't be long."

Once in the bedroom, Beth popped the blood to her fangs and then walked to the closet to survey her choices. That was when she realized she might take a little longer than she'd expected. She really had no idea what to pack. How long was she going to be stuck at the Enforcer house? What was she likely to need while there? Was there a possibility she'd go out for dinner or something—say, on a date? And what would look most attractive to Scotty?

Yeah, that last question told her just how deep she'd got into things. Beth had never worried about what a date would want to see her in before. She'd always dressed for herself. She was definitely starting to care a little too much for Laird Cullen "Scotty" MacDonald. And likely to get her heart broken unless she could figure out what his issue was with his mother and how that might stop him from claiming her.

Beth had originally thought his issue must have something to do with her profession as a mortal. A lot of people would have trouble with taking on a life mate who used to be a prostitute. But she couldn't imagine that Lady MacDonald had been a prostitute.

Sighing, Beth pulled the empty bag from her fangs and tossed it on the dresser for now. She then dragged out her overnight bags, only to turn around and put them back and retrieve a suitcase instead. Who knew how long it was going to take to sort out this business of someone trying to kill her? She might need clothes for a good long stay. Aside from that, she planned to pack for any eventuality.

"What?" Scotty stared at Mortimer blankly.

"I said Magnus took her to her apartment to collect some clothes," Mortimer repeated patiently.

Scotty shook his head, hardly able to believe what he was hearing. He'd woken up just moments ago, rolled over to reach for Beth, found the bed empty for the first time in two days and had a small panic attack. Honestly, Scotty had freaked out and pretty much dressed on the way downstairs to search for her, pulling his jeans on as he hopped to the bedroom door, and then donning his shirt as he hurried to the stairs. He'd managed to get it only half-buttoned by the time he'd hit the main floor, and had finished the job as he'd walked through the house, looking in each room. Not only had he not found Beth, but he hadn't seen anyone in the house at all until he found Mortimer and Donny in Mortimer's office.

"But she's no' supposed to leave the house," Scotty said finally.

"Beth was suffering a bit of cabin fever, and she wanted her clothes. She has Magnus with her," Mortimer said reassuringly.

"And Rickart," Donny added, and when Mortimer glanced at him in question, the younger man explained, "I saw them getting into Rickart's car with him as I pulled into the garage."

"There, you see?" Mortimer said, turning back to Scotty. "She will be fine."

"How long ago did they leave?" he asked at once.

"I am not sure," the head of the Enforcers admitted, glancing at his watch and then looking at Donny in question as he guessed, "An hour ago?"

"Closer to two," the younger immortal corrected him.

"Hmm, time flies when you are chasing after a bunch of cowboy Enforcers hunting rogues," he said dryly. Mortimer then glanced to Scotty and said, "They have probably already been to whatever fast food restaurant they chose in the end, so it's probably too late to put in an order, but I can call them and see, if you like?"

"Call them," Scotty said grimly. He was less concerned about placing an order for takeout than assuring himself that Beth was safe and on her way back to him. He couldn't wait to have her in his arms again, but not just in his arms. He wanted, *needed*, her in his life. Being with Beth was like nothing he'd ever experienced. The sex was mind-blowing, of course, but it wasn't just that. They'd also talked and laughed and just enjoyed each other's company these last few days, and he'd found they had a lot in common. They had many of the same likes, the same opinions on various subjects and even the same morals, which had been shocking to Scotty. He'd been painting her a scarlet woman all these years because of one part of her life, but Beth was so much more than the one-dimensional woman he'd been viewing her as. These last few days had added many colors to his vision of her. Hell, the time he'd spent with her since arriving in Canada had done that. Beth was a rainbow, a beautiful kaleidoscope of colors and shapes, and endlessly fascinating. Scotty felt a lightness of spirit when with her that he hadn't experienced since being turned. He'd felt as if a heavy weight had been lifted from his chest. He'd felt like he was no longer alone. Beth completed him.

Her past be damned, he thought grimly. There was no way to alter that. It was already written. He was the one who had to change if he wanted to hold on to the happiness he experienced with her. And he wanted that more than anything in this world. Scotty had come to that realization as he'd watched her sleep this morning, and before drifting off himself, he'd determined to tell her so when they woke up. He'd planned to tell her he was sorry for being such an ass, that she was a goddess among women and that without her he was nothing. He'd planned to beg her to forgive his stupidity, and to promise that if she'd only agree to be his life mate, he'd spend a lifetime making it up to her. Many lifetimes. Eternity, if they were allowed that.

But Scotty had never got the chance to tell Beth all of that and beg her forgiveness. He'd woken up to find the bed next to him empty, and had immediately had a terrible feeling he'd lost his chance, that something was wrong and he would never be able to claim the woman who possessed his heart.

The sound of ringing filled the room, and Scotty's attention shifted to Mortimer. The man had put the call on speakerphone, he realized as the sound stopped mid-ring and a deep voice announced, "This is Magnus. Is there a problem, Mortimer?"

"No, no," the head of the Enforcers said quickly, and then added, "Scotty's up."

"Ah," Magnus said in his wise voice.

"Yeah," Mortimer said dryly. "So, I think he wanted to be included in the takeout order, but you are probably almost home. Right?"

"Actually, we are still at Beth's place," Magnus said almost apologetically. "It took her longer to pack than expected. But we are just walking out to the car now. A quick stop for takeout and we will return."

Moving to the desk, Scotty leaned toward the phone and barked, "Do no' stop for takeout. Come straight back. Donny can go get takeout after ye return."

"We are only going to stop at the drive-through on our way back, Scotty," Magnus said in his patient voice. "It will be perfectly safe. I—"

"Come straight back," Scotty repeated sharply.

"Just a minute," Magnus said and must have placed the phone against his chest or covered it with his hand, because all they heard was a muffled, unintelligible conversation and some rustling.

Then Beth's voice, clear but distant, snapped, "Give me the phone. Just give me the phone."

Eyebrows rising, Scotty straightened and waited. He didn't have long to wait.

"Hey!" Her voice came sharp over the speaker. "Listen here, Cullen MacDonald! You aren't my boss, and you haven't claimed me as your life mate, so you have no right to order me about. I can go for damned takeout if I want."

Scotty's eyebrows rose at her agitation. Beth had mostly been calm and even-tempered since he'd arrived in Canada. Well, other than the fight they'd had in Vancouver. But now she sounded more like the old Beth, angry and hurting. Something had obviously stirred her up, and he feared it probably had to do with him. He really should have woken her up and told her everything this morning, rather than wait until they'd both slept. Since he hadn't said anything, Beth had no doubt concluded that nothing had changed and he was still a stupid ass unable to get over his hang-ups and claim her as he should.

"In fact," Beth continued sharply, "I can stay here if I want, and maybe I just will since you're being such a bossy bast—"

A loud explosion cut off her words, and then the line went dead.

Horror clutching at him, Scotty whirled toward the door. "Donny—!"

"I'm getting the SUV," the younger man assured him as he rushed out of the room.

Scotty followed quickly.

Fourteen

Beth opened her eyes, turned her head to the right on the pillow, peered at the pale yellow wall across from her and then closed her eyes on a sigh as she recalled the last time she'd woken up. She'd been groggy and in pain then. Scotty had been holding her in his arms, his expression one of deep concern and caring, and then Rachel had appeared and said something that she hadn't been able to understand. She'd then passed out again.

This time Beth wasn't in pain, but she was angry. She was sick to death of pain, of the attacks and of Scotty's shilly-shallying. First he was mean to her and then sweet, and then he was banging her like a bass drum, but she wasn't good enough to claim? Oh, and the best part—he still thought he could boss her around like he had claimed her when he hadn't. Not that she'd let him boss her around had he claimed her, but—

"How do ye feel?"

Opening her eyes again, Beth turned her head the other way to find Scotty seated in a chair next to the bed. There was no sign of the laughing lover, or even the concern she'd thought she'd seen earlier. He was leaning back as far as he could possibly get from her and had his distant face on . . . which annoyed the hell out of her. "I feel like I got run over by a semi."

"No, ye don't," he countered, unperturbed. "Ye're mostly healed now. Rachel refused to take the tranquilizer IV off until ye were."

"If you knew that, then why'd you bother asking?" she muttered and then raised an eyebrow in question. "What happened?"

Beth had no idea what had landed her back in bed. The last thing she remembered was bawling out Scotty on Magnus's phone, and then *pow*! A semi had hit her from behind. Or that's how it had felt.

Running a weary hand over the short hairs growing from his now healed skull, Scotty grimaced. "While he waited for you to get off the phone, Rickart decided to use his remote to start the car. The Mustang blew up."

"He has a remote to start the car?" Beth asked skeptically.

"Is that all ye have to say?" he asked with disbelief.

"No," she assured him, eyes narrowing. "I also want to ask, how do I get one? It would come in handy on cold days."

Cursing, Scotty shot to his feet and paced the length of the bed and back. "Ye could have been killed, Beth. Ye got lucky. Again! Ye were no' supposed to leave the house. We agreed—"

"*You decided*," she interrupted, suddenly calm now that he wasn't. Smiling, she continued, "I agreed to nothing. And really, all your stomping about and bellowing is only convincing me you maybe need some anger management training or something."

Scotty's eyes widened even as his mouth tightened, and for a minute Beth felt sure he was going to explode, but then he dropped to sit in the chair again and merely glowered at her, so she asked, "How are Magnus and Rickart?"

"Up and about and back to their normal selves," he answered shortly. "Ye were standing between Magnus and the car and shielded him with your body, and Rickart always was a fast healer."

"Lucky for them," she said mildly, and then asked, "The explosion wasn't a malfunction of the remote or something?"

"It was a bomb," Scotty said heavily. "It was rigged to explode when the car started. The person who rigged it obviously didn't know about the remote. Or maybe they were hoping he wouldn't use it. Who knows?"

"So it must have been set at the apartment building while I was packing," Beth said thoughtfully. "I think there are security cameras in the parking lot. I know there are in the parking garage."

"Fake," he said succinctly. "Both in the parking lot and garage."

"Seriously?" Beth asked with shock.

Scotty nodded. "They're only there to scare off potential criminals, not to record them. They're empty casings."

"Damn. Then there's no way to know who was behind the attack. Again," she added grimly. Beth scowled over that briefly, and then sighed and said,

"Well, if nothing else, this had told me that if I stay in Toronto, I should move to a new building. One with real cameras."

"What do ye mean, if ye stay?" he asked sharply. "I thought ye'd moved here to be close to Drina."

"Yes, but she spends most of her time in a little town south of here. It's supposed to be quite nice. Small town, everyone knows everyone, people can't follow you around and spy on you without someone taking notice," Beth added dryly.

Scotty scowled.

"On the other hand," she continued, "Toronto has its charms. Lots of nightclubs, even immortal clubs, and so many more people. I think I read somewhere that the Greater Toronto Area has more than six million people. That's three million men to play with, which is important to a single girl like me," she added sweetly.

Scotty's face went expressionless.

"And then there's the business I'm thinking of starting," Beth added.

"Business?" he asked with surprise.

"Hmm." Beth nodded. "I was thinking we should have a matchmaking service for immortals. I hear Drina's Aunt Marguerite is very good at recognizing possible life mates for immortals. So all that really needs to be done is to set up parties in different cities for all those interested in finding their mate, have Marguerite attend and meet everyone, and then she can tell us who are potential matches for whom. It might even turn out that some of us have more than one possible life mate. Wouldn't that be nice?"

"Nay, it wouldn't," Scotty snapped, standing up to pace again.

Beth raised her eyebrows as she watched him, and then sat up in bed. "Why not? You don't want me. Isn't it better if we find me someone else and find you someone more to your liking?"

Scotty frowned and turned to stare blindly out the window of her room. He didn't want someone else. He wanted Beth. But arriving at her apartment building to find her broken and bleeding from the blast had nearly killed him. He'd almost lost her again, and she was suffering *again*. He couldn't bear to see her in such pain. Scotty had sat here watching her sleep as she healed, and all he could think was that he wanted to take it all away for her, all the hurts of the past that he hadn't been there to spare her from, including this latest attack.

He knew it might mean losing Beth. That taking away her past might alter her to the point where he might no longer be a possible life mate for her and he would lose all that he'd just found. After all, she wouldn't remember him. He would remember her, though, and Scotty was quite sure he would love her to his dying breath no matter what. That he would spend the rest of his life alone and miserable, looking out for and yearning after a woman who saw him as a stranger. But he was willing to suffer that for her, to give her a chance for a life free of all the pain and misery she'd been dealt and so didn't deserve.

Turning abruptly, he asked, "Have ye ever really considered what it would mean to have yer memories erased?"

Beth reacted as if he'd hit her, her head going back and her expression going blank with shock. Finally she asked with disbelief, "What?"

"A three-on-one mind wipe could remove all the horrors o' yer life to date," he said, trying for reason. "Would ye no' like that?"

Beth shook her head and closed her eyes. "I can't believe this."

"What?" Scotty asked warily.

She opened her eyes and peered at him sadly for a moment, and then said, "You suggested that the night you saved Dree and me from Jamieson."

Scotty blinked in surprise at the change of subject.

"You dragged her away to talk, and I knew you wanted to talk to her in private, but she'd left her shawl and it was cold and . . ." Beth paused briefly and then cleared her throat and admitted, "And after what had happened I was terrified at being alone, so I used the shawl as an excuse to join you both. I headed toward the pair of you, but I could hear you arguing as I approached and stopped to listen."

Beth glanced down at her hands as she continued. "You were saying you should be reporting our presence at the house to the Council, that I was obviously mad and they'd want me executed rather than set loose on the world. You said at the very least I should be wiped using a three-on-one."

Scotty stiffened. Was there anything she didn't know?

"But," Beth continued solemnly, "Dree wouldn't let you. She said she'd take responsibility for me, that she was taking me back to Spain with her that very night, and if you tried to stop her, it would have to be at sword point. She'd not go quietly. She'd drag her brother and uncle into it and start a war if needs must, but she wasn't letting you touch me."

"I did no' ken ye heard that," Scotty said when she fell silent, and then added gently, "But ye were half-mad that night, lass. Perhaps wholly mad. The Council would ha'e insisted on putting ye down, and I thought if they wiped yer mind o' all the bad memories . . . I thought ye'd be better off without all the horrors that haunted ye."

"But it wasn't just the horrors that would've been removed, was it?" Beth asked softly, lifting her head to look at him again. "If you erased my memories all the way back to when I was ten, it could've removed my personality as well."

"When ye were ten?" he asked with confusion.

"Did you think the bad memories started with Jamieson?" she asked dryly. "He was just the first *immortal* monster in my life. There were many *mortal* ones before him."

Scotty frowned. The night he'd met Beth, he'd thought his inability to read her was due to madness brought on by the traumas she'd suffered under Jamieson. After what he'd seen inside the charnel house they'd saved her and Drina from, that had seemed the most likely explanation. It wasn't until Drina and Beth had already set sail for Spain that he'd realized his hunger for food was reawakening . . . and that his mind was suddenly easily read. Two sure signs that an older immortal had met their life mate.

Unfortunately, Scotty hadn't connected it with Beth. Mostly because he hadn't felt any sexual desire for her. He realized now that the situation and the bloody mess she and Drina had been at the time, literally, had not been conducive to sexual desire. Aside from that, they hadn't made physical contact of any kind. But he hadn't considered that then, and Scotty had looked closer to home for the life mate he knew he had recently encountered.

It wasn't until months later that Scotty had realized she was the one. He got news that Drina considered Beth recovered from her trauma and ready to train as a hunter. For some reason he even now didn't understand, he'd traveled to Spain to warn the Spanish Council that the woman was mad and shouldn't be allowed to train. And that was the only reason he'd realized the error he'd made.

It was the first night he slept on Spanish soil. He was staying at Drina's brother's home, and Drina and Beth had been in attendance, visiting before they left for training. He'd arrived late, just a couple of hours before dawn, but the Council had been waiting there for him, and he'd spent those hours before daybreak closeted with them, trying to convince them not to allow the woman to train. He hadn't fought that hard, though. Drina's brother had insisted Beth was sane and couldn't be judged on her reaction to one traumatic night, and it wasn't really his problem anyway. He'd already been questioning why he'd come all that way. If the woman was mad as he suspected, it would be the Spanish Council's problem. He had given them his assessment and that was all he could do.

It was dawn when the meeting ended and Scotty was shown to his room. He'd retired at once, but rather than restful sleep, when he lay down his night had been filled with erotic dreams full of a beautiful redheaded stranger. Scotty hadn't known they were shared dreams until he woke up and went in search of his host to thank him for his hospitality before leaving. He'd spotted Beth hurrying for the front door as he came down the stairs, and recognizing her from his dreams, had frozen halfway down. It was when she'd opened the front door and he'd heard Drina call out, "Hurry up, Beth. We will be late," that he realized who she was. Scotty had then stood there for several minutes in shock, unable to believe that she was the bedraggled and blood-covered madwoman he'd rescued.

When Drina's brother Stephano had found him there on the stairs moments later, Scotty had begun asking questions about Beth. That was when he'd learned that she'd been a prostitute before she was turned, that Drina had been her pimp, and that she was angry and bitter and still dealing with the horrors of her past, but Stephano hoped her working as an Enforcer would help her heal.

Scotty had been in a state of confusion when he left Spain, his thoughts and feelings torn in all different directions. He'd felt shock that she was his life mate, not someone in England, as he'd first assumed. He'd felt concern for her well-being, a desire for her to heal from the horrors of her past and, yes, even discomfort at her chosen career as a mortal. But Scotty had buried that discomfort under his other concerns for her, and had tracked her progress in training, and then as a hunter. He'd also sent Magnus to watch over her, and had interfered as he saw fit, trying to keep her safe.

When Magnus had questioned his actions, Scotty had admitted that she was a possible mate and had told him that he felt she needed to heal from her past before he could claim her. And he had actually believed that to some degree. At least, he had hoped it was true. Beth back then had been hard, angry and lashing out at the world, and he'd thought perhaps with time she could heal, and with time he could learn to accept her past. Unfortunately, rather than admit to his issues with her past and deal with them, he'd pushed them under and focused only on *her* struggles.

Sighing, he sat down and met her gaze. "Why would your memories have to be erased all the way back to the age of ten?"

Now it was Beth's turn to frown, and then she lowered her head and peered at her hands.

When she didn't speak, Scotty said, "I heard ye telling Rachel about yer childhood. About yer mother and sisters and the market and yer father being a drunk with a temper. Ye stopped when yer mother and Ruthie died when ye were ten. What happened next?"

Beth was silent so long, Scotty began to think she wouldn't answer his questions. But just when he was about to ask her again, she raised her head and spoke.

"When I was telling Rachel about it, I said that I sold all my pies the first time out at market after my mom died," she said quietly, and he couldn't help noticing that her accent had thickened again. Whatever she was about to reveal was emotional for her, he deduced.

"And that was true," Beth assured him earnestly, and then kept her head up but dropped her eyes as she continued, "But what I didn't say was that I didn't take home the coin I made." Her mouth twisted bitterly. "I was far too clever for that, or at least I thought so, certainly smarter than my mother. I determined that, unlike her, I wasn't going to let father get the money that he'd always beaten off my mother. I wouldn't let him drink all my hard work away. So, as the day passed, I paid some of the money to those we owed and bought the supplies for the next day on my way home. And then I tucked what little was left in one of Ruthie's old stockings and put it in a hiding place I had. Behind a brick in the wall, that I'd worked loose years ago," Beth explained before lowering her head again.

"I thought it was ever so clever," she repeated sadly, and then sighed and admitted, "I soon found out not. My father explained it to me. Mother too had paid bills through the day, and bought her supplies along the way home, but she'd always made sure to keep a couple coins behind for him. Just enough for him to have his tipple, and she let him slap her a time or two ere she gave it up, so he'd think that was all there was. He knew it wasn't, but didn't mind so long as he had what he needed."

Beth shifted on the bed so she could rest against the short headboard and then leaned her head back over the top of it and stared at the ceiling as she said, "The first time I came home with no money at all, he beat me something fierce. I couldn't walk let alone work for near a week."

Scotty clenched his hands at the thought of a grown man beating a young Beth so severely, but he kept his mouth shut.

"But the second time I came home without coin he merely said, 'You'll be sorry. You'll see.'" Raising her head again, she said sadly, "But I didn't see, because nothing happened until the third time I stubbornly hid the money and came home with none. That day he said, 'Now you'll see,' and then he grabbed my arm and he dragged me out of the house. He dragged me for blocks and blocks, into the worst part of the city. A part where Mother always said good girls didn't go. The house he took me to was quite nice compared to most of the others, and I had no idea what was coming until it was all but over and he'd sold me to a brothel owner."

Now it was Scotty's turn to lower his head, and he had to work to hold back the sound building in his aching chest for the ten-year-old innocent she'd been.

"It seems I wasn't so smart after all," she confessed dryly. "You see, when he didn't beat me the second time, I thought he was giving up. That all Mother had had to do was refuse him once, take one horrible beating, and he'd stop trying. But the truth was he hadn't beaten me the second time because he'd already decided what he was going to do, and he knew the brothel owner wouldn't pay much for me all black and blue and bruised."

Scotty raised his head in time to see her quickly wipe a single tear from her cheek, and then she cleared her throat and continued, "As it was, the bruises from the first beating hadn't completely faded yet, so she didn't pay as much as he'd hoped, but it was still quite a penny. More coin than I'd ever even imagined seeing."

Turning her head, she peered at him and said dryly, "It seems young girls under twelve, even common girls like me, were valued for our virginity. Lords and fine lairds would pay a high price for a young, untried girl. So the brothel owners bought us from greedy parents or other relatives to auction off to the highest bidder."

Returning her gaze to the ceiling, she shrugged. "As I say, though, they only paid my father mildly well. I still had some fading bruises, which meant they would have to wait for those to heal, feeding and clothing me the whole while before they could auction me off. Da wasn't pleased by that, but there was naught he could do.

"So for a week I was locked in a room, fed and bathed and taken care of until the day of the auction. That was scary," she admitted. "The first part wasn't so bad. I was bathed and perfumed, my hair washed and dried and brushed to a fine sheen, but then I was put in a white gown and paraded in front of a room full of what to me seemed like scary old men. The way they looked at me . . ."

Beth shuddered and Scotty had to swallow the bile in his throat.

"But then they told me to strip," she announced in a quiet voice. "I refused, of course, and struggled when they tried to forcibly remove the gown. In the end, it basically had to be torn from my body, and I was left to shiver and weep in front of those hungry-eyed men as they bid on me. After that I was rushed off by two of the brothel owner's women, force-fed a horrid-tasting drink and placed in a bed.

"The whole while the women were telling me how lucky I was that the man who'd bought me was kind and didn't wish a struggle or to have me screaming so was having me drugged instead. They said, 'A good many of them fine gentlemen like a fight, and even like to hurt a girl, ye see.' But I didn't see, and I didn't understand what was happening and I don't know what they gave me, but it made me feel all queer and I had little control over myself. I tried to get out of bed when the women left the room. The window of the bedchamber they'd kept me in prior to this one had been boarded up so I couldn't escape, but this one wasn't, and I thought if I could just get to it and climb out . . ."

Beth shook her head. "But I couldn't seem to master my arms and legs enough to even get out of the bed, let alone make the window, and then the 'kind gentleman' was escorted in and there was no escape."

She lowered her head to stare down at her hands as if they were the only thing in the world at that moment, and it made Scotty want to pull her into his lap and hold her until all her pain went away. Part of him wanted to tell her to stop talking, not to tell him any more, but he didn't and simply waited.

"He may have been a kind man, but no man likes to be laughed at," Beth said finally. "And I don't know if it was whatever they'd given me, or maybe hysteria, but when he stripped off his clothes and straightened, I thought him the funniest thing I'd ever seen."

Grimacing, Beth glanced up briefly as she admitted, "I'd never seen a naked man before. The closest was me father in his nightshirt, but even that hid everything except his hairy feet. But this . . ." Beth shook her head and lowered her gaze again.

"He was like a rooster, a sagging chin, narrow shoulders slouching into a big fat belly over short skinny legs, and for some reason, I just started to laugh. And then I couldn't stop, which infuriated him. He wasn't particularly kind or gentle because of it, I suppose, but at least he was quick and left me to cry myself to sleep."

Scotty watched her take a deep breath, and she seemed stronger as she said, "Of course, once I'd been bought and raped, my value dropped considerably. In fact, I was no longer useful to the brothel." Glancing his way, she explained, "This particular establishment only kept the most beautiful women."

"Ye're beautiful," he said almost too softly for her to hear him, but she did.

"Nay. I have red hair," Beth told him as if he might not have noticed.

"Yer hair is beautiful."

"The English don't like red hair," she countered.

"The English are idiots," Scotty growled.

"They also found my freckles unfortunate."

"I love yer freckles."

Ignoring that, Beth said, "I simply didn't measure up. Unfortunately, I also wasn't behaving myself."

Scotty couldn't help noticing she said that with satisfaction.

"Much to their displeasure, I kept trying to escape," she announced with pride, and then grimaced and added, "So I was auctioned off again, this time to a roomful of bullies."

"Dear God," Scotty breathed.

"The winning bidder was a man named Danny Olsen. He had three girls already. I was number four. He broke me in, which translates to he raped me for three days straight, and then he locked me in a room that he only unlocked for customers. I wasn't a very willing girl, ye see, despite his breaking-in. So he sent in the ones who didn't mind the fight in me . . . and for an extra quid they could bruise me as they liked so long as they didn't scar me permanent-like."

Scotty fisted his hands and briefly stopped breathing as rage flowed through him. He was angry, and hurting for her, and feeling so damned helpless because it was too late to change what had happened. Yet she was now telling it all rather emotionlessly, like she was recounting some tale she'd heard. It was as if Beth had separated herself from the events she was describing, and that just made the hearing worse.

"We girls were warned not to run away. Danny said he'd told the children on the streets that he'd pay a quid if they warned him when we ran away and told him where to find us. I was very nice to those children," Beth assured him. "I gave them whatever coin I could manage to squirrel away. The men would tip on occasion, you see. Usually it was the rougher ones. The rougher they were, the more the guilt, and the more likely they were to toss a coin or two extra on me battered body on the way out. I gave every one of those coins to the children on the street. I was hoping that when I tried to run away they would keep their mouths shut." Grimacing, she shrugged. "But it's cold on the street, and those children were always hungry, and in the end, a quid is a quid.

"Every time I ran away, they got a quid and I was dragged back, beaten viciously and locked in the room again. Still, I continued to try. I think I was seventeen when I made my last attempt."

"Seventeen," Scotty breathed with dismay. She'd

been locked in a room, beaten and raped for seven years, he realized with horror, and then blinked and asked, "Ye think?"

"Time began to blur in that room," Beth explained with a shrug. "I'm not sure how old I was that last time I managed to escape. Seventeen is my best guess."

Scotty swallowed again.

"Anyway," she continued, "Danny'd had enough by then. He was tired of hunting me down, tired of the trouble I caused. Besides, by that time he had thirteen of us girls and figured he'd hardly miss one . . . and I would serve as a fine example to the others of what to expect if they caused him too much trouble. So, when he caught me that night, he told me flat-out that he intended to beat me to death and leave my corpse in the alley for the rats to feed on, right where the girls would see me out their windows.

"Fortunately," Beth continued as Scotty buried his face in his hands, "Dree happened along then. She didn't know me, and didn't know Danny intended to kill me, but she saw him beating me and intervened. She tore him off of me like he was little more than a toddler, which infuriated him and probably scared him spitless. Foolishly, he pulled his knife and . . . well, that was a mistake. Dree just grabbed Danny and tossed him away up the alley like he was so much trash. He landed on his own knife and died almost instantly.

"When Dree then scooped me up and asked where to take me, the only place I could think was the brothel where the other girls were. She carried me there." Smiling wryly, she said, "I expect she thought she could just leave me and someone would tend my wounds, allowing her to go about her business. Instead, she found a house full of beaten and broken women, most of whom were younger than even me at that point. None of them knew what to do about my injuries. She had to stay and tend me herself.

"I think the other women shocked her," Beth admitted. "Dree probably thought they'd be grateful to be free of the man. Instead, they were frightened and panicky. They were terrified by the fact that our pimp was gone. Even a bad pimp was better than no pimp to their minds, and they blamed her for his absence. Instead of thanking her, they ran around crying, 'Who will protect us now?'"

Beth paused, pursed her lips and then said, "Except for Mary. Mouthy Mary, Dree used to call her, but affectionate-like," she assured him. "That first night Mary just stood up and announced that, seeing as how Dree had killed our protector, she'd just have to take his place." Beth grinned at the memory and admitted, "Basically the girls guilted Dree into acting as our protector and, by the time I healed enough to get out of bed, everything had changed."

Scotty peered at her curiously, noting that she was more animated now and seemed almost chatty as she said, "Dree at first tried to convince us all to leave the house and return to our families, or find a different line of work. But most of us didn't have families, and I wasn't the only one who had been sold into the business by family members. None of us had an education, or training. We would never be maids or shop girls—none of us knew the first thing about either—so we did the only thing we did know."

Scotty frowned at the realization that she'd stayed a prostitute even once she could have left it.

"But it was better now. No one beat us, not even the customers. Dree wouldn't let them. She lived with us, protected us . . . She even put her money into fixing the house for us. Everything was fine. Well, at first anyway," she muttered, her expression changing to dissatisfaction. "I suppose I knew things were going too well and it couldn't continue."

"What happened?" Scotty asked when she paused and stayed silent for several minutes.

"Oh." Beth glanced to him with surprise, as if she'd been so lost in thought she'd forgotten he was there. Giving her head a shake, she said, "Well, the girls were afraid Dree would leave us. And why not? Nothing was holding her there. She wouldn't take our coin. She wouldn't take payment in trade even from the girls who were willing. There wasn't anything keeping her with us, and none of us understood why she hadn't already just up and left. The girls were scared and started to . . . act up," she said finally.

"Act up?" he asked, now curious.

Beth grimaced. "Getting all catty, and nasty and fighting . . ." She rolled her eyes. "Dear Lord, the fighting!" She shook her head with remembered disgust, and then said, "But then one night, three drunk men attacked one of the girls as she was coming home. Dree was there at once to protect her, of course, but was terribly injured in the doing.

"All of us rushed out when we heard the cry and carted her back inside. We got cloths and water and such and the like, but every minute we were all sure she would die. We had seen the wound she'd taken. It was a wonder to us she'd managed to finish off the attackers before she died, and then a wonder she didn't die before we got her back in the house. But we were all positive she would die there with us . . . only when she didn't and we finally got around to cleaning the wound, it was already healing.

"Uneducated we may have been, but we knew there was something wrong with that. It just plain wasn't normal. We surrounded her and demanded answers. What we didn't know was that she was weak from blood loss and we smelled like mighty fine steak to her at that point. Desperate to get us away from her so that she could go find blood, she told us everything, all about immortals and that she was one."

Beth grinned. "I suspect Dree expected us to all be horrified, consider her a monster now and flee. No doubt she figured that later, after she'd found a blood source and recovered, she'd have to hunt us each down and wipe our memories. But not a one of us ran away, or screamed or even fainted. Instead, we were all oddly relieved."

"Relieved?" Scotty echoed with surprise, and she nodded with amusement.

"Yes. You see, finally here was a way we could repay her. She had taken care of us, and taken nothing in return. But she needed blood to heal, and we could give her that. When Mary asked, Dree admitted she needed to feed on blood regularly and hunted to get it, and again, we could give her that and save her the need to hunt. It could be an exchange instead of us being beholden to her and terrified she might up and leave one day. Dree would continue to keep us safe and we would keep her fed. Everyone was happy,"

Beth said as if it was simple logic. "And so we went for the next nearly twenty-five years."

"Ye were happy selling yerselves?" Scotty asked with a sort of bewilderment. That hardly seemed to fit with a woman who had repeatedly risked being beaten to death to escape.

Beth hesitated, but then blew her breath out and finally said, "No. I mean, it was not the life I expected to lead. As a child I thought I'd be like my mother, grow up, marry and have children," she admitted and Scotty suspected from her expression that it might have been the first time she'd ever admitted that, even to herself.

"But of course," Beth assured him, "I'd marry a good man, not someone like my father. I'd marry someone like our neighbor Mr. Hardy, who was always ever so kind."

"Then why did you not do that once Dree had saved ye from Danny?" he asked with confusion. "Dear God, ye risked being beaten to death to escape, and then simply settled into the life afterward. Why?"

"Because, as you know, no good man would want a whore for a wife."

Fifteen

Beth's words echoed in his brain. *"Because, as you know, no good man would want a whore for a wife."*

She'd sounded neither angry nor sorry for herself. She had said it as a simple statement of fact, and Scotty felt like she'd punched him. After all, it was exactly why he had hesitated to claim her, wasn't it? And they weren't merely two mortals who'd fallen in love. They were life mates with all that encompassed, and yet he had struggled with it. He was such an idiot.

"Yes. I tried to escape over and over," Beth said now. "But I knew I couldn't. I knew he'd drag me back. There was really nowhere for me to go. I think in truth I hoped he'd beat me to death, because I—no, not even just I—all of us felt like we were damaged goods. We were the refuse of society. We had been sold like cattle, abused and treated like trash. We felt sullied, not fit for a respectable life anymore, and everyone around us seemed to agree and made sure we knew it. The family members who sold us, the brothel owners and Danny who peddled us, the men who bought our time and then used and abused us, even the children who spat on us in passing for fun. And then there were the 'good women.' With never once a kind word or smile, they'd move as far to the side as they could in passing, sneering down their noses and gathering their skirts close as if we were diseased and whoredom was catchy."

She smiled sadly. "How could we even imagine that anyone would hire us for a respectable position? Or that a good man like Mr. Hardy would want a woman everyone else despised? Hell, after all of that, it was even hard to believe that Mr. Hardy was as good as he seemed. Perhaps he too beat and choked his wife at night because it was the only way he could perform."

Scotty cursed under his breath, wishing he could find and punish every single man, woman, and child who had made her feel this way. And then he closed his eyes in shame as he realized he was one of them.

"Besides," Beth said more cheerfully, "it did change. Now we could choose whom we accepted as our clients and were free to say no if we wished. And we did. We all worked much less than we had before. Dree somehow managed to have Danny's house put into our names, so we never needed to worry about a roof over our heads. All we needed to concern ourselves with was coin for coal, candles, clothing, and food and such. And without Danny or anyone else taking all our money, we didn't have to work as hard or as often. I myself was able to drop down to just two clients. Two of my regulars, who were kind men I liked, who were generous and who I knew would never hurt me."

"Why two?" Scotty asked carefully. "Why not one?"

"Because both wanted to move me to my own lodgings and take care of me," she admitted quietly.

"And ye didn't want that?" he asked.

"I . . . What if they changed their minds and threw me out?" Beth asked instead of answering directly. "Or what if, once they had me all to themselves, they became cruel and abusive?"

"Ye didn't trust them," Scotty said solemnly, and then added, "And why should ye, when yer own father sold ye into such a business."

Beth nodded solemnly.

"So ye kept two, so that . . ."

"Neither could think they owned me," she said quietly. "But those two were enough. For fifteen years I was basically a mistress to two men, but then one died and the other had a change in fortune, so I started making penny pies and going out to sell them as I had with my mother. I'd learned to make proper pastry by then," she added with a smile. "Mouthy Mary showed me."

"Penny pies in the market," he murmured.

Beth nodded. "That's where I found out that my father was dead. Our neighbor Mrs. Hardy still sold warm peas by the market, and she told me. He died just days after he sold me. He'd taken the money from the brothel owner and drunk himself to death." Her mouth hardened. "I didn't mourn him."

Scotty nodded in understanding, but simply waited. He knew how this story ended, just not all of the particulars.

"Life went on like that for another decade. A couple of the girls saved every penny they made, pooled it together and managed to buy a small pub to run together. Two more married and moved out of the house, and one died of pneumonia, but eventually all of us began to slow down. The girls took in less business, and I went to market less, especially in the winter. And then Dree convinced us to retire. She bought a house on the other side of London in an area where no one knew us and we could introduce ourselves as respectable widows, or simply old spinsters . . . whatever we chose. We could make friends and play gin and do needlepoint and be little old ladies.

"Dree put the house in our name. She said she'd recoup the money for the new house from selling the brothel, but she didn't sell it for years, and I suspect she probably only got half her money back when she finally did. Though, I didn't know it at the time. None of us had any idea how expensive that new house must have been. But we were so pleased with it," she said with a smile. "Charming it was, and beautiful. Dree had it decorated magnificently. She had come to love each and every one of us over the years and spared no expense.

"Once we were settling nicely into our new respectable lives, we suspected she might start to feel at loose ends, so we suggested she take a vacation. Have a nice long visit with her family in Spain, and maybe take a tour of the Continent or the like. It was something she hadn't been able to do while we needed her protection. She had hired a man named Cyrus to help protect us so that she could take short trips here and there over the years, but she'd never been gone for more than a couple days or a week or two before that. We felt she deserved a long vacation. So Dree decided she would go. She'd visit her family in Spain first and then perhaps take a short tour . . . but she wouldn't be gone long, she assured us. She'd come back to check on us soon."

Beth chuckled softly. "Now that I am immortal, I understand that time passes differently. Those decades she spent with us, while the better part of our lives and long in our minds, were not so long to her. But we didn't know that then, and Dree's short tour seemed interminable to us, though it only lasted a little less than two years. She wrote often, about once every week or two, and we wrote back if she said she would be somewhere for more than a couple of weeks. Anything shorter and she would be gone before our letters arrived," Beth explained.

Scotty nodded, but asked with curiosity, "In all the time ye'd known her, had none o' ye ever thought ye'd like to be immortal yerselves?"

"Oh nay," Beth said at once, and then frowned and considered it for a moment more before admitting, "Well, mayhap. On those mornings when I woke up sore and achy with age, or when I noticed I just wasn't as strong as I used to be and it wasn't as easy to lift that bucket of water, or cart those logs to the fireplace. And sure, once or twice when I caught a glimpse of myself in a mirror on passing and blinked in surprise at the gray hair sprouting and the wrinkles multiplying and then turned to look at Dree who was still as young, strong, and beautiful as the day we met her . . ." She smiled wryly. "Mayhap I considered it for a moment or two then, but the whole drinking blood thing quickly made me shake my head."

"And the others?" he asked.

"Ah." Beth nodded solemnly. "There were several of them who wept at the loss of their youth and looks and would have happily accepted immortality. But there were just as many who didn't want it at all, or only briefly considered it but feared it like me."

"Feared it?" he asked with a frown.

"This was the eighteen hundreds, Scotty," she said dryly. "*Dracula* may not have been out in print yet, but *Dorian Gray* was, and we were a superstitious lot. Nothing so fine as remaining young and healthy forever could be a good thing and without a steep cost."

Scotty smiled faintly at the words and nodded in understanding. He had lived through that era as well.

"Anyway, as I say, nearly two years passed. I know Dree didn't mean to stay away so long. Time flies when you're having fun, as they say, and there was no reason for her to think she had to come back. And although we missed her, we were also feeling guilty for how we'd monopolized her all those years. So in our letters we told her we were having a grand time and she should too. And we were," Beth assured him with a grin. "We enjoyed our new respectable rank. We made friends with the neighbors, had them in to tea and were invited into their homes as well. We did needlepoint, read books, played cards, and made up the most fanciful and tragic tales for each of us as to how we'd ended up widowed and in that house together.

"It was lovely," Beth said with a wistful smile, and then the smile faded, and she added, "Right up until the day Jimmy came."

"Jamieson Sterne," Scotty said solemnly.

"Aye," she murmured. "Apparently he'd seen Mary at the market. He'd considered making a meal of her, but when he slipped into her mind, he saw Dree there." Beth paused and focused her gaze firmly on him. "You must never tell her this, but he said that seeing her there in Mary's head was what made him follow her home rather than just feed. He used to be a privateer, you see, like our Dree, and they'd had something of a rivalry, but our Dree always beat him to the finest plunder. He hated her for always showing him up like that, and the way he saw it, by tormenting and turning us into his lackeys, he'd finally win."

"The turning ye part may have had something to do with Dree, but the tormenting was all him," Scotty said grimly. "He tortured all his victims. 'Tis what set us onto him. He had cut a wide swath of blood and terror through England forty years before."

"Odilia?" Beth asked at once.

Scotty wasn't surprised she'd recognized the similarities in their stories, and nodded grimly. "Jamieson killed her family and several others forty years earlier, and then disappeared. But we knew at once it was him when it started up again. He had slaughtered half a dozen families this time around ere he encountered yer Mary. If anything, finding Dree in Mary's thoughts may have kept him from simply slaughtering ye all outright and not turning ye. It was his habit to pick up on someone and follow them home and slaughter the whole clan in front o' each other, causing the most torment."

"Aye," Beth breathed. "And that's what he did, but without the killing. He just followed Mary in the door and said, 'Good evening, ladies. My name is Jamieson, and I've come for dinner.' And then, quick as a snake-like, he grabbed Mary, dragged her back and tore into her neck."

Beth swallowed, her eyes swimming with the memory. "It was nothing like when Dree fed. Blood squirted everywhere. More splashed on the walls than could have got in his mouth I'm sure, and then he slurped like a child at a Popsicle."

Scotty winced, his jaw tightening as he saw the remembered terror on her face.

"We were all too stunned to move at first. We were a gaggle of old ladies who'd seen and been through a lot, but this was . . ." She shook her head, took a deep breath and continued, "Then he tore open his wrist and pressed it to Mary's mouth for several seconds before dropping her like a rag doll and reaching for the next woman. It was only then that we regained our senses enough to start to move. Some simply made a run for it, some grabbed for anything that could be used as a weapon, but we were all screaming and shrieking and running about. In the end it didn't matter what our choice was, whether to run or fight. He was wicked fast, seemed impervious to our blows, and if anyone got close to the door or a window, he just took control of them. In no time at all, every last one of us was rolling on the floor in our own blood, screaming in agony as the turn began."

"His bleeding you first would have sped up the onset of the turn," Scotty said quietly. "The nanos would have recognized that your systems were in distress, needed urgent repair, and they would have started duplicating rapidly to attend to that."

Beth nodded, but told him, "Things got blurry after

that. All I remember is pain and blood and terrible nightmares. It went on for a really long time. Dree said it goes much more quickly when the turnee is given blood, and we obviously hadn't been given any, which drew out the process." Her mouth flattened briefly, but then relaxed again, and she continued, "When I woke up, I was lying on the parlor floor, covered in dry blood with no idea how I'd got there or what had happened or who the women around me were."

"Ye did no' recognize them?" Scotty asked, thinking that the horror of the mass turning must have been what had twisted her mind and made her mad, for the Beth he'd first met all those years ago had definitely been a madwoman. Her next words made him pause, though.

"No. Well, how could I?" she asked. "I may have lived with them for nigh on thirty years, but it had been a long time since I'd seen them young and healthy . . . Of course I did not recognize them."

"Oh, aye," Scotty said, smiling wryly.

"Except for one," Beth said suddenly, her expression turning sad. "Nelly hadn't survived the turn. She must've had a heart attack early on, because she hadn't changed much."

"I'm sorry," Scotty murmured.

"Yes, well, she may have been the luckier of us," Beth said quietly.

Scotty remained silent. He for one was glad that Beth had survived the turn. And while he'd already determined that her past wasn't important, hearing more of her history had sealed his acceptance of it. It wasn't learning that she'd been sold into the business as a child of ten. Or the fact that she'd tried to escape over and over again despite the beatings and abuse it brought on. What had finally sealed his acceptance was the reason she'd given for why she'd continued after Dree had arrived on the scene. Not because it was easy coin, or because she enjoyed the power of controlling men with her body. She'd continued in the business because she hadn't been able to envision another road for herself. Beth had seen herself as too damaged to be accepted as a wife and mother, or anything but the prostitute she'd been forced to become. She and the other women had all been made to feel that way by people like him, he realized with shame, and vowed never to be so judgmental and holier-than-thou again. All flowers did not have thorns, and all prostitutes were not heartless gold diggers. Elizabeth Sheppard Argenis was nothing like his mother.

Scotty closed his eyes briefly. God, he loved this woman. Unfortunately, everything she'd said had merely made him more determined than ever to convince her to agree to having her memories removed. He hadn't been there to protect her from her father's betrayal, or the years of rape and abuse. True, he had saved both her and Dree from the murderous Jamieson, but he hadn't been able to do so before the man had turned her home into a house of horrors and ensured the deaths of her friends, who were essentially her family. Scotty's heart ached for what Beth had gone through, and he wanted nothing more than to take that pain away for her. A three-on-one mind wipe would do that. It might also change her so that they weren't life mates anymore, as Matias had suggested, but he would risk that, for Beth. She deserved a future free of such horrors.

"Anyway," Beth continued on a sigh, "the others woke up just as confused and terrified as me . . . a state that didn't last long. Jimmy was quick to tell us that now that he'd made us all young and beautiful again, he owned us and we would do his bidding."

"Which was?" Scotty asked when she paused.

"We were to lure mortal men to the house with the promise of sex. But once there, we were to rob them and feed on them until dead," she said grimly. "Of course, none of us was willing to do that, but Mary was—"

"The infamous Mouthy Mary who told Dree she had to protect ye all?" he queried gently.

"Aye, Mouthy Mary," she said with a sad smile. "She was the only one brave enough to stand up to him. She said we'd not do it, and he could go to hell. She would go find Dree, who would fix him real good for what he'd done." Beth released a sigh. "The last word had barely left her mouth before Jamieson had crossed the room and ripped off her head. Quick as that," she added, sounding a bit bewildered. "None of us had ever seen anything like it. And none of us . . ." She shook her head. "In truth, I think we all just kind of shut down. Sank into shock or something. But none of us had the nerve to protest further at that point."

"What happened next?" Scotty asked solemnly when she fell silent again. The sooner the story was done, the sooner she could forget it. Hopefully forever.

"Jimmy had us clean ourselves up, make ourselves presentable, and then sent us out with the order to each bring back a man," Beth said and then admitted, shamefaced, "When I left that house, I was too scared and shocked to think anything but that I should do what he said. That anything was better than having me head torn off like Mary. But after walking half a block I began to regain my senses. My body was crying out for blood so bad it was hard to think, but I simply couldn't bite anyone, and I couldn't—*I wouldn't*—lure anyone back to that house of hell to be tortured and murdered. I decided I was going to run away, that I would find Dree somehow, but in the meantime, I would hide and not return to that house."

"And the other women?" Scotty asked, though he knew the answer.

"I tried to convince the others to come with me, but they were too afraid. They were going to do exactly what he ordered them to do. But I should go find Dree, they said, and bring her back to save them."

Beth sighed unhappily. "I tried so hard to convince them that doing what he said was the wrong thing to do, but they were all so terrified of him after what he'd done . . . and the bloodlust was on them too, I think." She looked down as if in shame, and murmured, "So I left them and fled."

"Where did you go?" Scotty asked quietly. He'd known some of what she'd told him, but not all of it.

"The only place I could think to go," she told him. "The old house, the brothel. I knew Dree wouldn't be there. She was still off on the Continent somewhere, but I needed to think, to figure out how to find her. And that, to me, seemed the safest place. At least it was somewhere familiar, and Dree hadn't sold the place yet, so I knew it was uninhabited at the moment, which seemed a very good thing indeed.

"That was a terrible trek," Beth admitted solemnly. "It was night, people were everywhere, and I was so hungry and they smelled so good. There were times I didn't think I'd manage to get to the house without attacking some poor passerby and biting them. But I did," she said, lifting her head proudly, and then a wry smile curved one side of her mouth and Beth admitted, "The problem was, I didn't know what to do once I got there. The bloodlust was so bad I could barely think. I certainly couldn't figure out how to contact Dree. I couldn't even remember which country she was visiting just then, or what her next stop was. I thought if I just had some blood, just a little, my mind would clear enough that I could figure things out. But I simply couldn't bite another human being."

"What did you do?" Scotty prompted gently when she fell silent.

"I fed on rats," Beth admitted with disgust. "That was how desperate I was. We had cats when we lived in the brothel, but we took them to the new house when we moved. Without the cats there, rats had moved in. For two weeks I stayed at the house, sleeping during the day and then waking up to feed on any rats I might be able to catch in the house, before slipping outside at night to try to find other small animals. Usually all I found were more rats or the occasional bird, once even a mangy old cat. None of it seemed to help, but I still couldn't bear the idea of biting another human being." She shuddered at the very thought.

"And then one night I was chasing a rat around the corner of the house when a carriage drove by. It slowed as it passed, and I glanced up and gaped at the woman peering out the window. It was Dree. For a minute, I couldn't believe me eyes, but it *was* her riding by, and the carriage had nearly passed the house. Terrified she would leave without seeing me, I just shrieked. Fortunately, she heard me and had the carriage stop. When she got out, I rushed over and threw myself at her."

Beth paused briefly and then said, "She's told me since that she didn't even recognize me at first, I was so filthy and haggard. But she said I was babbling incoherently about Mary getting her head ripped off and Nelly dying, and she sorted it out. She said she tried to get me to go to the retirement house right away, but I kind of freaked out. I don't remember that. Actually, it's all kind of blurry from my seeing her until a day or two later, but Dree told me that when I refused to let her take me to the new house, she ushered me into the old one and took care of me there.

"I was in a really bad way. Even so, I wouldn't feed when Dree brought a man in off the street for that purpose. She had to control both myself and him to get me to feed. She brought several people in over the next two days and did that again and again. Then she had me rest. I slept all day and most of the evening, but when I woke up I told her everything. About Jimmy coming and what he'd done, what he'd wanted us to do. I told her I tried to get the others to leave, but they'd feared if we all left he'd hunt us down one by one and do what he'd done to Mary, and that they were waiting for us to save them.

"Dree wanted to go to the house alone, but I wouldn't let her. I insisted on going with her. Once we got there, though, I was almost sorry I had."

Sighing, she leaned her head back against the headboard again and said, "You know what happened there. We thought we were only going to have to deal with Jimmy, that the women would be happy to see us.

Instead, the things Jimmy had made them do broke them, and the women had given in to madness. The house, our beautiful charming house, was a blood-spattered mess littered with corpses and body parts—not just of men, but of women and children too. And the stink . . ." Her nose wrinkled with disgust at the memory, and then she sighed unhappily. "Jamieson said 'Attack,' and they attacked at once. Women who had been friends . . . family for decades. They came at us like Valkyries, eager to rend us to shreds."

Beth turned her head and met his gaze. "We would have died that day had you and your men not rushed the house just then. You saved our lives, that's certain."

Scotty nodded. "We'd been tracking the man since his first attack on this second round of killings, but the trail had gone cold a couple weeks before that night. We realized afterward that it was because he'd gone to ground in yer house and sent the women out to hunt." Shaking his head, he continued, "The only reason we were there that evening was because we had intel that something was going on. People were disappearing in the area, many of them last seen entering that house, and there was a stench coming from it that was apparently unbearable and very telling. We were in a carriage across the street, just arming ourselves when the two o' ye arrived and traipsed in. We suspected ye had no idea what ye were walking into and followed quickly."

"I know I didn't have the presence of mind to say it at the time, but thank you for that," Beth said quietly.

"Me pleasure," Scotty said softly, and then cleared his throat before saying, "And I apologize if me suggesting the three-on-one mind wipe fer ye upset ye at the time."

When she merely nodded and closed her eyes, he added carefully, "But I still think it would have been—and might still be—best fer ye."

Much to his relief, Beth actually smiled at the words. But she didn't open her eyes and all she said was, "Do ye?"

"Aye," Scotty said. "Ye have so many horrible memories, Beth. I know they pain ye. A three-on-one would take them away so that they could no longer hurt ye."

"Do ye dislike me so much that you'd rather I was completely wiped, my personality completely removed, than to be the way I am?" she asked sadly, her eyes still closed.

"What?" Scotty asked with dismay. "Nay, I—"

"The way I see it, I'm exactly who I was meant to be," Beth said, grimly now. "And everything I went through? I wouldn't change a thing."

"What?" He gaped at her with surprise. "But you were raped, repeatedly, from ten years old on, and Danny near beat ye to death, and what Jamieson did to you and the other women . . ." Scotty shook his head, and frowned when he saw that she simply rested with her head back and eyes closed. He didn't understand why she wasn't jumping at the chance.

"Have you ever made a sword?" she asked suddenly into the silence.

"What?" Scotty asked with bewilderment.

"A sword," Beth repeated, neither opening her eyes nor moving. "I've never made one myself, but I gather they stick a steel rod into fire to soften it and then hammer it and hammer it and hammer it, only to stick it back in the fire again and hammer it some more. And they do that until they've made the finest, strongest, sharpest sword they can."

Scotty waited, expression blank, not sure what this had to do with anything.

"Some years back I decided God is like a blacksmith," she announced. "And I think all these horrible experiences are just him putting us in the fire and hammering at us, and then putting us in the fire again, and hammering some more until he makes us the strongest, finest, and sharpest we can be."

Beth smiled to herself, eyes still closed, and then admitted, "It took a lot of years for me to come to that conclusion. It took a lot of time for me to come to like myself too, and accept my past as being partially responsible for forming me. But now, I wouldn't change what happened to me for anything, Scotty. Not because I enjoyed it, for I surely didn't, at least not all of it, but because I like *me*. I like who I've become. As a child I thought I knew everything, knew better than my mother. I was arrogant as youth is. In my life I've been stubborn and stupid and selfish by turn, but everything that happened to me made me stronger and better. And usually taught me a lesson of one sort or another. And now *I like myself.*"

Sitting up again, Beth turned to face him, meeting his gaze directly. "So, you see, I don't want to forget. Because if all those things hadn't happened, maybe I'd be a different person. Perhaps weaker, perhaps more selfish, perhaps defenseless and dependent, or perhaps stronger and a queen," she said with a grin. "But I'd be a different person. I don't want to be a different person. I am who I am and I really do like, even love, myself now. So, if your efforts to get me to agree to a three-on-one are purely for my benefit, you can stop. I don't want that."

Beth was silent for a minute, letting that sink in, and then said, "However, I know that's not why. You were always cold and harsh with me, showing your dislike and disgust. I know it has something to do with your mother and your inability to accept my life before I was turned. And I'm sorry if the person I've become isn't good enough for you, and you feel that a three-on-one mind wipe would make me more to your liking. But the person I have become is good enough for *me*, and I'm the one who has to face her in the mirror every day."

"Beth, I'm no'—I just think—" he began, but she cut him off.

"It doesn't matter what *you* think," she interrupted, and then shook her head. "As I said, I've struggled with it this last century. It was hard work learning to accept myself for who I am. But I had got to the point where I *had* accepted myself. And then you came along and I started feeling not good enough again. I started hearing those taunts in my head—*dirty whore, nasty slag*. Who would want a dirty whore like me?"

Beth shook her head again. "I don't want to feel like that anymore, Scotty. I don't want to have to change to be acceptable to you. And I don't want to have to erase the person I've become to be good enough for anyone. The truth is . . . well, maybe the truth is *you're* not good enough for *me*. Maybe I don't want someone so small-minded and judgmental in *my* life. I think I'm better off without you. Because I don't want a life mate who makes me feel so small and soiled."

Leaving him sitting there, stunned, Beth stood and walked into the bathroom, closing the door quietly behind her.

Scotty just sat there for the longest time, his mind in turmoil. He couldn't believe the irony of it all. Finally he came to his senses, saw who she was and was ready to accept her, and she decided *he* wasn't good enough for *her*. And the hell of it was, he couldn't blame her. He *had* done everything she'd said. He'd looked down on her, and considered himself above her. Christ, he'd just added to her pain and suffering and made her feel small and soiled, and the knowledge shamed him. Scotty did not consider himself better than anyone else. At least, not normally. But . . .

But nothing. That's what he'd done . . . and he might have lost her because of it. The thought scared the hell out of him. All this time he'd been so busy fretting over *her* past and whether *he* could accept *her*, it had never once occurred to him that she might not accept him. After all, he was a catch, wasn't he?

God, he was an arrogant prick, Scotty thought with disgust. After all she'd been through, the last thing Beth had needed was him adding to her pain, and yet that's what he'd done. He needed to fix this. He needed . . . her.

Standing abruptly, he moved to the door and then hesitated. Scotty suspected he would have only one chance at this, if he even had that one chance. He didn't want to mess up . . . again.

Sighing, he took a breath, lowered his head and then knocked softly.

Sixteen

"Beth?"

Lifting her head, she peered at the door, but didn't respond. She couldn't. She was seated with her back against the wall between the toilet and the vanity, her arms wrapped around her knees and her heart breaking. Beth couldn't believe she'd done it, that she'd actually said what she had and walked away from Scotty, but it was really for the best. She had to take care of herself. That was something life had taught her—that ultimately you had to take care of yourself, because you couldn't always trust that someone else would do it for you.

"Beth, I know ye're upset," Scotty said now, his voice pained. "And ye've every right to be. I've been an arrogant and thoughtless prick. But please, ye do no' ha'e to let me in, but please just listen to what I'm going to say?"

Silence followed the plea, and Beth supposed he

was waiting for a response, but she didn't give one. She simply waited, and after a moment he began to speak.

"First, if I was cold and distant with ye over the decades, it was no' because I did no' like ye, lass. I might ha'e had trouble accepting yer past, but I never disliked ye," he said firmly. "I acted like that around ye because I was fighting the desire to drag ye into me arms and bed. Kenning, as I did, that ye were me life mate, it was a mighty struggle no' to do so, but I kenned ye were no' ready fer that."

There was silence for a minute, as if he was waiting for a response. When she didn't give one, he continued, "But ye're right. I've spent the last century or more being small-minded and judging ye when I had no right to. I did no' even know ye, lass. I just made judgments based on the little bit I did ken. I knew that ye'd been a prostitute as a mortal, and made me judgments based on that, because I've always had a certain belief about what kind o' woman would trade her body fer coin. But ye're no' that woman, lass. I ken that now."

Scotty paused again, but Beth remained silent. Waiting.

"And it's no' just because o' all ye told me. I'd come to that conclusion meself while we were healing from the fire, and I meant to tell ye soon as we rested, but when I woke ye were gone and . . ."

She heard his sigh through the door.

"Forgive me, lass, fer no' seeing ye clearly all these years. Ye've *shown* me the kind o' woman ye are in so many ways over this last century. I just was no' looking.

"Beth, ye're smart, and ye're brave, lass. Ye run into trouble to aid others without concern fer yer own well-being. I kenned that even ere this trip, though I don't think I admitted it even to meself then. But that first day here, I knew instinctively ye'd run into trouble to save that woman Walter Simpson had, despite knowing help was twenty minutes out. Ye could ha'e been beheaded and killed ere help arrived, and ye kenned it and rushed in anyway.

"And then there was Kira. Ye were so kind with her. Ye could ha'e just passed on the message Mortimer said to give her, and left it at that. But ye saw she was in pain and suicidal and ye made sure to give her a reason to live and convinced her to come here to Toronto.

"And the mortal at the dance club? She had nothing to do with ye. Ye could ha'e just walked back to the dance floor and left her to her own sorrows, but ye followed her to try to help.

"And then there's me. Lass, ye took on me pain to help me sleep and heal, and that was some terrible pain. Most women would ha'e run from it, but ye bore it to ease me suffering.

"Beth, the kind o' woman I decided ye were would ne'er ha'e done any o' those things . . . Me mother ne'er would ha'e done any o' those things."

Beth had lowered her head as Scotty spoke, but lifted it sharply and stared at the door at the mention of his mother.

"Magnus told me I had issues with me mother," he said solemnly. "He said that I was mixing ye up with her. I told him he was wrong, but now I see he was right. I was sure I had just learned well the lessons she'd taught me. But the truth is I was painting ye with the same brush as her because she was a cold heartless whore who traded her body for coin and anything else she wanted, and I thought any woman who was a prostitute must be the same. But ye're no' heartless, and . . . I was wrong," he said helplessly.

"And I swear, when ye finished telling me everything, I . . . this time I did no' suggest the three-on-one because I can no' accept yer past. That's no' true anymore. The truth is . . . it fair crushed me heart to hear all ye've gone through. I felt so helpless, kenning ye were on yer own through all that, and that I could no' help ye. I wanted to take away the pain I had no' been there to prevent.

"Lass," Scotty said solemnly, "Matias said that he wondered if ye would still be me life mate were yer memory wiped. That question has plagued me since he mentioned it. It still does. It bothered me then because, as much as I did no' feel I could claim ye, I could no' seem to let ye go either. But Beth, by the time ye finished talking, I thought if the mind wipe would give ye some measure o' freedom from the torments ye'd suffered, I'd risk it. Because I think I love ye, lass. And I'd rather spend the rest o' me life unmated and miserable, but kenning ye were happy and—"

Scotty stopped speaking abruptly and blinked in surprise when Beth suddenly opened the door. She hadn't been able to stop herself after the part about his thinking he loved her. She'd leapt up from the floor and opened the door and now faced him solemnly.

"I don't need my memories wiped," Beth said firmly. "My past doesn't torment me anymore. I like myself."

"No, I ken that now," Scotty assured her, looking relieved that she'd relented enough to open the door. "And I like ye too. I was just telling ye that. But I'm grateful ye do no' want it, lass, because I love ye, Beth, just the way ye are, and it truly would break me heart to lose ye now."

Beth almost threw herself into his arms right then, but made herself hold back and asked, "Will ye tell me about yer mother?"

Scotty closed his eyes briefly and sighed, but then nodded solemnly. "If ye wish it. Aye." He hesitated briefly and then said, "Did ye want to sit down while I do, or—"

"No," Beth interrupted. "I want to rest on the bed."

His eyebrows rose in surprise and then lowered with concern. "Are ye no' feeling well, lass? Rachel said ye were fully healed, but if ye're no' feelin'—"

"It isn't that," Beth said, stepping forward. She slipped her arms around his waist, but then leaned back to meet his gaze and said, "It's just . . . as stubborn, stupid and arrogant as ye can be, I think I love ye too," she admitted solemnly. "And I—"

That was as far as she got before Scotty closed his arms around her and ended her words by covering her mouth with his. Breathing a sigh into his mouth, Beth relaxed into his arms and kissed him back with all she had in her, hardly able to believe that it might work out. That he actually might love her and she him, and—

Her thoughts died and she gasped into his mouth when he suddenly scooped her up and carried her to the bed. He broke their kiss to set her on it, and then crawled onto it next to her, but when he reached for her again, she placed a hand on his chest. "Your mother?"

Scotty stilled, and then sighed and nodded. "Right . . . me mother."

Grimacing, he settled on the bed next to her to sit with his back against the headboard, and then waited for her to sit up beside him. Once she had, he raised his arm and put it around her, drawing her to rest against his chest. After a pause, though, he asked, "Do ye really want to hear this, lass? I ken ye're nothing like her."

"I want to hear it," she assured him solemnly. "Ye know my past. Let me know yours."

Scotty nodded, and then leaned his head back and said, "Well, to start off, I should give ye some history on me da first."

"Okay," she murmured, settling in against him and waiting patiently.

"Me da was married before he met me mother. His first wife was the love o' his life, and they were married for fifteen years ere she died. They were very happy together but for one thing—in all those years there was no hint o' a bairn fer them."

"How sad," Beth murmured.

"Aye." Scotty nodded. "And then there was me mother. She was a whore. No' professionally. At least, she did no' have a pimp or live in a brothel. However, she traded sexual favors for—" he shrugged helplessly, his chest moving under her "—basically for whatever she wanted. She slept with the king to gain favor for her father, and boost his—and by extension her—position at court. She slept with high-ranking officials, lairds . . . basically anyone who could do something for her that she wanted. And then she slept with me father."

"What did she want from him?" Beth asked with curiosity.

Pausing, Scotty frowned. "As I recall, the story went, she wanted some bit o' property he owned, for—" Scotty hesitated and then shook his head. "—for something. I'm no' sure I was ever told what she wanted the property for, or what it meant to her. All I ken is a bit o' land is the only reason I exist."

Beth raised her eyebrows dubiously at that, and Scotty smiled.

"Truly," he assured her, and then continued, "She showed up at the keep, in the midst o' a winter storm. Da later learned she stayed at a neighboring keep for weeks ere the storm hit, and the minute it set in, she left and traveled to our castle." Glancing down at her, he explained, "Hospitality was important in the Highlands, and turning her away would no' have been hospitable, so it was pretty much guaranteed she'd no' be turned away."

Leaning his head back, he continued, "She promptly set about what she did best and seduced me father. Afterward, she simply expected him to sign over the deed of the land she wanted to her. Just like that," he said with disgust.

"Thought that much of herself, did she?" Beth asked with dry amusement.

Scotty shrugged. "It had worked for her in the past. She was a beautiful woman, and apparently she was very skilled in bed."

"But it didn't work with your father?" Beth guessed.

"Me father was no' a stupid man. He knew if he gave her what she wanted, she'd be on her merry way. It was, he told me, an especially bitterly cold winter with little to do, so he hemmed and hawed, and said he'd think about it and such. Well, my mother simply saw that as a challenge. She was so vain she did no' for a minute believe she would no' get her way. This went on until the spring, by which point Father was growing bored with her, and as the mountain pass thawed, he was growing more and more eager to send her on her way sans the deed. But then he began to suspect she was pregnant."

"With you," Beth said with a grin.

"Aye." He smiled at her expression and squeezed her tighter briefly, then said, "Well, Da had always wanted children, or at least an heir. So to him, this was a blessed miracle."

"And to your mother?" she asked.

"A bargaining chip," Scotty said dryly. "In fact, to this day I do no' ken for sure that MacDonald was me father, or if she was sleepin' with one or several o' his men to get pregnant, and claiming it was his to have that bargaining chip. However, he believed I was his and that was all that mattered . . . to both o' us. He was a good father," he assured her.

Beth nodded solemnly.

"At any rate," Scotty continued, "once he realized she was pregnant, me da insisted she marry him. She refused, but said that if he signed that bit o' property o'er to her, she'd give me to him when I was born. But Father did no' trust her. He feared the moment he signed the deed o' property over to her, she'd find a way to be rid o' me."

Glancing down at her again, he explained, "She'd been pregnant a time or two before, ye see. And none o' those bairns had survived. Actually, I learned later that she had been pregnant many more times than even me father suspected. She was very fertile, but according to her maid, only three bairns survived to birth. Apparently she had a concoction that included wild carrot and I do no' ken what else that she would drink to rid herself o' unwanted babes. When that did no' work, she got rid o' the bairns by other methods after birth. One she apparently gave, along with some coin, to some peasants on her father's estate to raise. I gather she was fond o' the father o' that child," he said with a shrug. "Another she drowned at birth, and another she simply abandoned out in the cold on a winter night. She never knew if it froze to death, was rescued by someone or was killed by wolves. She didn't bother to check.

"So, me father kenned about the other bairns and did no' trust her," Scotty said, returning to the tale. "There was no way he was going to sign o'er the property ere she gave birth. He suggested she carry the baby to term, give it over to him, and then he'd sign the deed. She refused that offer and insisted he do it now, or the bairn, me, would no' make it to birth. A rather stupid threat to make if ye think about it," he pointed out. "I mean, she was alone with naught but her maid, who was no' very loyal, in someone else's castle."

"Yes, that does seem stupid," Beth agreed.

"Aye, but me mother was no' a stupid woman," he assured her. "I can only think that she was so frustrated that she was no' getting her way fer once in her life, that she lost her temper and ran off at the mouth." Scotty shrugged. "Whatever the case, me father's response was to lock her in the tower and ensure she was watched at all times so that she could no' concoct or take anything that might end the pregnancy, or otherwise rid herself of it. And then he waited, and on the day that she went into labor, he sent for the priest, and had him wait in the Great Hall while he went up to her room. He told her she was having the baby. Not only that, but he was ensuring it would survive by taking it away from her the moment it was born. He said he'd then announce my birth to the world and present me to the king as his child by her. She would be ruined . . . unless she married him and made me legitimately his heir."

"Just a minute," Beth protested. "Are ye telling me, with all her sleeping around and all the babies, she wasn't already ruined?"

Scotty grinned at her disbelief. "So long as it was only the men who knew what she got up to, she was safe. After all, they were all hoping to get into her bed again. But if a woman got wind . . ." He shook his head. "Then she would ha'e been ruined fer certain."

"Humph," Beth muttered with disgust, and then sighed and said, "She married your father?"

Scotty nodded. "I gather she argued, fought, cursed and swore. But in the end she had no choice. Were she ruined, he told her he would ensure she was sent to a nunnery where her hair would be shorn and she'd be on her knees the rest o' her days and kept far away from men. And he probably could have done that," he assured her. "He was good friends with the king, and if the king specified a certain abbey . . ."

"Your father played hardball," Beth said with approval.

"Aye." He grinned. "So she agreed. The priest was

called up, and me mother married me da just moments ere I came squalling into the world."

"I bet ye were a beautiful baby," Beth murmured, rubbing her fingers over his chest, and then she added, "And I bet you'll give *me* beautiful babies."

Hugging her tight, Scotty kissed the top of her head. "As many as ye wish and are allowed by law."

Beth chuckled into his chest. "Very romantic, m'laird."

"Hey, I'm the head o' the UK Enforcers. I have to include that last part," he said defensively.

"I suppose," Beth relented and hugged him back, before asking, "So, what happened next?"

"Me father still feared she might do away with me, so took me away from her at once, and handed me over to a nursemaid who raised me fer the first five years o' me life in a cottage on the estate."

"Away from yer father?" Beth asked with a frown.

"He visited daily," Scotty assured her. "And me nursemaid was a wonderful woman. She was his own nursemaid as a child. However, she was very old and died when I was five. My father then deemed me old enough fer it to be safe to allow me around me mother and brought me to the castle to live."

"And your mother?" Beth asked, suspecting she already knew the answer. After all, there was a reason he hated his mother.

"She loathed me," Scotty said solemnly. "And made no effort to hide it. Most o' me childhood after five was spent being tortured by her. There were subtle little cruelties that me father would no' notice, and then there were much larger cruelties when he was no' around, after which I was threatened that if I told him she would cut me tongue out, scalp me or kill me father . . . and so me childhood went," he said dryly.

"I'm sorry," Beth murmured, hugging him and wishing she could take those memories, and the pain they must have caused, away. The thought made her blink in surprise as she understood what Scotty had been feeling, but then he started talking again, and she pushed the thought aside to listen.

"Despite having married me da, the woman had no' given up her whoring ways. If she wanted something, or could gain something, she slept with whomever she thought could give it to her, or just anyone she wished. By that time me da would ha'e nothing to do with her and, I'm sure, sorely regretted marrying her. Although he would never admit it, at least no' to me. To me he said that all the misery she caused him was worth it to get me."

"I'm sure it was," Beth said solemnly.

Scotty shrugged and continued, "Da died when I was eighteen. To this day I suspect she poisoned him. He was a strong, healthy man, and there were no signs o' a weak heart before his attacked him. However, even if she did no' poison him, she was the cause o' his death. They were arguing, and she was spewing her venom all over him when he suddenly clutched his heart and fell over."

Beth hugged him silently, knowing how the loss must have hurt him. Scotty hugged her back and kissed her forehead before continuing.

"O' course, after having endured her viciousness and cruelties fer most o' me life, I hated me mother. But the final straw was when she tried to convince me to buy her fine new silk fer the funeral, by offering to bed me," he said with disgust.

"Her own son?" Beth asked aghast.

Scotty nodded, his mouth tight. "It was the only way she knew how to interact with a man, I suspect. But at the time I was so enraged . . ." He shook his head. "So the moment I was named clan leader, I made it clear to her that I would stand fer no more o' her nonsense. That she would be a good woman, and comport herself as a lady, or she would be cast out."

"And did she?" Beth asked. "Comport herself as a lady?"

"Fer two years," Scotty said grimly. "She had no choice but to toe the line. Her beauty had begun to fade, and her lovers had grown sparse. If I had cast her out as I promised, she would have had nowhere to go, and no sweet lover to rescue her from penury and rough living."

Beth nodded. "And what happened after two years?"

"She got wind o' a man she thought might help her. He had a certain reputation fer getting rid o' problems. And there were rumors that he had murdered a certain laird or two. So she sent a messenger to him with a parchment requesting his help. In it, she claimed I was cruel and abusive and so on and so forth. What she did no' realize was that he was an immortal. No' that she would've kenned what that was anyway, and she may not have even cared had she known. She probably would have tried to seduce him into making her one."

Scotty paused and frowned over that possibility and then gave a shudder before hurrying on. "As I say, he was an immortal and read the messenger's mind and knew there was something amiss. Apparently, all the messenger had on his mind was sex with me mother. His thoughts on me were respect and fear, but the fear made the immortal wonder, so he decided to find out what was what. Either he had a mother bent on filicide, or—"

"Excuse me?" Beth leaned up to stare at him with one eyebrow raised. "Filicide?"

"That's what 'tis called when a parent kills their child, whether 'tis mother or father, killing son or daughter. It comes from *filius*, the Latin word for *son*."

"Oh." She nodded solemnly and then rolled her eyes and said, "Well, la-di-da! Aren't we clever?"

"Aye. I learned Latin centuries ago," Scotty said with a grin. "Jealous?"

Chuckling at his teasing, Beth kissed his chest and said, "Get on with it. What happened with the immortal?"

"Oh." He paused a moment to shift his thoughts back to his story, and then said, "He let me mother believe that he would carry out her plan, and arranged to come to the castle. But he really intended to find out what was what. If I truly was a cruel, abusive bastard, he'd do as she requested. However, if she was bent on *filicide*," Scotty said, emphasizing the word with a teasing grin, "then he would warn me so that she could no' hire someone else to kill me once he refused the contract."

"Hmm, a killer with a conscience," Beth said with interest.

Scotty nodded. "So, he came to the castle while I was away for the day, and was seated at the table when I returned. Me mother, no' kenning he'd already read her mind and had her number, introduced him as Lord

Aequitas, just passing through, who would be staying the night, and—"

"Were ye angry?" Beth asked curiously. "Did ye suspect he was a lover or something and she was misbehaving?"

Scotty chuckled and shook his head. "He was only a couple years older than me. At least, he did no' look much older than me, so I did no' for a minute think he was interested in me old mother. And there was the whole hospitality thing, so I was no' angry that he was there."

"Oh," she said, almost disappointed.

"Anyway, me mother introduced us and then just sat there grinning. I think she actually expected him to slay me right there in the Great Hall in front o' one and all. Or perhaps she was just gleeful thinking I would soon be out o' her hair." Scotty shrugged. "Anyway, he did no' slay me in the Great Hall, and after dinner, me mother suggested the three o' us retire to the solar fer a drink. We did, but once there he turned to me and announced that me mother had hired him to kill me. He then handed me her letter with all its claims of abuse and such and crossed over to pour himself a drink."

Scotty grimaced. "Me mother had a fit, asked him what he was doing and ordered him to get over there and kill me. At which point he informed her that he had no intention o' killing me. In fact, he had come to warn me o' her plans so I might safeguard meself in future. He then went on to say that she was a base whore, with no conscience, and not a speck o' human warmth, while I was an honorable young man trying to do right by me people and, frankly, were he in the mood to kill anyone that night, which he wasn't, it would be her and not me." Scotty pursed his lips briefly, and then said, "Mother did no' take disappointment well."

"I suspected as much," Beth said solemnly.

"She sort o' grunted at the man with disgust, and then snapped, 'Give me that letter' and rushed toward me." Scotty paused briefly and then said, "I truly thought she was coming to grab the letter . . . and she did. She took it with one hand as her other hand came up with a knife in it, and she stabbed me in the neck."

Beth stiffened against him, a growl of fury sounding low in her throat. Scotty's mother was as bad as, and perhaps worse than, her father had been. Truly it was a wonder she and Scotty had turned out as well as they had.

"It was a mortal wound," Scotty said solemnly. "I would ha'e died, but the immortal, feeling responsible fer me situation, turned me. Although I did no' ken that was what he was doing at the time. All I kenned was that I was bleeding out on the floor o' me castle, and then he ripped into his own wrist, tore out a mouthful o' flesh and pressed the gushing wound to me mouth. It felt to me as if I were drowning on the blood, and . . . well, after that things got hazy. But I do recall his telling me mother that he was making me immortal. She could never kill me. He told her that I would never age or die, while she would fade away to a toothless, wrinkled old crone and then molder in the grave."

"Nice," Beth said with satisfaction, quite sure Scotty's mother would have been infuriated at that thought, but then tipped her head and asked with curiosity, "Who was this Lord Aequitas?"

"I do no' ken," Scotty admitted solemnly. "I never saw him again after that night."

Beth's eyebrows rose. That was bad. An immortal was never supposed to turn a mortal and leave them to their own devices, which made this guy a—"Rogue?"

Scotty considered her question with a frown, but then shook his head. "I do no' ken. I've wondered that meself. Sometimes I think aye, and other times nay."

"But he killed people, and he turned you and then left you alone. That's—"

"He only killed people known to abuse and kill people under their power," Scotty said solemnly. "I looked for him for a long time and learned that much about him."

"Oh," Beth breathed. That seemed kind of admirable. Lord Aequitas had been a sort of medieval character much like the Equalizer.

"And he did no' leave me alone," Scotty continued. "He did leave MacDonald, but he got a message to the closest immortal in the area, who happened to be Magnus Bjarnesen."

Beth's eyes widened incredulously. "Magnus? Did he know him? What was the message?"

"The message was that Laird MacDonald had been turned and needed assistance and training. Magnus headed for MacDonald at once to look into the situation. He found me and me mother, saw me mother buried and saw me through the turn, controlling me people as necessary to prevent interference. Once I was through the worst of it and able to talk, I learned he knew no Lord Aequitas, and he didn't recognize me description of the man." Scotty shrugged. "I never learned who Aequitas was, if that was even his real name."

"Oh yes," she murmured. The man probably hadn't been using his real name, she thought, and then she glanced at Scotty sharply. "Wait, he saw your mother buried? What happened? How did she die?"

"Ah." Scotty grimaced. "Well, when Aequitas said that bit about my living forever young, and her being an old crone and moldering in the grave, me mother was so enraged she attacked him. Of course, he just laughed and tossed her aside like a babe. He then repeated that there was no way she could murder me now, adding this time that once I had recovered, I would no doubt punish her properly fer trying to kill me and lock her in chains in the dungeon fer the rest o' her days. Me mother attacked him again. At least, that is how it appeared. But the truth is, I believe she deliberately ran herself through with his sword when she charged him, that she knew exactly what she was doing, and chose death rather than allow me to seek justice."

They were both silent for a moment, and then he peered down at her and said solemnly, "That is why I couldn't believe that the nanos would think ye a perfect life mate fer me. I loathed me mother and thought ye a mirror image of her because o' yer profession as a mortal. I was looking at the surface and no' the heart," he admitted apologetically. "And while this last time I suggested the mind wipe in the hopes o' removing all those painful memories o' yer past, I'm ashamed to admit that at first I thought perhaps if you were wiped to the stage of a tabula rasa, I could train you to become a better woman. But I was a fool. You are already a much better woman than me mother. And a much better person than me. I'm sorry, Beth, and

I'll spend me life making it up to ye, if ye give me the chance. Will ye be me life mate and give me that chance?"

Tears in her eyes, Beth swallowed and opened her mouth to respond, but then glanced to the door as a knock sounded.

Seventeen

"Maybe they'll go away," Scotty said with a frown at the door, and then grimaced when another knock sounded. "Or maybe not."

Smiling wryly, Beth slid off the bed and walked to the door to open it, her eyebrows rising when she saw Donny on the other side.

"Oh." The young immortal looked surprised and then smiled back. "You're awake and up. Rachel said you were better, but I expected you still to be resting."

"She will," Scotty assured him, walking up to stand behind Beth. "Were ye lookin' fer me?"

"Oh, yes, sorry," Donny said with a grimace. "Mortimer wanted me to find you and let you know he needs to have a word with you."

Scotty hesitated, and then asked, "Do ye ken what about?"

Donny shook his head. "Do you want me to go ask him?"

"No." Scotty sighed and then glanced to Beth apologetically.

"Go," she said quietly. "We can finish our talk later."

Nodding, he bent to press a kiss to her cheek and slid out of the room to hurry to the stairs with Donny on his heels. Beth turned back into the room, frowning and grabbing the back of her gown when she caught a draft. Damned hospital gowns, she thought as she closed the door. She hadn't even realized she was wearing another one until now. But her clothes had probably been ruined in the bomb blast, so Rachel had changed her.

Beth walked to the dresser and pulled out a pair of underwear and a bra, then grabbed some jeans and a T-shirt from the closet and stepped into the bathroom. A quick shower and change of clothes and then maybe she'd go down to see about something to eat if Scotty wasn't back yet. She was kind of hungry now that she wasn't distracted with emotional issues.

With food on her mind, Beth was in and out of the shower in a hurry and pulling on her clothes. She stopped long enough to brush her teeth and hair, but then headed for the door to the hall, and gave a start when she pulled it open to find Odilia there, hand raised to knock.

"Oh," Beth said with surprise.

"Sorry. I didn't mean to startle you," the woman said at once.

"No. That's fine. I've always had a high startle reflex," Beth admitted, and then added, "If you're looking for Scotty, he went downstairs a few minutes ago to see Mortimer."

"Actually, I was looking for you," Odilia said with

a crooked smile. "I don't know if you're aware of this, but it's Scotty's birthday next week."

"It is?" Beth asked with alarm. Jeez, she didn't even know when the man's birthday was. Or his favorite color, or his favorite food, or, or, or . . . They had a lot of talking to do.

"Yes, on Friday," Odilia said. "And I was kind of . . . Well, I had a big birthday party planned for him back in Scotland, but of course he will not be there so I canceled it, but I thought maybe we could plan something here. Something smaller, obviously, since we only have a week, but . . ."

"That sounds wonderful," Beth said quickly. "I'm in."

"Oh good, because I'm not sure what to do about—" She sighed with frustration and threw up her hands. "I have a list of venues and a bunch of samples to taste down in the garage. Speaking of which, I should get back there—I am on car duty today—but I brought the list and samples into work today and thought if you got a moment, maybe you could come down to the garage . . . ?"

"Actually, that's perfect," Beth assured her with a grin. "I happen to be hungry so the samples sound good. Do you want me to come down there with you?"

"That would be great," Odilia said with relief and turned toward the door. "Scotty is so difficult to plan for."

"Is he?" Beth asked with curiosity. Other than his bossy tendencies and the issues he'd had with her previous profession, she'd found him pretty easygoing.

"Yes, he—Oh, wait," Odilia said, catching her arm to stop her as they approached the stairs.

"What is it?" Beth asked with concern.

Odilia made a face. "I just want to make sure the

coast is clear before we go down. Like I said, I am supposed to be in the garage. Mortimer will be pissed if he sees me in here. I should have just called you or something, but I was not sure you would be up and about yet, and I didn't want to wake you if you weren't. I wish they had outdoor stairs here. I don't—"

"It's okay. Come on. We can avoid the house altogether," Beth said, turning to lead her back to her bedroom and thinking she hadn't realized how anxious Odilia was. On the other hand, the woman had endured a pretty traumatic childhood. At least Beth had been older when the entirety of what she considered to be her family had been attacked by Jamieson.

"Where are we going?" Odilia asked as she followed her into her room. "I really need to get back to the garage."

"You will. We'll use my balcony," Beth said easily as she crossed to the sliding glass doors in her room. They led to a small balcony overlooking the backyard. Beth opened the door, ushered Odilia out and then closed the door and moved to the rail. It was dark out. Nighttime, then, Beth noted. It had been afternoon when they'd gone to the apartment to get her clothes, but she wasn't sure if it had been just hours or days ago. Beth had no idea what day it was. She was really losing track of time with all these attacks and such.

"Now what?" Odilia asked.

Shaking herself out of her thoughts, Beth smiled and said, "Now we jump."

"Jump?" Odilia asked dubiously, peering at the bushes below with the rocks surrounding them.

"Try to hit the grass and not the rock garden," Beth

said with a grin and vaulted over the railing to land lightly on the grass in front of the bushes. Straightening, she glanced back up to Odilia and smiled encouragingly as she waved her down.

Odilia hesitated, but then gripped the railing and vaulted over it to land next to her. She straightened with a laugh and shook her head as they started to walk across the dark yard. "You would have been a nightmare to raise were you a teenager right now," she said with amusement. "You would probably be one of those girls who sneak out in the middle of the night to meet their boyfriends all the time," she teased.

"Yeah, I probably would," Beth admitted and smiled at the idea as she thought, especially if that boyfriend was Scotty. She would have taken every opportunity to slip out to see him, she thought, and then glanced around the empty yard and frowned. "I wonder where the dogs are?"

"Waiting in the kennels for me to feed them," Odilia explained, and added, "I'll have to do that and let them out before we try the samplers."

Beth shrugged. "I'll help."

"Thanks." Odilia sounded surprised, but smiled as she opened the garage door for her to enter.

"How did you get stuck on garage duty?" Beth asked as she led the way through the building to the door leading to the kennels and cells.

"I wondered that myself when I arrived and Mortimer assigned me to it," Odilia admitted as they passed into a hall with a door on the left and cells lining the right side. She paused at the door on the left, pushed it open and waved Beth in as she continued, "Donny has done it the last couple of days, and

I was surprised when Mortimer said I'd be doing it today, but . . ."

Beth had entered the kennels as Odilia talked, her gaze sliding over the excited dogs waiting to be fed, but when the other woman stopped talking, she started to turn in question, only to pause at a sharp sting in her side. Glancing down with confusion, she peered at the dart there and then shifted her bewildered gaze to Odilia. She saw the dart gun the woman held just before the lights went out.

"So you think one of the cameras from a convenience store by the apartment might have caught footage of whoever set up the bomb on Rickart's car?" Scotty asked with interest.

"We hope so," Mortimer said. "Magnus took Rickart with him to the store to get copies of the film footage from all four cameras. I asked Magnus why all four and why not just whatever one, or ones, might be pointing toward the parking lot, and he said—"

"—because we might get the license plate number or a closer image of the rogue as they were coming or going," Scotty said, nodding.

"Hmm," Mortimer said. "You two think alike."

Scotty shrugged mildly. "We've worked together a long time."

"Well, I appreciate your coming to help out and bringing your men," Mortimer told him solemnly. "Even I am learning off of you, because I would only have had them get film footage from the cameras that might have got the parking lot. I will know better in future."

Scotty smiled faintly, but then asked, "When do you expect Magnus and Rickart back?"

Mortimer glanced at the clock and pursed his lips. "They should be there now. But I am not sure how long it will take to copy the footage." He considered it briefly, and then said, "At a guess, maybe an hour or an hour and a half, depending on traffic."

Scotty stood up. "I'm going to go tell Beth, then."

Mortimer nodded. "If you are not back by the time they return, I will send Donny to get you, or text you."

"Thank ye." Scotty left the office, headed for the stairs. Halfway there, however, he detoured into the kitchen. Beth hadn't eaten for twenty-four hours. She could probably use more blood too, he thought and shook his head. It seemed that lately all they'd done was recover, eat, and feed . . . well, and make love. The thought made him smile. It *was* making love. He was pretty sure he loved her. She was a special woman, kind, generous, giving, brave, smart, sassy. He even liked the sassy. Maybe the truth was, he especially liked the sassy. A lot of people found him intimidating for some reason and few would dare to sass him, or say anything they feared he wouldn't like. Magnus was one of those few, and it was why they'd been friends so long. Beth also had no fear doing either, and he liked that, Scotty thought as he checked the refrigerator for possible snacks to take to Beth.

His gaze landed on the cheese and he grabbed it, collected a couple of plates and quickly sliced off several pieces for each. He then found the leftover apple pie from the night before and cut a wedge for each plate. He put both on a tray, grabbed a couple of bags of blood and then poured two glasses of milk.

He knew Beth would probably prefer coffee, but there wasn't any made at the moment, and he didn't know how to make it.

He'd have to ask Sam to show him how, Scotty decided as he gathered the tray and headed for the stairs. If Beth liked coffee, he'd learn and be pleased to surprise her with it when she woke. The idea of waking her with a kiss and a cup of coffee made him smile and think of lazy mornings in bed . . . and not-lazy mornings in bed, as well as a future full of both. Scotty seriously regretted that he'd been so stubborn and foolish for so long. He'd nearly lost her because of it. Thank God she'd been willing to listen to him and was giving him the chance to make up for it.

That thought had his smile widening as he moved down the hall to her bedroom. With his hands full, he used his foot to "knock" at the door, and then waited . . . and waited. Frowning, he lifted his foot to "knock" again, and then—concerned that Beth might be sleeping—Scotty shifted the tray to balance on one flat hand, freeing the other to open the door himself. He turned the knob, pushed the door open and started into the room, only to pause when he saw that the bed was empty. His gaze slid to the open bathroom door and the empty room beyond, and then he turned and headed back downstairs a lot faster than he'd gone up.

Scotty looked into the living room first and, finding it empty, started going from room to room. He checked in Mortimer's office last. The head of the North American Enforcers glanced up from the paperwork on his desk, his gaze landing on the tray, and his eyes widened.

"That looks good," he said, straightening in his chair. "Beth sleeping?"

"She's—I can't find her," Scotty said rather than what he'd originally intended, which was "She's gone." He really didn't want to say that. He had that bad feeling again and was afraid to give voice to it.

"She is not in her room?" Mortimer asked with a frown, standing up.

Scotty shook his head. "And not anywhere on the main floor. I didn't check the other bedrooms upstairs, though."

"Could she have gone to your room to surprise you?" Mortimer asked.

Scotty considered that briefly and then shook his head. "I told her I'd go back to her room after I finished talking to you. But I'll look and see," he said, turning away.

"While you do that, I will call down to the gate just to make sure she did not take a car and go out anywhere," Mortimer said.

Scotty didn't respond other than to nod as he hurried back to the kitchen to set down the tray. He jogged upstairs afterward, checked his room and then checked every other room on the upper floor as well, including double-checking her room again, before heading back downstairs. Mortimer was just coming up the hall from his office when he stepped off the stairs.

"Not there?" Mortimer asked.

Scotty shook his head. "The gate?"

"No. No one has left since Magnus and Rickart." Pausing, Mortimer turned to look around, and then said, "If you want to check the garage attached to the house, I'll check the basement. If we do not find her inside, then we will check the yard and the outbuildings."

Nodding, Scotty turned to head into the kitchen and the connecting door to the attached garage. It didn't take him long to assure himself she wasn't there, and then he went down to help Mortimer search the basement. Finding nothing, they headed outside.

"The dogs aren't out," Scotty commented as they started across the back lawn. It didn't take more than a glance to see that the yard itself was empty.

"Odilia is probably feeding them," Mortimer said. "You check the outbuilding and I will look in the front yard."

Nodding, Scotty continued on his way as Mortimer broke off and turned to walk around the house. Beth would be in the outbuilding, he told himself. She had to be. There was nowhere else to look for her.

He didn't see anyone when he entered the building, not even Odilia. Frowning, he scanned the vehicle bays, glanced into the offices and then opened the door to the hall that led to the kennels and cells. A quick look showed him that the cells were empty, and he was reaching to open the door to the kennels when it swung toward him. Backing up, Scotty frowned in disappointment when he saw that it was only Odilia.

"Is Beth with you?" he asked as she stepped out.

"Beth?" she asked with surprise. "Is she not still recovering from the explosion?"

"Nay," Scotty said, his mild concern turning to real concern as he realized she wasn't here either. "She's missing."

Odilia looked confused. "She cannot be missing,

Scotty. Did you look in the kitchen? Perhaps she was hungry when she woke up."

"We checked the house, upstairs, downstairs, even the basement and garage. This was the last place."

"You must have missed her," Odilia said with certainty. "Just give me a minute to let the dogs out and I will come up to the house and help you search it again."

"No." Scotty shook his head. "Stay here. Mortimer and I will look again."

"What about Donny?" Odilia asked.

"Donny?" Scotty echoed with confusion.

"Is he not helping you look for her?" she explained.

"I did no' see Donny either," he realized aloud.

"Well, maybe they are together somewhere. I know he has not left," she said with certainty. "His vehicle is still here."

Scotty frowned, but turned to head back out of the hall into the main part of the building. Now Donny was missing too? Or he might have been in the front yard when he and Mortimer searched the house. For that matter, Scotty thought suddenly, perhaps Beth was too. She had to be here somewhere. The car she'd rented until she bought another vehicle was still in the parking lot. He'd noted that from her bedroom window when he'd checked her room the second time.

His gaze slid around the yard. It seemed strangely empty without the dogs, and he now wondered how long they'd been in the kennels for feeding. The dogs, the fence, and the gate worked together to ensure the security at the Enforcer house. So long as the dogs were out, no one could get over the fence and around the property unnoticed, but while they were inside . . . that was another story. He should have asked Odilia that.

Eighteen

A sharp pain in her hands stirred Beth from sleep. She shifted with a moan, or tried to, and frowned when she found her movement restricted. She opened her eyes with confusion, peered around and began to wake up much more quickly as alarm slid through her. She was lying on her side on the floor of one of the kennels, her hands restrained behind her back, presumably with the same heavy chain she could see around her ankles. She was experiencing pain because she'd been bound so tightly, the blood supply to her hands and feet was cut off.

Beth raised her head and swiveled it first one way and then the other. The dogs were busy gobbling up whatever was in their food dishes, and paying her no attention at all. But she could hear voices coming from outside the room, and was just opening her mouth to call out for help when the talking ended on the sound of a closing door. Beth shouted anyway, despite knowing this part of the building was soundproofed so dogs barking and inmates shouting wouldn't drive anyone who had to man the office crazy.

Much to her surprise, the door to the hallway opened almost at once. Unfortunately, it was Odilia who entered.

"Awake, I see." Her voice was cold and calm as she walked over to stand in front of the seven-foot-high chain-link door at the end of the kennel. She peered at Beth with disinterest, and then glanced toward the dogs as they finished eating and moved to surround her. Odilia waited another minute for the last dog to finish, and then walked to the door at the opposite end of the room from the one she'd just entered and opened it. Beth knew it led directly outside, and wasn't surprised when every last dog went rushing through. Dinner was done—time to play and poop, she thought grimly.

Odilia let the door close and then locked it before turning to walk back to survey Beth. After eyeing her briefly, she commented, "I thought the kennel was an appropriate place to put you until we could leave. After all, you have been acting little better than a bitch in heat."

Beth stiffened, but then forced an uncaring shrug. "Wouldn't want you to be the only bitch in here."

She watched the fury explode on Odilia's expression and then ignored the pain in her hands and feet and shifted to a sitting position before asking, "Who were you talking to in the hall?"

Odilia's fury disappeared at once and she smiled slyly. "Scotty. He is looking for you. I asked if he needed my help, or if Donny was helping him look, and when he said he had not found Donny in his search either, I suggested perhaps the two of you are together." Her smile widened. "He will soon be imagining you are somewhere spreading your legs for the boy."

Beth's eyebrows rose and she said with amusement, "He won't think that at all. And the very fact that you think for even a moment that he would believe it possible tells me you know absolutely nothing about life mates."

"He will," she spat furiously. "You are a prostitute! A whore! You probably spread your legs for half of London back in the day, and half of Toronto since you got here. He will believe it, and he will see just how cheap a slag you are and how unworthy you are of him and the love he proclaimed for you."

"Where is Donny?" Beth asked rather than address her words. But she hadn't missed that the woman had basically admitted that she must have been listening to her and Scotty in her room earlier when they'd said they loved each other.

"Somewhere safe," Odilia said, calming at once. Her mouth even curved into a slight smile again. "Do not worry. You will be joining him soon enough."

Beth nodded, and then raised her eyebrows. "So, I'm guessing this means it was you behind everything?"

"Yes," Odilia said simply.

"Just so I'm clear," Beth said, "you were behind it *all*? The highway accident? The sword attack? The barn? Rickart's car? You were behind all those attempts on my life?"

Odilia nodded, but her expression was annoyed. "And you skated through every single damned attempt!"

"Well, I wouldn't say 'skated,'" Beth said modestly. "I mean, you almost hacked my arm off, and I was burned pretty good in the barn. I'm not sure what injuries I sustained from the bombing—nobody's told me yet—but I'm sure they were gruesome and painful too." She tilted her head. "I did survive, though. Sorry if that didn't jibe with your plans. I've been told I can be difficult to work with. To be fair, though, you didn't really tell me your plan, and it's hard to cooperate when I don't know the plan."

Beth watched the woman for a moment and could see the fury building quickly in her again. She was up and down like a yo-yo, with little to no control at all. Definitely off her rocker. Anger was good. Angry people made mistakes. Crazy people, though? Yeah, they were unpredictable and dangerous. A change of tactics was necessary.

"So you were already in Toronto when Scotty got here?" she guessed, and wasn't surprised to see the woman calm again at once.

"I arrived a day ahead of him. I was supposed to be checking out a tip about a possible rogue in Kirkwall in the UK. I called in the tip," she admitted with amusement. "And I called in regular reports that were completely bogus."

"How did you know we had gone to Vancouver?" Beth asked, very curious to hear the answer. That had been the stumbling block to connecting the attack in Vancouver to the others, after all.

"Scotty," Odilia said with a grin. "He called in and told Magnus that Mortimer needed help out here and to round up Rickart, myself, and three others. He said to send the three others to Toronto and that

Magnus, Rickart, and myself should meet him in Vancouver. He would contact us with the address as soon as he knew what it was."

Odilia shrugged. "As I said, I was supposed to be in Kirkwall, which is way up in the north of nowhere, so I said I would fly commercial to British Columbia from Scotland and meet Magnus and Rickart in Vancouver rather than fly to London, where they were, and travel with them. I followed you from the house that first day, caused the accident, and when that didn't work, I then hopped on a plane in Toronto. I probably landed an hour after you. I went to the Enforcer house there when Magnus texted me the address, and then followed you again, this time to the club."

"Right," Beth breathed. Well, they had kept saying only a hunter could know where they were. They'd been right; they just hadn't even considered the UK hunters. And why would they? She'd never even met Odilia before. This wasn't about her at all. It was about Scotty. Odilia was having a "little princess" moment. A "he's my daddy and I don't share" hissy fit, Beth thought with disgust, but simply asked patiently, "I presume there is a reason you've been doing all this? Scotty, perchance?"

"Of course, Scotty," Odilia snapped. "You are not good enough for him."

"Yeah, I've kind of heard that already. More times than I care to count, actually, and I'm really kind of getting tired of hearing it," she muttered.

"Well then, maybe you should start listening," Odilia said coldly. "You do not belong with him. He is mine."

Frowning, Beth tried reason. "Odilia, I realize Scotty raised you and is like a father to you, but—"

"Father?" she said with amazement. "We were lovers!"

Okay, that caught her completely by surprise.

"I thought you said he raised you," Beth said finally.

"I said he took me in," Odilia snapped. "I did not say he adopted me."

"Well then . . ." She stared at her with confusion.

"His house in London is huge," Odilia said with a shrug. "I was given a wing along with Mrs. McCurdy, the woman who was brought in to take care of me as a child. Scotty had his own wing. But he wasn't there often," she added irritably. "I saw him maybe a handful of times before I reached the age of majority and then mostly at a distance. But he wrote letters. I wrote letters. He kept tabs on me through Mrs. McCurdy. He was always out traveling, hunting, chasing down rogues. And then of course I had to leave London or risk exposure, because I wasn't aging. I traveled the Continent for a while, went to see the Americas, returned to the Continent . . . and then I heard that Jamieson was back in London. Scotty, of course, was hard on his trail almost immediately. It took me some time, however, to get back to England. The night I got there was the night they caught and killed him."

"The night I was rescued," Beth murmured.

Odilia nodded resentfully.

"I didn't see you there," Beth said quietly.

"I had gone to Scotty's house, but he had already left. It took me some time to find out where he was and follow. It was all over when I got there. The carriage taking you and Alexandrina Argenis to the docks was leaving just as I finally arrived. I could not find Scotty at first, though, so went into the house. I . . ." She closed her eyes, and Beth knew exactly what she'd found. Blood everywhere, Jamieson's remains, the bodies of the other women she and Dree had been going to save, the rotting corpses of men, women, and children strewn about and left to rot, and a stench so foul . . .

Beth lowered her head and closed her eyes briefly, trying to clear the smell and images from her mind. Just thinking about it put her right back in that house, in the middle of the madness and horror and—

"It was so like my home when I woke up after I turned," Odilia said unhappily. "Worse, really. I think I would have gone mad if Scotty hadn't come in when he did and ushered me out. He put me right into a carriage and sent me back to his house, promising he'd return as soon as he could."

Odilia's face twitched and she admitted, "Everything is kind of a blur after that until he came home. I remember getting to the house and going in, but everything felt . . . separate from me somehow . . . and I was suddenly so exhausted. The housekeeper tried to convince me to go to bed, but I wanted to wait for Scotty. I wanted to hear what happened. I needed to. I felt like . . . I was desperate to hear it, so she brought me a cinnamon bun and let me be. I was not hungry—I was still feeling unconnected—so just sat there, not doing anything or even thinking really, until Scotty got home and came to find me.

"He told me what had happened, but kept sniffing the air as he did," Odilia said with remembered amusement. "And then he finally asked what that cinnamon scent was and I said it was the bun the housekeeper had left out, but I did not want it. He picked it up, gave it a sniff and then took a bite, and seemed quite surprised that it was good. He just gobbled it up."

Beth didn't comment. She wasn't surprised. It made sense. She and Scotty had met earlier in the evening. They were life mates. His hungers would have been reawakened by that meeting. All of his hungers.

"I was shocked and just stared at him," Odilia continued. "I knew how old he was and that he didn't eat anymore. Yet he was eating. When I pointed it out to him, he kind of froze, and just sat there for a minute, and then he turned and stared at me for the longest time. I was about to ask him if he was all right when the butler came to inform him that Magnus had arrived.

"Scotty excused himself and left to speak to Magnus, but he hadn't quite pulled the door closed, and I heard them out in the hall by the front door. Magnus had come to inform him that a couple of the younger hunters had told him they'd been able to read Scotty's thoughts after the raid on the charnel house. He wanted to know why Scotty hadn't told him that he'd met his life mate. Scotty said he hadn't realized it until just now himself. That he'd come home and eaten a bun, and when he realized what he was doing, had tried to read me and could not."

Beth stiffened. "What?"

"He could not read me," Odilia said slowly and clearly as if speaking to someone hard of hearing. She followed it up with a triumphant smile.

"But—" Beth shook her head with bewilderment. That couldn't be. He was *her* life mate, not Odilia's.

How could he not read her either? The only time you couldn't read another immortal was if they were older, insane, or your life ma—

Oh, she thought suddenly. Beth had already deduced that the woman was off her rocker. She should have realized this wasn't a new status. But why hadn't Scotty known that back then? He'd . . . not raised the girl, she realized. Had seen her only a handful of times. Mrs. McCurdy had raised her and apparently never bothered to mention to her employer that the girl he'd put in her charge was a nutter. Great. But why hadn't he sorted out since then that the woman was insane?

"Magnus, of course, congratulated him," Odilia continued, drawing Beth's attention back to her story. "And told him he'd leave us be to enjoy our discovery of each other, and then he departed. I rushed out into the hall the moment he was gone and hurried to Scotty, and he took me in his arms and kissed me so sweetly."

Beth's eyebrows rose. She would not describe any of her own kisses with Scotty as sweet. Hot, passionate, hungry, devouring, frenzied, consuming, vigorous, even almost violent, yes. But sweet? Nope. Poor thing, she thought, eyeing Odilia with pity. The woman had no idea what she was missing.

"And then he swept me up in his arms, carried me to my room, and made gentle, tender love to me," Odilia said on a sigh.

"Sounds like a bad romance novel," Beth said dryly.

"It was beautiful!" Odilia shrieked. "The best night of my life."

"Lame life, then," she said with a shrug.

Odilia's face was purple, her eyes narrowed to slits, and Beth truly thought she'd pushed her too far. But then the woman suddenly relaxed and even gave a snort of laughter. "You are jealous."

Beth didn't deny that. Why bother? It was probably true. Oh, not of the night Odilia had just described. That might be a nice change in maybe five or six hundred years, but she preferred the passionate lover Scotty was with her. She *was* jealous that he'd slept with Odilia at all, though, which was silly. She'd had lovers over the last hundred years. Okay, so in her mind they'd unknowingly had his face in her bed, but still . . .

"It was so lovely," Odilia remembered softly. "And I was so happy. I worshiped Scotty. He was so handsome, so smart, so kind, and he'd taken care of me. He was wonderful, gentle, and caring. I had never had a lover who made me feel the way he did. For three months, every day was a sweet revelation."

Three months? Beth closed her eyes and hung her head. Man, had she gotten it wrong. What a mess. And what had Scotty been thinking?

"He was thinking I was his life mate," Odilia said with pleasure.

"But he wasn't, was he?" she said sharply.

"He should have been!" Odilia shrieked with frustration. "Look at you. You are nothing but a whore, and a *common* whore at that, while he is a *laird*! You are not good enough for him. I am a lady! My father was a baron. I have money. I was raised properly, and I would never sell myself for a couple of coins."

"No, I'm sure you wouldn't," Beth agreed. "But apparently you'll blow people up, cut them into pieces with wire traps and—Oh my God, you were willing to blow up Rickart and Magnus," she said suddenly.

Odilia shrugged her shoulders. "Collateral damage."

"But they're friends of Scotty's," she pointed out with disbelief. "And yours. You work with them."

"Collateral damage," she said again.

"Oh, wow," Beth said with disgust. "You're a complete and utter sociopath."

Odilia raised one eyebrow. "Really? You are going to say something like that to the woman who is going to kill you?"

Beth considered the question and then shrugged. "You can only kill me once. It's not like you can kill me for every insult I give you."

"No. But I can make it extremely painful and last a really long time to pay you back for every word you say that I do not like," she pointed out.

"Somehow I don't think you have the time," Beth said with certainty. "We won't be alone out here long enough for that."

"Oh, I am sorry. Did you think I was going to kill you here?" Odilia asked tauntingly. "No, no, no. You will only stay here for another half an hour, and then my shift is over and I am going to put you in the back of one of the vans and take you to my place, where I can kill you quickly . . . or slowly. The choice will be yours. Oh, wait," she added. "Actually the choice would be mine, so maybe you had better start being nicer to me."

Beth shook her head. "This isn't going to work at all, Odilia. Scotty will never love you. You're not his life mate and you don't really want him anyway," she added with exasperation. "If you knew what it was like to have a life mate, you wouldn't look twice at Scotty. Didn't Magnus and Scotty tell you that? Didn't they explain what it was like to have a life mate?" Beth closed her eyes even as she finished asking the question and then muttered, "What am I thinking? They're men. Men don't talk about stuff like that." Sighing, she raised her head and asked, "What about this Mrs. McCurdy? Surely she told you something?"

"Mrs. McCurdy was very old-fashioned," Odilia said primly. "She told me to wait for the right man. Scotty is the right man."

"No he's not," Beth assured her, and then suggested, "Read my mind. Since I'm a new life mate, I know you can. Look into my memories and see what I'm talking about."

"No," Odilia growled.

"Just read my mind," Beth insisted. "Or are you afraid to see I'm right?"

"Shut up!" Odilia snapped. "I hate you. I hate you so much. Everything was perfect, and then he went to Spain and had those damned shared dreams . . . Until then, he thought I was his life mate."

"I don't know how," Beth said with exasperation. "He should have known that lame-ass sex you two had wasn't life mate sex. Gentle and caring!" She snorted. "Did he ever want to be inside you so bad he ripped your knickers wide open just to get to you? Did he ever make you scream with pleasure so all-encompassing you passed out from the strength of it? *That* is life mate sex, not this insipid childish nonsense you keep prattling on about."

Beth shut up then, mostly because she'd become aware that Odilia was pale and quivering, her eyes stricken as she concentrated on Beth's forehead. The woman was reading her memories as she'd suggested, and Beth gave them to her with both barrels, remembering every encounter she'd had with Scotty and letting it replay inside her mind like a porno. Every position in the garage in Vancouver, the heated moments on the plane, the two days they'd spent in bed while he healed and after. Even the dream sex they'd shared that had started in the market and ended in the forest-green bedroom.

"That's why he changed the color of his room?" Odilia breathed, sounding beyond hurt. "For you? For a hundred years he has not allowed anyone to change it. He has it repainted the same color, has the sheets custom-made if he cannot find them in that color, and it was all for you?"

Beth's eyebrows rose. Odilia had seen all he'd done to her in that bedroom and *that* was what she was upset about? The color of the room. Scotty had said he'd decorated it that color because he'd known it would suit her. That she was—

"Fire and ice in a forest of green," Odilia breathed, and then rage filled her face again and she withdrew the dart gun from her weapons belt and shot her again.

"Maybe she and Donny went for a walk," Mortimer suggested, and then cursed and said, "This was a hell of a time for the cameras to go down."

"Somehow I do no' think that is a coincidence," Scotty growled.

"No," Mortimer agreed. He shook his head, looking frustrated. "They *must* have gone for a walk."

"I do no' think so," Scotty countered, shaking his head. "They have no' left the grounds, and we've been out in the yard and they were no' there. 'Sides, surely they'd have returned by now if they'd just gone fer a walk?"

He and Mortimer had been running around in circles trying to figure out where the pair could be since Scotty had returned and passed on what he'd realized while talking to Odilia—that Donny was missing.

Mortimer seemed to think that was a good thing. That it probably meant they were both fine. Scotty didn't agree. It made him more anxious.

"We did not check the airstrip. That is quite a hike. They would take longer to walk that," Mortimer pointed out.

Scotty stared at him in stunned silence for a moment, shocked that he hadn't thought of it himself.

"Come on," Mortimer said, leading him out of his office. "We can take the van. It is in the attached garage."

Scotty followed him through the kitchen to the door to the attached garage and headed for the passenger side, but paused when Mortimer threw him the keys to the vehicle. Scotty caught them instinctively and then glanced to him with surprise.

"I noticed that you like to drive," the man said dryly as he passed him to take the passenger seat himself.

Fingers tightening around the keys, Scotty hurried around to the driver's side. Mortimer had hit the remote on the visor to open the garage door before Scotty was inside. By the time he started the engine, it was already halfway up, and he had to wait barely a moment before he could slam on the gas and squeal out of the garage. He turned the wheel sharply the moment they were clear of the building, sending the van shooting around the house and along the lane toward the back of the property.

He spotted the door of the outbuilding opening, but didn't slow when he saw Odilia step out and glance around with curiosity. He was busy concentrating on the way the lane ahead narrowed as they surged into the trees. Mortimer's phone began to ring as the trees closed in on either side.

"It is Magnus," he said, and pushed the button to put the call on speakerphone.

"Mortimer?" Magnus's voice asked.

"And Scotty," Mortimer told him.

They heard Magnus grunt and then he said, "I thought you said the cameras at the apartment building were just empty casings? Fakes to deter criminal activity rather than working cameras to film it?"

"Yes," Mortimer agreed. "That is what I was told."

"Well, we were talking to the store clerk while waiting for the film to copy, and he asked us why we did not get the film footage from the apartment building. We told him what you had said about the cameras not being real and there not being footage, and he said sure the cameras are real. The manager of the apartment building drops in to the store all the time to buy cigarettes and is forever complaining about how he has to clean the camera lenses twice a week, or the picture on the film is so fuzzy you cannot see the faces of the kids who keep spraying graffiti on the walls."

"Did ye go talk to the manager yerselves?" Scotty asked at once.

"We are waiting for him now," Magnus said. "He—Just a minute. Here he comes."

Scotty frowned impatiently, but concentrated on not sideswiping one of the trees on either side of them. He now understood why they usually used the golf cart to drive people and luggage back and forth. The lane was crazy narrow.

They were just breaking out of the trees onto the airstrip and Scotty was scanning the empty tarmac when Magnus came back online. "The cameras are real and the manager says no one approached him about them."

Stiffening, Scotty glanced to Mortimer. "Who was supposed to check the cameras?"

"Odilia," Mortimer said quietly.

"Scotty," Magnus said, his voice full of concern.

"I know," he growled and, taking his foot off the gas, jerked the steering wheel of the van, sending the vehicle into a spin that ended with them facing the way they'd come. He hit the gas again at once, and they surged forward, rocketing back into the trees.

"Why would Odilia lie about that?" Mortimer asked quietly as he ended the call.

Scotty shook his head. He had an idea, but it wasn't a good one and he didn't want to talk about it. He just wanted to get back to the outbuilding. Beth had to be in the kennels. It was the only place he hadn't actually looked for himself. He'd just trusted Odilia when she'd said Beth wasn't there. Although she hadn't really said she wasn't there, he realized now. She'd just deflected the question with some comment about Beth still recovering.

This was all his fault, of course. He'd brought her here to Canada.

"But Odilia could not have caused the accident on the highway," Mortimer said suddenly. "She was not here before you flew to Vancouver."

"I wouldn't bet on that," Scotty said, his mouth tight.

"You think she was here even then?" Mortimer asked.

"She was supposed to be in Kirkwall, in Northern Scotland," he said grimly. "But she was on her own. She could have been here and said she was there. I know she insisted on flying straight to Vancouver from Scotland rather than fly back to London and travel from there with the men."

Mortimer merely grunted. They'd left the trees, and he and Scotty were both looking toward the outbuilding and Odilia's car. Scotty had started to steer toward it when Mortimer suddenly barked, "The van!"

Scotty followed his pointing finger toward the van presently pulling through the first gate. Even as he looked, Russell was closing the first gate and Francis was opening the second one.

"It has to be Odilia in the van. There's no one else here but Donny and Beth and they're both missing," Mortimer pointed out as Scotty took his foot off the gas, but hesitated to change direction.

Cursing, Scotty jerked the steering wheel again, this time steering straight up the driveway toward the gates. As he slammed his foot back on the gas pedal, he warned, "Ye'd best call and make sure the gates're open when we get there. I'm no' stopping. I'll drive right through the damned things."

"Lay on the horn," Mortimer said and quickly began tapping away on his phone. When a *ding* sounded, Scotty realized the man had texted rather than calling. Smart. Probably faster. Hopefully, Scotty thought, hesitating to hit the horn and give Odilia warning that they were giving chase.

Much to his relief, the first gate started opening almost at once and the second gate didn't close. Scotty shot through both and turned right, which was the direction Odilia had taken. Either she'd seen them careening down the driveway behind her, or she was just in a hurry, because she was already a good distance up the road. Scotty ground his teeth together and put his foot all the way down, but didn't expect the response he got. The van jumped and shot forward at a startling speed.

"Rogues do not usually come quietly, so I had my van hopped up just for chases like this," Mortimer explained, apparently noting his surprise. "One of the boys is a car enthusiast and switched out the engine for a Porsche turbo something or other. Fortunately, I only had my van and the SUVs tricked out like this and not the cleanup vans like the one Odilia is driving."

Scotty merely nodded, and concentrated on what he was doing as he steered their van up beside the one Odilia was driving. He slowed once he was beside her, and gestured for her to pull over, but she refused to even look in their direction.

"What now?" Mortimer asked.

Scotty was silent for a moment, considering all the alternatives.

"Odilia must know we've figured out she's behind everything now," Mortimer pointed out.

Scotty nodded. That meant she knew her fate if she stopped. Odilia was rogue. She'd killed one of Kira's bodyguards, injured and nearly killed Magnus and Rickart, and repeatedly tried to kill Beth. She'd be sentenced to beheading by the Council.

"She will not stop willingly," Mortimer pointed out. "She has nothing to lose."

"And she won't hesitate to take Beth with her rather than allow herself to be caught," Scotty growled. "And Donny too, if he's in the van."

Mortimer reached for his seat belt, and calmly did it up. Scotty didn't. He needed to be able to get out quickly once he got the vehicles stopped.

"Sorry about yer van," Scotty said with regret.

"The Council will replace it," Mortimer said with a shrug.

Nodding, Scotty dropped back a bit and steered into the van, bumping it gently at first, but continuing to steer to the right and forcing the van Odilia was driving toward the ditch on the side of the road. She caught him by surprise when she suddenly swerved to the left, steering into him now. Scotty held steady, but quickly realized she'd just been trying to distract him when he saw the tree ahead on the side of the road. He swallowed a sudden ball in his throat, fearing he knew exactly what she would do, and knowing for certain it was too late to prevent it from happening. Even now Odilia was turning sharply toward that large old oak tree.

Scotty slammed on the brakes at once, practically standing on them in his determination to stop the damned van as Odilia sent hers crashing into the tree. Even so, he overshot the accident, rushing past as the van crumpled against the tree, the engine in the front exploding on impact.

Cursing, Scotty jerked the steering wheel to spin the van again, just as he'd done on the tarmac of the air-strip, and drove back to pause behind the now burning van. Praying under his breath, he threw open his door and ran to the back of the other vehicle, nearly ripping the doors off in his desperation. Smoke immediately billowed out, but he spotted a pair of chain-wrapped feet, and grabbed one foot to drag the unmoving body toward him.

"It's Donny!" Mortimer said. "I have him. Get Beth."

Leaving the young immortal to Mortimer, Scotty crawled into the van and felt around until his hand found hair. Crawling further forward, he followed the hair to a head, and then a neck and finally a shoulder and arm as the smoke thickened and the heat increased, suggesting the flames were getting closer. Catching the body by one wrist, Scotty crawled quickly backward, pulling whoever it was along with him. It wasn't until he had climbed out of the back and pulled the upper body clear of the smoke that he was able to see and knew for certain it was Beth.

"Thank God," he breathed, scooping her up and turning to carry her quickly to the back of Mortimer's van. He gently laid her down next to Donny in the back, and then turned toward the burning vehicle, but Mortimer caught his arm.

"There's nothing you can do for her," he said quietly.

Scotty stared at the burning vehicle. The front was completely engulfed in flames that were slowly moving their way backward, eating up the interior of the van. There was no way Odilia could still be alive.

Swallowing, he turned back to Beth to look her over. From what he could see she had multiple bruises, gashes, and a couple of broken bones. But they would heal quickly enough. She was alive, and that was what mattered.

"I will drive," Mortimer offered.

Nodding, Scotty climbed into the back of the van and lifted Beth into his lap to cradle her on the ride back.

Mortimer closed the doors.

Nineteen

Beth turned onto her side with a little sigh, and then opened her eyes sleepily, only to scowl when she found herself staring at a pale yellow wall.

"Not again," she muttered. "I think I hate this room."

"Well, ye ha'e spent a powerful amount o' time in it, and no' at all fer the reason it was intended."

Rolling quickly onto her back, Beth swung her head around and stared at Scotty, her eyes quickly narrowing. "You."

His brow furrowed with concern. "Did I do something wrong, me love?"

"You slept with Odilia!" Beth accused. "Why the devil would you do that?"

Scotty lowered his head on a sigh, and muttered, "I thought she was me life mate at the time."

"I know that," she snapped. "And I even understand that first time. But once you'd actually bedded her, surely you sensed it wasn't quite right? She described it as gentle, caring and sweet, for God's sake," Beth said with disgust. "That is not life mate sex, Scotty."

"Nay, it's not," he agreed with a crooked smile, and then pointed out, "But I had nothing to compare it to at the time."

"Well, did you faint?" she asked, already knowing the answer. "That might have been a good tip-off."

Scotty grimaced. "I have heard o' cases where life mates do no' faint at first. No' until they learn to trust each other and are ready to let go emotionally."

When Beth merely glared at him, he said, "Truly, lass, I felt something was missing, but thought mayhap she just did no' trust me enough yet or something. It was no' until I experienced shared dreams with ye on me trip to Spain that I knew the mistake I'd made. When that dream sex was so hot and passionate and a million times better than *real* sex with Odilia, I knew I'd made an error."

"Uh-huh," Beth said grimly. "And apparently it completely slipped your notice that she was crazy as a loon?"

"Aye, it did," Scotty said seriously.

"You couldn't read her, Scotty," she pointed out quietly.

"I know, but I didn't try to read her again after that first night until I returned from me trip to Spain having realized she was no' me life mate. And I *was* able to read her then."

"Really?" Beth asked with surprise.

Scotty nodded. "She must have read me the minute I entered and realized what was coming. If she was mad even then, she must have fed me her thoughts rather than me reading them. Whatever the case, when

I could read her then, I decided my inability to read her before must have been because she was temporarily scattered by what she'd seen in the house we rescued ye from. I thought mayhap it had reminded her o' the horrors o' her childhood and she was in shock that night, or some such thing."

"Temporary insanity?" she suggested.

"Aye," he agreed. "And she seemed to accept it easily enough when I told her that I'd made a mistake and we were no' life mates, so . . ." He shrugged helplessly.

"Oh." Beth let her breath out on a small sigh, her irritation going with it. After a moment, she said, "So, the last thing I remember, I was on the floor in one of the kennels, and then Odilia shot me with her damned dart gun . . . again," she added dryly. Raising her eyebrows, she asked, "What happened after that?"

Scotty quickly and solemnly told her what she'd missed, and they both fell silent for a moment. Then Beth said simply, "I'm sorry about Odilia, Scotty."

He shook his head. "I think mayhap she was too traumatized by what happened to her and her family when she was so young. I fear I made a lot o' mistakes when it comes to you and Odilia. First I thought her my life mate when it was you, and then I thought you needed the mind wipe when ye did no', and now I think mayhap she is the one I should ha'e insisted on having a mind wipe. Mayhap had I done so, she could have found some happiness in this life."

"She found some happiness," Beth assured him solemnly. "That period when you thought her your life mate, she was happy. It wouldn't have lasted even if you hadn't sorted it out, but she was happy for a time."

Scotty looked down, and she wasn't sure if telling him that was good or just made him feel worse, but then he sighed and straightened to say, "We still have to finish our earlier conversation."

Beth stilled, recalling the conversation in question. When Donny had interrupted them earlier, Scotty had just vowed to spend his life making up for hurting her if she'd give him the chance and agree to be his life mate.

"But first," Scotty added before she could speak, "do ye need anything? More blood, mayhap? Or are ye hungry?"

Beth was going to lie and say no so that they could finish that conversation, but her stomach spoke up for her with a loud growl.

Chuckling softly, Scotty stood at once. "I'll go down and fetch ye something to eat."

Beth hesitated, but when he started toward the door, she quickly said, "I'll go with you."

Scotty swung back with surprise. "There's no need, lass. I'm happy to fetch something fer ye."

"Thank you, but *I'd* be happy to get out of this room. I'm thoroughly sick of it," she admitted, tossing her bedding aside. She then paused as she saw that she was wearing an overlarge T-shirt rather than the hated hospital gown. Beth peered at it blankly, not recognizing the top.

"Rachel put ye in a hospital gown, but I brought one o' me T-shirts in and had her change ye into it. I ken ye do no' like the hospital gowns, and while I ken ye prefer sleeping in the nude, I did no' want ye to think I was takin' liberties," Scotty explained as he moved back and offered her his hand to help her up from the bed.

Beth peered from the T-shirt to his hand, taking in his thoughtfulness with both actions. She then shifted her gaze to his face, stared at him solemnly for a minute and simply said, "Yes."

Scotty stilled, and for a moment she felt sure she'd have to explain what she was saying yes to, but then he asked hopefully, "Yes, ye will be me life mate?"

Biting her lip, Beth nodded.

"Thank God," he breathed and bent to scoop her out of the bed. Crushing her to his chest, he said, "Thank ye, Beth. I promise ye'll never regret it. I ken I've been an ass, but I'll spend the rest o' our lives making it up to ye."

"I'll hold you to that," she said, wrapping her arms around his shoulders and hugging him back.

The threat made him chuckle, but he drew back to peer at her, his expression growing serious before he said, "Ye'll no' have to, lass. 'Twill be me pleasure to treat ye as ye always should ha'e been treated."

"And how is that?" Beth asked with curiosity as he started toward the door.

"Like a queen," he answered promptly. Pausing for her to open the door, he added, "Or better yet, as the goddess ye are."

"Goddess, eh?" she asked with amusement as he carried her out of the room she was coming to hate.

"Aye," he assured her as he started down the hall. "Ye're everything to me, lass. All I could have ever wanted, and all I'll ever need."

"I guess that's why we're life mates," Beth said, wondering how the nanos knew such things.

"Ye're more than me life mate, Beth." Pausing suddenly, Scotty met her gaze and said seriously, "I love ye, Elizabeth Sheppard Argenis. I love ye, and everything about ye, and I'll thank God and the nanos and the universe itself every day o' me life fer gifting me with ye fer a mate."

"Oh," Beth breathed, blinking back the tears suddenly crowding her eyes. But then she said, "I love you too, Scotty."

"Ye do no' have to say that if it's no' true, lass," he said gently. "I hope someday it will be true, but I ken I've been an ass, and—"

"You *have* been an ass," Beth interrupted. "You've been stubborn, and bossy, and just plain stupid at times."

"Aye, I have," he admitted wryly.

"And if you hadn't been, we'd have reached this point long ago," she pointed out.

"True," he agreed solemnly.

"But you're also smart, and you have a wicked sense of humor, and you're strong and dependable and patient, and I can't imagine my life without you in it," she continued. Then she raised a hand, caressed his cheek and added, "And I don't want to. I do love you, Cullen MacDonald."

"Thank God fer that," Scotty breathed and bent to press a gentle kiss to her lips. At least, it started gentle, a heartbreakingly sweet caress that seemed almost a vow on its own. Beth felt that kiss to the bottom of her soul, and tears immediately pricked her eyes as her heart melted. But she wasn't Odilia. Beth was Scotty's life mate, and the sweet and gentle soon led to heat and passion. She wasn't even sure when it changed—perhaps when she sighed against his lips—but suddenly Scotty was urging her lips apart to allow him in.

Beth opened to him at once, her hands clutching at his shoulders as his tongue thrust forward to stake a claim. Her own tongue met his, welcoming and eager, and her body shifted restlessly in his arms, her back trying to arch as desire rushed through her.

Groaning, Scotty released her legs and let her dangle flush against him. He then pressed her against the wall and caught the backs of her thighs, urging her legs up. Beth immediately wrapped them around him, and then moaned into his mouth as he shifted and ground against her. Pinning her there against the wall with his hips, Scotty removed one hand from her legs so that he could find and squeeze one breast through the loose T-shirt she wore.

A long, low groan immediately slid from Beth's lips and she arched into the caress, her kiss becoming almost frantic. But when her legs tightened around his hips, and she shifted against the hardness pressing against her, Scotty broke their kiss on a curse and leaned his forehead against hers.

After taking a moment to catch his breath, he asked, "Lass, how hungry are ye?"

"Very, very hungry," Beth said breathlessly, and when he slumped against her, added, "For you."

"Thank God," he growled, and reached to the side.

Beth noted the door next to them with surprise as he turned the knob and thrust it open. She then gasped as he caught her against him and carried her into the room. Her gaze slid around the blue room as he paused to kick the door closed, and then she met his gaze. "Your room?"

"Our room," he corrected her as he walked to the bed, with her wrapped around him and clinging like a monkey. "Ye said ye were sick o' yer room, so we'll stay here. For now," he added, pausing next to the bed. He released the hold he had on her legs so that they dropped and she was flush against him again, and then set her gently on her feet.

"And then?" she asked, tilting her head to eye him with interest. She had just moved here to Canada, but he was the head of the UK hunters and would have to live there.

"And then, after we marry, we'll live wherever ye want," he said solemnly. "Here in Toronto, or that little town ye mentioned where Dree lives. Wherever ye want," he repeated.

"You'd give up your position as head of the UK hunters for me?" she asked with surprise.

"I'd give up everything fer ye, lass," he said solemnly. "Ye're me life mate, me love, and me whole world now."

Beth stared at him wide-eyed, touched beyond words.

Shifting under her gaze, he glanced toward the door and frowned. "Mayhap I should fetch ye some blood or—"

Beth covered his mouth with one hand and shook her head. "I don't want blood. All I want in this moment is you."

"Thank God," he growled, and was on her at once, his arms catching her up and bearing her down onto the bed beside them.

Beth went willingly with a laugh that was cut off when his mouth covered hers. But she could still hear that "thank God" in her head as his hands began to rove over her, and silently echoed it herself. Her life had been a long hard road at times, but it had brought her to this place and this man, and she thanked God for every trial that had led her here. If this was the prize, then it had been worth every moment.

Read on for a sneak peek at the next book in Lynsay Sands's Highlander series

SURRENDER TO THE HIGHLANDER

Coming February 2018!

The sound of a terrible explosion woke Edith. Blinking her eyes open, she glanced frantically around the room, and then jerked her gaze to her right as the sound came again. She gaped at the man slumped in the seat next to the bed. He was the source of the sound. Not an explosion at all, but a loud snuffling snort as the fellow snored in his sleep. Dear God, she'd never heard such a horrendous racket.

Edith stared at the man blankly, wondering who the devil he was and why he was in her room, and then she noticed the woman in bed next to her and peered at her with mingled confusion and concern. She recognized her at once as Victoria's maid, Effie. But finding her in her bed was somewhat surprising. The fact that the woman looked terribly ill just added to her bewilderment. The old woman was extremely pale, not an ounce of color in her thin, wrinkled skin, and she was completely unmoving too. Effie was so still,

Edith wasn't even sure she was breathing at first. She was beginning to worry the woman was dead when she noted that her chest was rising and lowering the faintest bit with slow, shallow breaths.

Relieved, Edith relaxed and then glanced around her chamber again. Her room was generally neat and tidy, but at present it looked like there really had been an explosion. An empty mug lay on its side on the bedside table, next to one standing up and two empty bowls. A bread crust and another cup and bowl were on the bedside table on the other side, and then a cask sat on the table at the far end of the room with several more metal cups and bowls between it and a small pile of browning vegetable peels. There was also what appeared to be a rabbit pelt, freshly skinned.

Wondering who had held the party in her room while she was sleeping, Edith glanced over the floor now, noting the sacks lined up against the wall. There were four in all with various items spilling out of them—cloth, vegetables, and weapons. And the rush mats on the floor were both crushed and kicked aside, showing a lot of use and definite trails from the door to both the bed and table, and then from both the table and bed to the fireplace, where a pot of something was bubbling over the fire.

Edith didn't have a clue what to make of all of it, or the fact that there was presently a man at her bedside like some very loud guardian angel.

Or perhaps just a guard.

That last thought was a bit disturbing. Edith knew she'd been sick for a while. The mess in her room suggested it had been quite a while. What had been happening at Drummond while she was out of her head with illness? Had one of the clans they were feuding with learned of the deaths of her father and brothers and decided to take advantage and attack the castle?

The idea was an alarming one, particularly since she had not been awake to aid in defending against such a happenstance. Her brother Brodie, much as she loved him, was spoiled rotten and not the most capable of men. He would be useless in such a situation, she was sure.

Biting her lip, Edith peered warily at the man slumped in the chair next to the bed. He was a big fellow, with wide shoulders and a youthful but not unhandsome face. He was also a complete stranger, not one of the Drummond men. Her gaze dropped to Effie again and she nudged her with her elbow, hoping the woman would wake and tell her what was going on and what had happened while she was ill. When the first nudge had no effect, she gave her a second, firmer poke, but that produced no response either.

Deciding to let the poor woman rest, Edith sat up, or tried. Honestly, it was an effort just to get herself into an upright position. She was as weak as a babe, and had to turn on her side and slide her feet off the bed so her legs hung off of it, and then push herself up into a sitting position.

Panting and sweaty from what should have been an easy task, Edith swayed where she sat on the edge of the bed and eyed the door with grim determination. Her chamber wasn't really that big. She knew from experience that the door was only six large steps or so from the bed. But after the struggle she'd had to sit up, even six steps seemed an awfully long distance to cross.

Unfortunately, while waking the snoring man in her room would have been the easier option, Edith wouldn't even consider it until she knew if he was friend or foe. Which meant that if she wanted to find out what was going on in Drummond, and whether she was safe or not, she needed to slip out into the hall and get a look around. Preferably without waking her guard.

Determined to do it, Edith took a deep breath, and then used every muscle at her disposal to get up. She pushed off with her hands and up with her legs, and for one glorious moment she was upright and standing, and then she fell flat on her face on a rush mat just as the bedroom door opened.

"Bloody hell, Alick! Ye were supposed to be watching—Laddie! Nay!"

Edith pushed one eyelid up and then immediately closed it again as she spotted the huge tongue just inches from her eye. She barely got it closed before the side of her face was lashed with a very large slimy tongue from chin to forehead. Nose wrinkling, she listened to the pounding of feet quickly crossing the room. She noted that the snoring had ended abruptly just before a second male voice, sounding startled, cried out, "What? Hey! Where'd she go?"

"Idiot," the man now kneeling next to her muttered. Edith wasn't sure whom he was calling idiot, and didn't particularly care. She was too grateful to have Laddie's affectionate licking brought to an end and opened her eyes to see a man dragging the dog back toward the door by his collar.

"Ronson!" he bellowed.

"Oh, hey! Niels? How'd she get out o' bed?" Edith

was quite sure it was the previously snoring man who asked that question since it came from the other side of the bed.

"How do ye think, Alick?" the first man growled and then bellowed again, "Ronson! Oh, there ye are. Get this mutt out o' here."

"Sorry, m'lord," Ronson cried, entering the room and hurrying to grab Laddie's collar. "He got away from me real quick. He's sneaky that way. But he's been missing Lady Edith and—Why is Lady Edith on the floor? What—?"

"Out," Niels growled. "Now!"

"Aye, m'lord," Ronson said, dragging Laddie with him as he shuffled backward toward the door. The boy beamed at Edith the whole way. "'Tis real fine to see ye awake, m'lady. Real fine. I'll bring Laddie back fer a visit when ye're feeling better."

The last word came muffled through the door as the man Alick had called Niels slammed it closed.

Edith could hear Niels muttering under his breath as she watched his large feet cross the room once more. It sounded like he was saying something about fools, lads, and dogs who were really horses, and then he knelt next to her, and she found herself turned and then scooped up off the floor and away from the nasty rush mat her face had landed on. It was dirty and beginning to mold, obviously in need of changing. She'd have to order the servants to take them away and make new ones.

"Sorry about that," Niels growled, drawing her attention back to him. "The dog tends to follow me around, but usually stops in the hall when I come in here."

"Aye, Laddie follows Niels everywhere when he

leaves the room," Alick told her solemnly. "So does young Ronson. They both seem to like him." Pursing his lips, he shook his head and added, "None o' us can figure out why."

Niels growled under his breath in response.

Edith glanced from one man to the other, unsure what to say. She had no idea if they were friend or foe. In the end, she merely nodded her head slightly. For some reason, that made the man carrying her smile, and she blinked in surprise as his stern face suddenly turned very handsome. He had an incredibly appealing smile. It lit up his whole face and made his beautiful blue eyes twinkle. Edith couldn't resist smiling back as her eyes slid over his high cheekbones, straight nose, full lips, and the wild long hair framing it all. He really was very attractive.

"I'm Niels Buchanan," he announced, and Edith stopped gaping at how pretty he was and met his gaze as she recognized the last name.

"Not Saidh's—" That was all she managed to get out, and it was nothing more than a breathy sound. Her mouth was so dry she couldn't even work up spit in it. Fortunately, Niels didn't have the same problem and understood what she'd wanted to say.

"Aye, one o' Saidh's brothers," he assured her, turning toward the bed. Setting her down in it, he added, "And ye're Edith Drummond, one o' me sister's dearest friends."

"Aye," she agreed in a whisper as he tugged the linens and furs up to cover her. Edith's smile widened ever so slightly. Drummond hadn't been invaded by enemies. They were being visited by friends. "Is Saidh . . . ?"

"Nay, she's no' here," he said almost apologetically as he straightened. "She was too far along with child to make the journey and sent us in her place."

Edith's eyes widened. "With child?"

"Aye, she is," the other man said, reminding her of his presence. Niels had called him Alick, Edith recalled as she glanced to him. Which meant he was the youngest of the Buchanan boys, Edith thought, watching the younger man grin widely as he continued, "And we think she's carrying more than one babe. She's only four months along but already big as a cow. Greer will no' even let her use the stairs on her own fer fear she'll lose her footing and roll down them like a great ball."

Edith's eyes widened at the news. She couldn't imagine rough-and-tumble Saidh not being able to walk down a set of stairs, let alone restricted from riding. She didn't imagine the woman was taking that well. But she didn't understand why Saidh hadn't mentioned being with child in her last letter. At least, the last letter she'd read, Edith thought, and wondered if she'd received others from her friend since falling ill.

"Alick, go tell Rory she's awake," Niels ordered, walking to the table where the cask sat.

"Aye," the younger man answered and then smiled at her reassuringly as he moved around the bed. "Our Rory's a healer, and the finest one around. Why, he's the one who sorted out that ye were no' ill but being poisoned. He'll have ye feeling right as rain in no time."

Alick Buchanan nodded at her cheerily and turned to hurry out of the room, leaving Edith staring after him with horror. Poison?

"Idiot."

That mutter drew her gaze to Niels. He'd finished filling one of the cups with liquid and turned to see her expression. Mouth tight, he shook his head and crossed back to the bed. "Forgive me brother. He has the tact o' a bull at the best o' times."

"Poison?" she whispered, her voice raspy.

Cursing, he settled on the edge of the bed and slid an arm under Edith to raise her up. "Aye. Poison. But drink this ere ye try to talk again, else ye may do yerself some damage," he said, holding the mug of liquid up to her mouth.

Edith hesitated, more interested in this poison business at the moment, but then she gave in and took a tiny sip. Once the cool wet liquid hit her mouth, she would have taken more, but wasn't given the option. She barely had a half mouthful of what turned out to be mead before he lowered the drink.

"Just a sip. Ye were no' able to keep it down when last ye woke so we'll go slow this time."

Edith's eyes widened at the claim. "I woke before?"

"Aye," he admitted with a grimace. "But ye were a mite confused and no' really alert. Ye drank some mead and then tossed it right back up all over me and passed out again. I'd rather no' go through that again."

Edith groaned and lowered her head with humiliation.

"There's naught to be embarrassed about," Niels said, and she could hear the frown in his voice. "I've four younger brothers who I've had to care fer as they tossed up their stomachs . . . and they were no' poisoned. It was just too much drink fer them. With you, well, at least ye had a good excuse."

Reminded of the poison, Edith jerked her head up on a frown. "Me father and brothers?"

Niels winced at her raspy voice and raised the mead again. "Another swallow o' this, I think. This time swish it around real good and wet all the corners. Ye're obviously dry as a bone."

Edith dutifully took another mouthful of mead, but the moment she'd swished and swallowed, she asked, "Me father and—"

"Aye. Rory can no' be sure o' course, but he believes they were poisoned too. They had all the same symptoms. Except fer the . . . er . . . stomach issues," he said delicately. "But Rory suspicions that's what saved ye. Ye reacted to the poison and tossed it up each time ye had it. There was no' enough left in ye to kill ye as it did yer father and brothers."

Edith lowered her head on this news, her mind awhirl with grief and anger. It had been bad enough when she'd thought she'd lost her father and two brothers to illness, but to know they had been deliberately killed—Jerking her head up, she asked, "Brodie?"

"Well and fine, as far as we ken," he assured her. "He feared getting it himself and took his bride and left fer safer shores when yer maid got sick."

Edith didn't comment. Now that he mentioned it, she recalled Brodie's leaving. She'd been rather annoyed at the time, thinking it less than laird-like behavior to flee the keep and all its people when they might be at the start of a crisis. She noted that Niels sounded disgusted by his actions too, but she merely asked, "Moibeal? She is—"

"Yer maid is fine," he assured her. "And fashing to see ye. I would no' be surprised does she no' ignore

Rory's orders to stay away and show up here once she learns ye're awake."

Edith's eyebrows rose. "Why was she no' allowed—"

She broke off and glanced to the door when it opened. Alick was returning with another man, and Edith found herself examining the three of them. They were all similar in looks with dark hair and those lovely blue eyes. But Niels was obviously older than the other two. He was also bigger, his shoulders wide, his arms thick and strong. Not that the other two didn't look strong, but Niels looked like a warrior used to wielding a broadsword, while Alick looked like he hadn't fully grown yet and Rory looked like . . . well, like he was a healer more than a warrior.

"'Tis good to see ye awake, Lady Edith," Rory said by way of greeting as he walked to the bed. "How do ye feel?"

"Thirsty," Edith admitted.

"I've only given her two small sips o' mead to see how she stomachs it," Niels announced, and much to Edith's disappointment, stood so that Rory could take his place. She wasn't sure why she was sorry he left, since she barely knew the man, but she *was* disappointed, and her feelings obviously showed on her face, Edith realized when Rory's eyebrows rose slightly and he glanced from her to Niels with a small smile.

Fortunately, he didn't embarrass her by commenting and merely asked, "How does yer stomach feel after the first couple o' sips?"

"Fine, thank ye," she whispered.

"Then Niels can give ye more in a minute," he said and leaned in to look into her eyes.

Edith stilled, fighting the urge to look away, and simply waited.

"Yer eyes are back to normal," he murmured.

Edith had no idea what that meant, but looked away with relief when he sat back again. She then frowned as her gaze fell on the woman in bed next to her. "Effie? Is she—?"

"She appears to have ingested the poison too," Rory interrupted, sparing her voice. "I think, like Moibeal, she did no' consume much o' whatever had the poison in it . . . else she'd be dead now. Howbeit she's old and frail enough that even a little might yet do her in."

"Ye ken what was poisoned?" Edith asked, her voice cracking in several spots. Her throat hurt, it was so dry, and the few sips she'd had of mead hadn't been enough to ease it.

"Niels, come give her more mead," Rory said, standing and moving around the bed to examine Effie now.

Edith frowned, thinking he planned to ignore her question, but when Niels settled next to her on the bed again and slid an arm under her shoulders to ease her to a sitting position, she forgot all about her question. Niels smelled like the woods in the springtime, a scent she'd always loved. Edith couldn't resist turning her head toward the curve of his neck and shoulder and inhaling deeply. When Niels stilled, she realized what she was doing and quickly turned her face back. Edith was quite sure she was blushing, but Niels merely smiled faintly and offered her the mug of mead.

"Thank ye," Edith murmured before taking a sip.

"Moibeal said she had a couple mouthfuls o' yer wine when ye did no' drink it the night she fell ill," Rory commented after she'd had several cautious sips.

Looking toward the other man, Edith saw that he had lifted both Effie's eyelids and was peering at her eyes silently. His words hadn't been a question, but she nodded and responded as if it was anyway. "Aye. I said she could. I did no' have the stomach fer it after tossing it back up so many times, so she gave me her cider and I let her have me wine."

"She said she did no' drink much, though. Is that right?" Rory asked, sitting up straight and turning his questioning gaze to her.

"Aye. She only had a couple drinks. She did no' care fer it," Edith recalled, noting that her voice was getting stronger. The mead was making her throat feel better too.

"And did Effie have some o' yer wine too?" Rory asked.

"I—" Edith paused, her gaze dropping to the woman before she shrugged helplessly and admitted, "I'm no' sure. She may have. I do no' recall much o' the last week or so since I fell ill again." Frowning, she explained, "At first I could no' keep anything down, but felt better once I'd purged. That kept happening, and finally I refused the wine and broth Moibeal brought." Eyes narrowing as she thought on it, she murmured, "Once I stopped having those, I was able to keep down an apple and some bread Moibeal brought me, and I started to feel better again . . . and then I wanted to build me strength so I had some stew and—" She grimaced with distaste. "It did no' seem to make much difference when that came back up. I was exhausted and weary and just wanted to sleep."

"Ye were weakening from no' being able to keep yer food down fer so long," Rory said solemnly.

"Mayhap," Edith admitted and glanced to the woman in bed next to her. "I have a vague recollection o' Effie trying to get me to eat or drink and saying I needed to build up me strength, but every time I did . . ." She shrugged and merely shook her head.

"Did ye ha'e wine with the stew while ye were tending Moibeal?" Niels asked, drawing her gaze his way.

Edith wrinkled her nose and shook her head. "Frankly, I fear I'll never want wine again after tossing it back up so many times. I did no' have anything to drink that night."

"So the poison was in both the wine and stew," Niels said grimly.

"It was?" Edith asked uncertainly.

"Aye," he assured her, his voice sounding angry. "Moibeal was poisoned from a couple o' sips o' yer wine, but ye fell ill again after eating stew. Both must ha'e been poisoned."

"Oh, aye," she said with realization and then noticed the grim looks Niels and Rory exchanged.

Still a bit fuzzy-minded, Edith wasn't sure what that exchange meant. Noticing her confusion, Rory explained, "We were hoping that perhaps the family wine had been poisoned in an effort to kill yer father and brothers, and ye merely had the bad luck to have some o' the poisoned wine. But if yer stew was later poisoned too . . ." He pointed out almost apologetically, "No one else fell ill from the stew."

Edith's eyes widened incredulously at those words. She understood what he was saying. After killing her father and brothers, someone had deliberately tried to poison her. Why would anyone want her dead? She was no one of import.

"Though," Niels added now, turning toward Rory, "the maids both being poisoned is most likely an unintended result o' trying to poison Edith."

"Aye," Rory agreed. "If Effie wakes up, I'm quite sure we'll find she ate or drank something that was sent up fer Lady Edith."

Niels nodded, his gaze shifting toward the table where the cask, vegetables, and rabbit skin sat. "So the liquid from the vial the maid was mixing into her drink is probably no' the poison."

"Nay. Probably not," Rory agreed. "Effie would hardly deliberately poison herself too."

"A little blue glass vial?" Edith asked, her ears perking up. She hadn't noticed it on the table, but it was small and there was enough mess with the mugs and whatnot that it might be hidden from her view.

"Aye," Niels said. "Effie was pouring the last o' it into yer drink to give to ye as we entered."

"Victoria gave it to Effie ere she left. She said it would help build me blood to aid in fighting the illness or some such thing," Edith murmured and grimaced. "It was foul. Just the smell o' it was enough to make me heave the first night Effie put it in me drink."

"Really?" Rory murmured, and the way he looked toward the table now with interest convinced her the vial must be there somewhere.

"It can no' be the poison," Edith assured them quietly. "Victoria does no' like me much, but she's no' stupid. She'd hardly give Effie poison to give me in front o' others like that."

"Nay . . . o' course she would no'," Niels murmured, but neither he nor his brothers looked completely convinced by her words. "Here, have more mead."

Edith hesitated, but then let him feed her more mead. She didn't think for a minute the tonic Victoria had given Effie could have poison in it. Her sister-in-law simply wasn't that stupid. Mind you, she wouldn't put it past the lass to have poisoned them all, just not in something that would lead directly back to her. Victoria might have seemed all sweetness and batting eyelashes when she'd first arrived at Drummond as Brodie's new bride, but once Edith's father and brothers had fallen ill, her ambition had shone through. Victoria wanted to be Lady Drummond with all that entailed, and had been terribly frustrated that the servants were not simply falling in line with her vision while the older brothers still lived. The woman had shown her true colors then, throwing a temper tantrum of epic proportions. Even Brodie had appeared taken aback by her behavior, and he was famous for his temper tantrums.

In truth, Edith had almost been glad to fall ill herself once her second brother, Hamish, had died. It allowed her to avoid watching the woman claim the position she was so greedy for. Edith was quite certain Victoria wouldn't have taken over graciously or kindly in an effort to secure the hearts of the people now under her charge. She had probably been spiteful and bitter as she'd barked her orders and demanded immediate obeisance. Edith couldn't have borne watching that.

Actually, she was no more eager to watch it now once her brother and his wife returned. Perhaps a visit with Saidh was in order so that she could sort out what she should do now. Edith was quite certain her days at Drummond were numbered. She had no doubt Victoria would want her out of there as quickly as possible, which probably meant a nunnery for her. If she wanted to avoid that, a visit with Saidh and the other girls where they might put their heads together and think up an alternative future for her was . . . well, really it was the only hope she had. Although, it was a slim one at best.

Edith swallowed the mead and then asked, "Has there been word as to when Brodie and Victoria will return?"

Niels shook his head. "Nay. I asked Tormod that very thing this morning, and he said no one has heard from them. He also said he did no' expect to, that Brodie comes and goes as he pleases without troubling himself to let others ken what he's about."

"Aye," Edith said on a sigh. "Brodie tends to be . . . impulsive. We did no' even ken he'd married until he arrived home with Victoria in tow. It seems he met her at court, fell madly in love and married her within a month."

"And her parents allowed it?" Niels asked with surprise.

"That was my first question," Edith admitted wryly.

"And his answer?" Rory asked at once.

"He said they were perfectly fine with it," she said, not hiding her doubt that it was true.

"Ye do no' believe it?" Rory asked with interest.

"Nay," Edith admitted solemnly. "And neither did me father. He sent a messenger to a friend at court, who immediately wrote him back with the true story as he knew it."

"Which is?" Niels prompted when she hesitated.

After a hesitation, Edith admitted, "Apparently, Victoria was contracted to marry another when she met Brodie. My brother wooed her with tales o' his being heir to the laird at Drummond." All three Buchanan men stiffened at this news and she rushed on. "Her parents found out and her father took him aside and told him he knew he was the third son and would never be laird, his daughter was contracted to another, and to leave his daughter alone or else. But I do no' think they troubled to tell Victoria that Brodie had lied, because according to my father's friend, the next thing anyone knew Victoria and Brodie were gone." She grimaced. "It seems the pair fled court fer Drummond and stopped in a pub along the way to exchange consent in front o' witnesses."

"So they're no' really married?" Alick asked with a frown.

"Oh, aye, they are," Niels said heavily.

It was Rory who explained, "According to canon law, all each party need do is give consent to be married. Ye need no' even have witnesses, although it helps if anyone refutes it."

"Then why is there always the priest prattling on and on?" Alick asked. "And what o' banns and—?"

"Not strictly necessary," Rory assured him. "Just preferred by most."

"Well . . ." Alick frowned and seemed at a loss as to why anyone would want such bother.

There was silence for a minute, and then Niels said, "So he claimed he was to be laird."

"And now he is," Rory added darkly.

Edith sighed. She'd just known that was what they would focus on. "Look, I ken it sounds bad, and frankly, me brother is a selfish, unreliable and spoiled lad . . . but Father is the last person Brodie would hurt.

He is the one who spoiled him so badly and let him go his own way so much growing up."

"And ye think he respected him fer that?" Niels asked curiously.

Edith stared at him blankly. "What?"

"Do ye think yer brother respected yer father fer spoiling him and letting him get away with so much, as ye put it," Niels asked, "or do ye think he just felt like mayhap his father did no' care enough to be bothered to discipline him and teach him to survive in this world as a man?"

Edith frowned. She'd often seen her father's indulgence of Brodie as hurtful to her brother, knowing it was doing him no favors, but she'd never considered that Brodie might see it as such too.

"Yer brother got lucky with Victoria," Niels added quietly. "If he'd tried the like with *our* sister and we'd caught up to him ere they exchanged consent, we would ha'e beat him near to death."

"Aye, and probably cut off his ballocks and fiddle to boot," Rory said coldly.

Edith's eyes widened incredulously at the threat to Brodie's family jewels. "Nay."

"Aye," Alick assured her with a grin. "We planned to do all that and more to MacDonnell after he sent a message saying he'd ruined our Saidh and planned to marry her." Pursing his lips with displeasure, he added, "I'm still no' sure why we did no' do it."

"Because MacDonnell's a laird, and he ne'er lied to Saidh," Rory explained dryly.

"Besides, Saidh was no' contracted to another," Niels added. "She had no better prospects. In fact, MacDonnell was a fine choice to husband."

"And she loved him," Edith pointed out.

"Nay," Niels said at once, and when she frowned, assured her, "'Tis true. She lusted after him and liked him at first, but did no' yet love him. She said as much herself right in front o' us."

"Really?" Edith asked, her voice almost a squeak of surprise.

"Aye," Rory assured her with amusement. "Though in truth, I think she probably was half in love with him when they married. She definitely loves him now."

"No' that it matters," Niels added quietly. "Had MacDonnell been a spoiled, lying third son unable to support her and any bairns they might produce, we would ha'e beat him to death rather than let him marry her . . . whether she loved him or no'."

"What?" Edith gasped, shrinking away from him with surprise.

Niels frowned at her reaction, but then asked, "Ye said ye do no' think Victoria's parents told her that Brodie had lied. Was it only because she ran off with him?"

"Nay," she admitted reluctantly.

"Then why?"

Edith blew her breath out unhappily, but then admitted, "Because she seemed shocked when they got here and Brodie introduced her to our older brothers."

"How shocked?" Niels asked.

Edith stared at him silently, suddenly suspecting he already knew the answer. If he'd talked to anyone here since their arrival, he probably did, she realized, and wondered just how long the men had been here and what all they knew.

"She fainted," Edith admitted quietly, recalling the

way Victoria had paled and then collapsed. Brodie had tried to brush it away as exhaustion from the trip as he'd scooped her up and carried her above stairs to his chamber, but they all heard the shouting coming from the room some ten minutes later when Victoria had apparently woken up.

Aware that no one had commented and the three men were watching her solemnly, Edith sighed and asked, "How long ha'e ye been here?"

"Nearly a week," Rory answered.

"A week?" she gasped with amazement.

"Only six days," Niels corrected him.

"But . . ." She glanced from man to man. "What ha'e ye been doing all that time?"

"Mostly taking turns guarding ye, hunting up game, making broth, and dribbling it down yer throat while ye were unconscious in hopes ye'd recover enough to wake up," Rory answered gently.

Edith stared at them, her mind spinning slowly. While Brodie had fled the keep with its threat of illness, these three men, who did not even know her, had been here nearly a week taking care of her?

"Why?"

The word slipped out without her conscious intent, and for a moment it just hung there helplessly in the air. Then Niels shifted her slightly so that she was looking at him and said simply, "Because ye needed our help, lass."

Perhaps she was still exhausted and drained from her illness, or perhaps it was the deaths of her father and brothers that she had not yet had a chance to grieve, but Edith's eyes suddenly glazed over with the sheen of tears. Just as she felt herself beginning to crumble in Niels's arms, the bedroom door suddenly burst open. Edith turned to see another man enter the room, this one as big and brawny as Niels and holding up two dead birds by their feet.

"I got a nice pair o' pheasants this time, Rory. If ye only use one fer broth, we can maybe get Cook to roast up the other and—" The man stopped and blinked as he noted Edith half-upright in the curve of Niels's arm. "Oh, say, ye're awake! Well, is no' that fine?"

MORE VAMPIRE ROMANCES FROM *NEW YORK TIMES* BESTSELLING AUTHOR

LYNSAY SANDS

UNDER A VAMPIRE MOON

978-0-06-210020-7

Christian Notte has seen enough of his Argeneau relatives taken down for the count, but he never imagined he'd let himself fall in love—until he meets the enthralling, charmingly skittish, and oh-so-mortal Carolyn Connor.

THE LADY IS A VAMP

978-0-06-207807-0

When Jeanne Louise Argeneau left work, she never thought she'd end up tied down—kidnapped—by a good-looking mortal named Paul Jones. More attracted than annoyed, she quickly realizes there is more to her abductor than meets the eye.

IMMORTAL EVER AFTER

978-0-06-207811-7

Anders felt a connection to the green-eyed beauty from the moment he cradled her bruised body in his arms. But before he claims Valerie Moyer as his life mate, he must destroy the vampire who almost stole her from him forever.

ONE LUCKY VAMPIRE

978-0-06-207814-8

Secretly playing bodyguard to sweet, sexy Nicole Phillips is turning out to be the wildest ride of Jake Colson's immortal life. He's barely had time to adjust to his new state when he must stop whoever's targeting her.

IMP 0811